Broken Road

Written By

ELIZABETH YU-GESUALDI

Copyright © 2012 Elizabeth Yu-Gesualdi

All rights reserved.

ISBN: 1479338117

ISBN 13: 9781479338115

Library of Congress Control Number: 2012917737
CreateSpace Independent Publishing Platform
North Charleston, South Carolina

*I would like to dedicate this novel to my sons, Jarrod and Alec.
Thank you for your never-ending love and for
inspiring me to be a better person.
You are my reasons for being born.*

*And to Dave...
my husband, my best friend, my one true love.*

Chapter One

*S*irens. He could barely distinguish between the police and those of the ambulances, but Jarrod knew that the loud, blaring wails of those sirens were fast approaching. Unable to move or open his eyes, he could feel the cold, wet trickle of blood and smell its rusty, metallic scent as it poured from his scalp onto his face. As he struggled to escape the suffocating blackness that was now engulfing him, he was able to call out to his brother.

"Alec...Alec," he mumbled in a voice rising barely above a whisper. With tremendous effort he tortuously attempted to turn his twisted body toward the backseat to check on Alec, but a sharp, searing pain ran through his ribs and chest area, rendering the movement impossible. "Alec, answer me," he grunted. He thought he heard a moan coming from the back, but he wasn't sure. Then he heard his name being called out. Was it the voice of the angel of death calling for him? Did he even have a voice, or did he just stand in front of his intended victim with his glowing, red eyes drilling holes into the soon-to-be-departed's heart while beckoning him to follow by simply waggling his long, flesh-less finger toward himself? Either way he would not respond.

He wasn't ready to die and leave everything and all those he loved behind. Not yet. It wasn't his time. The voice called out his name again, but this time Jarrod heard it with unmistakable clarity and knew whom it belonged to.

His brother was alive.

He knew help was on the way because the high-pitched cries of sirens were getting closer and closer. Closing his eyes in relief, he soon found himself losing the battle against consciousness as darkness began to make its wicked descent upon him. Just before unconsciousness hailed victory, he felt himself blissfully reliving the earlier hours that had led to this dark and horrendous moment.

He remembered baseball…

The day of the championship game had finally arrived. It was a beautiful Saturday afternoon and the weather was perfect for baseball. It was as if the baseball gods had discussed it and unanimously voted to do their part to make today as game friendly as possible. The sun was shining, but with just a few white, fluffy clouds scattered about so that it didn't become uncomfortably hot. A cool breeze was blowing, but not so strong that it might affect the outcome of where the ball headed after being hit. Perfect baseball weather.

Jarrod had spent the past few days studying for upcoming final exams and practicing to further tone up his baseball skills. He didn't hang out with any of his friends or see his girlfriend Morgan, except during school hours. He needed to focus. He was captain of his high school varsity team and they were competing for the state championship this afternoon. He already knew he would be the starting pitcher and thanks to Coach Leroux, he also knew there would be a scout for the Charleston Riverdogs, a Single-A minor league team for the New York Yankees, watching in the stands. He felt an enormous amount of pressure to perform well, as well as a combination of excitement, anxiety, fear, and nervousness at the prospect of all his hard work and dreams turning into reality. His nerves were as tight as his girlfriend's jeans, but he was ready. The opportunity to make one's dream come true only comes once in a lifetime. He realized this and would do whatever it took not to blow it.

The away game was scheduled to begin at one o'clock at the Secaucus High School field. Secaucus Patriots vs. Cliffside Park Raiders. He was dressed and ready by 9:00 a.m. Sitting on the edge of his bed while unconsciously tossing a ball into his glove over and over again, he silently prayed that his fastball have the speed of a Bugatti Veyron, that his curveball would break as if dropped from the Cliffs of Moher, and that his slider would dive down into the strike zone at the last second, the way his mom sniped the final bid on eBay with mere seconds left on an auction.

Glancing through Jarrod's bedroom doorway while en route to the bathroom, his younger brother, Alec, made an abrupt stop and leaned against the doorway, quietly watching him for a few moments before speaking. He knew how much this game meant to his brother. Secretly he was just as nervous. Had he not broken his right wrist two months ago in a basketball game with his friends, he would be playing alongside Jarrod today. Unfortunately his wrist was still bothering him, and the doctors felt it would be best for him to skip the season and give the injury time to heal properly. Alec also excelled in baseball as a catcher and loved the game just as much as Jarrod did. As happy as he was for his brother, it still killed him not to be able to participate in today's championship game.

Although Alec was a year younger and close to an inch shorter than Jarrod, he was his equal in muscular build. Being that they were so close in age, they shared many common interests, such as sports, movies, music, and friends. Both sons took after their father, Jim, in height, but only Alec resembled him in appearance, inheriting his lighter skin tone, soft yet thick brown hair, and eyes that were a rare combination of amber and green. Jarrod, on the other hand, took a stronger hold of their mother's genes, with the darker hair and olive skin tone. Janet's eyes were a warm brown, triggering her husband to lightheartedly tease that the blue-eyed mailman better not drop off anymore special deliveries at his house again.

Still leaning against the bedroom doorway, with his arms crossed over his chest, Alec asked, "How you holdin' up?"

Jarrod looked up at him with a small shrug and a tight grin. "Okay, I guess."

"You'll do fine today. Don't worry."

Looking back down at his ball and glove again, Jarrod said, "Easier said than done. I can't help but worry I'll screw things up. What if I work my ass off and I still pitch badly?"

"Just pretend it's you and me out there having a catch. Try not to think about who's in the stands watching. Focus and stay in the zone at all times. You do that and I guarantee you'll have a great game."

Appreciative of his brother's concern and advice, Jarrod simply nodded. Usually Alec was so laid-back and carefree, Jarrod instinctively knew it had taken a lot for him to say what he just did. He would probably need a nap later due to mental exhaustion.

"Alright, I'll see you there then. I'm going with Billy and Evan. I'll catch up with Mom and Dad at the field. Remember to just stay in the zone."

Alec was leaving the room when Jarrod called out to him, "Hey, Alec!"

"Yeah?" he asked, taking two steps backward and turning to face him in a tactical, military fashion.

"Sorry you aren't able to catch for me today. It won't be the same without you."

Alec nodded, gave him a slight grin, and said with a deep sigh, "Thanks. I wish I could be a part of it too. All I can do now is play the role of head cheerleader."

Jarrod smiled and said, "I also appreciate the pep talk. Never expected that from you."

"No problem. Just don't get all mushy on me, alright?" Alec shoved his left hand into his pants pocket and began to jingle the loose change, a perpetual nervous habit he'd developed years ago when faced with an awkward or uncomfortable situation. "I still think you suck as a big brother…but I gotta admit, you are one helluva ballplayer!" They both chuckled at his feeble attempt to lighten the moment.

The stands were filled beyond capacity on both sides of the field. People who couldn't find seats were standing along the first and third baselines with a few spectators set up in the outfield area. Some folks had even brought lounge chairs and seemed quite comfortable out there with their large golf umbrellas to shield them from the sun's biting rays and canned drinks to quench their steady thirsts. Both teams were warming up. Jarrod had already warmed his arm up and was sitting in the dugout just waiting. Every now and then, he would look up toward the stands to see if he could identify the scout. At one point he thought he might have figured out whom it was. A balding, elderly man who stood out from the crowd seemed to have that "scout" look, but then one of the players from Secaucus waved to him and yelled, "Hey, Gramps!" "Gramps" grinned brightly, showing off his perfectly shaped, porcelain-white dentures. He waved back and gave his grandson the double thumbs-up sign. Later another man kept looking down and shuffling some papers while simultaneously talking on his cell phone, but eventually Jarrod ruled him out as well. He overheard him ask the lady next to him how many innings there were in a high school game.

A voice over the loudspeaker welcomed everyone to the BCSL Championship Game. The voice thanked everyone for being there to show their support to the players and went on to wish both teams good luck. Everyone rose; those wearing hats removed them and placed them over their hearts while they listened to the scratchy recorded version of Whitney Houston's "Star-Spangled Banner."

"Play ball," the umpire yelled, and the Patriots took the field. The lead batter for the Raiders, Connor Dempsey, took his position in the batter's box. He glared unblinkingly at the pitcher as he wound up and threw the first pitch of the game.

"Ball!" yelled the umpire. Cheers, as well as hoots of disapproval, could be heard coming from both sides.

The game progressed and was quickly turning out to be a true nail-biter. Both teams were giving it their all. The scores crept up like the NASDAQ index on a good day. It seemed every time one team was ahead by a run or two, the other team came back swinging and knocked their socks off.

With a tie score of five-five and neither team scoring in the seventh inning, the game went into extra innings. After a scoreless eighth, Cliffside managed to scratch out a run in the top of the ninth. The score was now six-five, Cliffside. The first two batters in the bottom of the ninth were retired easily on routine ground balls to the second baseman and shortstop respectively. The Patriots were down to their last out. Jarrod gave up consecutive singles to the next two hitters and walked the third batter to load the bases.

Alec, along with his two friends, sat next to his parents. Janet grabbed his hand and held it tightly. He squeezed hers gently, letting her know he too felt anxious.

"C'mon, Jarrod," he whispered softly as he closed his eyes tightly for a brief moment and said a quick prayer.

With the bases now loaded and two outs in the bottom of the ninth, the batter worked the count to two and two. Jarrod wound up from the stretch and emitted a hard "Oomph!" as he released the ball.

"Ball!" screamed the ump. The tension and weight of the pressure on his shoulders was almost insupportable. He wiped the sweat from his brow with his right arm and took a deep, cleansing breath. "C'mon, Jarrod! You can do it, man!" cried the Raiders shortstop, Tim Watson. The Raider fans were all chanting, "Jar-rod, Jar-rod, Jar-rod!" Several people could be seen wiping away the nervous sweat from their foreheads while others simply lowered their heads, not able to watch him throw the next pitch.

Jarrod's shoulder and elbow were practically screaming to be iced down, and his arm felt like it weighed a thousand pounds. He looked up into the crowd, and his eyes met with Alec's. Alec winked at him and mouthed the word "zone." Jarrod gave him a small, hesitant smile and nodded.

There comes a point in time in everyone's life, however transient it may be, that determines the rest of it. Jarrod was fiercely aware that this indeed was his moment.

"Stop thinking," he mumbled under his breath while shaking his head. *Just breathe and focus*, he told himself. *Breathe in, breathe out. Breathe in, breathe out…*

Jarrod stared down the batter prior to his windup. For the three-two pitch, he went from the stretch position, came to a set, and delivered the pitch with all the strength he could muster after eight and two-thirds innings of intensive, exhaustive work. The pitch seemed to have some extra zip on it as the batter started his swing, but to his mortified chagrin, the ball found its way into the catcher's glove, resulting in the final out of the game.

"Strike three! Game over!" screamed the umpire from behind the plate. Cliffside won six-five on a game-ending, bases-loaded strikeout by Jarrod.

A good portion of the crowd jumped to their feet and began hugging one another, while others remained seated with their heads lowered in sorrow and disappointment. A combination of cheers, tears, and roars could be heard and felt throughout the entire area. The players from the outfield ran toward the pitching mound, where they met up with the infielders who were all embracing, jumping up and down, crying tears of joy, and raising their arms up high in victory. Obscured somewhere in that mass of joyous camaraderie was Jarrod.

"Congratulations, Jarrod. My name is Griffin Wyatt. I'm with the Charleston Riverdogs." Mr. Wyatt held out his left hand, and Jarrod eagerly shook it.

"Thanks, Mr. Wyatt," Jarrod said. "It's a real pleasure to meet you. I wish I could wipe this smile off my face, but I just can't seem to shake it!" Countless times he had dreamed about this moment, and in every one of his fantasies, he always envisioned himself handling the situation calmly and professionally. Reality was so much different. Here he was, at a pinnacle moment in his life, with a huge, silly grin plastered across his face that he simply couldn't get rid of. Surprisingly, Mr. Wyatt looked nothing like what Jarrod had expected a baseball scout to look like. Jarrod's mind had somehow formed the picture of an aging, balding, heavyset man sporting a baseball cap, with a half-smoked, cut-rate cigar dangling from his lips. Mr. Wyatt appeared to be no older than his early forties, fairly handsome, with a full head of fiery red hair. He wore fashionable glasses and a gold chain with a pendant that read "#1 Dad."

Mr. Wyatt responded with a loaded Southern drawl. "Nah, don't. You have a lot to be happy and excited about. That was some fine pitchin' I saw today. It takes quite a bit to impress me, and I'm happy to say, I'm impressed."

"Thanks again." He just couldn't believe what he was hearing. This absolutely was going down as one of the best days of his life.

"I like your mechanics, your motion, and your delivery. You've got a good, strong arm. And I must say, I was plenty awed by how you handled yourself when things got a little tense out there."

"Wow. I know I'm repeating myself, but thanks again." As Jarrod spoke to Mr. Wyatt, friends continually ran up to him and congratulated him, patted him on the back, or tousled his hair. He couldn't stop beaming.

"Listen, here's my card. It's got my cell number on it. I'd like to get together with you and your folks to talk. That is, if you're interested in the opportunity to perhaps play a little professional ball someday."

"Yes, sir, definitely. I'm real interested. When would be a good time to get together?" Jarrod asked with so much exuberance that he accidentally dropped the card and immediately bent down to retrieve it.

The scout smiled at Jarrod's zestful enthusiasm and said, "Well, looks like there might be some well-earned team celebratin' going on tonight, so why don't we just plan on gettin' together tomorrow? There's another kid in the area I'd like to check out, so I'll be 'round 'til Monday. Call me later on so we can set somethin' up, alright?"

"Yes, sir. I will. Thank you again so much."

Griffin Wyatt shook his hand once again and took off. Soon after that Jarrod was surrounded by his family, his girlfriend, Morgan, and his closest friends, each taking turns hugging and congratulating him. He was on an emotional high that he'd never experienced before and perhaps never would again in this lifetime.

That evening a family celebration was in order. After going home, taking a shower, and changing into a fresh pair of jeans and a black button-down shirt, Jarrod and his family headed out to dinner to one of the finest seafood restaurants in the area, the Waterfront. Jarrod's mouth was watering at the mere thought of digging into their famous surf 'n turf.

Close to three hours later, with bellies heartily filled beyond capacity, the Wentworths returned home. Jarrod asked if it would be alright for him and Alec to celebrate with a few friends at a party later.

"Yeah, sure," Jim replied. "But not too late, okay? You still have to meet with Mr. Wyatt sometime tomorrow, and I don't think it would be in your best interest for you to show up looking tired and haggard. And no drinking anything other than soda!"

"Yeah, don't worry. We'll just hang with the guys for a bit, and then come home. I'll call Mr. Wyatt now, before they pick us up."

"No Morgan tonight?" asked Janet, referring to his girlfriend.

"I'll meet up with her at the party."

"Oh yay," said Alec sarcastically. Janet gave Alec a stern look of warning while Jarrod opted to simply ignore him and headed straight for the phone in the kitchen, pulling Mr. Wyatt's business card from his back pocket. Before dialing he stared down at the card for a moment. He took a deep breath, closed his eyes, and whispered a quick prayer as he released the air. He nervously began to dial, but stopped because his hand was shaking so much. Janet, who was standing nearby watching him, quietly walked over. She gently took the phone and card out of his hand and laid her right hand softly on his cheek.

"It's going to be fine, you'll see," she said. "One step at a time, okay? Right now you're just calling to set up an appointment." Her soothing voice seemed to calm him down immediately. He took another deep breath and nodded. She kissed him gently on the cheek, returned the phone and card to his hand, and quietly left the room, allowing him privacy.

Jarrod dialed slowly this time and listened as the phone rang on the other end.

"Hello?" said Mr. Wyatt.

"Hi, Mr. Wyatt?" asked Jarrod.

"Yes, it is," said the scout.

"This is Jarrod Wentworth, sir."

"Ah, Jarrod. Glad you called. How you doin', son? All done celebratin'?"

"Not quite yet. Still working on it. I just came back from dinner with my family, and I'll be heading out in a bit to celebrate with the rest of the team and some friends." He nervously began to pace back and forth in the small kitchen.

"Good, good. Just don't overdo it, son. So, let's see. Why don't we set up our meetin' for tomorrow? I have a few things to do in the mornin', but do you think you and your folks could meet with me in the afternoon, maybe around three or so?"

"Yeah, sure. Whatever works best for you. Where would you like to meet? You're more than welcome to come to our house, or we can meet you at your hotel." Jarrod quickly ran over to the counter and grabbed a piece of paper and a pen so he could jot down the information.

"Why don't y'all meet me in the coffee shop here at the inn? I'm stayin' at the White Swan Inn on River Road in Edgewater. Do you know where that is?"

"Yes, sir. I do."

"Good. So then let's plan on that then. Three tomorrow in the coffee shop. I look forward to seein' you again and meetin' your parents."

"Same here, sir. Thank you."

"No problem, son. Now don't forget, don't overdo it tonight."

"I won't, sir."

"See you tomorrow, Jarrod."

"Goodbye, Mr. Wyatt," said Jarrod before hanging up the phone and turning around to find Jim, Janet, and Alec standing timorously in the doorway. The three of them looked as though they were about to drop to the floor from the anticipation.

After what seemed like forever, Alec finally asked, "What'd he say?"

"He says he can't make it. He changed his mind and is taking an earlier flight home."

"Liar," said Alec.

"Jarrod, if you don't tell us what Mr. Wyatt said right now, I'm going to drop dead from a stroke," Jim said. "I can feel my blood pressure rising as we speak. God, it's hot in here!" Janet absentmindedly nodded in agreement and began to pat his arm as if that would somehow help lower his blood pressure.

Jarrod gave them his best crooked smile and told his family of the conversation with Mr. Wyatt. Alec gave Jarrod a high five followed by a pound hug, while Janet and Jim smiled and hugged each other.

"That's great, hon!," said Janet as she embraced her son. Jim hugged him as well, then stepped away, cleared his throat, and said, "Well then, I believe I'll go take my Diovan now. I'm happy for you, son."

"Thanks," Jarrod said as he gave his father that one-of-a-kind, winning smile of his again and said, "Y'know what? I'm happy for me too." He looked at Griffin Wyatt's business card one final time and then placed it on the counter near the phone.

Chapter Two

Approximately half an hour later, Jarrod's best friend, Dante, pulled up in front of the Wentworth household and incessantly honked the horn of his '98 Eagle Talon. On a typical day, this would have been nothing out of the ordinary, but evidently today was an exception to the rule. The car was completely draped in black and red streamers, Cliffside's school colors. The back and side windows were covered in window paint declaring "Raiders are #1!" and "CP Raiders BCSL State Champs!" The power ballad "We Are the Champions" blared from inside the car.

Jarrod heard the honking and yelled up to Alec, who was upstairs in his room, "They're here! You comin' or what?"

"Yeah, I'll be right down," Alec responded as he quickly ran a comb through his hair. "Go ahead and I'll meet you out there in a minute."

Jarrod waved and muttered a quick good-bye to his parents as he headed out the door, letting the screen door slam shut. He walked quickly toward the car and saw that his other two close friends, Joey and Brendon, were in the backseat.

"Hey, what's up?" said Jarrod as he made himself comfortable in the front seat. Joey acknowledged his greeting by saying, "'Sup, superstar?" while Brendon smiled widely and said, "Left the front seat for you, my friend, 'cause we didn't know if there would be room enough for your big 'ol head back here!" They all laughed in unison. In the meantime, Alec made his way to the car and grudgingly squeezed into the backseat between Joey and Brendon, neither one willing to give up their window seats.

Smiling at Dante while lowering the volume on the car stereo, Jarrod asked, "Since when did you turn into Mr. School Spirit?"

"Since it gave me an excuse to party," he responded excitedly.

"And since when have you ever needed an excuse to party?" asked Brendon.

"This is true. But you see, today is special. Today is the day my best friend transformed himself from being just an ordinary kid from Jersey to…what exactly did you call him before, Joey?"

"I do believe I called him a *superstar*," responded Joey cheerfully.

"Yeah, a superstar. It's like Jarrod was a small, furry caterpillar just this morning, and now he's turned into a pretty little butterfly ready to spread his wings and fly away," he said jokingly. "What is that process called again, Professor Wentworth?" he asked loudly, inclining his head toward the backseat.

"Metamorphosis," Alec interjected with a grin.

"Thank you, sir," responded Dante. "Just think about it, Jarrod. Once you become famous and people realize that you're from Jersey, maybe they'll stop thinking of it as merely being the diner capital of the world, or worse yet, for having the most toxic waste dumps in any state in the nation."

Although Dante had originally come from Chicago, he had grown to love New Jersey and considered himself a native son of the state. Although they were best friends, they were such polar opposites of each other. Jarrod was tall, nearing six foot two, with an amazing athletic build, wavy hair that reached just above his neckline, in a color reminiscent of dark chocolate. His eyes were so blue that they could easily be compared to the beauty of the turquoise waters off the Caribbean Sea, inviting one to luxuriate in their warm depth. Dante on the other hand, had two inches on Jarrod and was exceedingly thin. As far as muscles go, if he had any, they were hidden deep within the long, loose, ill-fitting football jerseys he preferred to wear. He kept his light-blond hair cut short in a military style and wore a single small gold loop earring in each ear. But appearance was not where their contrasts ended. While Jarrod lived and breathed sports, Dante had absolutely no interest whatsoever in participating or watching, preferring to hang out with his buddies and to crash any party he could. He was also by far one of the most intelligent people Jarrod had ever met. He could discuss anything as mundane as the reason why prepubescent teenage girls were obsessed with love stories involving vampires to the more complex subject of President Obama's stand on foreign policies, without batting a single eyelash. Yet he refused to apply himself when it came to school. He had built a solid reputation as the class clown, and due to his infinite charm and sense of humor, was exceedingly popular with all — including the teachers who nevertheless continued to dole out Ds and Fs to him on a regular basis.

 Dante and his parents had moved to New Jersey from Chicago when he was only ten years old. The move from the wildly exciting Windy City to a small, suburban town in a state best known for farming tomatoes was taxing enough, but even more difficult was leaving his friends behind. His first day in his new school was, to say the least, challenging, nerve-wracking, and beyond terrifying. All the other fifth graders looked at him as if he carried some horribly contagious disease and would pass it on to them by merely imparting them with a passing glance. Except for Jarrod. He boldly came up to him during recess, introduced himself, and asked if he wanted to join him and two others in playing four square. Since Dante had never heard of the game, Jarrod quickly explained the rules. They played together that day and became fast friends. The friendship had only grown and flourished with each passing day.

"If Springsteen wasn't able to put Jersey on the map, I seriously doubt I'll be able to," Jarrod said. "Besides, let's not get ahead of ourselves here. We still don't know anything yet. Not until tomorrow."

"Oh c'mon, Wentworth! You want this so much, you'd give up Alec's firstborn for it," yelled Joey from the back.

"Hey," wailed Alec as he punched Joey in the arm. They all started laughing, but Jarrod became somewhat serious as he looked out the passenger side window, sighed deeply, and quietly whispered, "I do want it." Although it was barely audible, everyone seemed to either have heard it or sensed what he was thinking and kept silent.

After a few thoughtful moments, Dante said, "Dude, do me a favor and grab the AC/DC disc out of the glove compartment and put it in for me."

From the backseat you could hear Alec groan, "Not 'Thunderstruck' again!"

"Excuse me," exclaimed Dante. "I'll pull over right now and leave you here on the side of the road if you continue to make negative comments toward the Gods of Rock 'n Roll!"

Everyone chuckled at his retort since they all knew Dante's appreciation of AC/DC's music was longstanding and deep-rooted. He had always loved the group and knew the words to every song they ever recorded. "Thunderstruck" was his absolute favorite, and he called it his personal anthem. He would play it, or rather blast it, every morning in his car as he pulled out of his driveway.

Jarrod leaned forward and opened the glove compartment. He rummaged through it, pulling out various CDs, but could not find the requested one.

"It's not in here," said Jarrod.

"Sure it is," Dante said. "I listened to it just this morning and then put it back in there."

Jarrod rooted through the CDs again, shook his head, and said, "You may think you put it back in there, but you didn't. I checked twice. It's not in here."

Dante leaned over and started fumbling through the glove compartment himself. Every now and then, he would look up at the road and then lower his head again. "Man, I'm almost positive I put it back in—"

"Light!" Brendon screamed from the back.

Dante rushed to step on the brake, but it was too late. The last thing the four young men saw before the horrific, crushing blow was an approaching pickup truck heading toward the passenger side of Dante's car at full speed. The hard-hitting impact pushed the Eagle Talon across the double yellow lines before it abruptly stopped, sandwiching it between the truck and a parked car.

Aside from the horrified screams and cries for help from various witnesses, an eerie silence fell over the car like a soft hush. Five minutes later, in the far distance, light bars were flashing and the loud, high-pitched sound of sirens could be heard.

Chapter Three

"I don't understand why you can't just skip going to New Jersey this summer and stay here," Ileana said to her best friend. "You don't even want to go."

"I don't have a choice," Angel said. "My mom and dad are worried about my Aunt Helen, and they said it would make her really happy if I were to spend a few weeks with her. I think Morgan is being a pain in the ass again."

"Morgan was born a pain in the ass."

"I know. But there's nothing we can do about it." Angel looked in the mirror and frowned. "I think I'm getting a pimple."

"You never get pimples. You're perfect. I'd kill to have your looks."

Angel never thought of herself as beautiful. She considered herself passably pretty and found it surprising when people would say she was beautiful or gorgeous. Naturally she liked hearing the compliments, but didn't see what the big deal was. She would look in the mirror and see the flaws no one else seemed to notice, or if they did, were kind enough not to mention. Angel detested the three small beauty marks that formed a small triangle on her left cheek and she found that her lips were a little too plump. They almost looked as if she had injected Botox in them to give her that bee-stung look, but she hadn't. They were just naturally full. Oh, and there was that tiny scar above her right eye, barely visible to the naked eye, but she knew it was there. She had gotten that scar during a middle school gym class one day while playing touch football. She walked away with the small scar, but the girl she had collided into had lost her two front teeth. As much as she hated the scar, she knew she had been the lucky one that day. Her long, auburn hair was nice when blown out, but took so long to dry due to its thickness that sometimes it just wasn't worth the effort. More often than not, she let it dry naturally, revealing its natural, loose wave. The one thing she was grateful for were her eyes. She did like the color of her eyes. They were a deep green, remindful in color of a Douglas fir Christmas tree in all its splendor, but with little specks of gold surrounding the irises, making them appear almost ethereal.

"I'm far from perfect and you know it."

Plopping herself backwards onto Angel's bed, Ileana said "I don't mind you being perfect. As long as I get to pick up what's left of the discarded remains of your potential lovers, I'm okay with it."

Turning away from the mirror and facing her friend, she said, "Ile, why do you say things like that? First of all, I don't have any potential lovers, and second, you're absolutely gorgeous and do just fine on your own. In fact, you do a hell of a lot better than I do."

"It's by your choice that you don't have any potential lovers. And I'm not gorgeous. I have dull brown hair, humdrum brown eyes, and my skin is too dark. Even that's brown."

Ileana had an exotic Latin look going for her. Angel was altruistically jealous of her perfect olive tone skin that made her appear to have a healthy tan all year long. She wore her long, thick dark hair parted slightly off-center with side swept bangs that loosely and sometimes covered her left eye. Her hair was the envy of many girls and the rack and ruin of many men.

Thanks to her parent's skillful tutelage of their Cuban heritage, she was able to speak Spanish as well as English, knew the name of every patron saint in the Bible, and was able to prepare a mean dish of ropa vieja. Unfortunately, she also inherited from them her short stature, as well as her spirited temper that could scare Satan himself into leading a holy life.

"Alright, why don't we just agree that we're both perfect and gorgeous and the world is a better place because we're in it?" Angel said.

"Agreed," said Ileana with a slight smile, but then she became serious when she added, "I'm going to miss you so much while you're away. I hate that you're leaving."

"I'll miss you too. We'll just have to call and text one another every day so that we can keep each other updated on what's going on."

"This sucks."

Angel just smiled at her friend. They were incredibly close and shared everything, from clothes, to makeup, to secrets so intimate and confidential that the CIA wouldn't be able to lift a lid on them. They had been best friends since middle school, and they truly believed there was no subject matter that couldn't be discussed between the two.

Returning to her packing, Angel said, "I'll be back before you know it and then off to college together as planned."

"There is that," Ileana responded happily as she sprang back up into a sitting position. "Angel, it's going to be great. I'm so excited! I'm going to spend the entire time you're in New Jersey making plans."

"In the meantime, I'll be spending most of my time dealing with Morgan."

"I don't envy you there." Ileana had only met Morgan once or twice when she would come to Bradenton to visit for a week or so during summer vacations, but felt an instant dislike toward her. It was almost as if a dark nebula of negativity, cynicism, and contradiction hovered over her wherever she went. If she didn't get her way, she would throw tantrums, so usually people would give in just to avoid the ensuing hysteria. She tried it once on Ileana, but it didn't work. It had been during the summer of their sophomore year in high school. Ileana had saved up enough money to treat Angel to dinner to celebrate her birthday. They had planned on dining at Bo's Steakhouse for their deliciously famous porterhouses, but Morgan didn't want to go there. She had preferred to go to a swanky, posh, exorbitantly priced restaurant that Ileana could never afford. Morgan kept her whining and complaining up for hours even though Ileana had already informed her in no uncertain terms they would be going to Bo's, with or without her. Angel had unsuccessfully attempted placating and reasoning with her stubborn, selfish cousin; but in the end, the best friends enjoyed two of the most tender, juiciest, succulent steaks ever cooked, while Morgan remained home sulking and eating leftover pizza from the night before. The next day, Morgan returned to New Jersey.

"I don't understand why you're packing now anyway. You don't leave for another few weeks."

"I'm not really *packing,* packing. I'm just packing stuff I won't be wearing here before I leave. This is all new stuff that my mom and I bought for the trip."

"Yeah, but that skirt I could wear before you leave," said Ileana as she eyed the new floral mini-skirt that Angel had neatly packed away, as a butcher would eye a pig.

"You know the rules. No sharing 'til the owner has worn it first."

"I'll let you wear my new boots if you let me wear that skirt."

"Only you would wear thigh-high black leather boots in Florida. It's too hot here for boots."

"If being slightly uncomfortable is the price one has to pay to look good, so be it. Seriously, I absolutely positively need to borrow that skirt for my date tomorrow night with Ryan. That skirt is way too cute to be sitting in a suitcase for so long. Please say yes."

Rolling her eyes in feigned exasperation, Angel said, "Fine. Why do I always give in to you?"

"Because we're best friends and love each other. That's why."

Chapter Four

The doorbell rang at the Wentworth household at precisely 10:29 p.m. Janet was sitting toward the end of their black leather couch with Jim's feet resting comfortably in her lap. Jim had fallen asleep while watching *NCIS* and was snoring soundly. She gently lifted his feet and got up to see who was at the door at this late hour.

When she opened the door and saw the police officer standing there, dread and fear filled her heart. "Yes?" she said nervously while inadvertently bringing her hand to her chest.

"Are you Mrs. Wentworth?" asked the unfamiliar officer.

She nodded anxiously and turned her head toward the living room, while calling out loudly, "Jim. Jim, come here now." Jim jumped up off the couch at the sound of her panic-stricken voice and raced over to her. The minute he saw the officer, his heart began to race.

"My name is Officer Anthony Hernandez of the Cliffside Park Police Department."

Janet swallowed past the lump that was quickly forming in her throat and said, "What's happened?" She closed her eyes, knowing this visit would not be good. From the minute a mother-to-be finds out she is carrying a child within her body, worry becomes a constant in her life. From that moment on, the feeling of being carefree ceases to exist. Countless moments would cause her to torment herself with disturbing thoughts, and one of them was having the police standing on her front doorstep when her children were not home.

"Ma'am...sir...I'm sorry to inform you that there's been a car accident involving both your children." He gave the parents a moment to absorb that information and then continued. "Both boys are being treated as we speak. I'd like to drive you to the emergency room of St. Thomas's Medical Center right now."

Janet felt her knees begin to buckle beneath her and quickly held on to Jim for support. "Dear God, please tell me that my boys are alright," she said between sobs.

Officer Hernandez went on to explain to Jim and Janet that both their boys had been injured and sadly, there had been two fatalities, one being the driver of the other car involved in the collision.

Jim placed his arm around his wife's shoulder and pulled her close. He soothingly caressed her arm as he tried to comfort her while struggling to keep himself calm and continue to speak to the Officer. He swallowed hard and asked, "How bad is it?"

"I can't really say. But I do know both your boys are being well taken care of. You and your wife should come to the hospital right away."

"The other fatality. Who was it?" asked Jim. "You said there were two fatalities and one was the driver of the other car. Who..." Jim found he couldn't finish his question. He closed his eyes in fear and worry.

"I'm sorry, Mr. Wentworth. I just can't say at the moment. We're still trying to get hold of his family. They need to be notified first, but we're having trouble reaching them."

"Was it the driver?"

"I'm sorry, Mr. Wentworth. Please understand that I can't say. Please just come to the hospital." It was impossible for the officer to divulge information such as the name of the deceased without first informing the family. It was not only a matter of departmental procedure, but also a moral issue as well.

"I'll get my keys to the car," Jim said.

"Mr. Wentworth, it would be best if I drove you there. You and your wife are nervous, and it would be safer for everyone if I brought you both in the cruiser."

Jim nodded before gently pulling Janet into a deep embrace. He held her tightly as she cried uncontrollably. "They're going to be fine. I'm sure of it. We have to be strong now, okay?" he whispered into her ear.

Janet still could not control her tears and struggled to speak. "How...I don't understand..."

"We won't know anything for certain until we get to the hospital. The doctors are taking care of the boys right now." He took both her hands in his and said, "Sweetie, Jarrod and Alec need us. We have to go to them now. Can you be strong for them?"

Nodding, she said, "I will. Let's go," and then rushed to the hall closet to grab her handbag. By the time she turned around, Jim had already descended the front steps with the Officer.

It took only ten minutes to get to the hospital, yet it felt like eons. Both Janet and Jim rushed through the emergency room doors and raced to the nurses' station. Jim spoke first. "My name is James Wentworth. Both my sons were in a car accident tonight. Jarrod and Alec Wentworth."

"Yes, Mr. Wentworth," said the nurse. "I'm very sorry. The doctors are busy taking care of all the boys who were involved in the accident. I'll go have a look-see and find out what I can."

"Thank you. Could you get back to us as soon as possible?"

"Of course. Right away." The nurse stood up and headed toward the trauma rooms, through the doors to the right of the station.

Officer Hernandez, who was standing quietly behind the Wentworths, had overheard the brief conversation and was waiting a short while after its conclusion before advancing upon them. Another officer soon approached him, and they removed themselves to a more secluded area to speak.

A few minutes later, Officer Hernandez approached the Wentworths.

"Mr. and Mrs. Wentworth, I just want to say once again I'm sorry about all that's happened. I know this must be very difficult." The officer was tall, thin, and appeared to be very young. *He must have just recently graduated from the police academy*, thought Jim. He also began to wonder if they gave classes at the academy covering the proper way of addressing and handling a situation such as this. If so, he must have been at the top of his class, for he was extremely professional, yet sympathetic at the same time.

"Thank you," responded Janet as she reached out and gently placed a hand on his sleeve. "You're very kind."

"Is there anything else you can tell us?" asked Jim.

The officer removed his cap placing it on the counter of the nurse's station and pulled his hand through his short, dark hair while removing his notepad from his back pocket with his free hand. He flipped it open and while reviewing it, said, "It appears the driver of the vehicle in which your sons were passengers ran a red light. We have numerous witnesses that confirm that. It was hit by an oncoming pickup truck on the right side. The car was pushed a good distance before it…" He took a moment to clear his throat before saying, "stopped."

Jim closed his eyes briefly. When he reopened them, he looked the police officer squarely in the eye and asked, "When can you tell us about the fatality?"

Officer Hernandez looked at them sadly. "I can tell you now. I was just informed by another officer that we were able to reach his parents. They arrived not too long ago and are with their son right now. I'm sorry to inform you that the deceased's name is…Dante Malone."

Janet gasped and grabbed Jim's arm for support. "No!" she wailed as she turned her body into her husband's arms, where he held her tightly. Sobbing, she cried, "No, no, no… not Dante! Oh, Jim… this just can't be happening. Dear God, what about Janice and Mike? How are they going to handle this?"

Jim could no longer hold back the flood of tears that had begun to well up behind his eyes. He had known Dante since he was a young boy. He'd spent so much time at the Wentworth home, it was almost as if Janet and he had three sons rather than just two.

"We have to help them through this," he told Janet in a hoarse voice laced with sorrow. "They're going to need their friends more than ever and that's where we come in." Jim closed his eyes and two thoughts immediately came to his mind. He remembered the last time he had seen and spoken to Dante just a few days ago. He had walked into the house as if he owned it, jumping over the back of the couch and landing into a comfortable cross-legged sitting position while smiling at Jim the whole time. "What's up, Papa Jim?" he had asked, still smiling but adding a nodding motion to his head reminiscent of a bobble head doll.

"Get your shoes off the couch," responded Jim while continuing to read the sports section of the paper, causing an even wider smile to appear on Dante's face.

He also remembered the first time he had met Dante. Jarrod was in the fifth grade, and Jim had gone to pick him up at school that day because Janet was tied up showing a house to a potential buyer. Jarrod ran up to him with Dante at his side and introduced him to his father by saying, "This is my new best friend, Dante." Jim smiled and shook the young boy's hand and thought to himself how funny kids were. It seemed as though every week they had a new best friend. This one would probably last that long, if not less. But Jarrod had proven him wrong. Those two had been stuck to each other like glue from the moment they had met, experiencing jointly all the trials and tribulations that adolescent life offered.

And now Dante was gone. Gone forever. How would Jarrod handle the loss of his best friend? His confidante? His second brother in spirit?

Officer Hernandez walked away quietly, allowing Jim and Janet the privacy they needed. Stopping to join the other officer, he turned to look at the Wentworths once again. Lowering his head in sadness, he watched as they stood there looking into each other's eyes as if they were hoping to find a fragment of calmness or inner peace in the other rather than the fear and desperation that was indubitably reflected back.

Twenty minutes later the nurse returned. "I'm sorry for taking so long. The doctors were busy, and I had to wait for an update. I didn't want to come back without some information for you."

"Thank you," Jim said. "What can you tell us?"

"Well, it seems that your youngest son—"

"Alec," stated Janet. She gently placed her hand on the nurse's arm and said, "Please tell me he's alright."

The nurse quickly covered Janet's hand with her own.

"It seems Alec was fortunate enough to only suffer some minor injuries. He was sitting in the backseat, between the other two boys, so he had some…how can I put this?…well, he had some cushioning from the blow. It appears as though he only suffered a broken arm and two broken ribs. I know that sounds bad, but really it isn't. He will need to spend the night for observation, but I wouldn't worry too much about him. The doctors believe he'll be fine."

"Thank God," they both uttered simultaneously. Janet briefly hugged the nurse and then said, "What about our other son, Jarrod?"

The nurse lowered her eyes for just a brief moment, took a deep breath and obviously hating this part of her job, softly said, "I'm so sorry to say it's more serious with Jarrod. He was sitting on the side of the car that took the full brunt of the impact; therefore, the blow was tremendous to his body. There's been significant trauma to the right side of his body; he also has a collapsed lung. He hasn't awoken yet. He'll be taken down for a CT scan once he is stabilized and will be scheduled for further tests—"

"When you say he hasn't awoken yet, do you mean he's in a coma?" asked Jim as he desperately tried to hold back his tears. If he broke down now, Janet would never be able to make it through this.

The nurse paused for a moment. She looked him straight in the eye and said slowly and clearly "At this point, we're not certain. As of now he isn't responding to stimuli. The doctors are performing complete physical and neurological evaluations to determine whether he is or is not in a coma. I'm so very, very sorry. I wish I had better news for you. Hopefully the doctors will know more by the time they are able to speak with you. If you need anything at all, please feel free to let me know. My name is Kayla."

"Thank you, Kayla," said Jim. Kayla walked toward the nurse's station and sat down behind it. In her eighteen years as an ER nurse, she had seen many injuries such as the ones their eldest son had sustained, and not once did any of those patients survive. She was desperately hoping he would be the first. As she had done countless times before, she said a silent prayer for the young man whose ravaged body doctors were painstakingly trying to save at this very moment—a body deprived of strength, power, and capacity, which lay torpid only a few feet away behind closed doors.

Janet and Jim stood alone in the long, empty hallway of the hospital. The distressing circumstances, combined with the nauseating odor brought on by the blend of medication and disinfectants, caused them both to suffer a sickening sensation. Janet leaned her back against the wall and slowly lowered her body into a sitting position on the floor. Somewhere in the background, people could be heard, but nothing made any sense to her. Some were moaning from pain, others were complaining about insignificant matters such as the lengthy wait, and a few fortuitous souls were just content to finally be leaving. It felt as if she and Jim were alone in a dark, dismal tunnel that existed only to siphon their spirits of all happiness and joy. All they could feel now was misery, hopelessness, anguish, and despair.

"We're losing him."

Voices. Some were yelling, others were whispering. So much commotion. Doctors giving orders and nurses anxiously following them. Why did that one doctor say, "We're losing him?" Who were they talking about? This was clearly a hospital. What the hell was he doing in a hospital? Was someone hurt? Where was Alec? Where were the guys?

Jarrod's thoughts were meshing all together, causing so much uncertainty. His head was spinning, but yet it didn't hurt. He felt fine. No, he was better than fine. There was no pain, no pressure, and no worries. His body felt weightless and buoyant, as if he were a boat drifting aimlessly on the water.

The doctors were hovering over a body, but whose body was it? He wished that one nurse would just move an inch or two to her left, and then he would be able to see who it was.

From the corner of his eye, he noticed an illuminating beam of light. He turned to look at it, but it was so bright, it forced him to squint. Where was that light coming from, and why did he feel such an urgent need to reach out to it?

"Clear!"

The voice distracted Jarrod momentarily and he turned toward it. The nurse had moved, and he had a clear view of the body on the gurney. It was *him*. No. That was impossible.

He looked again. It *was* him. How could that be? How was it possible that his body was lying there, covered in blood and appearing lifeless, when he was just fine standing there watching them? Something was wrong. Terribly, terribly wrong. Perhaps someone had slipped a mickey into his food or drink at the restaurant where he had dined earlier with his family and it was now causing him to hallucinate. That had to be it. That was the only rational explanation. Either that or he was dreaming. *Wake up! Wake up already*, he thought to himself.

The light. It was even brighter and stronger now. So inviting and warm. He felt an immense pull; it beckoned him and drew him closer as he found himself walking, no floating, toward it.

"We have a pulse."

And suddenly, just like that, the light was gone.

Chapter Five

Two long hours after arriving at the hospital, Janet and Jim were finally allowed to see Alec. He was lying on a gurney in one of the trauma rooms, his arm in a cast, his eyes closed. He had a few scratches and bruises on his face and neck area, but aside from that, he looked well enough. Janet leaned over and kissed him gently on the forehead. Alec opened his eyes slowly. He looked at her for a long moment, and then a lone teardrop gradually escaped from his eye and rolled down his cheek. "Jarrod?" he asked in a gravelly voice.

Janet wiped away his tear, while Jim placed his hand soothingly on his shoulder. He couldn't really get past the tightness in his chest, so he was only able to grunt out "He'll be okay."

"The guys?" Alec asked as he timorously looked from one parent to another.

"Brendon and Joey were hurt, but they'll be fine." Janet cast a quick, meaningful glance to Jim and decided that it would be best for Alec not to hear about Dante's passing until later, when he would be stronger and more lucid. She told him the doctor had insisted on them staying only a few minutes so as to not tire him out, therefore they only had time to check on him, and they would talk about everything after he rested.

Alec was so tired and woozy from the medication that he had been given; he did not have the strength to argue. All he was able to get out before falling asleep was, "Call…Wyatt. Jarrod can't…appointment."

Jim and Janet looked at one another wide-eyed. They hadn't even thought of that. A few short hours ago, Mr. Wyatt and tomorrow's meeting was the most important thing in the world to them. Now it was at the lowest point on their totem pole of priorities. "I'll call him later," said Jim.

A few hours later, Drs. Matthew Anderson and Nicholas Arcao escorted the Wentworths to a small conference room located near the emergency room. When they had all made themselves comfortable, the doctors explained that Alec would be released the following morning if there were no complications throughout the night. X-rays were taken to evaluate the extent of damage to his left arm, and it was determined that he had suffered a closed fracture of the humerus, which is the largest bone in the arm. He would need to wear a hanging arm cast that would be suspended by a sling looped around his neck for possibly three weeks and would require additional X-rays to make sure the bones stayed aligned. In addition, Alec had suffered trauma to the chest area, causing two of his ribs to break. Usually broken ribs healed completely in about two months. They recommended rest, ice, and over-the-counter medications to relieve any discomfort. He was to avoid any activities that would aggravate the injuries. No long-term damage was expected.

Both Janet and Jim drew deep breaths of relief. But that sensation would be short-lived. They noted how both doctors seem to stiffen a bit and look at each other before speaking. Dr. Arcao looked down at the file before him, cleared his throat twice, and then looked up at Jim. There was such sadness emanating from his eyes. "I wish we had good news with regard to your eldest son, Jarrod. But unfortunately, we don't." He cleared his throat once again, took a sip of water from a glass he had poured just a few minutes earlier, and then finally spoke.

"Due to where Jarrod was seated in the vehicle, he absorbed the most impact from the collision. The result is that he is suffering from what is called traumatic pneumothorax or in layman's terms, a collapsed lung. He also has an acromioclavicular separation, which is an injury to the area between the collarbone and the shoulder. He has a broken arm and leg, as well as…" The doctor took a deep breath and then continued, "bleeding in the area between the brain and the thin tissues that cover the brain. This is called a subarachnoid hemorrhage." Jim abruptly stood up, not able to listen any further, and cut the doctor off by asking, "Is my son going to die?"

Dr. Anderson looked him straight in the eye. "We don't know for certain, but sadly, there is likelihood that he might. It might be a good idea for you both to prepare yourselves for this possible outcome. We're so sorry. We truly are. It goes without saying that we will do whatever we possibly can to save your son."

Janet wiped her tear-filled eyes with a tissue and asked, "Is he in much pain?"

Dr. Anderson stretched slightly forward across the conference table and placed his hand over Janet's. "No. I truly believe he is not in any pain. Presently, Jarrod is in a coma. The trauma to the head, based on the results of the CT scan, appears to be significant. Dr. Christian Silverstein is reviewing his file and scan results and will determine what the next step should be. I should tell you that Dr. Silverstein is one of the most prominent neurosurgeons in this field. Your son Jarrod is in great hands. He'll be able to explain in much better detail what needs to be done next."

Dr. Arcao followed with, "Mr. and Mrs. Wentworth, we're not going to lie to you. For a brief moment, twenty-five seconds to be exact, we lost Jarrod. He flat lined and had no pulse. We were able to bring him back, but we do not know what long-term effect those twenty-five seconds may have had on him, should he wake up from the coma."

"*When* he wakes up," said Janet. She wasn't crying or panicking anymore. She simply sat there fingering a small gold cross around her neck, all the while looking calm, stoic, and resolute. She was determined that her son was going to wake up and be fine, and because of this, Jim felt better. When Janet was determined for something to happen, it happened.

After speaking with the doctors, Jim and Janet spent the next few hours at Alec's bedside. He was sleeping peacefully, thanks to the pain medication he was being given. Every once and awhile, he would wearily open his eyes, let out a soft groan, and then fall right back to sleep again. The nurse, Kayla, had come by once or twice to let them know if there had been any changes in Jarrod's condition. Unfortunately, there hadn't been.

At 6:22 a.m., they were finally allowed to see Jarrod. Although Kayla had forewarned them of what to expect, they still had not been prepared to see him in this state. When is any parent prepared to see their child lying in a bed, helplessly hooked up to numerous machines and IVs? They both gasped as they approached him.

Janet leaned over, as she had done with Alec, and kissed his cheek tenderly. His head was wrapped in a turban of white gauze, and there were numerous cuts and abrasions evident across his cheeks, chin, and neck, with scatters of dried blood encased in the wounds. His face and lips were swollen beyond recognition. This unconscious man-child lying helplessly in the hospital bed barely resembled their beautiful son.

"Baby, it's Mom," she whispered in his ear. "You're going to be fine. We'll get through this one step at a time." Janet suddenly realized that those were practically the exact same words she had said to him earlier that day, prior to him making the call to Mr. Wyatt. She gave Jarrod a tentative smile, because she knew she had been right then, and she was going to be right again. "I love you," she said, and she kissed him once again.

Soon after they met with Dr. Silverstein. It turned out that he not only was considered a champion surgeon in his field, but was also the chief of neurosurgery at St. Thomas's Medical Center. He elucidated in further detail the results of the tests and examinations. He also informed them that immediate surgery was required; otherwise Jarrod's outlook would significantly worsen.

Chapter Six

Jarrod was prepped and taken into surgery that afternoon. The Wentworths were informed that the surgery would last approximately four hours, and they spent that time alternating between Alec's room and the hospital chapel. At one point Jim went home to place the dreaded call to Mr. Wyatt, but was back at Janet's side within a short hour.

The surgery went amazingly well, with no complications arising. Dr. Silverstein was able to relieve the pressure building in Jarrod's brain by removing the amassed blood. Now, only time would tell. He would be monitored around the clock by a team of doctors and nurses. All Janet and Jim could do now was hope and pray for Jarrod's safe and quick recovery.

Services for Dante Malone were held that Tuesday morning at Holy Trinity Church. It seemed as if every resident of Cliffside Park was in attendance to pay their respects. The church was overflowing with mourners, and people stood outside on the sidewalk, quietly listening to the priest via a loudspeaker that had been turned on. Family, friends, and even strangers stood under a sea of umbrellas as they tried to protect themselves from the bleak rain, appropriate weather for such a dismal, oppressive occasion. Many embraced one another while trying to reconcile themselves to the fact that something so tragic could have happened to such a decent, well-liked, and admired young man.

Upon entering the church, Alec noticed Morgan was in attendance, but had opted to sit in the last pew with a few of her friends. *She probably chose to sit there due to its close and convenient proximity to the exit door,* he thought. For someone whose boyfriend was lying in a coma after a horrific accident, and who was attending her boyfriend's best friend's funeral, she didn't appear too heartbroken as she whispered and giggled into her friend's ear. Alec turned away from her revolting display of dispassion and joined his parents, who were sitting morosely in the fourth pew. The Wentworths had already expressed their sympathies to Dante's family the night before when they had visited them at their house after leaving the hospital. The meeting had been sad and discomfited. Janice and Mike were inconsolable and rightfully so. Between tears they apologized to the Wentworths profusely, for they not only felt sadness, but also regret as well for the physical state of all the boys; especially Jarrod, whose life was dangling by a string. They also felt an abyssal sense of remorse for the tragic death of the other driver.

Wiping away her tears, Janice lifted her head and looked at Alec. "I just don't understand how he could have run a red light," she said. "He was usually so careful driving. Alec, you were there. Please tell us what happened?"

Alec, who had just been released from the hospital the day before, looked at his parents for support. He didn't want to tell them their only child had died because he was busy looking for a CD in the glove compartment. At the same time, he understood that as Dante's parents, they had the right to know every step that had led up to their son's death. Janet softly touched his shoulder. "They need to know. Tell them."

Alec glanced down at the floor and said in a soft voice, "He was reaching into the glove compartment to look for a CD."

Janice and Mike both looked shocked. Mike closed his eyes, bit his lower lip while shaking his head in denial, and excused himself from the room.

An unending stream of tears poured from Janice's eyes. As she wrapped her arms around her middle, she rocked herself gently back and forth.

Janet turned her eyes toward Jim, and they stared back at each other, feeling powerless. Her heart broke for her friend, but all the while she couldn't help but be thankful her two children were still alive. Broken and battered, but mercifully still alive. Janet quickly walked over to the sofa where Janice sat and wrapped her arms around her. Janice leaned into her, seeking comfort and solace from the pain that was destroying her.

"How could he have done something so irresponsible? A CD? My son died because he wanted to listen to a damn CD." She sobbed uncontrollably out of pain and anger. "Why didn't he just ask someone to—"

"He did," said Alec. "He asked Jarrod to look and he did twice but couldn't find it."

"Oh..." She took a few deep breaths to calm herself down, wiped her nose with a handkerchief that she clutched tightly in her fist, stood up, and slowly walked toward the fireplace, where she stood momentarily staring at a family portrait that hung above the mantel. Dante had only been three years old when the photo had been taken. He had been so uncooperative that day. Although the photographer was able to make him smile for that one snapshot by repeatedly hitting himself on the head with a plastic cane, if one were to look closely, one would notice the gleam of unshed tears in his eyes.

"Which CD?" she asked, never taking her eyes off of the portrait.

Alec looked up at her and said, "Excuse me?" He couldn't understand how that mattered.

"Which CD did he want?" she repeated softly.

"Umm…" he hesitated. "AC/DC."

A slight smile broke through her pain and she said, "'Thunderstruck'?"

He nodded and speaking softly said, "Yes." Now he understood why it mattered. Dante's mother knew as well as everyone else how he had loved that song.

Mike had reentered the room unnoticed and stood silently in a corner with his head down and his arms folded across his chest. Upon hearing what was said, he lifted his head and slowly walked over to Janice and pulled her into his arms. They held each other silently for a few moments and then Mike turned toward the Wentworths and said, "Again, we're so very sorry. We feel horrible that so many lives were impacted due to Dante's recklessness. I hope you can accept our apology and forgive Dante."

Jim walked over to stand behind Janet and placed both his hands squarely on her shoulders. "You have nothing to apologize for. It was an accident. These things happen. Think of how many times we've all done the same exact thing. You just never think that something will come of it. Dante never meant for any of this to happen." He drew in a deep breath and continued. "We have no choice but to accept things and move forward. The boys, in time, will heal. The two of you need to heal as well, and the only way for that to happen is for you, not us, to forgive Dante and let his spirit be at peace."

Janet and Jim walked toward Dante's devastated parents, and they embraced one another in conjoined pain as Alec looked on. As he turned to readjust himself in the chair, he inadvertently let out a soft moan of discomfort. His medication was wearing off and he desperately needed to lie down.

Janet, seeing that Alec needed rest, made their excuses and said their good-byes. Though it was not mentioned, they all knew they would see each other again in the morning at the funeral service.

As Janet sat in the church wiping away her tears, she bombarded heaven with silent prayers for Dante, his parents, and all the boys involved in the accident, as well as Clyde Lambert, the young father of three boys who had been driving the pickup truck that had crashed into Dante's car. She had read in the newspaper that morning that his funeral was being held today as well. Brendon and Joey were still hospitalized due to their injuries, but the outlook was good for them both. Jarrod came through the surgery and now all anyone could do was wait and see.

The service lasted almost two hours and had all the major components that would generate a tearjerker movie. Various students, teachers, and relatives spoke briefly in turn of Dante's high-spirited and exuberant love of life and all that it offered, his undying devotion to family and friends, maddening obsession with reality TV, and ultimately his prodigious fondness for a really good party. The final eulogy, given by his father, was heart-wrenching as he spoke of the love and pride he and his wife felt and would eternally cling to in their hearts for their beloved son. He broke down twice while speaking, but never quit. As difficult as it was for him to stand in front of hundreds of witnesses as he bid his final farewell to his only child, he persevered as would be expected from this man who held a remarkable sense of true honor, strength, and dignity. His worthy tribute was followed by the melodious voice of Luciena Alderoni, who had secretly harbored a crush on Dante for the last two years. She sang the stirring, devotional words of the "Ave Maria" while his coffin was slowly and gently carried out to the waiting hearse that would transport his body to its final resting place, Mount Hope Cemetery.

The Wentworths did not attend the burial service or the gathering that immediately followed it at the home of the Malones. They were physically and emotionally spent and could not bear to watch while Dante's body was lowered into the ground. After the funeral Jim took Alec home so he could rest, while Janet headed directly to the hospital to be by Jarrod's side.

◊ Broken Road ◊

When Janet walked into the intensive care unit, suddenly a nurse rushed up to her, smiling brightly.

"Mrs. Wentworth, I'm so glad you're here. We've been trying to reach you at home and on your cell since this morning."

Janet could sense the nurse was about to give her spectacular news. She began to feel nervous and excited at the same time.

"We were at a funeral earlier today and my husband and I turned off our cells. I'm so sorry. I don't know what I was thinking. Has something happened? Is Jarrod okay?" She mentally beat herself up for not putting the phones on vibrate rather than turning them off. Her mind seemed to be scattered in a million directions since the accident, and simple thoughts and actions evaded her completely.

"Yes, he's better than okay. He's woken up."

"Oh my God!" She quickly embraced the nurse in her excitement and ran toward Jarrod's room. As she was halfway down the hall, she looked back and hollered, "Thank you."

The nurse started behind her, still needing to give her additional information. "Mrs. Wentworth! Wait! Please wait." She caught up to her before Janet entered the room. She stopped her by placing her hand on her arm "Mrs. Wentworth, wait a moment, please."

"Why? Is something the matter? Didn't you say he woke up?"

"Yes, he did and everything seems to be great, but I just wanted to forewarn you that he's been asking about the accident and the condition of his brother and friends. We've been able to avoid answering him, which has not been easy, but we thought it would be best for the news to come from either you or your husband."

"Yes, you're right. Thank you so much. I appreciate it," Janet responded worriedly. She began to bite the nail of her left thumb as she debated whether to call and wait for Jim to arrive so they could tackle telling Jarrod the heartrending revelation together, or if she should just go in alone. She just couldn't bear waiting another moment to see him.

"You should also know we were able to speak with your husband just a little while ago, and he said to tell you that he and your other son are on their way." *Maybe I can wait just a tiny bit longer,* she thought. Just as she finished thinking those words, Jim came rushing through the doors of the ICU, with Alec following as quickly as his injuries and pain would allow. Jim caught up to Janet and hugged her tightly.

"Have you seen him yet?" he asked.

"No, not yet. I just got here myself. I can't believe I was stupid enough to turn my cell phone off. What the hell is wrong with me?"

"Not just you. Me too. We're just overwhelmed and frazzled with all that's happened. As soon as I turned mine back on, I listened to my messages. The hospital had called six times. I called right back to let them know I was on my way."

"The nurse says he's been asking about the accident and of the condition of the boys. No one has said anything, so we need to be prepared to tell him."

"Let me do it," said Alec in a somber tone as he reached them.

"Are you sure you're up to it?" asked Jim, worry and concern etched across his face.

"No," Alec said definitively. "I just feel it should come from me."

The parents looked at each other and then turned to Alec, replying simultaneously "Alright" and "If you're sure." Jim added, "We'll be right there if you need us."

"No. I'd rather it just be him and me when I tell him." The parents agreed, although their faces reflected their reluctance.

The three of them followed one another into the room. Jarrod appeared to be sleeping, which frightened Janet. Her eyes clouding with tears, she whispered to Jim "She said that he had awoken."

"I am awake," muttered Jarrod. He opened his eyes slowly and turned his head slightly toward them. He groaned softly. The slight movement hurt terribly, and he found that his vision was blurred. He blinked several times, trying to focus and clear the superimposing images of their bodies.

Janet rushed to his side and reached to touch his hand. She leaned forward and kissed him softly. "Hi, sweetie. Welcome back." She squeezed his hand gently and wiped away her tears. "I've missed you. How are you feeling?"

❖ Broken Road ❖

"Okay…just thirsty." His throat ached and his lips felt dry and cracked. He tried licking them, but even that small movement hurt.

Jim quickly grabbed a clear plastic cup from the night table, filled it with water from the pink pitcher that sat next to it, and placed a bendy straw in it. He positioned the straw in Jarrod's mouth, helping him to drink. "Drink slowly, son," he said, pausing just a moment to swallow past the lump that had formed in his throat. "I'm so happy you're okay."

Jarrod stopped drinking and gazed at his parents and then his brother. "You alright?" he asked his younger brother.

"Yeah. Better than you. How are you doing?"

Jarrod closed his eyes for a moment and did not respond to his question. Instead he looked up at his brother and said, "Tell me."

Jim cleared his throat and said, "We'll leave you two to talk." He grasped Janet's hand as they hesitantly took their leave from the room.

The brothers watched in silence as their parents left. The silence continued for a few moments as both boys were deep in their personal thoughts.

"Go on," said Jarrod as he took a deep breath in preparation, but only caused himself pain in doing so. He grabbed his chest in distress and did his best to restrict a cough he felt coming on, but failed. The pain was excruciating. He moaned and tears came to his eyes as he continued to hold his chest, hoping somehow that would ease the ache. Alec was by his side in seconds, feeling utterly helpless as he watched his brother struggle through the discomfort.

Once Jarrod was feeling better, Alec stepped away from his side and walked slowly toward the window, which looked out onto the Hudson River and the beautiful New York skyline. The majestic beauty created by the varying ranges of style, size, scope, and extent of the skyscrapers never failed to astound and affect him in an overwhelming and wondrous manner. He felt himself pulled toward and fascinated with the architectural allure and charm of the Empire State and

Chrysler Buildings as they stood towering in their spellbinding glory. As he looked south toward Lower Manhattan, he felt sick at heart when viewing the area that once was characterized for the omnipresence of the Twin Towers, but now appeared barren and dispiriting.

"Brendon and Joey will be alright. They're both here at the hospital and will be for at least another few days, maybe even a week for Joey. Both guys were pretty banged up, but the doctors say they'll be fine. Joey had surgery on his knee yesterday, so he'll be laid up for a bit. But all in all, they're fine."

Jarrod nodded and closed his eyes. He knew in his heart what the answer was going to be to his next question. He didn't want to hear it, but he had to ask it. "Dante…?" A soft sob escaped while tears began to gently stream down his face. He closed his eyes more tightly, trying to obliterate the words he was about to hear.

Alec took his time responding. Still unable to muster up the strength to face Jarrod, he continued staring out the window as if fascinated with the view. Knowing he was about to tear his brother's heart in two, he cleared his throat and forced himself to face him. Their eyes locked. "We just came from the funeral," Alec whispered.

Jarrod turned his head away and let the tears spill over as he gasped for air, repeating Dante's name over and over again. Alec walked over to him and simply placed his hand on Jarrod's shoulder. They cried together in silence, for there was nothing Alec could say or do at this time to ease the pain in his brother's heart.

Four days later Brendon was released from the hospital, and two days after that, Joey followed suit. Both boys visited Jarrod on Tuesday, exactly one week after Dante's funeral. They hobbled in on crutches, Joey's left knee wrapped in a protective knee brace. They stood on opposite sides of Jarrod's bed and all three gazed at one another in silence until Brendon spoke. "Hey," he uttered. "How you doin'?"

Jarrod raised one eyebrow slightly and said, "How do I look like I'm doing?"

"Not so good," responded Joey. "I mean, we look like crap, but compared to you, we look like we just spent a week at a spa."

"Yeah, well, believe it or not, I feel worse than I look. Every bone, muscle, and joint in my body aches. How about you guys?"

"I'm alright," said Brendon. "Alec and I were the luckiest of the five."

A deafening hush hovered over them akin to a black cloud. At that precise moment, everyone's thoughts went straight to Dante. Jarrod closed his eyes and pinched the bridge of his nose as if trying to prevent the tears from flowing. He failed."God, guys, what are…we…what are we going to do?"

Both his friends were crying as well and unable to speak. After a long pause, Brendon wiped his nose on his sleeve and said, "I still can't believe it. I mean, it just doesn't seem possible."

"It's like a freakin' nightmare," added Joey. "I just want to wake up and find that the accident never happened and everyone is fine."

"And Dante's still alive," Jarrod said.

"Yeah…and Dante's still alive," reiterated Brendon between whispered sobs.

Chapter Seven

Jarrod was released ten days later with detailed instructions for his follow-up care. He would need to wear the leg and arm casts for approximately two months and avoid strenuous activity to allow his injuries to heal, as well as visit his numerous specialists on a continual basis and begin physical therapy rehabilitation as soon as his injuries permitted.

Jim wheeled him into the house in his temporary wheelchair. He would only need it for a short while, until he felt stronger and was able to move around on his own.

"Do you want to watch a little TV?" asked Jim.

"No, thanks," responded Jarrod so softly that Jim had to lean forward to hear him. He looked around the living room of the house where he had grown up. So much had changed in his life within the past few weeks; and yet, as he studied the room, so much still remained the same.

"How about a nap then?" Jim said, interrupting Jarrod's thoughts. "I can make up the couch and you can just lie down for a bit…" Jarrod shook his head gently, letting his father know he had no interest in taking him up on that offer as well.

"Well then…um…is there anything I can get you? A soda? Sandwich?" Jim felt there must be something he could do to help his son.

"Dad, I'm fine. Don't worry about me. I'll let you know if I need anything. What I would like, if you don't mind, is for you to help me up to my room. I just want to be alone."

"Sure. Not a problem," Jim was just so delighted to be able to do something for his son that it didn't really faze him that being asked to be left alone was what Jarrod wanted more than anything else.

He helped Jarrod out of his chair and slowly they both ascended the steps, with Jarrod leaning heavily on his father. By the time they reached the top, they were both out of breath.

As Jarrod tried to get comfortable in his bed, Jim asked once more if there was anything he could get him or do for him. Jarrod responded with a negative shake of the head and a quickly mumbled, "No thanks."

Soon after Jarrod heard the faint sound of a telephone ringing. Moments later his father quietly opened the door to his room and softly whispered, "Jarrod? Jarrod, are you awake? Morgan's on the phone." No response. He heard his father say into the phone as he was walking back out of the room, "Morgan, he's sleeping right now. I'll have him call you later, okay?"

Jarrod wasn't sleeping. In fact, he hadn't slept soundly since…well, since he woke up from the coma. He only pretended to be sleeping because the last thing he wanted to do was speak to Morgan. He remembered her last visit to the hospital and how badly that had gone.

"What do the doctors say?" she had asked as she nonchalantly placed the bouquet of flowers she had sent earlier that week in front of all the others that were quickly taking over the room.

"Not much. At least nothing I want to hear." He watched her pull out a dying flower from another arrangement. "Did you color your hair again?"

Smiling, she turned to face him and quickly raised a hand to her hair. "Yup. I had it done last night. You like?"

"It's okay. I thought you said you had a ton of homework and that's why you couldn't stop by to visit last night."

"I did have a lot of homework, but it didn't take me as long to do it as I had thought it would," she said while turning her back to him to look through some of the cards he had received from well-wishers. "You're changing the subject. Answer my question. What are the doctors saying?"

"I told you. Not much. I have to take it easy for awhile, but once I'm better, I need to start physical therapy. That's it."

"Will you ever be able to play ball again?" she asked casually as if she were asking him about the weather.

"Ouch. Man, you don't believe much in mincing words, do you?"

"Nope."

"I don't know," he said and then added, "I don't really want to talk about that, if you don't mind."

"You can't just ignore it. I mean, you need to find out what they think. You had plans. Dreams. Goals…and if you aren't able to play…"

"Morgan, I said I don't want to talk about it, alright? Just drop it," he said loudly.

Exasperated, she let out a deep sigh and nodded. "Fine, I'll drop it. For now."

A tense, awkward moment ensued until Jarrod asked, "Have you seen or spoken to Mr. and Mrs. Malone yet?"

"I saw them at the funeral."

"How are they?"

"How do you expect them to be? They're sad."

"I mean…well, what did they say? What did you say?"

"Jarrod, I expressed my sympathies and they said thank you very much. What else is there to say?" She plopped herself down in the chair next to his bed.

"You didn't say anything more? You just expressed your sympathies and that was it?"

"Yeah, that was it. Look, I've never been any good at that kind of stuff. I hate funerals, I hate wakes, and well, I just hate anything dealing with death, period. Everyone is so sad and moping around like it's the end of the world or something. I was uncomfortable being there, so I said as little as possible and then got the hell out of there."

"For some people, like the Malones, it is the end of the world. Nobody is comfortable talking about or dealing with death, but it's something we all have to deal with at one time or another."

"Well, that's how I choose to deal with it, and just because it's not how you would, it doesn't necessarily mean I'm wrong. It just means that we're different, so you can stop looking at me like I'm some sort of monster or an alien from a different planet…oh, hey, are you going to eat that pudding, or can I have it?" she asked, looking at the untouched tray of food that had been sitting there idle for over an hour.

"You eat it. I've had enough crap for one day."

That had been four days ago. He hadn't seen or spoken to Morgan since then. Funny thing was, he found he didn't miss her all that much and didn't mind the lack of contact. *That can't be a good thing*, he thought to himself. It definitely didn't say much for their relationship.

As Janet pulled into the driveway after taking Alec to a doctor's appointment, she heard loud music blasting from Jarrod's room. As she came around to the passenger side of the car to open the door for Alec, she looked up toward Jarrod's open bedroom window.

"What in God's name is he doing?" she said. "He's playing that music so loud, it can be heard two towns away."

"Mom, leave it," said Alec as he looked up toward Jarrod's window.

"I can't just leave it! He has to lower it. It's way too loud! The neighbors will call the police. If he wants to listen to music, he should put in his ear thingamajigs and listen to it on his iPhone."

Alec continued to stare at his brother's window and simply uttered the words, "He wants it loud for a reason. He's grieving."

"Pardon me?" Janet asked.

"That's Dante's song. 'Thunderstruck.' He played it all the time. It was his favorite." He fell silent for a brief moment and then said to his mother, "Mom, listen closely. Really closely. Beyond the music."

Janet did as her son requested and it slowly dawned on her what Alec was able to hear that she hadn't. She wiped an errant tear from her eye as she listened to the mournful cries of her eldest son beyond the deafening music.

As days turned into weeks, not much seemed to change within the Wentworth household. Jarrod still remained in his room most of the time, only leaving it to go to the bathroom or take a shower. One night, as a special surprise that she hoped would please Jarrod, Janet ordered Chinese food from their favorite local takeout restaurant and brought two separate trays loaded with his favorite appetizers and entrees up to his room. Alec followed her into the room and sat down at a small snack table his father had brought up earlier that day.

"Mind if I join you for dinner?" asked Alec.

"I was wondering why Dad brought up that table. Yeah, sure." Actually, he did mind. He would have preferred if Alec ate downstairs with the rest of the family as he usually did, but he didn't want to offend him. He didn't feel like dealing with incessant prattling or hearing the latest gossip or rumor that was going around. He didn't want to exchange pleasantries or make small talk about inconsequential, banal topics. He preferred to eat alone, sit alone — to be left alone. Why couldn't they just understand that? He simply did not want company.

Alec picked up an egg roll and began to eat, while Jarrod unconsciously mixed his beef lo mein with his sweet and sour chicken. He continued doing so while unknowingly being observed by his brother.

"You plan on eventually eating that mishmash, or are you going to create some new recipe like Mom does?" Alec finally asked.

"Not really hungry today," Jarrod responded as he put down his fork and moved the tray aside. He raised the volume on the television set, hoping that Alec would get the message and cease with the small talk.

Alec took a deep sigh and asked, "What are you thinking about?"

So much for subtle hints, thought Jarrod. He lowered the volume and said, "I'm thinking I need to see Dante's parents." He had been thinking about paying them a visit since he was released from the hospital. He just wasn't sure if they could handle seeing him in a wheelchair. On good days he was able to hobble along on crutches, but those days were few and far between.

"I'd wait a bit if I were you. I think it's too soon." Alec put down his fork and stopped eating as well.

"For whom? Them or me?" Jarrod asked irritably.

"Both."

"Why do you say that?"

"Dude, they just lost their only son. They need time. You were his best friend. It'll kill them to see you." Alec knew Jarrod was suffering. Aside from the physical pain he was enduring, he had lost his best friend, and that was an agony that all the rehab in the world would not be able to heal. On top of everything, the uncertainty of his future lay before him. What if he could never play baseball again? That thought had to be driving him crazy with fear and worry.

Alec could only imagine the pain Jarrod was feeling as he watched his ambitions, dreams, and hopes wither away. He only wished his brother would open up and talk about his sorrows and concerns. Not that there was anything he could do to change the situation, but at least he could be there for Jarrod as a venting outlet. He also wished Jarrod would take a moment to think about the pain others were enduring. He wasn't the only one affected by the accident. The anguish his parents were bearing by watching their son undergo such physical, mental, and emotional pain was horrific. And now he'd decided it was time to visit the Malones. What about their pain? Could he not, for just one moment, see that by him appearing on their front doorstep, he would be reopening a wound that hadn't yet begun to heal?

"I can't ignore them forever," said Jarrod.

"Nobody's telling you to ignore them; not now, not ever. I'm just saying to give them a little more time. The fact that they haven't come to see you yet is proof that they aren't ready. Plus, you need some time too."

"I'm fine," Jarrod responded coldly and definitively. That seemed to be Jarrod's response to everything lately. Everything was always fine; he was always fine. *What a load of crap that was,* thought Alec. Pure, unmitigated crap. His brother wasn't fine, and he wasn't ever going to be fine if he remained a recluse in the seclusion of his room, hiding from the world and all its unfairness and cruelty.

"No, you're not," said Alec, knowing he was about to draw first blood. He could sense that Jarrod was getting angry and that he was treading thin ice, but he felt that the conversation could not be left incomplete, so he continued on by adding, "Jarrod, you and the Malones are both mourning the loss of a really special person in your lives. That's not an easy thing to get over. It takes a lot of time—"

"So now, all of a sudden, you're Dr. Phil? Alec, do me a favor and just mind your own business and stay out of this," Jarrod said abruptly, cutting his brother off. He stared straight ahead at the television and once again raised the volume.

"I'm not saying that I know everything…," said Alec loudly as he tried to be heard over the theme to ESPN's *SportsCenter*.

Jarrod lifted the tray of uneaten food with his good arm and threw it angrily across the room, hollering, "You don't know anything! You don't know how I feel; you don't know what I'm thinking!" He screamed again, "You don't know shit! Just get out! Get out of my room now!"

Shock silencing him, Alec slowly got up from his chair and quietly walked out of his brother's room. It was going to take a lot longer than he thought for his brother to get through this. As he closed the door to Jarrod's room, he could still hear Jarrod screaming, "Why can't everyone just leave me the hell alone?"

His mother was running up the steps and stopped suddenly when she saw Alec leaving the room and heading toward his own.

"What's going on?" she asked anxiously.

"You heard him. I wouldn't be surprised if the whole neighborhood heard him. He just wants to be left alone."

"Are you alright?" Janet asked. She was shaking and kept looking toward Jarrod's room, where profanities and roars of anger were still being unleashed.

"Never better, but I wouldn't go near him right now if I were you," he responded dryly as he walked past her into his room. Before shutting the door behind him, he turned to face her and added, "And just so you know, he's decided to redecorate his room, starting with the walls. He's opted to go with an Asian motif."

Janet stood on the steps for a long moment, glancing from one closed door to the other. Eventually she sat down on one of the steps and began to cry. Jim sat alone at the dining room table and cried softly as well.

Time continued to pass and the situation did not improve. The only evidence that Jarrod resided in the same home as the others was that the stereo in his room would blast for hours on end, playing the same song over and over again. Alec tried repeatedly to get him to talk or at least leave his room, but it was useless. He decided to give his brother what he had asked for, and he left him alone to wallow in his sorrow. At least for a few days. He spoke with his parents about doing the same during dinner later that evening.

"I think it's best if we just do as he says and leave him alone," Alec suggested to his dismayed parents. He lifted a forkful of lasagna to his mouth and watched as they looked at each other, dumbfounded.

"How can you expect us to do that?" Jim said. "He's our son and he's hurting. It's our job to help him through this."

"I understand, but I think if we just let him be for a few days and stop hovering over him, he might get past it a little quicker," Alec said confidently.

"Why do you say that?" said Janet as she passed him the bottle of soda for his empty glass.

"Thanks," said Alec. "I think he feels suffocated. We keep—and I say we because I'm just as guilty as the two of you—we keep asking him if he's okay, or if he needs anything, or if there's anything we can do for him. We ask him if he wants to talk…does he need his pillow fluffed…for Christ's sake, Mom, yesterday I heard you ask him if he needed to pee."

"I asked him because he needs help getting up. He has so much trouble—" Janet said before Alec cut her off.

"Mom, he doesn't need that much help. True, he has a difficult time getting around, but he can do it. I've seen him get up and go to the bathroom by himself plenty of times. He doesn't get any help in the shower, does he? I'm just saying that by offering so much help, we're basically telling him we don't think he's capable of doing anything on his own. And why should he? We're more than willing to do everything for him."

"Are you saying he's enjoying it?" asked Jim.

"No, not at all. If anything, he probably hates it. But maybe he's starting to believe that he can't do any of the things he once did and that's only making him more depressed." He took a long swallow of his soda. "It's just too much. Instead of letting him just be, we keep reminding him of everything that's happened, all that he's lost, and even worse, all that he might never be able to do again."

Janet nodded. "Losing Dante was and is a devastating blow."

"It's more than that," said Alec. "Not that that's not enough of a blow, but you need to remember one thing. He's probably thinking his career as a baseball player ended before it even had a chance to begin." He stood up and walked into the kitchen to grab the butter from the refrigerator. When he returned, he looked at his father and said, "Have you even thought about that?"

"Only about a million times a day," said Jim. He never brought it up simply because he felt the family was struggling with enough issues and didn't need the extra worry and stress; but the thought weighed heavily on his mind.

"Try multiplying that number by another million, and that's about how many times he's thought of it, I'll bet you," said Alec as he buttered his roll.

"I just don't know how or if I can just leave it be," Janet said. "He's my son and I worry. I worry about the both of you. You've been through so much as well. You just seem to be handling it better. Are you, love? Or is it just my wishful thinking?" She leaned over and placed a soft, warm comforting hand over his.

"I suppose I am. I mean, yeah, I think about what happened a lot. I'm thankful to be alive, but it just kills me when I think of Dante being gone. It's got to be so much worse for Jarrod than for me." He hesitated before speaking again. "I guess we do handle things differently, though. I sort of see that the future still holds a lot for me, but I don't think he sees that for himself anymore. Then again, he was so close to having his dream come true and then this happened. I don't think he's ever even considered doing anything else other than play ball professionally. He's got a lot on his mind and a lot to figure out."

"And you think leaving him alone, when he has so much bringing him down, is the right thing to do?" Janet asked. "I just don't see how that can be for the best."

"I'm not saying to never ask him how he is or if he needs us to do anything for him. I'm just saying that for a few days, we need to stop pestering him. Just give him a little breathing room."

Janet and Jim looked at each other, searching for either a look of agreement or disagreement. Ultimately, concurrently yet reluctantly, they nodded in affirmation.

"Hey, I have a question for you," said Jim. "When did you get to be so smart?"

Alec smiled meekly and said, "It's in the genes."

For the next few days, the Wentworths stuck to their plan. Janet stopped asking him what he wanted to eat and instead would just bring up a tray of whatever everyone else was eating that evening. Jim stopped offering to help bring him downstairs for a change of ambiance and would just stop by and stand in his doorway to say hello every now and then. If Jarrod wanted anything, that would be his opportunity to ask. He never did.

On the fifth day, Alec stopped by his room. He knocked on the door and waited for Jarrod to respond. He did note that for the first time in days, Jarrod was not blasting the stereo. Instead he heard the faint sound of the television.

"Come in," said Jarrod. He was lying on his bed with his head resting on three pillows as he continuously flicked through the channels with his remote. This was the part of the day he most hated. Either soap operas or game shows could be found on the regular channels, and repeats of shows that he had already seen a thousand times were on cable. The premium channels kept repeating the same movies over and over. A person could watch *Die Hard* or *Shawshank Redemption* just so many times.

"Hey," said Alec.

"Hey yourself," responded Jarrod, never looking away from the television and still clicking away. "I don't need anything, if that's why you're here."

"That's not why I'm here," said Alec. He ventured into the room a little more and picked up a baseball that was collecting dust on top of Jarrod's desk. He began to toss it gently in the air and catch it.

"Put it down," said Jarrod without emotion.

"Why?" asked Alec as he continued with the soft toss.

"Just put it down," Jarrod said with a little more force. He finally looked away from the television and said to his brother, "If you're not here to find out if I want anything, then why are you here?"

Alec put the ball back on the desk and said, "I was wondering if I could borrow your car."

"No. You can leave now." The bitterness in Jarrod's voice caused Alec to flinch. Jarrod finally stopped changing the channels and left it on a Spanish soap opera.

"What the hell are you watching?"

"*Lagrimas de Sangre*," Jarrod responded while simultaneously destroying the beauty of the language with his atrocious accent.

"You watch this every day?" asked Alec, dumbfounded.

"Most days."

"Do you understand any of it?"

"Nope. I make up my own storyline based on their reactions." Closing his eyes and tossing his head back against the pillows, he asked in a bored manner, "Why do you want to borrow my car?"

"Joey and Brendon don't have cars."

Jarrod abruptly turned his head toward Alec and asked suspiciously, "Where are you guys going?"

Without showing any hint of satisfaction over the fact that Jarrod was finally exhibiting more or less some form of interest in something other than lying in bed, he simply said, "Cemetery."

Jarrod said nothing. He turned off the television and turned his head to stare out the window. Unfortunately, from where his bed was located, his only view was of the tall, leaf-resplendent, oak tree that stood directly outside it. He was so damn tired of looking at that stupid tree.

"Yes or no?" said Alec.

"What?" Jarrod responded as his thoughts returned to Alec and his request. His mind had wandered far away, as was becoming the norm recently.

"Yes or no? Can I borrow the car?"

Jarrod turned his face toward his brother and nodded. Then he said, "I'm coming too."

Chapter Eight

The four friends surrounded Dante's grave in total silence. A heat wave had recently hit a large portion of the East Coast, and as Jarrod stood there drenched in sweat, he found it almost impossible to breathe. He looked at the large mound of raw earth stretching the length of the grave, which stood a bit higher than ground level and was covered in both desiccated and fresh flowers, the bright, colorful unsullied flora lying atop the dried-up, old, decaying ones. There was no headstone, just a simple wooden marker with his name on it. Alec noticed the irritated scowl on Jarrod's face as he stared at the marker and said, "I heard Mom tell Dad that Mr. and Mrs. Malone ordered a nice headstone. I guess it's going to take a while for it to be made."

Hearing this, Jarrod seemed to relax.

Joey staggered back quietly to the car, opened its windows, and then placed a CD in the player. He raised the volume to the maximum, and as the music began to play, he rejoined his friends. As the boys stood quietly surrounding their friend's grave, AC/DC's "Thunderstruck" could be heard in the background. A solemn tribute to their friend.

Alec wiped away a tear, cleared his throat, and spoke first by saying, "We miss you…" But he wasn't able to continue. He tried swallowing past the aching lump that had formed in his throat, but just couldn't get past it.

Joey lowered himself as best he could and gently placed flowers on the grave. He looked up toward heaven and said, "I hope you're invited to every rockin' party held in heaven." Then he rolled his eyes slightly and added, "But, then again, if you're not, I'm sure you'll crash them all anyway."

The friends chuckled slightly and quickly became somber again. Brendon also brought flowers. He tossed them on the others and quietly mumbled, "Rest in peace, dude. We love you."

All became silent again with the exception of the music still blaring in the background. Jarrod spoke softly and asked his friends and brother if he could have a moment alone. They all nodded and Brendon said, "Sure…no problem." They headed toward the car, and once in, Joey lowered the volume of the music and raised the windows so Jarrod could have a moment of privacy.

Jarrod stood there alone in total silence, aside from the dulcet chirping sounds emanating from a few birds nestled in the trees surrounding the graves. He took a momentary look at his surroundings and noticed how peaceful and calm it was there. He and his family had been to this cemetery many times before when they would visit his grandmother's grave on Christmas and Mother's Day, but he had never taken in the serenity of the environment. A few large trees were scattered about, along with benches lining the narrow pathways for people to sit and rest—maybe even pray for the souls of their departed loved ones.

After a minute or two, he quickly glanced behind himself to make sure he wasn't being watched or listened to. He saw and appreciated that they were generously allowing him to have a personal moment with his friend. Looking up toward the sky, he was forced to momentarily squint due to the sun's blinding rays. He closed his eyes and briefly enjoyed the soothing, soft breeze that suddenly passed over him. He began to speak, but choked up and had to begin again after clearing his throat twice.

"I miss you, guy. I miss you so much, I can barely breathe…" He stumbled over his words and found himself trying to get words out while taking small gasps of air between sobs. "I don't know what to do…I'm so scared." He roughly wiped his tears away and took a steadying breath. "Sometimes I just want to pick up the phone and call you…but I can't. Or I listen for your car horn outside my window…but nothing."

All of a sudden, Jarrod lost his hold on his crutch and fell to the ground. He heard the car doors open, but he immediately lifted his hand in a stop motion and said loudly and firmly, "No. I'm alright." Within a few seconds, the doors closed again. But he knew that his friends and brother were now watching him.

Jarrod grimaced in discomfort as he attempted to get himself into a somewhat comfortable position. Physically uncomfortable and emotionally spent, he sat silently a few moments while lost in tormented thought. After a brief period of plucking fistfuls of grass and tossing them to the side, he cast a passing agonized glance at his friend's grave while desperately trying to calm his breathing down. His spectacular blue eyes were now swollen with grief and the whites were bordered with red streaks.

Rubbing his face brusquely and then letting out a massive grunt of anger, he said, "God, I'm so friggin' pissed at you. How could you leave me? How could you leave your mom and dad? You were supposed to fight, goddamnit! You weren't supposed to die." He stopped to take a steadying breath. "Why didn't you fight? Did you even try? Didn't you even give a shit?"

He cried so hard and for so long that he thought he might just dry up and turn to dust; yet oddly at the same time, it felt somewhat cathartic to finally let it all out. For much too long, he had been trying to hold the pain and fear in so as not to show his despair. Because of this, he now found himself mentally and emotionally drained. But after this release, he felt to some extent somewhat spiritually and psychologically purified.

❧ Broken Road ❧

Composing himself enough to lower his voice to a calmer level, he said, "Damn it, Dante. You're killing me here. What am I supposed to do without you? You were the only person who understood me and I could be myself with. You and I…we had no secrets. You knew everything about me. You knew about my dreams, my hopes…my fears. You just knew everything." Wiping away at a fresh onset of tears, he said, "I feel so lost. I don't know what to do. Everything I ever cared about is gone. You're gone, my future is gone…I just don't know anything anymore." Another warm breeze washed over him, and he suddenly began to remember something his mother had told him and Alec when they were just small children growing up. She had explained that there were three paths that could be taken in life: the good, the bad, and the "need to make a change" paths.

The good path would lead you to all the right things. If one were to follow this road without perpetual deviation, good choices, good future, and ultimately a good life were all for one's taking.

The bad road, well, that one just always seemed to lead to a life in prison. She was effective in using terms such as "life sentence without parole," "death penalty," and her personal favorite, "never drop the bar of soap." As youngsters, Jarrod and Alec had no idea what she was referring to, but intuitively knew that body wash was the way to go.

Then there was the last road she talked about: the "need to make a change" path. This was the road most frequently travelled, simply because no one is perfect, and mistakes and bad choices are invariably made in one's lifetime. Attempting to never make it onto this path was like asking Helen Keller to play a round of Marco Polo. It simply was impossible. The good thing was that if you did find yourself on this trail, all you had to do to be led directly back onto the highly revered good path was to simply correct your ways and move forward.

Jarrod suddenly realized there was a fourth road that she had failed to tell them about: the road that led a person to nowhere. There was no beginning, and it felt as if there was no end in sight to this trajectory. Realizing he was now irrevocably on this path and having no idea how to get off, he felt suffused with panic and dread. Breathing became labored again as he broke out in a cold sweat and his skin became pale as ashes. What was he to do? He had no internal GPS tracking device; there were no exit signs, no directions. Nothing.

He felt as though he were walking through total darkness and couldn't depend on anyone or anything to help him by shedding a ray of light toward an escape. Life felt aimless, without importance or purpose. He didn't know if he was coming or going, but the worst part was, he simply didn't care anymore. All his dreams that had once been within his grasp were now nonexistent through loss and destruction. In his current state of mind, life as he once knew it was completely and irretrievably lost.

He sat there for a few minutes on his own and waited for the tears to dry up. When they finally did, he spoke again.

"I love you, man. I'll miss you forever, and I'll never...ever forget you." He placed his hand over his aching heart and said, "You'll always be right here." He wiped away one last stray tear that had escaped and said, "Goodbye for now. I'll see you someday."

He motioned for his battalion to assist him, and they all rushed out, although rushing for them was akin to a turtle trying to get out of the way of a speeding car. When they finally reached him and helped him up, he turned around one last time as they were walking away and said so quietly that no one other than Dante could have heard, "One more thing. When you come across the pretty angels...save one for me." Then he gave a lopsided half smirk. It was the closest thing to a smile he'd revealed in over three weeks.

As time continued on, normalcy was slowly beginning to slink its way back into the lives of the Wentworths. Jarrod and Alec had begun physical therapy and were both beginning to feel stronger and more agile. They no longer depended on their parents for every little thing, which gave them both a considerable sense of independence, thus improving everyone's disposition by quite a bit.

One Thursday afternoon, upon returning home after having seen Dr. Silverstein for a follow-up appointment, Jarrod asked his mother if she would drop him off at the Malones' house. Janet seemed nervous at this request and stumbled over her words when she said, "Are you sure about this? Do you think this is a good idea?"

"Yeah. I've let some time pass, but I don't want to wait too long. I'm ready to see them. I just hope they're ready to see me."

With uncertainty etched across her face, she nodded and said, "I'll take you there now. Janice has called a few times to see how you are doing. Maybe they are ready."

She made a right at the next traffic light, drove down a few blocks, and then made another right onto Dewey Avenue. The Malones lived a few houses down on the left. Upon pulling up in front of the familiar bright-yellow, Colonial-style house with green wooden shutters the color of Granny Smith apples, she noticed the lawn was in dire need of being mowed and that the flower beds were unkempt and dying. Fighting back the desire to burst out in tears, she bit her lower lip and blinked away tears that were forming anyway. She knew that had the table been turned and it had been either Jarrod or Alec who had perished in the accident, she too would have ceased caring about anything and everything and would have let the world fall to pieces.

Opening the car door and stepping out with great effort, Jarrod gave his mother a sideways glance from the corner of his eye. From the look on her face, he knew she was dying to jump out and assist him, but instead painfully contained herself and watched in tormented silence. He thanked her by simply saying in typical Dante fashion, "Much obliged, ma'am." Mistaking his gratitude for the ride, she responded, "No problem. Call me when you're ready to be picked up." She smiled encouragingly at him as he closed the door and began to walk slowly, leaning heavily on his one crutch, up the driveway toward the front door.

Jarrod rang the doorbell and within a minute, Janice opened the front door. As her gaze fixed on him, her eyes instantly began to well up. She opened the screen door to let him in and immediately noticed the arm in a sling and the cast on his leg. He was walking with most of his body weight leaning solely on one crutch. She held the screen door wider and helped him up the last step into the house. Once inside, words were not spoken immediately. Instead she leaned forward and hugged him tightly, holding on with great intensity. Neither one wanted to let go, but eventually Janice gently broke the grasp.

"I'm sorry," she said. "I don't want to hurt you anymore than you're already hurting." Taking both her hands and placing them squarely on both sides of his face, she looked into his eyes and said, "I'm so glad you came by. I've missed you."

Chapter Nine

Looking up in exasperation from his book, Jarrod said, "Dad, I'm begging you. Please can you get me the SparkNotes? I don't understand any of this Shakespeare crap."

Jim lowered the newspaper he was reading and tilted his head forward a bit to look at Jarrod over his wire-rimmed glasses resting near the tip of his nose.

"No SparkNotes. Read the play. If you have any questions, you can ask your mother later."

"Why not you?"

"Because I don't understand any of that Shakespeare crap."

In order to graduate, Jarrod needed to comply with state and local school board curriculum requirements. Still unable to attend school on a daily basis, Jarrod and his parents had opted for home tutoring so he would be able to receive his diploma as planned and not have to repeat his senior year. Within five minutes he gave up and closed his book, leaving Macbeth in the midst of a raging fit aimed at an empty chair and a ghost named Banquo. Looking at his father, who appeared captivated by some article in the paper, Jarrod asked, "What exactly did Mr. Wyatt say again about me calling him?"

"You know exactly what he said because I've told you about a hundred times." Taking pity on his son, he folded the paper and placed it on the coffee table. "Mr. Wyatt said that it would be fine for you to give him a call when you're feeling better."

"Do you think it would be alright for me to call him soon?"

Enduring the trappings of cabin fever, Jarrod constantly felt confined, restless, and antsy. Even though, for the most part, he was able to get around without assistance from others, not being able to attend school or leave the house with regularity was enough to drive him to the nearest insane asylum. He still wasn't sleeping well through the night, for he was haunted by agonizing thoughts that would keep him up for hours. He missed his friend and he missed playing baseball.

There was nothing he could do to bring Dante back, and that fact left him feeling hopeless and desperate. He would find himself tossing and turning in bed, alternating between lugubrious thoughts of the friend he had lost forever and despairing concern for his own questionable future. So many feelings and none of them good. His heart felt heavy with anger, despondency, and even loneliness. Yes, loneliness. Even though he knew he had immeasurable support and love from his family and friends, he still couldn't help but feel he was in this boat alone and would have to use strength of will as oars to pull himself out of this whirlpool of misery. He needed to do something and felt that since he was progressing so well with his physical therapy sessions, he might be ready to begin his baseball training.

"Jarrod, when I spoke with him to let him know you were out of the coma and healing, he was happy and said for you to call him when you were better. What he meant by the word 'better' was, when you're ready for another tryout. You're not ready for that yet. I'm sorry, son, but you have a long way to go before you can stand in front of him and attempt to pitch. Your body hasn't fully recovered yet." Jim regarded his son with a look of combined sympathy and pride. He understood how difficult it must be for Jarrod and was amazed at how well his progress was going; but he knew it would be awhile before he'd be able to pick up a ball again, much less pitch.

"I know I have a long way to go, but I'm going nuts here. There must be some sort of light training that I can do," Jarrod said, his spirit slightly daunted.

"I understand how you feel; however, you can't do anything until the doctors say it's okay to start training. If you push your body before it's ready, you'll end up doing more harm than good. Just try to be patient. I know it's hard, but you can do it. You have to learn to walk before you can run."

"Yeah, I just wish we could squeeze in some baseball between the walking and the running. What about jogging?"

Jim rolled his eyes, smiled, and said, "No jogging on hard pavement. Just on the treadmill at rehab."

"Dad, I need to get out of the house."

"Go for walks. Walking is good exercise and not too strenuous."

"Walking is for old people."

"Your mom and I go for walks every night."

"My point exactly."

Chapter Ten

"So what do you think of Jersey so far?" Morgan asked her cousin, who had arrived from Florida just a few days ago.

Angel lowered the volume on the television set and smiled brightly at Morgan. "I like it. I mean all I've seen of it so far is Cliffside, but it's nice."

"It sucks. Especially this town," responded Morgan. Cliffside Park was a small town nestled in the northeast portion of New Jersey. One could make it into New York City by car, bus, or train in as little as fifteen minutes, barring any traffic on the George Washington Bridge or Lincoln and Holland Tunnels. Due to the ever-growing population and popularity of the town, new homes were forever being built in duplex form so as to accommodate more families within limited space. The older, existing homes were so closely situated that if the neighbors had something to say to each other, all they needed to do was open their side windows, and they could literally touch one another.

The entire town had only three school buses, and each one was half full at best. Usually kids were dropped off at one of the three elementary schools in the morning and picked up at the end of the day. As crowded as the town was, the residents still continued to enjoy a small, close-knit environment, with just about everyone being on a first-name basis with one another. Unfortunately, everyone knew one another's business as well. Two types of people lived here, the first being known as the Townies. They were the group that would forever remain loyal and loving citizens of this small community atmosphere. The individuals that made up this band were born and raised in Cliffside and would bear and raise their own brood here as well. Many of them already had their plots selected and paid for in advance in the town's only cemetery, Mount Hope. The second group was known as the Bolters. They were the select group who bolted out of town so quickly after being handed their high school diplomas that they would leave the Townies standing in the wake of a breeze caused by their departures for days on end. Morgan was planning on becoming a Bolter as soon she possibly could.

"Well, I don't have much to compare it to. It's not like Bradenton is the…"

Morgan rolled her eyes in boredom and cut her off by saying, "Whatever." Plopping herself beside Angel on the sofa, she grabbed the remote control from her hand and began flipping through the channels, never remaining on one for more than a few seconds. Not saying a word, but inwardly brewing, Angel heaved a quiet sigh and stood up to leave the room.

"I have to stop by my boyfriend's house later on for a bit. Will you be alright while I'm gone?"

"It'll be tough, but I'm sure I'll survive," said Angel sarcastically. "Tim seems like a nice guy."

"Tim's not my boyfriend."

"Oh. I thought he was. When he came over last night, you two seemed…I don't know…sort of like a couple."

"He wants to be. I'm just letting him woo me a bit. I may have to end things with my boyfriend so I can make Tim's dream come true," she said with a chuckle.

Surprised, but not shocked, at Morgan's revelation that she was allowing someone to "woo" her, although she had a boyfriend, Angel simply stared at her cousin in dumbstruck fascination. Sitting back down, she turned toward Morgan.

"What about this boyfriend of yours? Where does he fit in?"

"You probably won't even get a chance to meet him. He's been laid up for a bit because of an accident he was in. He's doing a lot better now, but all he does is mope around when he could be out and about. He keeps saying he's not well enough yet, but I just think that's a crock of shit. He's never been much of a partygoer; he prefers to stay in a lot. I don't see him in my future anymore."

"If that's the case, wouldn't it be wiser to just break up with him rather than two-time him?"

"I'm not two-timing him. Tim and I haven't even kissed. We just flirt around a lot."

"You were holding hands last night. That's two-timing."

"Not in my book," Morgan said as she stood up and tossed the remote control onto Angel's lap. Grabbing her handbag, which lay on the floor near the front door, she stopped to inspect herself in the mirror in the foyer. Satisfied with what she saw, she turned her face toward Angel.

"Not everyone is as wholesome, sweet, and good as you, Angelise. Some of us like to live life to the fullest, and if that entails breaking what you might consider to be rules, then so be it. See ya. Tell Mom I'll be home late." With that as her parting line, she left.

Twenty minutes later Morgan was at Jarrod's house. She had been dropping by to visit two, perhaps three, times a week and would stay only a short while each time. That day she walked in the door and greeted Jarrod's parents and Alec, who were watching TV in the living room. After asking if it would be alright for her to go upstairs, she turned toward the steps and hesitated at the bottom step before moving forward. Alec noticed the brief wavering and frowned slightly.

When he heard Jarrod's bedroom door close, he turned toward his parents and said, "She's going to break up with him."

"What?" responded Janet in a shocked voice while Jim simply stared at his youngest son in a curious manner.

"I've heard some rumors and none of them are good."

"Why do you want to break up?" said Jarrod as he lay motionless on his bed. He didn't seem upset, just curious.

"It's just that I feel we've reached a standstill in our relationship," Morgan said as she stood stock-still at the foot of his bed. "Could you please stop changing the channels and pay attention to what I'm saying?" In a disinterested manner, Jarrod complied with her request and tossed the remote on the bed next to him. With slight difficulty he righted himself into a sitting position and folded his hands over his stomach while patiently waiting for her to speak. He watched as she unsuccessfully attempted to pull her pink and white midriff below her pierced belly button, finding it somewhat amusing to watch it ride back up the minute she removed her hands from it. Her tight denim jeans rode low on her waist, emphasizing her curvaceous body.

Upon noticing how he was watching her, she began to feel self-conscious, so she turned away to face the mirror and tousled her short, brown hair to give it that natural, messy, windblown look that usually took over an hour to perfect. When she was certain her hair looked its best, she wiped away a smidge of black eyeliner that had smeared below her big, brown eyes. Big, brown, *boring* eyes, she thought to herself. Why couldn't she have had blue, green, or even hazel eyes? Brown was so dull and unexciting. Angelise had beautiful green eyes. Jarrod had gorgeous blue eyes. Even Alec, Jarrod's nimrod brother, had nice eyes. Everyone did but her. It didn't seem fair.

"Go on. You were saying we've reached a standstill. How do you mean?" he asked, impassively bringing her back to matters at hand.

She turned to face him and said, "Meaning that I...I feel that maybe...the time has come for us to move forward and...I just don't see that happening for us together." Beginning to feel irritated by his indifference, she began to mentally count to ten, which is what she would do whenever she felt she was about to lose control. She was expecting, perhaps even hoping, for him to feel hurt, frustrated, or even angry, but definitely not this coldness and apathy. He appeared to be aloof and dispassionate and that bothered the hell out of her.

"Why? Because I can't get around well enough to take you to the mall, movies, the prom..."

"No...no, that's not it. It's just that...well, it's just that..."

"Just say it," he said as he picked up a copy of the *Sports Illustrated* Swimsuit Edition that was lying on his bed, paying particular attention to page seventy-five.

As she watched him peruse the magazine, she thought to herself that he was probably the most arrogant, coldhearted son of a bitch she had ever had the misfortune of meeting. She was glad as all hell that she was breaking up with him.

"On second thought, maybe yes, just a little. Jarrod, I'll be eighteen in less than a week. I'm young and I want to do things, go places, and have fun. I feel terrible about all that's happened to you, but I can't be expected to sit around and wait for you to heal..."

Tossing the magazine aside and glaring at her, he said, "You think this is easy for me? You think I enjoy lying here waiting patiently for my body to give me a sign that it's ready to start 'moving forward,' as you put it? Well, news flash. It's not! I'm in fuckin' hell here."

I finally hit a nerve, thought Morgan.

"Jarrod, please...calm down. You need to understand."

"I totally understand. You're coming in loud and clear. You want out of the relationship and that's fine. I won't fight you on it."

"I don't want you to be angry. I'm hoping that we can—"

"Be friends?" He lifted his brows in a questioning manner.

"Yeah. Do you think that it might be possible?"

"Whatever." After a brief, awkward silence, he added, "You should go now."

"Jarrod, you may not care at the moment, but I want you to know I'm sorry…I really am." Walking toward him, Morgan slowly leaned over to place a light, tender kiss on his forehead before turning and walking out the door, shutting it softly behind her as Jarrod coolly picked up the remote and once again began clicking away.

When she made it down the stairs, she quickly glanced into the living room and noticed it was empty. Taking a deep sigh of relief and releasing it softly, she headed for the door as quickly and as quietly as she possibly could. As soon as she opened it, she found Alec sitting on the top step of the front stoop. He turned toward her and said, "Thought you were in the clear, huh?"

"What do you want, Alec? I'm not in the mood today for your bull—"

"What did you say to him?" he asked, cutting her off. He stood up and blocked her path down the steps.

"It's none of your business," she retorted. Alec had made it obvious from day one that he didn't think highly of Morgan, and she was tired of trying to change his perception of her. When Jarrod and she first started dating, Morgan had tried hard for Alec to see a different side of her; but no matter what she did or said, he still always saw her as a scheming, conniving, malicious bitch and treated her like one.

"He's my brother and unlike you, I care about him. I have every right to know what kind of crap you just fed him."

She gave Alec an exasperated look and said, "I told him we needed to end things because our relationship had reached a standstill and it was time to move forward. Blah, blah, blah. Now that you know what I told him, would you please get the hell out of my way, so I can leave?"

"As much as I would *love* to see you go, no. Did you tell him you've been screwing around with Tim Watson?" He gave her a fierce look while she stood stunned by his accusation.

Regaining a slight fix on her composure, she defiantly lifted her chin in a resolute manner and brusquely said, "You have no idea what the hell you are talking about. I haven't been cheating on Jarrod."

"Yet. It's just a matter of time. Everyone knows that you've been throwing yourself at Tim."

"Just stay out of my business Alec," she said while trying to get around him, but he continued to block her way by moving in the same direction.

"Just tell the truth and you can leave."

"I am telling the truth. I haven't been with Tim. Yes, he's shown interest, and yes, I sort of like him, but we haven't been together. I haven't been cheating on Jarrod." Morgan was livid now. How dare he interrogate her like this? She owed him absolutely no explanation and didn't know why she even bothered to tell him what she did. She just wanted to leave, but he was making it so difficult. Why did he have to be so big? Little brothers were supposed to be small and puny, not powerful and well built like Alec.

"I know you, Morgan. You may have everyone else fooled, but not me. I know what you have planned. You know damn well you're going to hook up with Tim eventually, so you decided to break up with Jarrod before you do, so no one can ever say you cheated. I'm right, aren't I? Just admit it."

Feeling like a mouse trapped in a corner, she blurted out, "I don't know what I'm going to do. I just know that being with Jarrod right now is not the right thing for me. I have big plans for my future, Alec, and things have changed so much that it can no longer include Jarrod." She quickly realized she had said too much, but it was too late to take it back now.

"Go on."

At that point she would have said anything to get out of there and away from him and his condescending, holier-than-thou attitude.

"Fine, if you're so intent on knowing, I'll tell you." Taking a deep breath and closing her eyes briefly in hopes of gaining a smidgen of control over her raging temper, she leaned back against the white porch column with her arms folded across her chest. When she opened her eyes, a sudden gleam appeared over them as she looked beyond him toward her anticipated future.

"I want the finer things in life. I want to someday be married to a rich man, have a big house on the cliffs overlooking the skyline and a nice, expensive car or two. A Ferrari would be nice. I want to wear the finest designer clothes and be able to shop as much as my heart desires and not worry about where the money is coming from." Now smiling softly as though she were experiencing this description of what she foresaw as her future, she added, "I want to be able to pack my Louis Vuitton bags and travel all over the world whenever I feel the whim to blow this pop stand of a town. I want everyone to envy me and say, "Oh look. There goes Morgan Billings, the luckiest girl alive.'"

Now looking at Alec, she said without a trace of emotion, "I almost had all of this with Jarrod, but let's face it, now that he injured his arm as badly as he did, the potential for him playing ball and giving me all this is no better than nil. I can't waste my time with him anymore. Like I said, it's time to move on and that's exactly what I'm doing."

Alec was silent at first, causing Morgan to believe that she had shocked him. But on the contrary, he expected something like this of her. He knew she was shallow and materialistic; therefore, her actual reason for breaking up with his brother came as no surprise to him.

"First of all, what makes you think he would have married you?" said Alec calmly.

"He would have," she said overconfidently.

"I doubt it," he responded.

"He would have done the right thing."

Alec paused, realizing what she was getting at. "Are you saying you're pregnant?"

"No. But if it would have guaranteed a gold ring on my finger from him, I would have made sure I was." It was true. If Jarrod hadn't been in that accident, causing all of her plans to pulverize like concrete into dust, she would have gone to whatever extreme measures were necessary to ensure the realization of that marriage, even if it included getting pregnant. It wouldn't have bothered her to pop out a baby or two; that's what nannies were for.

"Man, I always knew you were nothing more than a worthless piece of shit, but I had no idea you would go as far as that to get what you wanted," said Alec with cutting derision.

"Your flattery warms my heart. Where do you come off judging me anyway? You don't know the first thing about me," she responded fiercely.

"I know you're a conniving, lying bitch. I know my brother is too good for you, and the best thing that could have happened to him is you breaking up with him. I know someday you're going to regret the choices you've made, and I'll be celebrating with a bottle of the finest, most expensive champagne money can buy when you do." He moved to the side, allowing her to leave. "Just get out of our lives, Morgan. I don't want my brother or anyone else I care about poisoned with your venom."

Without saying another word in her own defense, she walked past him and headed toward her car. She got in, drove away, and never looked back.

As Alec turned and walked back into the house, he never realized Jarrod had been standing directly above him and Morgan the entire time, listening through the open window of his bedroom. Strangely, he wasn't absurdly troubled by what he had just heard. Rather, he felt a strong sense of amazement mixed with respect stemming from Alec's fervid defense of him. It suddenly dawned on him that he did have somebody he could turn to when he needed to talk or share his thoughts. He smiled as he became conscious of the fact that for the past sixteen years, Alec had been his truest friend-in-training.

Chapter Eleven

Graduation day arrived and Jarrod was unable to attend the commencement ceremony. Although he was feeling stronger every day, his energy level diminished greatly after short periods of activity. He was able to attend doctor's appointments, as well as engage in his physical therapy sessions, but usually after those commitments, he would be physically drained and needed to rest.

Brendon and Joey had returned to school two weeks prior and were able to don their caps and gowns and receive their diplomas with the rest of the graduating class of 2012. Fortunately, Jarrod had completed the necessary school requirements to graduate while being tutored at home; therefore, he would be able to receive his diploma as well. Mr. Ortiz, the high school principal, had called the family the week before and suggested Alec be Jarrod's proxy during the ceremony. The family discussed it over dinner that night, and Alec agreed to do it when Jarrod conveyed to him that it would mean a lot if he did. In reality Alec was not too pleased to play the role of a stand-in, but he felt Jarrod had already been through enough and it was the least he could do for him. Although nothing had been mentioned, he knew his brother was feeling a little bummed over missing the senior prom and now graduation.

Commencement was being held on the football field directly behind the high school. Seating arrangements were set up so that family and friends would assemble on the metal bleachers that faced out toward the makeshift stage that included a podium centered on it. Wooden folding chairs were set up in seven horizontal rows to the left and to the right of the stage. This is where the students would sit while awaiting the announcement of their names and where they would return to as graduates of Cliffside Park High School.

The day was perfect for an outdoor ceremony. By late afternoon the sun had already begun its move toward settling in the west, leaving behind a cool penumbra over the field.

The graduating students made their processional entrance onto the field while the school band coarsely played the "Pomp and Circumstance March." The boys wore black caps and gowns, while the girls all wore red. The ceremony began with a welcome introduction given by Mr. Ortiz. The national anthem played while everyone stood in silence. After everyone was seated, Mr. Ortiz stood at the podium and paused a moment before speaking.

"As many of you already know, our town and school were recently devastated by the tragic loss of one of our most endeared students, Dante Malone. Dante would have been a member of today's graduating class and was a bright, well-liked student and a good friend to many. He was taken from us much too young, and we will forever mourn his loss. His life should be celebrated, and we should be thankful for the special moments he left us. He will not be forgotten, for he was an amazing young man who touched us all and will continue to live on in our hearts and minds."

"What is it that we remember the most when we think of Dante? I think we would all agree it was his sense of humor. He always knew how to make us laugh. I would like to take this moment to reiterate to his family how very sorry and saddened we are for their loss. His passing was a great loss to many and our hearts and prayers go out to his family and friends."

He took a small sip of water from a glass that was hidden on a shelf within the podium and continued, "I would also like to take this opportunity to make a special announcement. Starting today this field will no longer be known as Cliffside Park High School Field, but rather will now be recognized by its new official name, the Dante Malone Memorial Field."

Cheers were heard throughout the field, while a huge white tarp that was covering the scoreboard at the back of the field was being removed by the maintenance crew. There, written in large black lettering, was "Dante Malone Memorial Field."

There wasn't a dry eye to be found. Students embraced, while family and friends held and comforted one another. The Wentworths were seated beside the Malone's as they held hands tightly. Janice and Mike had originally not planned on attending the ceremony, but Mr. Ortiz had called them the night before and requested they be there for a special announcement. He hadn't indicated what it was, only saying he believed they would be pleased. Both women were dabbing their eyes with tissues while the men fought back tears.

As the ceremony progressed, names of the students were called out in alphabetical order. Applause and cheers were heard as each student walked onto the stage, shook hands with the principal and the superintendent of schools, collected his or her diploma, and finally, as indication that they were now graduates and no longer students, flipped the tassel hanging from their cap to the other side.

There was much applause and shouts of "God bless you!" and "Congratulations!" and "Be strong!" as Brendon and Joey received their diplomas. As Brendon collected his, he quickly turned toward the microphone set up at the podium, raised his diploma up high, and said loudly, "Dante, we love...you." The tears began to flow once again, commencing with his own as he faltered and choked on a sob before continuing on and adding, "Party on."

Mr. Ortiz continued calling out names and shaking hands. "Lauren Wang...Christopher Waylons...Sofia Webster...Jarrod

Wentworth. On behalf of his brother who sadly was not well enough to attend the ceremony today, Alec Wentworth will be accepting his diploma. Susan Wilson…Michael Womac…"

After further speeches by the valedictorian and the superintendent of schools, songs were sung by the chorale group and lastly, a final benediction was given by Father Anton of St. John the Baptist Church. Mr. Ortiz took to the podium one last time and said, "Thank you one and all for joining us today here at the Dante Malone Memorial Field to celebrate the graduation of the Class of 2012. We wish our former students much success as they embark on a new journey in this we call life. Good luck and God bless. Congratulations!" As he said these last words, a mass of black and red caps were flung into the air like confetti on New Year's Eve.

When the Wentworths returned home, Alec walked in still wearing the black cap and gown, holding the diploma in his hand and humming the tune to "Pomp and Circumstance." Jarrod, who was lying on the sofa watching MTV, turned to look at Alec.

"It appears that congratulations are in order," said Jarrod as he slowly lifted himself into a sitting position.

"Congratulations," replied Alec.

"Thank you. Now where's my diploma?"

"Here you go," Alec said as he passed the diploma to his brother.

"Wait! Let me get a picture of this," said Janet as she rummaged through her handbag and pulled out her camera.

Jarrod looked at her as if she had two heads and said dryly, "Ma, you're kidding, right?"

"Do I look like I'm kidding?"

"Ahhh, c'mon, Mom," Jarrod responded.

"Oh, stop your bellyaching. I understand why you weren't able to attend the ceremony today, but it's still your graduation day, and it's a big deal, so I want a picture of you holding your diploma." She gave him a fierce, unswerving glare that would have turned a cow into sour milk.

"I'd do it if I were you," chimed in Jim. "Otherwise, you'll never hear the end of it."

"Fine, fine." Jarrod stood up slowly with some help from Jim, and a picture was taken of Alec handing the diploma over to Jarrod, while shaking his hand. It turned out to be a lovely picture with both boys smiling widely. Only one thing was wrong. Alec still wore the cap and gown.

Jarrod continued going to his physical therapy sessions and seeing his doctors on a regular basis. Physically, he was feeling much better and with all casts finally removed, he was able to move about easily and get things done without feeling hampered in any way.

Before the accident occurred, he had applied to various colleges and was accepted by all. He decided, after discussing it with his parents, that he would attend the University of Florida in Gainesville. His plan was to major in physical education and minor in business. Hopefully, if everything worked out as he planned, he would be well enough to try out, and God willing, make the baseball team.

Jarrod was not afraid of hard work, and he knew what was in store for him. His parents had instilled excellent work ethics in him since he was a child, and he was planning on utilizing those skills to the max.

He got into a routine of visiting the cemetery every Sunday, and then he would go to the Malones for a typical Italian dinner, which was usually eaten at three o'clock. Alec usually tagged along for the dinner portion of the day. Mrs. Malone would make a big meal consisting of antipasto salad, stuffed mushrooms or shrimp cocktail, pasta, meatballs, bracciole, vegetables, and dessert. They would stay for hours after dinner just talking and catching up. Sometimes they would bring over a DVD and they would watch a movie together. The Malones loved their weekly visits and looked forward to them with great eagerness. For Jarrod, it was a way to hold on to the memory of and still feel a connection to his deeply missed best friend.

One night after leaving their house, Jarrod and Alec were walking home when they bumped into their friend Billy, who was driving down the same block.

"Hey, what's up? Haven't seen you guys in awhile. How are you feeling?" asked Billy, addressing both brothers.

Both boys said, "Fine," with Jarrod adding, "How 'bout you?"

"Good. I'm heading over to Evan's house. There's a party going on. Why don't you guys come? Everyone will go crazy when they see you. You two are like those weird, furry animals that look like rats…y'know…the ones that hide in their holes and rarely come out."

"Prairie dogs," chimed in Alec.

"Yeah, that's it. C'mon, guys. Poke those little heads out and come join us for some fun."

Both Jarrod and Alec looked at each other and Jarrod said, "I'm game. Beats watching C-SPAN with Dad again. What about you?"

"Yeah, sure. Let me call Mom first and let her know so that she doesn't worry." Alec pulled out his cell phone.

"Ahhh, that's so cute. You gonna call your mommy?" teased Billy laughingly as he leaned over the passenger side and opened the door so they could get in.

"Screw you!" and "Shut up!" were the responses he received from his laughing friends as Alec got in and sat in the front seat while Jarrod made himself comfortable in the back.

When they arrived at the party, the house was packed. Music was playing loudly and people were dancing everywhere. Some with partners, others without.

"Man, now I know what it feels like to be a sardine in a can," Alec screamed to Jarrod so he could be heard above the music. "I can barely move."

"What? I can't hear you," Jarrod hollered back.

"I said I can barely move."

"Still can't hear you. Man, I can barely move!"

"Never mind," Alec said, exasperated.

"What?" Jarrod shouted.

Alec simply rolled his eyes and motioned for him to move on. They walked around a little bit, found a somewhat quieter room, and sat with some friends. It was good to see everyone again. It had been a long time since they had simply hung out. Jarrod stood up to get another soda and walked toward the kitchen. He was distracted by someone hollering his name and waving to him. As he waved back and turned the corner leading into the kitchen, he bumped into someone, causing her to spill her drink on her blouse.

"Oh, man, I'm so sorry. Are you alright?" Jarrod asked.

She was looking down at her blouse and then slowly looked up at him, revealing the most startling green eyes. They were the most beautiful, haunting green eyes he had ever seen. For a brief moment, it was as if time stood still. In that timeless moment, they simply stared into each other's eyes; she marveling at the captivating sensual blueness of his, while he allowed himself to be drawn into the beauty and depth of hers.

"Yes, I'm fine," she said softly. *What a beautiful voice*, he thought to himself: tender, soft, and feminine. He couldn't seem to tear his eyes away from her face, for she was strikingly gorgeous. Her hair was soft, long, and of a titian hue that just beckoned one to run his hands through it. And God, those lips; they were just so unbelievably full and naturally rose colored. She barely wore any makeup and had no need to. Jarrod couldn't speak. He was mesmerized by her beauty.

Her voice startled him back to reality, and he mumbled, "Excuse me?"

"I just said thank you for saving me. You see, my aunt gave me this blouse for my birthday, and honestly, it's just not my style, but I didn't want to hurt her feelings. This fruit punch stain will never come out, so you see, you saved me." She gracefully favored him with the most wondrous smile he had ever seen. "So, thank you."

"You're welcome." Jarrod felt as though his tongue was ten sizes too big for his mouth and his brain had turned to total mush. Nothing made any sense, and he was afraid to say more than two words, risking the chance she might think he was a bumbling idiot. He looked at her and noticed she was carefully pouring more of the fruit punch on the front of her blouse.

"What are you doing?" he asked, grinning.

"Just making sure the stain takes," she sweetly responded.

"Do I know you?" He was hoping he didn't sound too imbecilic for using such a cliché line when she responded, "No, I don't think that's possible. I'm not from New Jersey. I'm just visiting my aunt and cousin for a couple of weeks, and then I leave again."

"Where are you from?" asked Jarrod.

"Florida," she said.

"Really? I'll be going to college there at the end of this month."

There was that smile again. "Small world. Which college? Florida State, University of Florida…Miami?"

"University of Florida."

"So will I. I actually live in Bradenton, Florida…Oh, I'm sorry, I haven't introduced myself." She quickly switched her glass to her right hand and lifted her left to shake his hand. "My name is Angelise, but everyone calls me Angel."

"Angel," Jarrod repeated as he shook her hand, holding on to it a bit longer than necessary. Silently he sent up a quick thank you to Dante for saving that one Angel for him. He couldn't take his eyes off of her. He was totally captivated by her alluring grace and charm. It was as if he were looking directly into the eyes of Venus, the Roman goddess of love and beauty.

"It's weird, but I just have this feeling as if we've already met," he said.

"I know we haven't."

"I'm not so sure. I think we may have…once upon a time in my dreams."

A slow smile made its way to her mouth. "I'm impressed. How long have you been working on that line?"

He chuckled and said, "Awhile now. How'd I do?"

"Not bad. Not bad at all. But maybe next time you might consider adding a sexy, smoldering look when you say it," she said as she gave him a sly wink.

"By the way, my name is Jarrod," he responded while chuckling.

She nodded. "I already knew your name from when you told me in *my* dream." And then she let out a soft, lilting, almost musical laugh.

"Hey Jarrod!...oh, excuse me...," said Alec as he approached the two.

"Alec, this is Angel. Angel, this is my brother, Alec," said Jarrod.

"Nice to meet you," said Angel as she shook his outstretched hand.

"Same here," Alec responded. He turned toward Jarrod and said, "Listen, I don't mean to interrupt, but I just wanted to forewarn you that Morgan is here with Tim."

"Hmm...awkward. Alright, thanks for the warning."

"Morgan Billings?" asked Angel unobtrusively.

"Yeah. Do you know her?" responded Jarrod, a little surprised.

"Yup," she said and then added, "She's my cousin."

"Talk about awkward," said Alec, chuckling. "This party might turn out not to be such a dud after all."

Angel looked at Jarrod and said, "Is it safe to assume there might be some history there?"

Alec, not giving Jarrod a chance to respond, injected, "Anatomy too."

Jarrod gave Alec the look of death, which prompted his younger brother to immediately excuse himself and leave to join some friends in the kitchen.

"Anatomy, huh?" said Angel with a slightly disappointed smirk.

"My brother has a big mouth and a little brain, so I wouldn't put much value into anything he says," he responded.

At that moment Morgan approached them and presented them with her most impressive, artificial smile. She had seen them talking to each other from across the room and would have gotten to them sooner had she not been held up by about a hundred people or so.

"Hi there," she said, looking at Jarrod. *Mmm, he looks good. Really good*, she thought. She bit her lower lip as she perused him thoroughly, as one might do when purchasing a car.

"Morgan," responded Jarrod coldly with a slight nod of the head.

"Hi, Morgan. I'd introduce you to Jarrod, but I believe you already know each other," said Angel, smiling halfheartedly.

"We do. How are you feeling, Jarrod?" He looked more handsome and more muscular than before, she thought to herself as she continued to scrutinize him from top to bottom. Total eye candy. "You look good. Really, really good," she added as she passed her tongue in a slow, sweeping motion against her upper lip.

Angel's mouth dropped open in shock. Did Morgan just lick her lips at Jarrod? *My God, she is openly flirting with a guy while her boyfriend is in the same room.* Angel quickly glanced around and saw that Tim was busy talking to someone; therefore he was oblivious to his girlfriend's misdoings. Luck was on Morgan's side. This time.

"Better," he replied. He smiled at Angel and remained fixed on her. He'd much rather look at her than her wicked cousin of the East.

Morgan noticed the apparent attraction between her cousin and Jarrod. How could one not? A person on a plane, forty thousand feet up in the air, would have noticed. She didn't like this one bit. Looking at the two of them together made her feel like an outcast, something she was not used to. If anyone didn't belong there, it was Angelise, not her. Suddenly someone rudely bumped into her while making his way toward the kitchen. Morgan decided to take advantage of the circumstance and over-exaggerated the contact, forcing herself directly in front of Angelise. Now Jarrod had no choice but to look at her, she thought.

"Good. I'm happy to see that the casts are finally off," said Morgan as Jarrod moved slightly to the right and helped dislodge Angel, who was stuck between the wall and her cousin.

"Thank you," said Angel. "Casts?" she inquired.

"I was in a car accident," Jarrod said warmly to Angel.

Why isn't he looking at me? Morgan silently and angrily thought. *He must still be angry or hurt. Poor thing.* Her mind started picturing them together again, and strangely, she found the thought extremely pleasant. If he looked this good physically, perhaps he would soon be able to play ball well again. So many thoughts were whirling through her mind.

"I'm sorry. Are you alright?" Angel asked, genuinely concerned. Jarrod nodded and said, "I'm doing much better now."

Facing Morgan, Angel asked, "Is this your…the boyfriend… I mean, is Jarrod the one that was in an accident?" Upon Morgan's acknowledgement, Angel added, "I didn't know."

"He's fine now," cut in Morgan coldly, "but it didn't look so good for awhile. His best friend gave up the ghost in the accident."

Jarrod grimaced at the nonchalant manner in which she spoke of Dante's passing. He couldn't help but wonder why she suddenly seemed resentful and on the defensive, when it had been her decision to end things. Could Morgan be jealous? Not that it mattered. He had no desire to get back with her. He had seen her true colors and found them as favorable as a black and gray rainbow.

"Oh my God. That's terrible. I'm so sorry," Angel said sincerely. "This must be such a hard time for you."

"It hasn't been easy, but I'm getting through it. Thanks." He almost felt as though he should take her in his arms and console her as her eyes became somewhat misty and threatened to spill over. Beauty and a heart. What more could a man ask for in this life? If she didn't mind watching ESPN, he would get down on one knee at this very moment and propose.

Morgan was fast becoming irritated. This was not good. There was no way she was going to allow her cousin to date her ex-boyfriend. She would have to speak with Angelise later about that.

"So, Jarrod, what plans do you have for college?" asked Morgan. "Will you be able to go this year, or do you need more time to recover from the accident?" She hoped he would say he needed more time.

"I'll be attending at the end of the month."

Morgan seemed surprised and to Jarrod's utter bewilderment, almost disappointed. She cleared her throat and began working on creating that infamous bogus smile of hers once again.

"That's nice," she was able to utter between her clenched teeth. "Where?"

"University of Florida."

She choked on the sip of Coke she had been taking and released a spray of it all over Angel and her new blouse. Angel didn't seem to mind and just smiled at Jarrod. He couldn't help but return the smile.

"Isn't that...isn't that where you're...going?" she directed toward Angel while in the midst of a coughing fit.

"Yup," responded Angel as she took a dry napkin that Jarrod offered her and began to wipe some of the soda off her face.

"Haven't even packed my bags, and I've already made a friend in college," he said bitingly toward Morgan. "Isn't that nice?"

"Yeah, real nice. Angel, we need to leave now..."

"We just got here and I was hoping to get to know Jarrod a little better," she said, slipping him a conspiring wink while Morgan looked away.

Ah, so she was beginning to have fun with this, thought Jarrod. *Not only was she gorgeous, sexy and sweet, but now she was also covering the cool market as well.*

"Now," Morgan responded. "Goodbye, Jarrod. Good luck with college." She grabbed Angel by the hand and began to pull her away. They had only moved a few inches when Jarrod gently placed his hand on Angel's arm to stop them and said to her, "Before you go, I was wondering if I could have your phone number so we can maybe get together in Florida. Or maybe even sooner, if you're not leaving right away."

"I'd like that," she responded and gave her number to Jarrod, who immediately entered the number in his cell phone.

"There. Now I can't lose the number," he said as he smiled tenderly at Angel and then turned a cold stare toward Morgan.

"It was nice meeting you," Angel said.

He gently took her hand, lifting it slowly to his lips, and softly placed a feather light kiss on top. "It was like a dream."

Chapter Twelve

"You cannot date him!" hollered Morgan. "I forbid it."

"You forbid it? First of all, you have no right to forbid me from doing anything. You're not my mother. Second, I never said I was going to date him. I'd just like to get to know him better. He seems sweet." *And gorgeous to boot,* Angel thought privately.

Tim, who was driving, was quickly becoming irritated with Morgan.

"Why do you give a damn whether Angel dates Jarrod or not? You're with me now, not him."

"I know, baby, but it's just a silly rule we girls have. No dating ex-boyfriends of friends, or *cousins*." She emphasized the last word for Angel's benefit.

"Well, the key word in that sentence is 'silly,' and I would add 'stupid' to it as well," he said, obviously bothered by the entire conversation.

"Don't be jealous. You know you're the only guy for me. I just don't like the idea of Angelise dating my ex-boyfriend." She turned toward the backseat and said to Angel while shooting daggers out of her eyes, "Why would you want my sloppy seconds anyway? I don't want the two of you sitting around talking trash about me."

"Morgan, I would never talk trash about you, and I'm hurt that you think I would," said Angel resentfully. Besides, if she got together with Jarrod, she was positive there were a million other things they could do other than discuss her cousin, so why would they waste their time doing so?

"He's still off limits," said Morgan forcefully. "You're absolutely not allowed to date him."

"Enough," said Tim forcefully. "Angel doesn't need your permission to date Jarrod. She can make her own decisions and she doesn't need your approval."

"Thank you, Tim. Very nicely put," said Angel. She turned to look out her window and smiled shyly as she reminisced over her encounter with Jarrod. Dear Lord, he was handsome. So tall and muscular, yet not excessively so. He was just right: lean and fit. His jaw was firmly set and perfectly carved, while his eyes were unbelievably clear and blue, as if they were inviting her to dive into the deep abyss of his soul. She loved how his dark, thick hair fell into short waves and longed to run her hands through it. And he was so charming—and masculine—and gentlemanly. He was undeniably and irrefutably the most perfect specimen of a man she had ever had the pleasure of meeting.

She turned her head and looked toward her cousin, who was sitting in the front passenger seat, seething. *Well, it was just too bad if she wasn't happy about this*, she thought to herself. Jarrod was a prize that her cousin took for granted, and she was not going to be that stupid.

And then she thought about how he had taken her hand and kissed it, and she felt shivers run up and down her spine. He was so romantic. "Like a dream," he had said. Ohhhh… what it must be like to feel his lips on hers. She closed her eyes and let her fantasy sweep her away.

"So, you and Cruella's cousin seemed to hit it off," said Alec as they were heading home after the party.

"Yeah. She's gorgeous, don't you think?" asked Jarrod.

"No doubt."

Jarrod stopped walking for a moment. Alec was forced to stop and took a few steps back. "Hey. Can I talk to you about something?" Jarrod asked hesitantly.

"Yeah, sure."

"It's pretty heavy stuff. You might even think I'm nuts."

"I already think you're nuts," Alec responded matter-of-factly.

"I'm serious."

"Fine. Spill your guts. I'm listening."

"Remember when Dad told us that I had…well, that I had… flatlined…the night of the accident?"

"Dude, why are we talking about that? You know how it creeps me out." Alec noticeably shuddered.

"I know, but something happened. I haven't told anyone about it. Not even Mom or Dad."

"What? What happened? Are you able to heal the terminally ill with a touch of your hand now, or better yet, can you bring back the dead?" Alec raised his hands in praise and shouted, "Praise the Lord! Hallelujah, brother!"

"Jeez, Alec. Would you please take this seriously?" Jarrod said, irritated.

Alec quickly realized Jarrod wasn't joking around and that he was having a hard time getting this out, so he decided to take his brother up on his suggestion and take it seriously. "Alright. Sorry."

Jarrod pointed to a park bench across the street. They crossed over and sat beside each other. Alec leaned back while stretching his legs out in front of him and crossed his arms over his chest, waiting for Jarrod to speak.

"It's a little weird, and I don't even know what to make of it…" The older brother took a deep breath and continued on by saying, "I'm pretty sure I had a near-death experience."

Alec glanced at Jarrod quickly and then turned away just as rapidly. After a few seconds, he turned toward him again, this time allowing the gaze to linger. "What exactly do you mean when you say you had a near-death experience? I mean, you weren't 'near' death; you were dead for twenty-five seconds."

"Alright, if you're going to get technical about it, I'm pretty sure I had a 'full twenty-five seconds of death' experience."

"I'm listening," said Alec. He seemed interested in knowing, but at the same time, a bit wary. He never was a big fan of anything related to the paranormal. Nervously, he scouted his surroundings and suddenly became extremely aware of how dark it was and how alone they were. There were very few stars that could be seen, but that was normal. Cliffside's close proximity to the city meant it suffered the ramifications of the light pollution that existed there, which virtually destroyed any thoughts or plans for casual stargazing. Alec involuntarily jerked when a furry, little squirrel scuttled by and quickly scampered up a nearby tree. Without being too obvious, he inched his way closer to his brother on the bench.

"I saw a bright light and felt unbelievably at peace when standing in it. As if nothing bad could ever happen. Just serene like..."

"Was Grandma there?" Alec asked, completely engrossed now in the conversation.

"No. I just saw a light."

Alec again moved closer to his brother and surprised even himself when he calmly asked, "So, what exactly happened during this experience of yours?" This was getting creepy, as far as Alec was concerned. A chill ran through him and he shivered slightly. He tried moving closer to his brother, but Jarrod stopped him.

"Would you get off of me? You're practically sitting on my lap." Alec nodded and moved slightly to his right, leaving only a few inches between the two of them.

"Answer my question. What happened?" asked Alec.

"Nothing. All of a sudden, the light was gone, and I didn't feel anything anymore. Next thing I know, I'm waking up in the hospital hooked up to about a hundred machines and in total agony. The weird thing is that the feeling I had...when I was...well, dead...I sort of had the same feeling tonight when I met Angel. Just for a second, when we were looking into each other's eyes, I felt at peace, safe and light. No pain, no pressures, no sadness. It was as if a warm blanket had been placed over me and all my troubles were suddenly gone. Crazy, huh?"

Alec didn't respond. He sat there in silence, not moving. Jarrod realized his younger brother was terrified. If Alec got any closer to him right now, they'd be conjoined twins.

"I wonder why there's always a light," Alec said, wide-eyed and mouth agape in wonder. "People are always saying there's a light."

"Who says?" asked Jarrod, grinning just a bit.

"People," Alec stated flatly.

"Which people?"

"I don't know," Alec said, frustrated. "People that have died and come back. People like you."

"Well...whomever these people are...they're right. There definitely was a light. I wanted to head toward it, but then it was just gone." He took a deep sigh. "Alec, it was just the most incredible feeling ever. I felt safe there. Remember when we were little and we'd get sick or fall down and get hurt?"

"Yeah," responded Alec, completely fascinated with Jarrod's account.

"Remember that feeling you had when Mom would take you into her arms and just hold and soothe you?" Jarrod stared straight ahead into the darkness as he mentally relived those comforting moments of his childhood.

Alec smiled at the fond memory and nodded. He instantly recalled the many times that his mother would comfort him after a nasty fall. No matter how bad the scrape, sprain, or strain was, her love and warmth always seemed to ease the pain and make it bearable.

"Just imagine that feeling, only infinitely stronger," Jarrod said.

Suddenly, a black cat wildly streaked past the brothers with lightning speed, causing Alec to leap to his feet and shriek like an eight-year-old girl. Jarrod immediately began laughing hysterically.

"What the hell is wrong with you? That wasn't funny," wailed Alec.

"I'm sorry," Jarrod responded with his head thrown back laughing. "I'm sorry, but I just can't help it! You were so scared." He struggled to rein in his laughter, but every time he looked at Alec, he would begin again. Alec glared at him and angrily plopped himself back on the bench, this time leaving approximately two feet between them.

"Just go on with the story," Alec said stoically.

Jarrod finally regained a semblance of self-control and said, "That was it basically. Weird, huh?"

"Unbelievable is more like it. I mean, don't get me wrong, I do believe you…it's just that…yeah, you're right…it is sort of weird."

"Crazy as it sounds, I almost feel as if there's a connection between what happened that night and meeting Angel. I mean…first I have this indescribable feeling upon meeting her, and then when she told me her name, I almost freaked. Seriously, how many Angels have you met in your lifetime?"

"None until tonight. Do you think she sensed anything?" Alec asked, uncertain.

"No. Definitely not in the sense of something otherworldly. But I do think she felt some sort of a connection. You know, like an attraction between the two of us. I mean, I definitely felt it."

"Yeah, we all kind of felt it. It was obvious there was chemistry between the two of you. What do you plan on doing?"

"I'm going to call her and take it from there. Do me a favor and don't mention any of this to anyone, alright?"

"Nobody would believe me anyway," Alec said.

Letting out a soft groan as he stood up, Jarrod leaned forward to rub his right knee. Mildly worried, Alec asked, "You okay to walk, or do you want me to call Mom or Dad to come pick us up?"

"I'm okay. It's just that some days I feel as old as…well, as old as Dad."

"That old, huh?"

"Yup. That old. I have to admit, though, it felt good to laugh. I haven't laughed that hard in a long time."

Alec nodded and then said, "Damn cat scared the shit out of me. I think I may have peed on myself just a little bit." Once again, Jarrod burst out laughing.

Chapter Thirteen

"Has he called you yet?" Morgan asked Angel as she stood leaning against the doorway of the guest room Angel was staying in. The room was small, but Angel thought it perfect. Aunt Helen had decorated it simply, yet tastefully. The curtains that hung on the one window were of a soft, beige lace, very feminine. The matching dresser and nightstand were purchased at a flea market, but had an antique, distressed look to them that Angel found utterly charming. Helen had originally purchased them for Morgan's room, but she wouldn't hear of having the secondhand, battered "junk" anywhere near her. Angel knew the sheets and comforter were new, because they still felt stiff and scratchy. A few washes and they would be just right.

"Has who called me yet?" She knew exactly whom Morgan was referring to, but she wasn't about to let her know that.

"You know who. Jarrod." Morgan said with an impatient sigh.

"Nope, not yet... no big deal, though." Like hell it wasn't. It had been three long days. She was beginning to wonder if he would ever call. He seemed so interested that night. Why did she feel this overwhelming connection to him? She had dated plenty of guys before, but she had never felt such a strong pull for one as she did for Jarrod. Angel's mind was being driven to madness because he hadn't called yet. Over the past few days, she had found herself willing the phone to ring more times than she cared to admit and had lost count of how many times she had checked the battery charge level.

Morgan sauntered over to the mirror and began to brush her hair. She was trying to behave indifferently to the whole situation, but in reality it was eating her up inside. Rumor had it that Jarrod was doing well and was even planning to commence training again for baseball in a few short weeks. She was beginning to have second thoughts about the breakup. What if he did recover completely from all the injuries he had sustained in the accident and was eventually able to play ball again? Perhaps she had been too hasty and acted impetuously when making her decision to end things.

If she could choose between Jarrod, who was healthy, strong, and extremely handsome and might make it to the big leagues someday, and Tim, who was equally healthy and strong, but not as physically blessed in the looks department, but who would someday definitely take over his father's highly successful restaurant business, whom would she pick? That was simple. She would pick Jarrod. Jarrod was a thousand times better looking. Plus, the life of a professional baseball player's wife seemed much more exciting than that of a local restaurateur. But how was she to get Jarrod back? She should probably first end things with Tim, but what if she did and Jarrod didn't want to reconcile? Then she would lose both men.

Plus, now there was the matter of Angelise. Sparks were definitely flying between the two of them the other night. She would somehow have to take Angelise out of the equation. But how? She'd already asked her numerous times not to see him, but she had never agreed. Then again, Morgan never did ask. She demanded. Perhaps she should go about it differently. Maybe what she needed to do was appeal to Angelise's more sensitive, familial side. Yes. That was it. She would appeal to her sense of honor and loyalty to her family…

"I want Jarrod back."

Angel had been looking down at a magazine when she heard Morgan speak and looked up immediately upon hearing those words.

"What?" Angel asked warily.

"I said I want Jarrod back."

"All of a sudden you want him back? What about Tim?" She closed the magazine and laid it next to her on the bed. She'd have to get back to all the dramatic, tension filled madness of Teresa Giudice's latest antics on *The Real Housewives of New Jersey* later.

"I've been thinking about it for awhile. I mean, I've been missing him. I think…no…I know I made a bad decision in breaking up with him. I now realize that I love him. I always have."

She walked over to the bed Angel was sitting on and sat down facing her. She took both of Angel's hands in her own, looked down at them for a moment, and worked hard to well up a tear or two, but failed miserably, only being able to achieve a glassy-eyed look.

"I've made a terrible, terrible mess of things. I love him so much and I need to be with him. We were meant to be together. He misses me as well. I can tell. Don't you see why he paid so much attention to you? He's hurt and angry at me for breaking up with him, and he wanted to get back at me. What better way to achieve that than to make a play for my own cousin? I'm just so sorry that he used you that way."

She grabbed a tissue from the box on the nightstand and wiped away a nonexistent tear. In the meantime Angel was so hurt and shocked by what she had just heard that all she could do was stare at her cousin, wide-eyed and openmouthed.

"Please don't be too angry at him," Morgan said. "He's usually very nice. It must be the pain that I caused him that made him do it."

Angel wanted to take her cousin by the shoulders and shake her until her head fell off, but her body wouldn't respond. She wanted to scream at her at the top of her lungs and tell her that she was a mean-spirited fool and an idiot to boot, but her mouth wouldn't allow the words to escape.

"As far as Tim goes…well, I just don't know what to do. He's so sweet and he doesn't deserve to be hurt, but what choice do I have? I know that he loves me and I do care for him, but just not the same way I care for Jarrod. Angelise, what should I do? You're so kind and thoughtful, I'm sure you would know what would be the right thing to do."

"I…you…I…" Dear God, what was the matter with her mouth? Why couldn't she just say what she was thinking and how she was feeling?

Morgan stood up and walked toward the door. She turned toward Angel and said, "I'm sorry. I know I just threw a lot at you. I mean, here you are thinking he was interested in you and now here I am telling you that I still love him and need your help in getting him back. I'll leave you alone for a bit. Maybe you can think of a solution to my problem. I just can't seem to think anymore."

As she walked out of the room, closing the door behind her, she smiled as she thought of the Academy Award performance she had just given. She wanted to laugh out loud when she realized how easy it was to fool Angelise, thus ensnaring her in her web of deceit and stratagem.

Angel sat there for a long while thinking and doing her best to fight back tears, but that seemed to be a battle lost. How could she have been such a fool? The one time she felt a physical and emotional bond with someone, it turned out he had just used her to hurt her cousin. Yet, something still just didn't feel right. He hadn't known they were cousins when they had met. Or had he? Was it possible he had set the whole thing up and had purposely bumped into her? Her head was spinning. She didn't know what to think. She liked him. But, yet, her cousin was in love with him. They were once a couple and she had heard it said many times that where fire once burned, embers lingered. What if she had gotten to know Jarrod better, maybe even fallen in love with him, and then he left her to be with Morgan again?

Damn it, she was just getting ahead of herself. He hadn't even called, and it had been a full three days since they had met. He probably had never even planned on calling. Morgan must be right. He did make a point of glaring spitefully at Morgan when he took Angel's phone number. What a fool she had been by assisting him in his evil plan by egging Morgan on. And to top things off, she had winked at him. He probably hadn't called her because he was still too busy laughing at her ridiculous stupidity.

There was nothing left to do but forget they had ever met. She told herself she was fine before she met him and she would be fine now. She didn't need him in her life. She would just have to forget how he made her feel. And forget the gentle timbre of his voice that reminded her of the soft, muffled tones of a musical instrument. And she would have to force herself to forget about ever coming across his inordinate blue gaze, which made her heart skip beats. And most of all, she would have to forget the feel of his tender lips on hers and the passion he'd awoken in her as he deepened the kiss…oh wait…that part she had just imagined. But nonetheless, she would have to forget it.

Later that evening, during dinner, Aunt Helen noticed Angel barely touched her food. She tried, for her aunt's sake, to eat a few bites, but she had absolutely no appetite. She continued to move the food around her plate with her fork.

"Is something the matter, Angel?" asked Aunt Helen as she looked at her niece with concern.

"No, I'm fine," she responded with a spiritless smile.

"I've noticed you're not eating much tonight. I thought you loved steak."

"I do and it's delicious. It's just that my stomach is bothering me a little," she lied.

"I'm sorry, sweetie. If you don't feel well, don't force yourself to eat. Would you like a cup of tea instead?" asked Aunt Helen sweetly. She truly loved her niece. Angel was like a rare gem as far as Helen was concerned. Her outward appearance sparkled like a diamond, but her inner beauty was more gentle and serene, similar to the beauty of a precious and treasured pearl.

"No thanks. I'll be fine," replied Angel.

"You overcooked the meat again," Morgan commented dryly.

"No, I didn't. I cooked it medium rare, just like you like," responded Aunt Helen. "There's just no pleasing you."

"Then you bought the cheap meat again, because it's dry and tough, just like I hate. No wonder Angelise won't eat it," Morgan said callously.

"That's not true. The meat is fine. I'm just not feeling well. Really, Aunt Helen, your dinner is delicious as usual." Angel tried to make amends for the hurt Morgan was once again causing her aunt. Sometimes Angel just couldn't understand how wounding Morgan could be. She never seemed to take anyone's feelings into consideration other than her own. How she turned out that way, Angel would never know. Aunt Helen was such a sweet, kind, and loving person. She always went out of her way to please others, even at her own expense. Even when things had been difficult for her, like when her husband abandoned her and their two-year-old daughter for another woman, she had never been bitter and had never turned hard. She worked two, sometimes three jobs, so she could give her daughter the best she could; yet her efforts were never appreciated.

Morgan constantly demanded the best of everything. It began when she was just a toddler demanding the most expensive and hard-to-find toys, and still had not stopped when she recently informed her mother she wanted a new car, because she simply could not be seen driving around town in her mother's beat-up Toyota. While Morgan wore designer labels, her mother was forced to shop at consignment shops for her own clothes. It did not go unnoticed that while she and Morgan were served steak tonight for dinner, Aunt Helen's meal consisted of a grilled cheese sandwich and a bowl of canned tomato soup. That thought brought Angel back to reality, and she began to feel guilty for not eating the steak.

"Aunt Helen, why don't you eat my steak instead of the sandwich? I wish so much I could eat it, but I'm just a little nervous that it might not sit well." Angel hated to lie, especially to Aunt Helen, but she knew if she didn't, she would never accept the steak.

"Are you sure, love?" asked Helen.

"Absolutely." She passed the plate to Aunt Helen, who immediately pushed the plate sitting in front of her aside and began to dig in to the steak.

"Angelise, did you happen to give any thought to what we were talking about earlier today?" Morgan asked.

Angel abruptly looked up at Morgan, shocked that she would bring something like that up in front of her aunt.

"Morgan, I'm not feeling well enough right now to get into such a deep conversation. Aunt Helen, if you don't mind, I think I'll go lie down for a bit."

"Of course, hon. Go ahead and rest. I'll come check on you in a bit."

Angel stood up and glared at Morgan while Aunt Helen continued to enjoy her repast. As she turned to walk away, she could have sworn she heard Morgan giggle.

Chapter Fourteen

Jarrod sat on the edge of his bed holding his cell phone in his hand. He sat there for nearly ten minutes simply staring at it, sometimes breaking up the drab monotony of that by switching the phone from one hand to the other. Alec entered his room and promptly sat down beside him and watched him do this for a few minutes without saying a word. Finally Jarrod said, "I'm going to call her now."

"You mean you haven't called her yet?" exclaimed Alec. "It's been over a week."

"I thought it might be best to take it slow."

"If you take it any slower, you'll both be collecting Social Security checks down the pike. The only thing you may have achieved by taking it so slow is to have given Morgan time to poison Angel's mind."

Jarrod hadn't thought of that. Why should Morgan care or do something like that when it had been her decision to end the relationship in the first place? Plus, what could she say to Angel that could possibly poison her mind? He had always been honest, respectful, polite, and courteous to her the entire time they had dated. Jarrod cringed when he realized that the description he just gave of his courting graces better described a Boy Scout than a boyfriend.

"God, I hope not," said Jarrod.

"Call her and find out," Alec said as he leaned back and made himself comfortable on Jarrod's bed.

"Do you mind?" Jarrod said with raised eyebrows and a scowl upon his face.

"Not at all. Go right ahead." Alec fluffed up the pillows and made himself even more comfortable.

"Go!" said Jarrod.

Alec slowly stood up, making sure to first take the time to stretch his arms exaggeratedly and yawn deeply, dust some invisible particles off his pants, glance out the window to watch the birds take wing from one tree to another, take a sip out of Jarrod's day-old soda can, and then finally walk slowly out of the room, shutting the door behind him.

Jarrod listened for a moment and then said loudly "Get away from the door, Alec." A moment later, he heard the mumblings of what sounded something like "Whatever," and then heard footsteps as they faded away down the steps.

He picked up the phone and pressed Contact List. The first name to appear was Angel's. He pressed the dial key and it began to ring.

Two miles away, Angel was busy folding and packing her clothes into a suitcase. She was scheduled to leave that night on an 8:15 p.m. flight departing out of Newark Liberty Airport. She stared at the ringing phone and debated whether to answer it or not. It was him. Who else could it be? The number shown indicated it was a local call. Aside from Morgan and Aunt Helen, no one else from this area had her number. Well, he certainly did take his sweet time. She decided not to answer and let the call go to straight to voice mail.

"Hi. This is Angel. I'm not available to answer your call at the moment. Please leave your name and number, and I'll get back to you as soon as I can. Thanks for calling!...beeeeeeep..."

"Um, hi, Angel. This is Jarrod. Jarrod Wentworth. We met at my friend Evan's party last week. I hope you remember me... anyway, I'm sorry it took so long to call. It's just that I've been busy…I've been going to physical therapy every day and it sort of wears me out. I still tire easily. Anyway, I was hoping we might be able to get together before you head back to Florida. If you can, give me a call. Well, I guess that's all for now. Hope to hear from you soon. Bye."

Jarrod hung up and just stared at his cell phone for a bit. He had wanted to take things slow, but perhaps he had taken it to the extreme by not calling even a day or two sooner. He truly hoped he hadn't messed things up.

Angel waited for the phone to signify that a message had been left. When she heard the alert, she retrieved and listened to the message Jarrod had left.

He sounded sincere, she thought. But then again, he had sounded sincere last week. Why was she happy to hear he was feeling well enough to go to physical therapy every day? Morgan had mentioned in passing that he was a good athlete with a lot of promise before the accident. Why should she care that he wasn't giving up on his dream like so many others would have? Perhaps physical therapy was just an excuse he came up with for not calling sooner.

Oh, how she wanted to call him back, but she knew she couldn't. Morgan was, after all, her cousin and her loyalty lay with family. But what if he didn't want to be with Morgan? What if he was interested in her like she had hoped? Or perhaps he wasn't interested in either one of them and was just having some fun via payback? Once again she was developing a headache from so much thinking. Rubbing her temples, she tried convincing herself that things would be better once she was back in Florida. She needed to get away from here, although she would miss her Aunt Helen terribly. Nonetheless, it would be better for her to separate herself from this situation.

Morgan walked into the bedroom unnoticed. She stood in the doorway and watched as Angelise listened to her message and then stared at the phone after pressing the End Call button.

"Need help packing?" Morgan asked. Startled, Angel dropped the phone on the floor, immediately bent down to pick it up, and then nonchalantly tossed it into her handbag.

"You scared me," said Angel.

"Sorry." She couldn't have cared less.

"Thanks for the offer but I don't need any help. I'm almost done." Angel continued packing the few remaining items and then closed the suitcase. She went over to the desk and grabbed her ticket, which she placed in her handbag. She looked at Morgan, who was still standing in the doorway, and motioned for her to come in and close the door, which she did.

"Morgan, we need to talk," said Angel.

"I agree," Morgan responded and then sat down on the bed. "Who starts?"

"I will, if you don't mind," Angel said and sat on the bed beside Morgan and faced her. She looked away from Morgan's eyes and began to trace with her finger the outline of one of the flowers on the floral comforter she knew her aunt had purchased specifically for her visit. "I've thought about what you told me the other day, and I've made a decision. I've decided not to…not to…encourage a relationship with Jarrod. I won't call or see him."

"Thank you so much, Angelise," Morgan exclaimed as she leaned forward to eagerly embrace her cousin.

Forced to stop tracing, Angel returned the embrace and said, "But…if you're going to pursue some sort of a reconciliation with Jarrod, then I highly recommend you end things with Tim first. One, Jarrod will never take you seriously if you still have Tim dangling on a string, and two, it's just cruel to string Tim along like that. He is a nice guy and deserves better than that."

"I know you're right, but what if Jarrod doesn't want to get back? If I give up on Tim now, then I might end up with neither."

"I think it's a risk you will have to take," said Angel in a clear-cut tone.

"You're right. I'll have to find a way or rather, find an excuse, to give Tim for ending things. Maybe I'll just use the same one I used on Jarrod." She chuckled.

Angel frowned at that comment and said, "What excuse did you give Jarrod?"

Realizing she may have just committed a blunder, she quickly answered, "I just told him we were growing apart, and it would be best for us to go our separate ways."

"Okay, so that was the excuse you gave him. Now, what's the real reason you ended things?"

Morgan just wanted the conversation to be over before she gave away too much information, so she hurriedly responded, "It doesn't matter. All that's important is that I've changed my mind and now I have to fix things. Angelise, thank you again." She leaned over and hugged her again and threw in for good measure, "I'll miss you." She then left the room.

An hour later, when Angel was in the shower, Morgan quietly slipped back into the room, pulled Angel's phone out of her bag, and listened to her voice-mail message. When she was done, she deleted the message and his number from the received calls list and gently placed the phone back in the bag.

She smiled as she walked away, knowing that even if Angelise changed her mind about getting together with Jarrod, she would not be able to get in touch with him.

She was walking down the steps, humming happily, when horror struck. She suddenly remembered Jarrod and Angelise would both be attending the same college. What if they were to have some of the same classes together? What if they were to bump into each other on campus? What if Jarrod called her again? She hadn't thought of that when deleting the message. There was no way of preventing that from happening. Hopefully he would get the message that Angel wasn't interested when she didn't return his call, and he would give up. But that would be too easy and nothing ever came easily for Morgan. More than likely, Angel would cave and call him. Damn. This was going to be more difficult than she had thought.

Chapter Fifteen

Angel sat on the plane next to a short, portly old man who, based on the amount of perspiration emanating from his body, was quite nervous about flying. Directly to his left sat a young, stressed-out mother nursing her newborn, colicky baby. It was going to be a long three hours.

To pass the time, she tried perusing through a magazine, but soon found herself comparing all the young, hot-looking male celebrities to Jarrod. Unfortunately for the celebrities, they kept coming up short.

Bored out of her mind and with nothing to do, she leaned her head against the small window beside her and stared absentmindedly at the clouds. Suddenly what normally appeared to her like huge puffs of white floating cotton balls or whipped cream undeniably had taken on the appearance of either baseball gloves or bats.

Finally she gave up trying to not think of him and just let her thoughts succumb to their fantasies. She imagined him holding her in his strong arms, lifting her face toward him, and gently placing a kiss on her lips. He would start slowly, deepening the intensity as the passion grew stronger and more heated.

Then she imagined them strolling along a deserted, palm-lined Caribbean beach. They would be holding hands as they walked in silence, and then he would slowly stop, turn to face her, take her face in both his hands, and gingerly place a soft, tender kiss on her lips.

She even imagined their first argument. It would be about which movie they would go see. She wanted to see a romantic comedy starring Channing Tatum, filled with tenderness, relationship dilemmas, obsession, and passion. Lots and lots of passion. He, in turn, wanted to see a recently released action war epic jam-packed with shooting, explosions, guts, and blood. Lots and lots of blood.

She would argue he just wasn't romantic, and he would counter her argument with the allegation that she was not willing to make an effort to do the things he enjoyed doing. They would go back and forth bickering for a bit, and then they would compromise and agree to see a mystery film where the man saves the woman he loves while steadily dodging bullets and bad guys along the way. Afterward, as he bid her good night, Jarrod would press his body up against hers, lift both her arms up, and wrap them around his neck as he kissed her hard and long. It would be the kiss of all kisses, an unsurpassable kiss that would leave all other kisses in the history of the world lacking and wanting. A kiss so intense…

"Excuse me, miss? Miss?"

Angel was abruptly brought back to reality and responded, "Yes?"

"I need you to fasten your seatbelt," said the pretty, young flight attendant. "We'll be landing in Tampa in approximately ten minutes."

"Sorry…thank you," said Angel as she did as requested and let out a soft groan of disappointment that she would have to wait until later to see how that fantasy ended.

She looked to her left and the portly old man smiled mischievously at her. She returned an unsure smile, wondering if she had in any way given indications of what she had been thinking while she had taken her short trip to fantasyland.

As soon as she landed, she checked her cell phone and found Jarrod had called twice during her flight, but had only left one voice mail message. As she listened to the new message, she felt slightly despondent over the fact she could not return his calls.

"Hi again, Angel. It's Jarrod. I'm sorry to be bothering you by calling so often, but I promise to stop hounding you if you call me back. I hope everything is alright. Call me, okay? It's my cell number, so don't worry about calling late and waking anyone up...bye."

She loved the sound of his voice, although he did seem a little less animated this time around. He must be getting the message. She hated being rude by not returning his calls, but then again, if there was any truth to what Morgan had said about him using her to make her jealous, she shouldn't be concerned about his feelings. He obviously wasn't worried about hers.

She placed the phone back in her handbag, looked toward the mass of people gathered behind the security checkpoint, and saw her father waiting and waving. She smiled and waved back.

As they sat in the car during their drive home to Bradenton, Willie Skyler asked his daughter how her trip had been.

"It was fine," responded Angel, staring out onto the dark highway.

"Anything exciting happen?" her father asked.

"No, not really. Aunt Helen seems fine. A little tired, I think. She works really hard."

"Yes, she does. She's had a pretty rough time of it. It can't be easy raising a child alone with no support from the father," he said as he took a sip of the coffee he had purchased at the airport. He offered Angel a sip, but she declined with a shake of her head.

"I'm sure. She does try hard, though. I just wish Morgan wasn't so...so..."

"So what?" her father asked, his curiosity peaked.

"I don't know. It's hard to explain. She just wants so much and is so demanding and is never grateful for anything anyone does for her…she wants everything done her way and expects everyone to bow down to her…she treats everyone like she's better than—"

"Whoa. Hold on, killer. I'm detecting some animosity here. What exactly happened in New Jersey between the two of you?"

"Oh, Daddy. It's so complicated." Tears began to well up in her eyes and she found herself desperately trying to quell them. As she fought against the tightness in her throat, she explained to him in detail everything that had happened since her arrival. Beginning with a simple shopping expedition that turned into a fiasco due to Morgan's incessant negative comments about every item Angel selected and ending with the sad situation involving Jarrod, Morgan's ex-boyfriend.

Willie continued driving, silently listening to everything his daughter was saying. They had always been close and were able to discuss more things than most fathers and daughters did. When Angel finally fell quiet, he gently placed his hand over hers and said, "I understand how you feel. This can't be easy. I mean, who are you supposed to believe? Your cousin or a total stranger?"

"A stranger who makes me feel so unbelievably incredible or a cousin who is known for doing and saying anything to get her way."

"True. My only advice is that you give it a little time. Maybe then things might seem clearer, although it does seem as though you've already made your decision based on the fact that you haven't returned any of his calls."

"I've made a decision that I'm not comfortable with," she responded sadly.

"You can always change your mind."

"I suppose. Believe me, I'm struggling with that choice." Her eyes began to tear up again, but she refused to let them spill over.

Willie stifled a grin. "Didn't you just meet him a few days ago?"

"Yes, but Daddy, it's so hard to explain. I swear I've never felt an emotion so strong or so quickly for anyone before. I feel like a magnet being pulled by some invisible force toward him. It's a little frightening."

"You know, you're never going to know the absolute truth about his feelings unless you speak to him. Yes, he might be lying to you as Morgan says, but then again, perhaps she's the one lying to you to get you to leave him alone so she can swarm in for the kill."

"Nice way to speak of your niece," she said with a slight grin as she gave him a sidelong glance.

"She's my niece and I love her, but I'm not blind to her faults. She's always been selfish, egotistical, and too ambitious for her own good. I'm sure her own mother sees it, but just doesn't want to admit it."

"I suppose I can understand that. It must be hard to see your only daughter turn out to be so opposite of what you tried to raise her to be. I just don't understand it…Aunt Helen is such a sweet, unselfish, and giving mother. How is it possible her daughter turned out this way?"

"Perhaps she was too giving," he said solemnly.

"How do you mean?" Angel asked curiously. Based on her father's reaction, it was obvious this was a subject he had given much thought to.

"She never said no to her. Whatever Morgan wanted, Morgan got. She doesn't know what it's like to not get things her way. I'm sure your aunt meant well, but I think she may have done her more harm than good by not letting her learn firsthand one of life's more important lessons, which is that one doesn't always get what one wants."

"Is that why you and Mom constantly say no to me and Luca?" she said, once again smiling.

"First of all, we do not 'constantly' say no. As I recall, you and Luca have never wanted for anything…"

Angel smiled and chuckled before saying, "I'm only kidding, Daddy. You and Mom have been extremely generous to us."

Ah, that smile of my daughter's could melt an iceberg, he thought. He smiled back.

"Yes, we have, but to be honest with you, there were many times when we could have and wanted to say yes, but opted to say no to teach and prepare you both to deal with disappointment. It also taught you to be grateful for what you do have."

"Boy, you two are smarter than I give you credit for." She looked at him while he stole a quick glance at her and then she squeezed his hand gently and said softly, "Thanks."

Chapter Sixteen

"If you don't fold those, they'll wrinkle," said Janet. Jarrod turned to find his mother standing directly behind him while he stuffed clothes into his suitcase. She was so quiet that he hadn't heard her enter the room.

"I'll just iron them when I get there."

"Sure you will," she said sarcastically. "Why don't you just let me do that?" She gently pushed him aside and began to take over the packing. Jarrod didn't argue with her. He hated the task of packing, so the less he had to do, the better. She began to take everything out he had already placed in it and started over again.

"Are you okay?" he asked her, looking concerned.

"I'll be alright. It's not easy watching your son leave home." She blinked away tears that were beginning to form.

"I know…but you did have eighteen long years to prepare for it."

She gave him a halfhearted smile. "A hundred years wouldn't have been long enough."

He stood behind her and wrapped his arms around her tiny waist and whispered in her ear, "You did a great job raising me.

Thanks." Then he gave her a quick peck on top of her head. She just smiled past the tears that were already flowing, having lost the battle to control them, reached behind, and lightly patted his cheek with her hand.

Shortly after dinner Alec asked Jarrod to join him for a walk around the block. The evening was warm and humid with a few scattered stars making an unusual appearance by besprinkling the night sky. As they walked together, side by side, Alec said, "Y'know, it's not going to be easy around here without you."

"Is this your way of saying you're going to miss me?" Jarrod asked, grinning.

"No. It's just that you're the buffer between me and the folks. Now with you leaving, I'll have no buffer."

"So you'll just have to learn to deal with them on a mature basis. You know, like a grown-up would do."

"Yeah, whatever," Alec said, rolling his eyes.

Jarrod just smirked and said, "So, what's going on? I know you didn't ask me to join you for a walk just because you suddenly felt the urge to get some exercise."

"Just wondering what's been going on with you and Angel. You haven't spoken much of her lately."

"Nothing much to say. I had to stop calling," Jarrod said as he bent down to pick up a penny from the ground.

"Heads up or tails up?" Alec asked as he leaned over to see the penny.

"Heads up," Jarrod responded as he placed the penny in his pocket.

"Cool. So, why did you have to stop calling her?" Alec asked.

"She changed her number."

"Ouch."

"Tell me about it," Jarrod said, frustrated.

"Listen, there's something I want to tell you. A rumor I heard."

"What rumor? I knew something was up." Jarrod slowed his pace a bit. He had been feeling some discomfort and stiffness in his leg since early that morning, which he surmised was brought on by the humidity and the likelihood of rain either later that evening or the following day. After the accident it seemed as though he was able to predict oncoming bad weather as well as, if not better than, a meteorologist.

"I heard from a reliable source that Morgan broke up with Tim and she's looking to get back with you."

"Who's the reliable source?" asked Jarrod inquisitively.

"Can't say. I've been sworn to secrecy. I gave my word as a gentleman not to say…"

"Who?" Jarrod asked loudly and impatiently.

"Angelo Sardone," Alec said without compunction.

Lifting his brows and grinning slightly, Jarrod tittered at how quickly his brother ratted his friend out and said, "Remind me never to rob a bank with you. You can't be trusted with a secret."

"Too late. You already did," Alec reminded him.

"That's true. You didn't tell anyone, did you?"

"Nope. I'm more loyal to family than acquaintances."

"I guess I'm lucky to be family then," Jarrod said, smiling.

"I've always told you you're lucky to have me as a brother."

"Repeatedly."

"You don't seem surprised by the info," Alec stated.

"I'm not."

"Why not?"

"Morgan's been calling me and leaving messages telling me how sorry she is and how she regrets breaking up with me. She told me she wants to get back together and that she'll do anything if I'd just give her another chance."

"Have you called her back?"

"Nope. I have no reason to. I haven't any interest in getting back with her," Jarrod said matter-of-factly. He stopped and bent down to rub his knee.

"Do you want to stop and rest?" Alec asked.

"Nah. I'm fine," he said as he loosely shook his leg and then began to walk slowly with a slight limp. Alec noticed the limp and decided to cut the walk short and turn around.

"Let's head back. We can finish our conversation on the way," he said to Jarrod. Jarrod nodded, and they turned back.

"I'm glad to hear you have no interest in getting back with her," Alec said. "She's no good for you."

"I know. Listen, there's something I haven't told you."

Alec stopped dead in his tracks and said, "Oh God, now what?"

"Nothing weird…just that I overheard the conversation you and Morgan had that day she broke up with me."

"You mean, when she and I were outside?" Alec asked nervously.

"Yeah," replied Jarrod.

"How?" asked Alec tentatively as he began to walk again.

"My bedroom window was open, so I was able to hear everything."

"Dude, I'm sorry. I should have checked first." He felt terrible remembering the things Morgan had said. *It must have been crushing for Jarrod to hear*, he thought.

"Nah…that's fine. I'm glad I heard. At least I know the truth and my eyes were opened to what kind of person she is."

"Yeah. Not very pretty, huh?"

"That's being kind."

Alec paused and took a deep breath before saying, "There's more to the rumor."

"Really? What?"

"She's going to Florida."

Now it was Jarrod's turn to stop cold.

"What the hell do you mean she's going to Florida?"

"From what I hear, she's basically going out there to follow you."

"Please tell me you're kidding?" Jarrod said hopefully.

"I wish I were."

"What the hell is wrong with her?" he asked angrily.

Alec placed his hand over his heart and pretended to swoon and then said in a mocking voice, "She's in love…"

"She's nuts is what she is."

"I won't argue with you there."

"Man! What am I going to do?" Jarrod rubbed his face brusquely and began to walk fast, causing his limp to intensify.

"I think you better call her and find out if there's any truth to that part of the rumor."

"Doesn't look like I have much of a choice, does it?" He shook his head in total annoyance and said, "This sucks." He then dug into his pants pocket, removed the penny that he had found, and threw it angrily across the street.

Chapter Seventeen

Morgan was quietly sitting at her desk in her room writing an e-mail message on her laptop to her friend John. She reviewed it and smiled, liking what she had written, and quickly clicked Send before logging out. She hoped he would respond quickly as she was eager to know what his reply would be to her request. In truth John was more of a friend of a friend. She had met him at a party that her friend Annette had thrown last year. He was an acquaintance of Annette's older brother and was visiting from a city in Florida named Alachua. She remembered the name because it sounded like a sneeze and she was tempted to say 'God bless you' every time he mentioned it. He and Morgan hit it off immediately, and he gave her his home and e-mail addresses so they could keep in touch, which never did happen. She had, however, placed the information in her handbag but had forgotten she even had the small slip of paper until just recently. After retrieving it, she Mapquested the distance between the two cities and found out that they were in close proximity to one another. Hopefully John would agree to let her stay with him until she could find a place of her own. She remembered he had mentioned that he had roommates, so she assumed he would have to speak with them first. She would keep her fingers crossed and maybe even consider saying a prayer or two.

Her phone rang, and she rushed to pick it up, first checking to see who it was. She smiled and released a small squeal of excitement. She cleared her throat twice and took a deep, calming breath before answering.

"Hello?" she said casually.

"It's me," said Jarrod into the phone.

"I know. Took you long enough to call back," she said while attempting to sound cool and aloof.

"Is it true you're planning to go to Florida?"

"What?" *Amazing how quickly news travels through Mayberry*, she thought.

He repeated the question and then added angrily, "Stop playing games and just answer the damn question!"

"I don't know...," she said, bewildered by his anger. She did not appreciate the attitude. Wasn't it enough that she had called numerous times apologizing and asking—no, begging—for a second chance?

"Why would you even consider it? Are you suddenly planning to attend college there?"

"No." She walked over to her bedroom door and quietly closed it and then returned to sit on her bed with her legs crossed. As their conversation continued, she began to examine her small, drab, colorless room with detailed attention and suddenly became charged with the notion of leaving it behind and moving forward toward change and possible excitement.

"Then why?" he asked.

"Why haven't you called me back? I've left you tons of messages."

"Don't change the subject. Answer my question," he said crossly.

"You answer first," she retorted. How dare he yell at her like this. And how the hell did he even find out about her plans?

She had only mentioned it to a few friends that she trusted implicitly.

"Fine. Because I have absolutely no interest whatsoever in getting back with you, so there was no need to call you back. Now you answer my question."

Bastard. Where did this mean streak come from? It was so unlike him. She must have hurt him terribly, she thought. He can't seem to get past the pain and move on. Rather than make his life easy and reconciling with her, he was dragging the ache on by just trying to get back at her.

"You didn't return any of my calls. I'm willing to do whatever it takes for us to be together again."

"You're nuts."

"Why don't you want to get back together? I told you on my messages how sorry I am and that I miss you. Jarrod, I love you—"

"Stop. I don't want to hear your lies. I've heard enough of them to last a lifetime."

"What do you mean?"

"I mean, I know about the conversation you had with Alec after you broke up with me."

"I should have known that he would say something," she said heatedly.

"He didn't say a word. I overheard the two of you speaking through my open window."

"Oh God…"

"Don't bother following me to Florida. You'll just be wasting your money on the flight."

"Jarrod, I don't understand why you're being so mean." She needed to change his mind and convince him they should get back together. Once she did that, everything would be fine. From what she had heard, Jarrod was doing great and had already started training again for baseball. He wasn't quite at the level where he was before the accident, but was progressively getting better with each session. If everything worked out as she planned, within a year or two they would be living happily ever after as Yankee and wife. But how was she ever going to get him to believe she was truly sorry, even though she really was only sorry that he'd caught her?

Tears. Every man was a sucker for tears. She needed to cry, but for some reason, the tears just weren't coming. She was too nervous and angry to cry. She looked around the room and found her tweezers lying on her nightstand. Oh, this was going to hurt, but sometimes sacrifices needed to be made to achieve one's goals. She picked up the tweezers, rushed over to the mirror hanging above her dresser, and yanked at a hair nose. Ouch! Well, that worked. Her eyes immediately began to tear up. She yanked again and then the tears began to flow freely. "Jarrod…please don't tell me you…(sniff)…don't want to get back…(sniff)…together."

Was she crying, thought Jarrod? No way. This woman wasn't capable of shedding real tears. In all the time they had spent together, he had never once seen her cry. Even when her mother had lost one of her jobs and was distraught with worry and uncertainty, Morgan hadn't shown any concern or empathy toward her mother's situation. Oh, there were plenty of times when she would scrunch up her face and grimace as though she was trying to look like she was crying, but actual teardrops never made an appearance. You have to have feelings for that to happen.

"Are you crying?" he asked incredulously.

"Of course I'm crying. You're breaking my heart!"

Jarrod rolled his eyes and, without a trace of emotion, said, "Cut the crap. I know you're faking."

"You're being such an ass. I'm not a monster, y'know. I have feelings too."

She really was crying. He could tell the tears and sniffles were undeniably real. No matter. He wasn't going to allow himself to be pulled into her labyrinth of underhanded deception and treachery.

"Listen, I don't have time for this. Just accept the fact that we're not getting back together. Ever. You were the one who wanted to break up, so now deal with the consequences. My feelings for you are completely dead, so don't call me anymore and don't follow me out to Florida."

Anger stirred up in Morgan, and she shouted into the phone, "Have you been in contact with my cousin? Did Angelise call you? I swear I'll kill her if she did."

"It's none of your business if she called me or not," he responded angrily.

"The hell it isn't. She promised me she wouldn't, and if she broke—"

"You made her promise not to call? You had no right," he screamed in fury.

"I have every right. You're mine, not hers."

"I'm not yours and I never will be. You need to stay the hell out of my life, do you understand? Stay out of it!"

"We'll see about that, you bastard." In full-blown rage, she repeatedly pressed the End Call button on her iPhone as hard as she could, but using the angry hang up strategy on someone just wasn't the same as with a landline. She cursed modern technology.

The following day Morgan made all the arrangements necessary to leave for Florida. John had responded and said she was more than welcome to stay with them. He informed her that he had spoken to his two male roommates and they were both fine with her staying, as long as she contributed toward rent and food while living with them. She would be leaving in four days. Now it was time to break the news to her mother.

Helen was mopping the kitchen floor when Morgan strolled in, not caring that the floor was wet. Her mother just looked at her and said, "Morgan, do you mind? I'm mopping and your shoes are leaving tracks—"

"I'm leaving," she said as she grabbed a banana and began to peel it.

"Alright. What time will you be home?"

"No. I mean, I'm leaving for good. I'm going to be staying with my friend John in Florida for awhile." She watched her mother while taking a big bite of the banana.

Helen just stared at her in shock. She knew this day would come, but didn't expect it so quickly after graduation. "When are you leaving?"

"Friday afternoon. I'll need you to do laundry on Thursday so that everything will be clean by the time I'm ready to pack."

Her mother nodded and then said, "Why Florida? You never mentioned wanting to go there. In fact, you always say Florida is for old people."

"Things have changed. Maybe the state needs some young blood to stir some life into it." She tossed the banana peel into the garbage can and started to walk away.

Helen had a bad feeling about this. Why this interest in going to Florida all of a sudden? And why the hurry? "Do you have a job lined up?" she called out to Morgan.

Morgan stopped but did not turn around to acknowledge her mother's question. "No. I'll find something once I get there."

"How did you pay for the flight?" Helen asked suspiciously.

Morgan turned to face her mother and imperturbably said, "Credit card. Yours. Hope you don't mind."

"Morgan, I do mind. How could you do something like that without checking with me first? I'm trying so hard to keep the bills down, and I'm having a difficult time making the payments as it is…"

"Please spare me the sob story. You don't have to worry about me spending your damn money anymore as of Friday, so consider it a going-away present to me."

"I just don't understand you. Has something happened to make you want to leave so suddenly?" Helen asked worriedly.

"I'm just sick and tired of this small town life. I need excitement…"

"So you pick Florida for excitement?"

"I'm sure there's more to do there than there is here." *Yeah, like nab myself a husband*, she thought.

"Well, then, let me ask you something. Why stay with your friend John when you could stay with your aunt and uncle in Bradenton? I'm sure if I call them, they'd love for you to stay with them. You could stay in Angel's room now that she's leaving for college…"

"No. I don't want to go to Bradenton. Speaking of Angelise, I was wondering if you happen to have her new cell phone number? I've tried calling her, but she changed it and she's never called to give me the new number."

"No, I don't have it."

"Could you get it? Just call Aunt Laura. She'll give it to you," she said, surprisingly sweet. Better not let anyone in on her real feelings toward Angelise.

"Fine," Helen said. She was tired. Tired of arguing with Morgan. Tired of always trying to please her and always coming up short. Tired of her hurtful jibes. Just plain tired of it all. It was easier to just give in and do as she asked.

"Could you do it now? I'd like to call Angel and see how she is doing," Morgan said, knowing she never would call her cousin.

"Would it be alright if I finished mopping first?" Helen asked dryly.

Morgan smiled at her mother's lame attempt at defiance.

"Fine. Gotta go. Just don't forget about having the laundry done by Thursday, okay?" She turned and left while Helen just stood in the kitchen, wet mop still in hand, as she watched her only child walk away.

Morgan arrived home after midnight and found a piece of paper on the kitchen table with Angel's new cell phone number written on it. She took the piece of paper and immediately put it into her handbag for safekeeping. She then climbed the steps to her bedroom, humming softly once again.

Chapter Eighteen

John helped Morgan carry her bags into the house. She looked around and wondered if all the sacrificing she was making was worth it. It was obvious that only men resided there. The house was completely run down and unkempt. The paint on the walls was peeling, the rugs were stained, and the stale odor emanating from the room was strong enough to make her scrunch up her nose in disgust.

"Yeah, I know. Smells, huh?" said John.

"A bit. Do you guys ever open the windows and let the house air out?" she asked.

"Sometimes, but we forget a lot of the times."

"Apparently. So, two other roommates, huh?"

"Yup. Nate and Benjamin. Nate's cool. You'll get along fine with him, but…um…I should forewarn you about Benjamin."

"Why? What's up? He's not some serial killer or a deranged sex feign is he?" She popped her head into the kitchen and quickly turned away in disgust.

"No…I don't think so," he said thoughtfully.

Morgan abruptly turned her head toward him and cautiously asked, "You don't *think* so?"

"It's just that he's a little on the strange side. He prefers to keep to himself. Doesn't interact with people unless absolutely necessary. Rarely looks you in the eye and almost always has his head down like he's studying the dirt on the ground or something."

"Great."

"By the way…don't ever call him Ben or Benny or anything other than Benjamin. I called him Ben once and he totally freaked out. I thought he was going to jump me or something."

"You know, it might have been nice if you had told me about this nutjob before I got here…oh, it doesn't matter. I'm not planning on becoming chummy with anyone anyway. I've got more important things to focus on."

She continued following him until he reached a closed door and opened it. She walked in, looked around and said, "Please don't tell me this walk-in closet is supposed to pass as my bedroom?"

"We'll expect two hundred and fifty dollars every first of the month. That should cover food and board." He smiled at her and leaned against the doorway with his arms folded across his chest. "Morgan, it's nice seeing you again. I'm glad you finally decided to get in touch with me, even though it was only because you needed something from me." He gave her a sad, little pout she found endearing.

"I'm sorry, John. It was wrong of me. It's just that my boyfriend would have freaked if I had contacted you." Even though it was a blatant lie, it was less hurtful than telling him the truth, which was that she found him completely unattractive and had no interest whatsoever in pursuing a romantic relationship with him.

"And he doesn't mind now?" he asked curiously.

"He doesn't care about anything I do anymore since we broke up."

"Sorry. It's his loss. Besides, you're far too pretty to be tied down to a Jersey loser. We Floridian men are much more sophisticated."

She smiled at his comment, but decided it would be best to avoid responding to it at this moment.

"How much did you say the rent and board is?" she asked in an attempt to change the subject.

"Two hundred and fifty dollars a month." He watched her when she wasn't looking and noticed she may have gained a few pounds since he last saw her. Not a lot, perhaps five or ten pounds only, but definitely all in the right places. He loved her short, dark, hair, which gave her that spunky, in-your-face look. She had big, brown, puppy-dog eyes that sometimes seemed a little sad. She wasn't too tall, which was great, since he was only five ten. He hated it when the girls he dated were taller than him. She turned toward him, so he quickly diverted his eyes from the brief study he was administering on her ample backside and smiled at her.

"Then expect me to eat a lot because this room isn't worth ten dollars a month," she said and sighed resignedly.

While Morgan was busy inspecting her new living accommodations, just a few miles away, Jarrod was on the phone speaking to Alec.

"So, how's college life treating you so far?"

"No complaints yet," Jarrod responded. "Then again, I just got here."

"Have you seen Angel yet?"

"Shhhhh…I don't want Mom to know," Jarrod scolded.

"She's not even in the room. She's upstairs crying over her eldest son abandoning her…"

"Dude, seriously?" Jarrod's voice was laced with concern.

"Nahhh…just kidding. She just stepped outside to get the mail."

"Good. To answer your question, no, I haven't seen her yet. It's crazy. I keep hoping I'll bump into her, but *nada*."

"I see you learned something from watching that Spanish soap opera. So go find her."

"I'm trying but it's not easy."

"Yeah, well, while you're out there searching for your one true love, just watch your back for your former love."

"Huh?"

"She's there," Alec simply said. Jarrod froze while desperately hoping Alec was not referring to Morgan.

"Not Morgan? Please tell me not Morgan," Jarrod pleaded, knowing all along that that was exactly who Alec meant.

"Morgan."

"Dammit."

"Listen, I'm serious. Be careful. Who knows what she's capable of?" He was worried for his brother. As far as he was concerned, Morgan was bat-shit crazy.

"Yeah, I will. Do you happen to know if she's in or near Gainesville?"

"I don't know. I'll do some investigating and let you know what I find out."

"Thanks. Whatever you find out, any little thing, just call me and let me know, okay?"

"Definitely. Hey, and let me know when you find Dreamgirl."

"I will. Talk to you soon," Jarrod said before hanging up.

Chapter Nineteen

After numerous letters, phone calls, and incessant pleading by the two young ladies, Angel and Ileana still failed in their endeavor to become roommates. They were both terribly disappointed, but nonetheless happy to be attending the same college and fortunate enough to be in two of the same classes. This was no surprise, since they had both decided to major in advertising, in hopes of someday opening up an agency together. As they were heading toward Broward Beach to enjoy the sun after a lengthy two-hour marketing research class, they spoke of inconsequential topics such as the latest rumor concerning Britney Spears and her latest love interest, the pros and cons of wearing a thong, and a nauseating overview concerning the key ingredients found in head cheese. The conversation concluded in the culmination of a debate over the merits of ingesting Gingko Biloba in liquid or pill form.

"Didn't you take it in liquid form for awhile?" asked Angel.

"I don't remember," Ileana stated flatly while looking perplexed.

"Obviously you didn't take it for a long-enough period," laughed Angel.

They sat down under a tree and plopped their books down beside them. Ileana leaned back on her elbows with her legs outstretched, crossing her ankles one over the other. Angel sat with her legs crossed in a yoga-like meditation style.

"I don't know how you find that position comfortable," said Ileana. "I would end up with the worst leg cramps if I sat that way for more than a minute." She sat up for a moment to place her hair into a ponytail with a hair tie she pulled out of her back pocket.

"I'm flexible," Angel responded with a wicked smile and a wink.

"Yeah, right. Too bad you don't put that flexibility to good use."

Angel just smiled and closed her eyes, lifting her head toward the sky to feel the warmth of the sun on her face. When she had awoken that morning, the day brimmed of promised rain, but thankfully that promise had been broken and the sun now stood proudly in the sky, favoring all with its brightness and beauty. She took a deep breath just as Ileana let out a long, disgusting belch. Angel got a whiff of what presumably had been Ileana's now fully digested lunch. She scrunched up her nose in disgust.

"Jeez, Ile, that's disgusting. You smell like…like…hot dogs. At least forewarn me when you're going to do that."

Ileana chuckled and said, "Sorry." One of the benefits of being so close to someone was that you could totally be yourself and let loose, literally, and still be loved by that person. "Girl, you need to open your eyes. You're missing all the hot guys and their gorgeous, toned bodies."

"I have only one gorgeous toned body on my mind," stated Angel with a deep, depressed sigh.

Ileana turned to look at her friend and felt sorry for her. Based on how Angel had described this Jarrod fellow, he sounded almost too good to be true. No one was that good-looking or sweet or romantic or funny or any of the other twenty or thirty laudatory adjectives Angel had used in describing him. Damn that horrible cousin of Angel's.

"Have you seen him around campus yet?" she asked.

Angel opened her eyes, staring straight ahead at nothing in particular and said to her friend, "No, but I keep looking, though. It's so weird. I want to see him, but at the same time, I'm terrified that I will."

"There's nothing weird about that. You like him and you want to see him. The problem is, you know that if you do, it's going to be super awkward. I mean, you were kind of mean to him by not returning his calls and then changing the number so he couldn't call you anymore."

"He was mean to me first. He used me to make Morgan jealous."

"You're basing that allegation on what Morgan told you. You know you can't believe a word that bitch says. I don't even know why you bother with her."

"She's never done anything to hurt me," Angel said, not fully understanding why she was defending her cousin.

"Until now."

"We don't know."

"Exactly. We don't know and we never will know unless you speak to him." She hesitated in continuing but did so anyway by adding, "Angel, you know I love you. You are by far the most special person in my life, aside from my family."

"I hear a 'but' in there…"

"*But* you're too good. Don't you see what your cousin is doing to you? She wants Jarrod and she won't hesitate to do anything and everything in her power to get what she wants, including lying to her cousin."

"I don't know what to think. I should just forget about him. I mean, it's not like we even dated…but I just can't help but feel that he's special. It's like…when I think of him, I feel all warm inside. It's like he…he…"

"If you dare say he completes you, I swear I'll throw up right here," Ileana said, throwing herself backward onto the grass.

"Shut up," Angel said, laughing, but then suddenly became serious and said, "But yeah, I sort of feel like if given the chance, he could."

"Be forewarned," said Ile.

"Forewarned about what?" and all of a sudden, Angel heard what sounded like a foghorn sounding off a warning signal to an oncoming ship. The smell that followed it collided into Angel with a staggering blow. "Good God, Ile! By chance, was that hot dog smothered in chili and raw onions?"

Close to a month went by and still no sightings of Jarrod or Angel had been made by either one. Angel thought that should be a relief, but she was becoming more and more frustrated as time passed. Her mind began to work on overdrive again. Did he transfer to another college to avoid seeing her? Did he and Morgan get back together and he decided to stay closer to home to be near her? Perhaps he was not physically well enough to be on his own and was forced to delay furthering his education. So many questions, so few answers.

Jarrod returned to his dorm room at Murphree Hall after a training session at Perry Field. Physically speaking, he was feeling great. His arm felt good and his pitching strength and power was returning at a considerably progressive rate. A few more months of intense training and practice, and he might be ready to give Griffin Wyatt a call.

Mentally speaking was a different story. He kept searching for Angel and couldn't find her. He had asked around, but nobody seemed to know her. Even when he'd described what she looked like, they still didn't know who she was, but every guy he'd asked was more than willing to keep an eye out for her. Unfortunately, Jarrod was pretty sure they weren't planning on getting in touch with him if they did indeed find her.

As he entered his dorm room one night, he found his roommate sound asleep in his bed with the television blasting. Dave Johnson looked like a colossal giant sleeping in the small twin-size bed furnished by the university. He was massive in every sense of the word. Approximately six foot three in height and powerfully built, he had been the star linebacker of his high school football team and was attending UFS on a full ride. Extremely intelligent, he was majoring in engineering with a minor in physical education. He amazed Jarrod with his ability to juggle his school workload, athletic commitments, and "diversified frolics," as Dave would call it. The teddy bear of a brute was a walking encyclopedia of useless, but quite interesting, information and funny as all hell. He sometimes reminded Jarrod of Dante, and he imagined they would have liked each other quite a bit. Dave kept Jarrod in stitches, which was a good thing, seeing that Jarrod wasn't finding amusement and distractions anywhere else. His juggling ability wasn't as impressive as his roommate's.

Jarrod turned the television off and placed his equipment bag on his bed. When his cell phone rang, he checked to see whom it was before answering. Alec. He picked up and said, "What's up?"

"Not much. What's going on?"

"I just got back from the field. My arm and shoulder feel pretty good."

"Glad to hear it," said Alec as he sat on the front steps of the house watching the cars go by. It was a nice evening, although a bit on the chilly side.

"How are Mom and Dad doing?" Jarrod asked.

"You mean, since last you spoke?"

"Yeah."

"They've had dinner."

Jarrod chuckled and said, "That's good. Nice to know they're eating well."

"I didn't exactly say they were eating well," responded Alec dryly. "I just said they ate. Mom cooked."

"I see what you mean."

"Hey, I just wanted to let you know I spoke with Morgan's mom today. I bumped into her at Walmart."

"How is she doing? She's a nice lady." He did like Mrs. Billings. She was nothing like her daughter. Whenever he went to her house, she'd offer to cook something for him or immediately switched the television channel to ESPN. She was always trying to please him, and he sensed it truly gave her pleasure when he'd accept the offer of a sandwich or simply thank her for letting him watch sports.

"Really nice. But I don't think she's doing too well. She looked sad and she's lost a lot of weight. She looks…kind of old."

"Why? Is she sick?" Jarrod asked, concerned.

"Probably just sick and tired of having an ass for a daughter."

"What's up? Did she say anything? Is Morgan back in Cliffside?" Jarrod desperately hoped Alec's answer would be in the affirmative.

"No. Unfortunately, she doesn't know too much. I was able to find out that Morgan left about a month or so ago and has only called her mom once or twice. She said she left to stay with her friend John in Florida, but she doesn't even know what town she's in. Morgan won't even tell her that. Mrs. Billings keeps calling and leaving messages on her cell, but Morgan rarely calls her back unless she needs money. She's worried sick and—"

"I can't believe someone could hurt her own mother that way," interrupted Jarrod. "It makes me sick."

"I know. I feel bad for her," Alec said sorrowfully.

"Me too. Y'know, the more and more I think about it, I can't figure out what the hell I ever saw in Morgan. I mean, how could I not see this side of her?"

"Love is blind."

"I was never in love with her," Jarrod said forcefully.

"Lust can be just as blinding."

"Yeah, maybe. But when you think about it, she isn't all that hot either. I mean, she's definitely pretty, but not 'out of this world' pretty."

"You mean like Angel?" Alec asked.

"Yeah," he responded sadly, "like Angel."

"Anything going on there?" Alec felt bad for Jarrod. His brother so wanted to find Angel and truly believed it was his destiny to be with her, but he just couldn't find her, no matter how hard he tried.

"No. I haven't seen her and no one seems to know her...I don't know what else to do." He began to rub his face in aggravation.

"It's a big campus. Umm, are you rubbing your face?" Alec asked.

"No, I'm not rubbing my face." He immediately stopped rubbing his face. "You're right about the campus being big, though. Looking for Angel is like looking for a diamond in a mound of broken glass."

"Have you gone to the housing office to find out if they can tell you what dorm she's in?" Alec asked.

"Yeah. It was one of the first things I did. Big mistake."

"Why, what happened?"

"They started asking me about a thousand questions. I felt as though I was being interrogated by the police. I think they thought I was some maniac stalker or something. I knew I wasn't going to get any answers, so I just got out of there before they called the UFPD and had my butt hauled into jail or something." Jarrod gave a slight chuckle at the memory.

"Smart move. Listen, I gotta go. Mom's yelling at me from inside the house because I need to work on a paper that's due tomorrow. I'll talk to you next week, unless something new comes up."

"Alright. Bye."

After they both hung up, Jarrod took a long, hot shower, studied for about an hour and then went to bed exhausted. He was so tired, he even slept through Dave's thunder-like snoring.

The next morning, as they were getting ready for classes, Dave asked Jarrod if he would like to join him and some friends that evening to hear a new rock band play at the Tenth Inning Pub, which was located not far from their dorm.

"Nah, I don't think so," Jarrod responded. He was looking through his closet hoping to find a clean shirt. He hadn't done laundry in over a week, and a pile of dirty clothes in the corner of the room could easily hide a family of four.

"Why not? C'mon, you'll have a blast. You need to get out and have some fun. All you ever do is go to classes, play baseball, study, and then go to bed."

"That's what I'm here for." He found a clean shirt, pulled it out to look at it, and placed it back in the closet. His mother must have packed it because he never would have. What was he thinking when he bought that green-striped rugby shirt? If he wore that, he'd seriously be mistaken for that guy on *Blue's Clues*.

"Yeah, but there's a lot more to the college experience than just studying and playing ball. Seriously, you'll have a good time. I guarantee it."

"Who's going?" asked Jarrod.

"T.J., Mark, Melissa, Niko, Parker, Paul, and some other people you haven't met yet."

"Sounds a bit crowded." He walked over to the pile of dirty clothes, picked up a T-shirt he had worn a few days ago, gave it a whiff, and seeing that it didn't smell, put it on. Dave gave him a look of disgust, but Jarrod just shrugged.

Dave fell to his knees, placed his hands together in a placating mode, and said in a beseeching voice, "Pretty please? Oh Jarrod, please say you'll come out and play with us!"

"Fine, if it'll shut you up," Jarrod responded with a laugh.

"Good. Meet us there around eight tonight," said Dave happily as he stood up. He grabbed his books and headed toward the door, but said before leaving, "It might be a good idea if you do some laundry before meeting us. I'm sure everyone will appreciate it. I know I certainly will."

Chapter Twenty

That evening Jarrod returned to the dorm after doing his laundry, took a quick shower, shaved, and dressed before heading out to the Tenth Inning Pub. As he walked in the door, he was met by Paul, a friend he had met through Dave. Paul's hands were occupied with holding drinks, so he casually nodded and smiled at Jarrod and said "Hey! Glad to see you made it, man. Everyone's sitting over there," as he gestured toward the center of the room. "Follow me."

Jarrod acknowledged by nodding and then followed him. The pub was overly crowded, with all the tables and stools at the bar being taken up by college students out to have a good time—most with high hopes of forgetting about failed exams, research papers that were due soon, possible lost scholarships due to poor grades, or as in Jarrod's case, beautiful, heavenly looking girls that simply could not be found.

A jukebox in the corner of the room blasted Springsteen's "Glory Days," which suddenly brought on a slight case of melancholy for Jarrod. The Boss was considered a living icon in New Jersey where he was born and bred, and it would be hard to find a fellow Jersey native that wasn't truly proud of that fact. When Jarrod finally reached the table where his friends sat, just about everyone at the table began to mockingly cheer and clap. He smiled and sat down next to Dave, who immediately leaned over and put one arm around him and began introducing him to those at the table he had never met.

"And this lovely *señorita* sitting directly across from us is Ileana Mendez...Ileana, this is my roommate, Jarrod."

Ileana looked at him and recognized him immediately based on her friend's description. Angel hadn't exaggerated after all. He was gorgeous and muscular and had these piercingly blue eyes that were absolutely mesmerizing.

"Hi, Jarrod. It's nice to meet you," she said as she leaned forward to shake his hand.

Jarrod half stood so she wouldn't have to lean forward too much and shook her hand.

"Nice to meet you too," he said as he sat back down. *Pretty girl, but with a slightly annoying tendency to stare*, he thought to himself.

"If you don't mind me asking, where are you from?" she asked, still gaping at him.

"New Jersey," he responded uneasily. He wished she would stop looking at him so intently; it made him feel incredibly self-conscious. As she ogled his nose, Jarrod automatically rubbed it with his hand and began to wonder if he should have taken the time to trim his nose hairs after his shower. She moved on to his mouth, and he found himself closing his lips and passing his tongue over his teeth in fear there may have been remnants of the salad he had had with dinner earlier.

Ileana could not stop staring at him. It had to be him. It was too much of a coincidence. But she had to be absolutely sure, so she asked, "What town? I know someone from New Jersey."

Blink lady. Just blink once, he found himself silently wishing. "I'm from a small town called Cliffside Park. You've probably never even heard of it."

"I've heard of Cliffside. The girl I know is from that town." Barely pausing and with complete assuredness, she added, "She's a total bitch-ass and her name is Morgan."

Jarrod looked at her in shock. It couldn't be the same Morgan. Or could it? Same town, same name. It must be the same bitch-ass. It had to be her. Jarrod shook his head in disbelief.

Ileana finally blinked, her gaze losing some of its intensity.

"I have the misfortune of knowing her because she just happens to be my best friend's *cousin*." She placed an emphasis on the word *cousin* to see what sort of reaction he would give. She wasn't disappointed.

Becoming increasingly hopeful and optimistic that he may have finally found a way to contact the woman who had been haunting his thoughts and dreams for what seemed like forever, he straightened up and nervously asked, "May I ask what your best friend's name is?"

"Angel," she said.

He smiled widely, exposing beautiful, straight, glistening white teeth and then said, "Would you like to know my new best friend's name?"

"Sure," she said, returning his smile.

"Ileana."

She motioned for him to take the empty seat next to her. He did as she requested and then she began by saying, "I know all about you. Angel told me about how the two of you met."

"Do you have any idea why she never returned any of my calls? I know Morgan made her promise not to, but I just want to know if that's the only reason. Maybe I just imagined her being interested and in reality she's not."

"I do know," she said sorrowfully, yet at the same time apprehensively. She always felt Angel did not handle the situation correctly by not taking his calls, or not returning the numerous messages he left, but even worse, for changing her phone number to avoid his calls completely. That was just rude and so unlike Angel. But on the other hand, if what Morgan had said was true, then she shouldn't feel sorry for him. It would serve him right for using Angel that way.

"Can you tell me?" he asked.

"Not really. I would be betraying her confidence if I were to do that."

"Oh," he said, disappointed. "I can understand that, but I'm just confused. I mean, I felt like there was some sort of an intense connection between the two of us, and I was so sure she felt it too. I called her a few times, but she never returned any of the calls. Then she had her number changed, so I got the picture that she wasn't interested. It's just so damn confusing."

"Not everything is as it seems."

"Well, that clears things up for me," he said half jokingly.

With a slight grin and minor hesitation in her response, she said, "I just don't know why, but for some reason, I have a good feeling about you. It's strange, but even before meeting you tonight, I just sensed maybe you weren't the villain in this situation."

"How can I be the villain? I never even got the chance to do anything—bad or good."

"Morgan certainly did."

Leaning slightly forward, he looked directly into her soulful brown eyes where he thought he saw a glimmer of empathy. "Please…I need you to explain. I need to know the truth behind all of this."

She was torn. If she betrayed Angel by telling him what Morgan had said and it turned out to be true, Angel would look and feel like a fool. How could she place her best friend in that situation? But if it was all a lie, then maybe, just maybe, she would be doing Angel a tremendous favor. She stared at Jarrod for a long moment and then closed her eyes as she took a deep, resigning breath. When she opened them again, she saw he was staring tentatively at her as if all his hopes lay within her merciful power. Then he softly uttered one simple, yet effectually convincing word. He said, "Please."

Damn him, she thought.

"Angel will be so mad at me if I do, but yet, if this has all just been a horrible misunderstanding between the two of…" She was reluctant to continue, but dropped her head in complete defeat and said, "God, I'd hate for the two of you to miss out on a good thing simply because I was afraid of pissing her off."

"So would I."

Looking back up, she said rather forcefully "I just need to know a few things first. Are you and Morgan back together?"

"No, definitely not. Once we broke up, that was it. She and I are completely over."

"Good to know. Now, I need to know another thing. Do you have feelings for Angel, or did you just pretend to be interested in her to make Morgan jealous?" At that moment, Ileana glanced across the table and caught Dave staring at her. She smiled at him and he returned her smile, but looked away quickly. His mood seemed to have changed from earlier. He seemed distant and a bit sad. She wondered what might have happened to make him feel this way when he seemed so happy and was joking endlessly just a little while ago. Slightly distracted, she returned her attention to Jarrod.

Jarrod seemed surprised by Ileana's question. Where did that come from? "I truly have feelings, very strong feelings, for Angel. I have no reason to make Morgan jealous. I just want her out of my life forever."

"What about payback? Did you show interest in Angel just to get back at Morgan for hurting you?" she said as she bit her lower lip in nervousness.

"No...to be honest with you, it didn't hurt all that much when she broke up with me. I think what hurt was why she ended things. She basically didn't have any faith in me and my ability to come back swinging, literally, after a bad car accident I was in. It was difficult because I was at the lowest point in my life and I, myself, wasn't even sure if I would ever be able to play ball again...but losing Morgan, the person, didn't hurt. Just her actions did. They forced me to question my own abilities."

Ileana intensely studied his face for sincerity and unequivocally found it there. She just needed to know one more thing before she took this giant leap of faith that could possibly destroy her friendship with Angel forever.

"Tell me one more thing. Tell me about your feelings for Angel."

He sat there looking at her quietly for a moment.

"Without going into too much detail, I can tell you this has been the worse year of my life. I've had to deal with loss, fear, worry, anger...you name it, I felt it. Before that night—the night I met Angel—I honestly didn't give a shit about anything anymore. Nothing seemed to matter, or if it did matter, I felt as though it was lost to me forever. Then I met her. For some reason she made me feel like things could be better again in my life. I know it sounds crazy, especially since we only spent a few minutes together, but I just feel that if we're not together, neither one of us will ever know or experience...that deep, intense feeling...of...of..."

She cut him off by asking in a shocked tone, "Jarrod, do you think you're in love with her?"

He slowly blinked and raised his eyes to her and she noted that they were slightly fogged over with something she could not describe, as if he were in a trance.

"I can't explain it. God, we only spent ten short minutes together, but you have no idea what I'd give to experience those few moments just one more time—just to spend a little more time with her. Since I got to Florida, I've spent whatever free time I've had trying to find her, but I haven't had any luck until now."

He paused and shook his head as if to clear it and continued by saying, "Am I in love with her? Love at first sight seems like such a cliché. I have no idea. I've never been in love before, so I don't know what it feels like. What I do know is that I've never experienced such a strong connection toward someone, and I feel that she and I deserve the chance to explore our feelings and find out where they might lead. I feel like that opportunity was taken away from us."

As she listened to his words, simple yet so powerful, she knew in her heart that he and Angel needed to be given that chance. She indisputably knew that what Morgan had callously stolen, she would have to give back to them. She just hoped things would work out as she anticipated and Angel would find a way of forgiving her betrayal.

"God, she's going to be so mad at me!" she said as she closed her eyes hard and threw her head back.

Jarrod smiled, placed his hand over hers, and simply said, "Thank you."

The band, Desperate Souls, had already been announced and was on stage ready to begin their set. They began with a startlingly good rendition of Guns N' Roses' "Welcome to the Jungle." The patrons were all singing, shouting, and clapping in unison and the clamor reached a thunderous level.

"I think we need to go somewhere quieter to talk. How about the coffee shop across the street?" Ileana suggested loudly to be heard over the ear-piercing music.

"Good idea. Let's go," he agreed.

They said their quick good-byes and received looks of shock and dismay from all. Dave made a point of pulling Jarrod aside and saying, "Dude, you don't waste time, do you?"

"Nah. It's nothing like that…"

"Listen, I know it's none of my business, but she's a nice girl. I've gotten to know her and she's a sweet kid. I don't want to see her get hurt—"

"Dave, stop talking for a second and listen to me. I'm not interested in her. Don't get me wrong, she's very pretty and nice, but it's her best friend I'm interested in. A lot of stuff has gone down, and I'm hoping she'll help me try to work things out with her friend. So don't worry. She's in no danger of me breaking her heart or vice versa."

Dave seemed exceedingly pleased with that bit of information. "You have no idea how glad I am to hear you say that. Well, then…umm…good luck with everything."

Jarrod and Ileana walked across the street and found a quiet booth in the corner of the small coffee shop. A young, pretty waitress with long dark hair pulled tight into a ponytail came over to the table to take their order.

"Hi! What can I get you tonight?" she asked with a pleasant smile.

Ileana ordered a coffee and Jarrod asked for a Coke.

"Are you hungry? Would you like something to eat?" Jarrod asked.

"No, I'm good. Thanks." *How thoughtful of him to ask*, she thought. She could definitely see him and Angel together. She truly hoped she was doing the right thing and not making the mistake of a lifetime.

The waitress left to get their drinks and smiled appealingly at Jarrod as she did. Ileana didn't miss the one-sided flirtation and instantly wondered if that happened a lot. Of course it did. Jarrod was an astonishingly good-looking guy and she was certain hundreds of girls found him completely irresistible and had probably thrown themselves at him. And yet he'd chosen Angel above them.

"First, let me start off by saying that Angel is more than just my best friend. She's the sister my parents never gave me. I would walk through fire for her and I know she would do the same for me. That said, I want you to know that what I'm doing right now by sitting here talking to you is putting our friendship on the line. She spoke to me about you in total confidence, knowing that I would never, ever betray that confidence. Yet, here I am…"

"You're doing it because you know that it's the right thing to do. She'll understand and be happy that you did," he hoped.

"I hope you're right. Jarrod, I usually have a good sense of people's characters, and my first impression of you is good… but I could be wrong. There's always a first time for everything. Please don't make me regret doing this."

"I won't hurt her, if that's what you're worried about. On the contrary I'll do my best to make her happy. If she lets me, that is." He knew how hard this was for Ileana to do and wholly appreciated her bravery.

The waitress placed the coffee and soda in front of them and they thanked her. Ileana watched her walk away and then took a deep breath and said, "Here goes then…"

She began by explaining how Morgan had told Angel she was still in love with Jarrod and wanted to reconcile with him. She also told him Morgan had led Angel to believe that the sole reason Jarrod had shown any interest was because he had wanted to make Morgan jealous, while at the same time make her pay for the pain she had caused him. That thought hurt Angel beyond belief. She believed he had used her, and that was why she had chosen not to return any of his calls. She was not about to aid him further in his quest for revenge, while at the same time opening up a window that would allow her heart to be broken in the process.

Jarrod was speechless. He now understood why Angel hadn't returned his calls and it infuriated him to know she had been hurt. He tightened and released his fists in anger and then rubbed his face in frustration.

"You okay?" Ileana asked.

"Yeah… I'm pissed off, though," he responded heatedly.

"I can see that. My dad does the same thing when he's frustrated."

"Does what?"

"Rubs his face. He usually does it while paying the bills." This comment brought an endearingly crooked half smile to Jarrod's face.

"I'm glad you're smiling. I was afraid that vein in your forehead was about to burst." Ileana motioned toward the protruding vein with a nod of her head.

Jarrod immediately touched his forehead and said, "Oh yeah. That damn vein…It's always been a dead giveaway to my moods."

He suddenly became serious and said, "Thanks for telling me all of this, and I want you to know that everything Morgan told Angel was a lie. The absolute, one and only true reason why I showed interest in Angel is simply because *I am* interested in her. Not because I wanted to hurt or make Morgan jealous. She'll go to no ends to get what she wants." He got so angry that he took his fist and pounded the table.

"Take it easy, cowboy," she said laughingly.

He leaned back in his seat and ran one hand through his hair, making it appear disheveled. The look made him appear boyishly sexy. *Angel certainly has good taste in men*, she thought to herself.

"I'm sorry," he said. "It's just that I get so angry when I think of how she manipulated Angel with her lies. It doesn't faze her in the least bit to play with other people's lives as if they were puppets. I mean, this is her own cousin…family… her own flesh and blood…and she couldn't care less."

"So, now what do we do about it?" Ileana asked gravely as she took another sip of her coffee.

He gave Ileana his most impressive and magnificent smile and said, "You get Angel to meet with me."

Chapter Twenty-One

"I can't believe I'm doing this," Ileana cried. "I swear if you two end up getting married, you better name your firstborn after me!"

"What if it's a boy?" he said, laughing.

"You two figure something out." She started biting her nails for the third time since Jarrod showed up.

Jarrod gently reached over to take her hand out of her mouth and said, "Nails are hard to digest."

"These are fake, so I should have a lot to look forward to in about two hours."

Jarrod laughed again and then said, "Tell me how you got her to meet me."

"I didn't tell her you were coming. In fact, I didn't tell her anything. I just asked her to meet me here for coffee. I know, I know. I'm a spineless, yellow-bellied chicken." She had phoned Angel that morning before classes began and asked her to meet her at four o'clock that afternoon at Java Joe's, the same coffee shop where she and Jarrod sat together two nights ago. Of course, she hadn't mentioned that part to Angel.

"You didn't tell her? What if...um..."

Ileana nervously played with a lock of her long hair by continually twirling it around her forefinger, but suddenly stopped as she looked past him and opened her eyes wide.

"What if…um…nothing. Gotta go. Bye and lots of luck to you."

She jumped up from her seat and smiled at Angel, who was waving to her. She quickly walked toward her and when face-to-face, pressed a quick peck on her left cheek, and whispered in her ear, "Last booth on the right. I'm sorry and…I love you. Now go." And then Ileana walked briskly toward the exit, never stopping to look back.

Angel watched her friend run out the door and across the street with a perplexed look on her face. She slowly turned around and hesitantly walked toward the last booth. A man sat with his back facing her. He appeared tense. He sat ramrod stiff, reminiscent of those bronze statues you sometimes see in front of office buildings, the ones so lifelike that people constantly confused them for real people.

When she reached the table, she looked at the man, but his head was now bent forward causing his hair to cover a portion of his face. He looked up at her, and she immediately stepped back. Her eyes widened in surprise and shock, and her mouth fell open, but words did not come out.

"Hi, Angel," he said.

Ah, that voice. Although she'd listened to his undeleted voice messages over and over again, she would never tire of hearing it. It was so masculine and sensual, just like he was. Still she said nothing; she simply turned her head toward the front door, looking to see if she saw Ileana anywhere. When she didn't, she looked at him, confused.

"Why don't you sit down?" he said.

She shook her head no, but did not turn to leave.

He shimmied across the seat and slowly stood up. He motioned toward the other side of the booth with his outstretched arm and said, "Please?"

Angel stared at him and then agreed without saying a word. She simply sat on the other side and placed both her hands in her lap. At first she kept her head lowered, but then slowly raised it to face him.

"I don't understand," she said softly.

Ah, that voice. He'd missed hearing it. He had only heard it the day they had met and the few times he had called and listened to her voice message, but he'd remembered everything about it. He recalled its tenderness, but his memory failed to evoke the beauty of the soft and lilting timbre it held. He was captivated by everything about her. There were moments when he'd thought his imagination had over-exaggerated her appeal, but seeing and hearing her now, he knew it hadn't. She truly was as magnificent as he'd recalled.

"I met Ileana the other night. We were introduced and she was able to put two and two together based on your description of me as well as information she got by asking me some direct questions."

"Ile is direct, if nothing else."

"Definitely. Anyway, we got to talking and she explained some things to me."

Placing a bent elbow on the table, she leaned forward and covered her face with one hand while nervously asking, "What sort of things?"

"Things that made her fear you enough to run out of here like a bat out of hell."

Looking up she said, "I'll kill her," and then quickly leaned to her side to see past Jarrod. She was looking for her intended victim, but she was nowhere to be found. Coward.

"That's what she keeps saying, but I don't think you will when you hear what I have to say. She set this meeting up because she cares for you and wants you to be happy. She took the time to hear me out, and I'm only hoping you will too."

The same waitress as the other night stopped to ask them what they would like. Angel requested a coffee and Jarrod ordered a regular Coke. The waitress eyed Jarrod curiously and asked, "Weren't you just here the other night?" As she awaited his response, she slipped a brief glance to Angel and immediately realized she was not the same dark-haired girl he had been with that night.

"Yeah, I was," he said, never looking up at her. He couldn't seem to take his eyes off Angel. Endless weeks had turned into endless months of him hoping, praying, and wanting to see her. Now that she was sitting before him, he wasn't about to waste a second looking at someone else.

"Busy guy, aren't you?" said the waitress, whose name tag identified her as SueEllen.

"Excuse me?" he said, still looking only at Angel.

"Never mind. Anything else besides the drinks?"

Jarrod gave Angel a questioning look.

"No thanks," she said.

SueEllen mumbled something under her breath as she walked away, causing Jarrod to turn toward her for a brief second, curiously wondering what she had just said. When he turned to face Angel, she was chuckling. Whatever SueEllen had said, it was definitely not complimentary.

"Are you here to apologize?" she asked, becoming serious.

"Apologize for what?" he asked.

"Do I have to say it?"

"Yeah, actually, you do. You see, I know I didn't do anything wrong. You were made to believe that I did by your cousin, but the only thing I'm guilty of is being attracted to you…strongly attracted."

Angel didn't know whether to believe him or not. Did he mean what he just said or was he still simply toying with her feelings?

"I'm listening." Although she seemed willing to listen, it was acutely apparent she was feeling apprehensive and mistrustful of the situation. He could sense it in her demeanor as well as her posture. She held her head high, looking straight at him, and her back and shoulders were pressed firmly against the seat of the booth. *This was not going to be easy*, he thought.

"According to Ileana, Morgan told you she wanted to get back with me. That part is true. She tried contacting me a few times, but I never answered her calls or returned her messages. Except one time. I called her back because I had heard she was planning on following me to Florida and—"

Without thinking, she cut him off by lifting a hand to silence him and said, "Hold on. Are you saying Morgan's here in Florida?"

"Yes."

SueEllen returned with the coffee and soda and hastily retreated after serving them. She glanced back at Jarrod once and shook her head before heading toward the long counter to begin the tedious task of marrying the ketchup bottles.

"How do you know? Has she called you again?" She wondered if her parents knew Morgan was here. No, they wouldn't know. If they had, they would have mentioned something to her over the phone last night.

"No, she hasn't called in awhile. My brother bumped into her mother the other day and she told him."

"Aunt Helen," she said quietly.

Jarrod took a long sip of his soda and continued. "The night I called Morgan was to find out if it was true, if she was planning on coming to Florida. That was the only time I've spoken to her since the party where you and I met."

"But she had been calling you and leaving messages during that time?"

"Yes."

"And you never once called her back?"

"No. Just that one time."

"Why didn't you return her calls?" she asked curiously. She added a pack of Equal to her coffee, stirred it, and took a sip. It was hot, and the liquid burned her tongue and throat on the way down. "Ouch," she exclaimed as she closed her eyes in pain and grabbed for her throat.

"You okay?"

"Yeah. It's just really, really hot. Go on. I'm fine." She began to gently blow on her coffee.

"I had no reason to call her back. I have no interest in getting back with her, which brings us to her first lie. According to Ileana, Morgan told you the only reason I showed any interest in you was because I wanted to make her jealous. Is that true?"

"Ile talks too much."

"Nonetheless, did Morgan tell you that?"

She nodded and then took another sip of her coffee, this time with the utmost care. Jarrod looked at her without saying a word until she was forced to look back at him. They stared into one another's eyes for a long moment and then he said, "Do you believe that? I walked away from you that night thinking and hoping you had felt the same connection I did." He looked away and mumbled under his breath, "I guess I was wrong."

Placing the cup back on the table, she took a deep sigh before saying, "Jarrod, I did feel something that night. Something so strong and so new to me, it made me feel too many different emotions at the same time. I was happy, yet sad because I was leaving soon. I felt nervous, anxious, scared…"

"How about we focus on the happy part," he said with renewed hope.

She smiled for the first time since she got there. It wasn't one of her big, brilliant smiles that he remembered, but it was close and he'd take it.

"I felt happy," she said. "Very happy." Her smile faded. "Until Morgan told me she was still in love with you and that she wanted the two of you to get back together. She told me you had only shown interest in me because you wanted to get back at her for hurting you…"

She looks so sad and hurt, he thought. He wanted to see that smile of hers again badly, and the only way to achieve that would be by straightening things out with the truth.

"Lies," he said.

She looked at him with hope, wanting to believe him, but terrified he may be the one lying now. In exasperation, she let out a frustrated huff and said, "I just don't know what to believe anymore."

"Angel, I know she's your cousin and maybe there's a side to her you see that we don't…"

"Who's we?" she asked curiously, tipping her head to the side.

"Every living and breathing soul on the planet earth, with the exception of you and her mom."

"Jeez…"

"I swear what she told you is not true. I don't even believe the part about her loving me. I don't think she's capable of that emotion."

She thought about how badly Morgan treated Aunt Helen and had to somewhat agree with his assumption. Anyone that could treat her mother, a mother as wonderful as Aunt Helen no less, the way she did was definitely not capable of loving.

"If she doesn't love you, then why would she want to get back together so badly? I mean, for her to follow you all the way here—"

"I overheard her talking to my brother outside my window the day she broke up with me. She had given me some lame excuse about how we had grown apart and that it was time to move on. I didn't argue with her, because to be honest, I just didn't care one way or the other." He took another sip of his soda and motioned for the waitress to get them another round. Then he continued by saying, "We had a good time while dating, but I knew it would never go further than that. My feelings weren't growing for her."

"So you used her for a good time," Angel said not too happily.

"It was mutual. She got just as much out of the relationship as I did, and I'm not just talking about sex. We went to parties, school events...hung out with friends...movies...just a bunch of stuff. She enjoyed the attention we received as a couple."

"So you..." She couldn't bring herself to ask. She wanted to know, but at the same time, she didn't. She couldn't stand the idea of them being together in *that* way.

"Are you asking me if we had sex? Is that what you want to know?"

She blushed profusely. She could feel the heat rising from the bottom of her toes to the tip of her head.

"Never mind. It's none of my business. I don't want to know."

"Yes, you do. But I think that's a discussion we should leave for another time. Right now I just want to concentrate on clearing things up. As I was saying, I overheard her and Alec speaking. She was more honest with him than she was with me and confessed to him her real motive for ending things."

"What was the real reason, if you don't mind me asking?"

"I don't mind telling you at all. I want us to be open and honest, so whatever you want to know, I'll tell you. She believed that any potential I might have had for a career as a professional athlete was lost, therefore any potential she might have had of being a professional athlete's wife had also fallen through the cracks. I was hurt so badly in the accident that it didn't seem possible I would ever pick up a ball again, much less play professionally."

"But you seem to be doing great."

"Yeah, for everyday stuff. But to play pro ball, well…that's a whole different story."

"How badly were you hurt?" she asked.

He turned his head to his right and stared out the window for a moment before speaking. It was still difficult for him to think about the accident, much less discuss it. He slowly turned to face her.

"Pretty bad…I was in a coma and surgery had to be performed to relieve some of the pressure that was building up in my brain. Otherwise I would have…well, let's just say I wouldn't be here sitting with you today."

Angel's eyes opened wide and she quickly brought her hand to her mouth to cover the gasp of shock she felt escape. She had to blink away tears that were forming.

"I also had a collapsed lung, broken arm, dislocated shoulder, broken leg…," he continued.

Angel raised her hand to stop him and said, "Enough." She swallowed past a lump that had formed in her throat. "I'm sorry. It's just that I didn't realize how badly hurt you were. You've come such a long way."

"I still have a much longer way to go. If I want to get back to playing ball and make something out of myself, I have a lot of work ahead of myself."

She smiled and simply said, "You can do it. It won't be easy, but you will." She cleared her throat and said, "I'm happy to see you're not giving up on your dream."

"Sometimes I think it would be easier if I just did. I still worry and wonder if it's ever going to happen for me."

"It will. You just have to work hard and not give up, no matter how difficult it gets. You have to believe in yourself as well as in your dream." Sensing the conversation was going in a different direction and still wanting to clear things up about Morgan, she asked, "What about Morgan? What will you do if she tries to contact you?"

"She hasn't called yet, so I don't think she will at this point."

"She will. When Morgan sets her mind to something, she usually gets what she wants."

"Not this time. She's travelling down a one-way street when it's a two-way street she wants and needs to be on."

She gave him a shy smirk and said, "But what will you do if she does call you?"

"I'll just continue to ignore her calls or messages like I did back in Jersey."

"You'll just make her angry. Have you ever seen her mad? It's not a pretty sight." Angel slowly pushed her coffee cup aside, having had her fill. Her stomach was beginning to act up and she wasn't sure if the cause of it was the coffee, her nerves, talking about Morgan, or a combination of all three.

"Yeah, I've seen her mad plenty of times. It's like dealing with a two-year-old."

They both chuckled and then Angel said in a serious tone, "So, the question is, what exactly do you want from me, Jarrod?"

"A chance."

She paused a moment before answering. "I don't know. It seems like there is so much negativity surrounding us. Is that how we want to start a relationship? I mean, if it begins with so much trouble, it could only get worse, don't you think?"

"No, I don't. I really don't. All that negativity stems from one source. Morgan. As long as she's out of the picture, there will be no more negativity."

"She's my cousin. She'll always be in the picture."

"Yeah, but in time she'll get over it. It's just too fresh for her right now."

She bit her lower lip as she contemplated his statement. Jarrod leaned forward and gently took her hand in his.

"We could take it real slow," he said. "As slow as you want. You set the pace."

She looked into his dazzling blue eyes as he gazed right back into her smoldering green ones and then she quietly said, "I can't start anything until I find Ile."

"You still want to kill her?" he asked sadly, still holding her hand and caressing it with his thumb. He looked down at their clasped hands, afraid to hear what her answer might be.

"No. I need to thank her."

Morgan sat low in the driver's seat of John's car, which she had borrowed earlier that day. She had been following Angel during her time off from work for the last few weeks. She had almost begun to think Angel had kept her promise, but watching the two of them sitting there together in that coffee shop, holding hands, proved otherwise. She was furious. No, she was beyond furious. She was livid, beside herself with rage. If they thought she was just going to sit back and allow them to continue with their little fling, they had another thing coming. They had unleashed the fury in her and were about to pay. Obviously they didn't know what she was capable of.

Chapter Twenty-Two

Angel awoke to the sun streaming through her window. She threw the covers off, jumped out of her bed, and ran to the window. It was a beautiful, sunny day with only a few swollen, white clouds dusting the gloriously blue sky. Although she hadn't slept well, due to the scores of overwhelming thoughts that invaded her mind throughout the night, she awoke in high spirits. In fact, she couldn't wait to get to her first class, because the quicker she got through the day, the sooner she would be able to see Jarrod. They had agreed to meet tonight after his workout at Perry Field.

She grabbed her clothes and toiletries and practically ran toward the shower down the hall. As soon as she was done and dressed, she snatched up her handbag and books and headed toward class. As she approached the massive, tree-shaded brick building that was surrounded by beautifully maintained grounds, she saw Ileana waiting for her at the bottom of the steps, appearing exceedingly nervous.

Angel was contemplating whether to have some fun and make her suffer a bit or letting her off the hook from the get-go, but when Ileana turned and saw her, the look in her eyes indicated she had suffered enough. She stood up and ran toward Angel.

"I'm so sorry," she said, her eyes tearing up quickly. "Please, please forgive me."

"I do," said Angel as she quickly hugged her best friend, who looked as if her legs were just about to give out. "I know you meant well and I appreciate what you did for me." Closely watching for her reaction, she added, "We both do."

Ileana immediately pulled out of the embrace and exclaimed, "We?"

"Yes…we," said Angel, smiling.

"As in…you and Jarrod?" she asked incredulously.

"Yup."

Ileana pulled her best friend back into a bear hug and said, "I'm so happy for you. I just knew it would all work out. He does seem as amazing as you described him. I didn't think it was possible, that there even existed a man like that, but he does. He's terrific."

"Well, we'll see. Right now we're just going to take it real slow and see what comes of it."

"That's good. Slow is always good." Ileana had a triumphant beam pasted on her face. She took Angel's arm, hooked hers with it, and together they walked that way to class.

Meanwhile, approximately three miles away, Morgan was sitting on her bed in her makeshift room, idly brushing her short, dark tresses. The room was eerily silent. All that could be heard was the sound of the brush as it passed slow and rhythmically through her hair.

She heard someone enter the house, and she immediately put the brush down and opened the door slightly to her room. She peeked out and saw it was Benjamin standing stiffly beside the kitchen table as he sifted through the mail. The time had arrived to put her newly devised plan in motion.

She stepped out of her room and walked toward the kitchen area, stopping near the doorway, and said, "Hello, Benjamin."

Although he didn't respond, she noted how his back stiffened upon hearing her voice.

"I said hello, Benjamin," she tried again, raising her voice just a tad.

Still not looking at her, he quietly responded, "Hello." Gently placing the mail back on the table, he began to draw some sort of design on a dusty portion of the table with the tip of his finger.

"I've been waiting for you to come home. I wanted to speak to you about something."

He ceased his doodling and turned to face her, still keeping his eyes downward and began to clench and unclench his fists in nervous agitation.

"W-what about?" he said. He barely spoke above a whisper, so it was difficult to hear him.

"I thought you might be interested in knowing something," she said as sweetly as she could muster. "I heard something about you today and thought that you might want to know." Turning away from him, she walked into the living room and sat down on the couch.

He followed her into the living room and stood motionless in its center.

"A-b-b-bout me?" he asked as he quickly lowered his head again to stare at his shoes.

"Uh-huh." She nodded and added, "I was at work today, and two girls came in to look for dresses. One of them was very, very pretty."

"What d-does that have to d-d-do with me?" he stuttered.

"I happened to overhear one of the girls tell her friend there was someone she was crushing on. Want to know who that person is?"

He shrugged. Since he wasn't looking anyway, Morgan rolled her eyes at him and gave him a dirty look. "It was you, silly," she said.

He looked up at her and pushed his glasses back, but this time he didn't lower his head again. *Finally a reaction from the wackadoodle*, she thought.

"Me?" he asked, surprised and shocked.

"Yes, you. Isn't that exciting? She's so pretty too. Long dark hair, beautiful green eyes, and a nice body too. You two would make such a nice couple."

"Um…m-maybe she was t-t-talking about someone else… a-another Benjamin?" His stammering was getting worse, and he was beginning to perspire. In an attempt to calm his nerves so that his speech would flow more smoothly, he took a deep breath and exhaled slowly.

"No. She was definitely talking about you. She mentioned your full name. Benjamin Langdon. Plus, she described you to a tee." What a weirdo. Jeez, if Angel were ever to find out she was behind this plan of setting Benjamin onto her, she'd have a conniption.

"Really?"

"Yeah. Definitely. You should check her out, see if you like her and then let her know you're interested."

"I could n-never ask her out." Oops, there went the head again. It almost seemed as if his head was connected to an invisible string that was attached to an imaginary hand. Every now and then, the hand would pull the string taut so that the head would be raised, and then it would abruptly let go, so that the head would drop like a rock.

"Why not? Benjamin, you already know she's interested in you. In life you have to take the bull by the horn and make things happen for you. You just can't sit around and wait for things to be served to you on a silver platter. That's just not reality. You have to go out there and get it yourself."

"N-n-no. I d-don't think that's a g-good idea…," Benjamin stammered again.

She stood up from the couch, picked up a pen from the coffee table, and used it gingerly to lift a dirty sock that had been left on the floor. With her arm outstretched in front of her as if the sock had been contaminated by radioactive material, she carried it into the kitchen and dropped it, along with the pen, into the garbage can. Returning to the living room, she found Benjamin exactly as she had left him. Head bent down, yielding to his unending obsession with his damn Chucky T's.

"Benjamin, why don't we sit down? Please?" she asked in a soothing, trusting tone.

He shook his head and began to fretfully scratch his head. She noted how he'd begun to slowly sway back and forth, switching his weight from his left leg to his right, while nervously clenching his pants leg into a tight fist.

Speaking in a cautious, hushed tone, she continued, "Listen, I just want to help you. You seem like a nice guy and you should…no…you deserve to be with someone special." If he believed that load of crap, she'd love to talk to him about investing some money into a fund she created a few years back that was still going strong—the Morgan Billings MasterCard Fund.

"How are you g-going…to help me?" he asked sheepishly.

"Are you kidding? There's so much I can do for you. How about I start by getting you a picture of her? Then you can see for yourself just how beautiful she is. If you like her, we can start off slowly. Maybe send her some flowers. Every girl loves flowers. What do you think of that?" She spoke to him as if he were a child she was trying to convince to be a good little boy and share his toys.

"Um…okay. I g-guess."

"Good. Then it's settled. I'll get a picture of her for you."

"How?" he asked.

"She comes to the store all the time. She's one of our best customers. I'll sneak the photo with my cell phone when she's not looking." *Angel will never know what hit her*, she thought to herself while smiling maliciously and hoping to God she had a picture of her cousin stashed away somewhere.

⸺⸺

Three days later and with no luck in finding a current photo of Angel, Morgan had no choice but to follow her to the mall, where she met up with Jarrod. When Morgan saw them together, it took all the restraint in the world to not run up to the two of them and scratch their double-crossing eyes out. She made sure to get at least one photo of her without Jarrod in it, which was not easy, because he always had his blasted arm around her.

As she showed the picture to Benjamin, she noticed how wide he opened his eyes and how his demeanor seemed to change. He almost appeared excited.

"Pretty, isn't she?" she asked while closely scrutinizing his reaction.

He nodded rapidly and then became grim with concern.

"Why would she w-w-want to be w-with me?"

"You underestimate your appeal. Listen, every woman out there has a type that she likes. My type, well, my type is outgoing, tall, athletic, and handsome. Some women prefer the brainy, quiet, shy type. You obviously are her type."

"W-what's her name?" he asked.

"Angelise."

"Pretty n-name," he said and then added, "She l-looks l-l-like an angel." He never took his eyes off the photo. Morgan rolled her eyes at his apparent display of infatuation and cleared her throat loudly to gain his attention.

"What should I d-do now?" he asked gravely.

"How badly do you want her?"

"B-badly," he said, lowering his head to the ground for the first time since they began speaking.

"Good. I was hoping you would say that." She turned away from him and smiled deeply. Then she quickly turned toward him again and said, "Let me take care of everything. I'll just let you know what you need to do and when you need to do it, okay?"

"Okay. Um…thank you, M-m-morgan."

"You're welcome. This is going to be loads of fun for me."

"Morgan?" he said, stopping her as she was beginning to walk away.

"Yes?"

"Why are you doing this f-for me?"

"I like you, Benjamin. I just want to see you happy, that's all."

"D-do you think you can…get some m-more pictures? P-please?"

This was going to be easier than she thought. He was like putty in her hands. "I'll try my best," she responded as she walked away feeling triumphant.

Chapter Twenty-Three

Angel and Ileana were in Angel's dorm room studying while drinking frozen cappuccinos they had bought at the coffee house across the street.

"Has he kissed you yet?" asked Ileana, never lifting her head from the book she was reading.

"He's tried. A couple of times," Angel responded. "Switch," she said, and without even looking at each other, they swapped drinks, Ile trading the vanilla-flavored beverage for Angel's caramel.

"And you didn't let him?" she asked, now looking up at her still-studious friend.

"No. I sort of turn my head and he gets my cheek a lot."

"Girl, are you nuts? Why don't you want him to kiss you?"

"I do want him to kiss me. I'm dying for him to kiss me."

"You enjoy confusing me, don't you?"

"I simply want to take it real slow. Don't forget that phase one of our relationship didn't exactly start off with a ticker-tape parade. He needs to earn my trust. If I let him know just how interested I am so early in the relationship, he won't have to work at anything."

"Hmm…I guess that makes sense in a demented, masochistic sort of way. Just don't play too many games. That's a sure way to lose a guy in record time."

Angel smiled and winked at her, but quickly turned away in response to a knock on the door. She went over, opened it, and was informed by another female student that flowers had been delivered to her and that she needed to go downstairs to sign for them.

"Flowers. Let's go," cried out Ileana as they both raced out the door, tripping and practically knocking each other over in the process.

"They're beautiful," Angel said as she looked at the stunning bouquet of white roses intermingled with small bunches of baby's breath within the flora. She inhaled deeply as the scent besieged her.

Ileana quickly reached for the card and opened the envelope. As she read the card, she said, "Oh my God. He's so romantic. I'm dying of jealousy right now." She grabbed Angel's hand and pressed her fingers to the side of her neck and said, "See, no pulse. I'm dead."

Laughing at Ileana's crazy antics, she snatched the card out of her hand and jokingly asked, "You mind?" She read aloud in a hushed voice so no one other than her friend could hear, "Until I am able to hold you lovingly within my arms, I am but half a man—with only half a beating heart."

Both girls sighed in unison. Angel cradled the bouquet in her arms as they both walked back to her dorm room.

"You look like Miss Universe holding the flowers like that," Ileana said. "By the way, how did he know white roses are your favorite?"

"I don't know. I didn't tell him. I thought that maybe you had." Angel was baffled. Both girls looked at each other in complete bewilderment.

When they arrived at her room, Angel's roommate, Ava, was there. She looked up from her laptop as they walked in and said, "Hi! Wow! How beautiful!"

"Aren't they?" Angel responded happily.

"Who are they from? Oh God, it's not your birthday, is it?" Ava turned toward Ileana and said fretfully, "Please tell me it's not her birthday."

"It's not her birthday," said Ileana with a smile. "They're from Jarrod. You've got to read the card. You have got to read the card. It's unbelievable!" She yanked the card out of Angel's hand and showed it to Ava.

Ava read it and provided the requisite "oohs" and "aahs" that were mandatory in a situation such as this. "Are you sure they're from Jarrod? There's no signature."

"Of course they're from him. Who else would send them?" Ileana responded.

"I'm sure," said Angel. "They're perfect, just like he is… although I can't help but wonder how he knew white roses are my favorite." She looked at Ileana, who just shrugged her shoulders.

Jarrod picked Angel up promptly at seven thirty that evening. They were planning on going to the movies to see the new thriller starring Johnny Depp. Angel rushed up to him and gave him a big hug and a quick peck on the cheek. He seemed pleasantly surprised and said, chuckling, "What was that for?" as he opened the car door for her.

"For being so sweet. And of course, for the flowers. They're absolutely beautiful. Thank you so much. How did you know white roses are my favorite?"

Flowers? What flowers? He didn't send any flowers, but based on her reaction, maybe he should have. Although he would love to take the credit for them, he knew better than to lie. He'd rather appear to be an inconsiderate, cheap bastard of a boyfriend than a lying one. He closed her door and walked around to his side of the car and got in.

Before starting the ignition, he said, "Angel…I…uh…I didn't send any flowers."

She seemed totally stunned and bemused.

"Really?…um…sorry." She was now completely at a loss. "Well, if you didn't send them, then…who did?"

"Good question. Was there a card?" he asked, not too happily.

She nodded. "You may not like what it says."

"Try me," he said, his words clipped.

She pulled the card out of her wallet and showed it to him. She was right. He did not like it.

He paused a moment and asked forlornly, "Angel, what's going on here? Are you seeing someone else?"

"No!"

"Then who sent them to you?"

"I don't know. I just assumed it was you."

"Well, according to this card, there's a man running around town with only half a heart beating," he said angrily as he held the card out to her. She gingerly retrieved it and placed it back in her wallet. She looked up at him and watched as he stared straight ahead at nothing. She could tell he was upset by how tightly he was squeezing the steering wheel, and it was apparent he was struggling to gain control of his emotions.

They'd only been dating a short time, and it appeared that they were having their first argument. Strange, but she didn't imagine their first argument being over someone else. It was supposed to be over which movie they would go see. Goes to show you, one can never truly rely on fantasies. They were just too unreliable.

"I swear I don't know who sent them. I don't have anyone's heart—half or whole."

"You have mine." Although he said it angrily, she couldn't help but smile inwardly. She didn't say anything, because he seemed too upset at the moment, but she would remember it for later when she was alone and could escape into her fantasy world starring Jarrod Wentworth.

"I don't like this," he said. "I'd like to know who the hell sent them." He wasn't angry at her; he was jealous. Even though Angel wondered herself who might have sent them, she was secretly pleased to see him jealous. Good. It would do him good not to be too sure of her.

"Why don't we just try to forget about it," she said. "It's no big deal..."

"It was a big deal when you thought I'd sent them."

"Yeah...but..."

"Did you say this person sent you your favorite flowers? White roses?"

She had hoped he hadn't picked up on that. *Make way for that anger again*, she thought.

"Yes," she said.

"So this person must know you fairly well. Who do you know who would be privy to that kind of information?"

"My dad."

"Angel, I'm serious."

"Jarrod, I don't know," she said, frustrated. "That's not something that comes up in everyday conversation. I don't recall mentioning it to anyone recently."

"I'll stop by the florist shop tomorrow and see what kind of information I can get from them," he said more to himself than to her.

"Can't we just leave it alone?"

"I don't feel comfortable with someone, an unknown someone, sending you flowers. What florist did he use?"

"Evie's on University Avenue," she said stoically. She was just as curious as he to know who had sent the flowers, but was incredibly uncomfortable having this conversation with him.

"Do you want to come with me tomorrow?"

"Sure. They probably won't tell you anything unless I'm there anyway," she said as she glanced down at her watch. If they didn't hurry up, they would be late for the movie.

"That's true. Make sure you bring some form of ID and that damn card. I'll pick you up after your last class."

"You have physical therapy tomorrow afternoon," she reminded him.

"I can skip one session."

"No, you can't. I won't let you. We'll go after that, okay?"

"I'd rather not wait that long."

"We either go after your session or we don't go at all. I don't want you missing any of your therapy treatments," she said with finality.

"Fine," he acceded.

"So, can we go see the movie now?" she asked brightly.

They went to the movies, but Jarrod wasn't able to concentrate on what was happening on the screen. Angel noticed his preoccupation and leaned over to whisper in his ear. "Stop thinking. Just enjoy the movie," She placed her hand over his. He turned his hand over and interlocked his fingers with hers. They remained that way throughout the remainder of the film.

After the movie ended, they rode silently in Jarrod's car while he drove. When they approached her dorm building, he parked the car and walked around to open her door. She stepped out, and they walked hand in hand toward the main entrance. When they arrived, he took both her hands in his, looked around to ascertain that they were alone, and leaned in closely.

"Angel, I want to kiss you," he whispered.

She nodded her head and said, "I'd like that."

He smiled and timidly asked, "You won't turn your head this time?"

"Not this time."

And so he gently pulled her closer and tilted her chin upwards toward him as he slowly bent his head and brought his lips closer to hers. He tenderly positioned his lips upon hers and then gradually pressed harder until she opened to him. His tongue lightly entered her mouth and found hers. They softly intertwined until a soft moan escaped from Angel's throat. He deepened the kiss as their passion began to swell and pulled her tighter against him. He felt his breath quicken as she wrapped her arms around his neck, pulling his body so close to hers that a sheet of paper could not have been inserted between them.

His hand, splayed like an open fan, wove a slow and sensual path up and down her spine. He placed his other hand in the heavy mass of her hair, gently pushing it aside, and rained kisses along her neck until he reached the hollow behind her ear. She moaned again as if in pain, but the only pain she was feeling was that of pent-up desire. He took her mouth again and kissed her slow and easy, then hard and greedily. Suddenly she pulled away, breaking the kiss.

"What's the matter?" he tenderly whispered as their foreheads gently pressed together.

"Nothing. Absolutely nothing," she said quietly as she tried to regulate her breathing.

"Then why did you pull away?"

"It was too nice. I was enjoying it too much."

"We're supposed to enjoy it," he said as he lavished soft kisses upon her cheeks, making their way to her still-closed eyes.

"I know. But…I was just feeling so much…too much…" Her breathing was beginning to quicken again.

"It's called passion. Passion is good."

"Ummm…so good," she said, and now the acceleration of her heart rate was competing with the rushing of her breath.

And then he kissed her again. This time there was no gentleness to it. He pressed her back against the wall and kissed her with voracious intensity. He found himself inwardly moaning and wanting desperately to be one with her.

She broke away again. "Jarrod, we have to slow down."

"Angel, I'm dying for you. You're so beautiful…"

"This is all so new to me," she said, trying to slow her mind and body to a normal pace.

"You've never kissed a man before?" he asked, shocked, although he knew the answer to that. Of course she'd been kissed before. No novice could kiss so well.

"I've kissed before. What's new to me are the feelings. I've never felt so much, so quickly or so strongly before. It scares me."

"I know. Me too." He found he was having a difficult time getting his body to behave and cooperate. He couldn't seem to get enough of her. He tried kissing her again, but she pressed both her hands on his chest and pushed slightly.

"Jarrod, no."

He took a deep breath and said, "Okay. You're right. We'll take it nice and slow." He slowly backed away, but still held her hand. He brought it up to his lips and said, "Until tomorrow" and then he kissed it.

He watched her walk into the building. Once he knew she was safely inside, he turned and walked toward his parked car.

In the meantime Morgan watched furiously as she hid within the darkness of a dark alley across the street.

The following day Angel decided to surprise Jarrod by meeting him at the rehab center. He was already in session when she got there. He hadn't noticed her when she arrived, so she stayed out of the way to avoid distracting him. He was sweating profusely and breathing heavily as a result of the heavy exertion, but he never gave up. It was obvious he was in pain, based on the grunts and moans he was making, but he dealt with it and moved forward, never complaining. Her heart ached for him, but it also swelled with pride at his dedication and commitment.

When he was finally done, he sat exhausted in a chair, trying to catch his breath as he wiped his sweat with a towel and gulped down water from a bottle. He didn't even notice when she quietly sat beside him in an empty chair.

"Tired?" she asked.

He turned in surprise and smiled. "When did you get here?"

"About a half hour ago."

"Why didn't you say something?"

"I didn't want to bother you. How are you feeling?"

"Exhausted."

"I'm sure." She glanced around the facility and took note of the number of people, varied ages, and legion of diverse injuries that were being treated. As an elderly woman limped past them, Angel took a deep whiff and said with a melancholic smile to Jarrod, "She smells like my grandma."

"Huh?" he asked.

"The little old lady who just passed us. She smells just like my grandma. Jean Nate Splash."

With a hint of a smile, he said, "That's Mrs. Pierce. She's a sweet lady. She fell in her bathroom and broke her hip a few months ago, so she comes here twice a week for therapy." He chuckled and added, "Give her half an hour, and I guarantee she won't smell like your grandma anymore. More like Kobe Bryant after an intense game."

Angel smiled and said, "Anyway, I saw how hard you were working out. Exactly what type of treatment do you receive when you come here?"

"We basically focus on range of motion, strengthening, and conditioning. The therapy is sports-specific and is designed to help me regain full function so I can perform at my best level."

"I'm impressed. I do ten sit-ups and I'm practically laid up in bed for a week," said Angel.

"Crazy thing is, I used to be able to work out a thousand times harder than this, and I'd barely break a sweat. Now…"

"Now you're taking a body that's been through the wringer and you're reconditioning it. That's not an easy thing to do, but you're doing it. Just be patient and don't give up." Then she kissed him tenderly on the lips and whispered, "I'm proud of you."

"Thanks. Proud enough to give me another kiss?" he said, smiling.

Grinning, she leaned over again and gave him another soft kiss, but this one lingered just a little bit longer than the first.

"That's all for now," she said as she sat back, favoring him with that brilliant smile that he had quickly learned to love. "You smell like Mrs. Pierce will in half an hour."

He sighed, stood up slowly, and then groaned mutely as he rubbed his aching shoulder. "I'll go take a quick shower and then we can head out."

"Take your time. I'll just sit here and entertain myself by watching all these young, hot, firm, sweaty men working out."

Jarrod quickly glanced around and realized there were indeed a few young men scattered about.

☙ Broken Road ☙

"I'll be back in ten minutes. Behave," he said laughingly as he walked away.

Forty-five minutes later they arrived at Evie's Florist. The exterior of the building was of no special architectural or artistic makeup. It was a simple, white stucco edifice with little character. On the other hand, once one entered the shop, it was an entirely different story. The shop smelled heavenly and was beautifully decorated with white gossamer chiffon and layers of twinkling lights amidst the flora and greenery. Angel felt as though she had mistakenly walked into a magical enchanted forest. Michael Buble's rendition of "The Way You Look Tonight" was playing softly in the background, lending an air of elegance and quiet sophistication to the establishment. A middle-aged man stood behind the counter perusing through a stack of orders. As he noticed the young couple approaching him, he pleasantly asked, "How may I help you today?"

Jarrod explained the situation to the gentleman and was informed in a nice, professional manner that he could not supply him with the information he was requesting.

"I understand your concern, but it's a privacy issue. I remember taking that order because of what she wanted written on the card. I also remember her saying, in no uncertain terms, that her identity was not to be revealed."

"Her?" Jarrod and Angel both said.

"Yes, but she said she was ordering it for her boss. She intimated that the flowers were not for his wife and this is where the confidentiality issue prevails."

"Her boss?" said Angel. That would mean the man who sent her the roses was older than she, and married as well. "That's weird," she said. She had barely been in the area a few months and definitely hadn't developed a relationship with anyone older than herself. Aside from Jarrod and Ileana, the only other person she interacted with on a daily basis was her roommate, Ava.

Jarrod rubbed his face in frustration.

"Is there any way at all you can help us out? I'm worried about my girlfriend's safety." That was the first time Jarrod had referred to Angel as his girlfriend. Angel felt a mixture of pride and happiness with that small detail that was insignificant to anyone other than herself. Jarrod looked at her and smiled, knowing she had picked up on his territorial declaration. He felt as much pride in saying it as she did in hearing it.

"I understand. I do. I wish I could help, but I don't want any trouble. It could be bad for business. I have a reputation for respecting the privacy of my customers and I don't want to do anything that would put that in jeopardy. I'm sorry I can't help."

"What if the police were to ask you to give them that information?" Jarrod asked.

"Then, without hesitation, I would cooperate as the law dictates," said the owner. Then he added, "But you're not the police."

Angel quickly turned her head to face Jarrod and said, "The police?"

"Don't worry. I'm sure it won't reach that point."

They thanked the owner and walked out. Once outside, Angel turned to Jarrod and said, "Now I'm worried."

"Don't be. I won't let anything happen to you."

"I know," she said as she leaned into his open arms and felt warm and safe as he wrapped them around her. She looked up into his eyes and said, "But don't you think it's strange that a married man is sending me flowers?"

"I'm more worried about what he wrote on the card. If it was just the flowers, it could be just about anything. Maybe you did something nice for someone and he sent the roses as a thank you, or maybe someone wanted to wish you good luck in college...anything, really. But the fact that this man said what he did about being half a man, with half a heart...well, that bothers and worries the hell out of me."

"That's true," she said.

They walked toward his car and he opened the door for her. As she settled in, he walked around and got in himself. He started the car, but didn't put it into motion.

"Can you remember at any time meeting an older man and getting a feeling he was interested in you?" he asked.

"No, not at all."

"What about a professor?"

She thought hard. "No. No one."

"Alright. Well, let's not go crazy over this. Eventually we'll find out who your secret admirer is. In the meantime I want you to be extra careful, okay? No staying out late unless you're with me. No going anywhere alone, not even during the day. Start paying closer attention to your surroundings and those around you and…"

"And I promise not to take any candy from strangers or help them look for lost puppies either," she said jokingly.

"Very funny. But seriously…"

"Seriously. I promise to be careful. Scouts honor," she said as she raised her right hand in an oath-making gesture.

"That's my girl," he said as he leaned over and pressed a light kiss on her lips. He pulled out of the parking space and drove toward her dorm.

Chapter Twenty-Four

Morgan was seething as she paced back and forth in her room. Unfortunately, her bedroom was so small that her treading only allowed her to take four steps forward before she was forced to turn around and take four steps back. The small area rug she had purchased just last week was already showing signs of wear with a slightly faded path right down the middle.

Every time she pictured them together or remembered how he had kissed Angelise, she wanted to squeeze the life out of them both. Especially her cousin. She was supposed to be loyal. Hadn't she ever heard of the phrase, "Blood is thicker than water?" What a backstabbing traitorous bitch her cousin had turned out to be.

She heard a car pull into the driveway and raced to the window to see who it was. It was Benjamin. She didn't know of anyone else on this planet who would be seen driving a car like his. Not only was the man disturbing, but he had no taste. She watched him open the door to his once cherry red but now lukewarm copper 1988 Dodge Shadow. How it still ran was a mystery to her. Compared to his car, her mother's Toyota was a match for a brand-new Turbo Porsche 911. He stepped out of the car, stopped to wipe his glasses on his filthy, stink-ridden denim jacket, and walked around the house to enter through the back door. Morgan wondered why he always used the back door rather than the front door, which was closer to the driveway. She also wondered why he always wiped his feet exactly thirteen times and twisted the doorknob three times before opening the door and entering. Everything about this man gave her the creeps. His obsessive compulsions, the weird way he would pull at his hair when he thought no one was looking, and his lack of concern for personal hygiene. His dark black hair was forever greasy and constantly leaving a light coating of dandruff on his dark clothing. His eyebrows were so bushy; she was dying to take tweezers to them. She grimaced at the thought of tweezers. Every time she saw or even thought of that torturous tool of hair removal, the memory of when she was forced to yank out her nose hairs to build up a few measly tears for Jarrod's sake would hit her like an express train at rush hour. It made her sick to think of all the physical and emotional pain she'd been required to endure since Angelise and Jarrod met. Damn her for ever coming to New Jersey in the first place.

There was a soft knock on her bedroom door. She turned away from her thoughts and went to open it. As she had guessed, it was Benjamin.

"Benjamin," she stated flatly.

Staring at the ground, he responded, "Hello, Morgan."

"What's up?" she asked irritably.

"I was w-w-wondering if there was…um…anything…"

"Spit it out, Benjamin," she said, annoyed at his sickening pauses. She wasn't in the mood to deal with his stammering, boorish ways today. She had too much on her mind and felt as though she was running out of time. The more time Jarrod and Angelise spent together, the harder it would be to separate them.

"Anything new on…the p-pretty…"

"Angelise, Angelise, Angelise. Why don't you ever use her name? I've given you like a gazillion pictures of her, and you still just call her 'the pretty girl.' Why?"

"I haven't...m-m-met...her yet. It's not...r-right," he sputtered.

"But it's fine to send flowers and collect photos of her?"

"You sent the flowers and...you t-t-took the pictures of her."

"For you. I'm busting a gut trying to help you get the girl and you're doing absolutely nothing," she said angrily.

"What do you w-w-want me to do?"

"Talk to her. Ask her out on a date. I don't know...just do something," she wailed, flailing her arms in the air.

"I c-can't," he said, finally looking up at her.

"Why not? If you want to get together with her, you'll have to eventually ask her out. I'm not going to do it for you. Plus, what are you so worried about? You know she likes you." At this point she had told so many lies that she was almost beginning to believe them herself.

"It's too soon. I need just a l-little m-m-more time. Please."

"Fine. One more week is all you're getting out of me. Then you're on your own. Got it?"

"Okay."

Morgan attempted to close her bedroom door when he spoke again. "Morgan?"

She shut her eyes tightly and said in a bored and bothered tone, "What?"

"I need m-m-more...pictures," he requested.

"Jeez, you are one sick, demented—"

"*Don't say that!*" he screamed. He began to pull at his hair and walk in small circles. "D-d-don't...say that. D-d-don't..."

"Fine!" she screamed back, slamming the door to her room. She immediately locked it as well. Dear God, this man was nuts. Well, she only needed him long enough to scare Angelise sufficiently to send her and her packed bags back to Bradenton. After that she would have all the time in the world to work on getting Jarrod back. After all, he still had his college education to think of. He wouldn't be able to follow her out there. Eventually he'd get lonely and find himself in need of female companionship, and lo and behold, Morgan would be there waiting with open arms, more than willing to let him find comfort in them. She threw herself on her bed and stared unblinkingly at the ceiling while she fervently hoped all her plans would turn out well.

⁓

The next day Angel picked up her mail and was thumbing through it when she noticed a large manila envelope that did not include a return address. She sat down at her desk and opened the envelope. In it she found an eight by ten photo of herself. The photo was taken of her last week. It had been Tuesday, because she recognized the exterior of Smathers Library, where she had gone to research information she needed for her Expository and Argumentative Writing class. She was sitting on the front steps, wearing her favorite turquoise tank top and jeans, looking out toward a group of students that had convened and were laughing wildly. Angel stared at the photo as her eyes began to blur. A large heart had been drawn in red marker around her face and written next to it, in black ink, was the word, "Mine."

She looked at the envelope again and then looked inside to see if there was a note. Nothing. All of a sudden, her phone rang, causing Angel to jump. She shook herself out of her thoughts, retrieved her phone from her handbag, and answered it.

"Hello?"

Silence answered her.

"Hello?" Angel said again, only a bit louder.

This time there was something, but no words were spoken. Just breathing. Heavy, concentrated breathing.

"Hello," she repeated in anger.

More deep breathing.

"Stop it. I don't know who you are or what you want, but I want you to stop it. Don't call me or send me anything again or I'll call the police. I mean it. Just leave me alone." She hung up the phone angrily and found herself shaking and began to cry. Who was doing this? She sat down on her bed as she tried to calm herself down. She took slow, deep breaths and walked over to the mini-fridge she and Ava shared and grabbed a bottle of water. She started to drink from it when the phone rang again. She jumped once again, and some of the water splashed out.

"Damn," she said. She looked at her phone and saw it was Ileana on the other end. She picked up and said, "Hi."

"Hi! What's up?"

"Nothing good," Angel said as she sat down and wiped her eyes and dabbed at her nose with a tissue.

"Trouble in paradise?"

"I wish it were that simple."

"I don't understand," said Ileana.

"Ile, I think the person who sent me the flowers is more than just a secret admirer," she said as she began to cry again.

"What do you mean? Angel, are you alright?" Ileana heard Angel sniffling and immediately sensed there was trouble.

"I mean, I think, he might be a…stalker."

"I'll be right over. Don't go anywhere," Ileana said before hanging up.

An hour or so later, Angel and Ileana sat together on the large sofa in the common room in whispered conversation. The atmosphere was implausibly boisterous with so many students milling about; some chatted, while others watched television or played games such as foosball or pool. They would have preferred to have stayed in Angel's room, but Ava was studying for a big exam and required total silence, so they opted to sit in the common room.

"Have you told Jarrod about the picture?" Ileana asked. "More importantly, have you called the police?"

"No to both your questions. I just received the picture today and I haven't spoken to anyone about it besides you."

"You need to tell Jarrod."

"I'm not sure I want him to know."

"Why not? He's your boyfriend. He has a right to know. Besides, he can help you."

"How can he help me?"

"Gee, let me think…duh, by protecting you," Ileana said, annoyed and worried. She adored Angel, but sometimes her stubbornness and naïve way of seeing only the good in everyone was beyond exasperating. Here she was, receiving flowers, threatening mail, and unnerving phone calls from a total stranger, and still she found no need to inform her boyfriend or the police. Why? Because in her uncorrupt heart, she truly believed no harm would ever come to her, simply because she didn't think anyone was malicious enough to want to hurt her.

By choice she rarely watched the news or read the newspaper, saying when she did, she was left depressed due to all the dismal occurrences that were happening in the world today. It was almost as if she preferred to live isolated in a bubble of unassailable goodness. Unfortunately, Ileana was now terrified that someone, a complete Section Eight, was out there somewhere planning on bursting that bubble.

"I don't need someone to protect me. I can take care of myself."

"I disagree. You are way over your head here. You need to tell him and also the police. You can't deal with this alone." She paused for a moment and then added, "What about your parents? They need to know what's going on."

"No way. Absolutely not. I don't want to worry them unnecessarily. If they knew about this, they'd be here so fast, they'd break the sound barrier. Besides, I'm not alone. I have you."

"Angel, I love you to death, but we have to be realistic here. What the hell can I do to protect you? I'm even smaller than you and you're no bigger than a flea. I'm like a gnat."

"I think gnats are bigger than fleas," said Angel with a half grin.

"Really?" Ileana asked. "No, I don't think so. I'm pretty sure fleas are…oh, what does it matter anyway? My point is that we're both tiny. Together we couldn't bring down a Chihuahua."

Angel chuckled at her paradigm. Then she said, "I'm just not sure yet. Don't say anything to him when you see him. If I decide he should know, I want to be the one to tell him. And I mean it, Ile, don't you dare go behind my back again…"

Ileana raised her hand to stop Angel from continuing and said, "Yeah, yeah. I got it. But I strongly recommend you tell him immediately. That's my advice to you as your best friend. You should listen to me for once. Sometimes, believe it or not, I know what I'm talking about."

Chapter Twenty-Five

John entered the house and soon realized no one was there. Aside from the monophonic ticking of the kitchen clock, there was complete silence. It was rare for the house to be completely empty. With three roommates, all with different work schedules, he could almost always find someone home. This was the perfect opportunity to do something he had wanted to do for quite some time, but had never gotten the chance. He walked toward Benjamin's room and knocked on the door. No answer. Turning the doorknob, he found it was locked.

Surveying the area one last time to ensure that the coast was clear, he quickly pulled out his driver's license from his wallet and began to jimmy the lock while turning the doorknob. He worked hurriedly, stopping every now and then to listen for sounds of approaching roommates. Surprisingly, he had only spent a few minutes performing this process when suddenly he heard a click.

"Yes," he said while slowly turning the knob and glancing around once again before entering. Once he did, he wished he hadn't. John was shocked to find the walls covered with pictures of a beautiful auburn-haired, green-eyed girl. She was gorgeous. But what frightened him was that these were not photos of a model or a celebrity taken from magazines. No, these were candid photos, and it was apparent this woman was not aware the photos were being taken. There were pictures of her lying on the grass, sitting on steps, getting into a car. There were also snapshots of her eating in a restaurant, leaving the theatre, and getting off of a bus. She must be a student at the university because in many of the pictures, she was carrying what appeared to be textbooks. She looked so young and innocent.

John wondered about these photos and about the girl. Was she in danger? He knew that Benjamin was strange, but was he crazy in the clinical sense?

Hundreds of photos were displayed, but when John looked closely, many were copies of the same photos. It was almost as if Benjamin was planning on wallpapering the entire room with them.

"Holy shit," he whispered as he continued to survey the room. He carefully opened the top drawer of Benjamin's desk, but found nothing of interest. Just a few pens, a roll of tape, and blank sheets of paper. He closed the drawer and proceeded to open the other two, finding nothing but junk. On top of the desk was a plastic bag from a local bookstore, the Book Haven, and John quickly looked inside. The bag contained three new books, all relating to the subject of angels. He placed them back in the bag and carefully returned the bag to the desk exactly as he had found it. He looked around the room and saw a Bible on the unmade bed. Numerous pages were dog-eared in the sacred writ, marking pages of interest. John quickly perused the noted pages and realized that the names of various angels had been highlighted. What was this sudden obsession with angels?

Just then he heard someone turning the doorknob to the back door. He quickly placed the Bible exactly as he had found it on the bed and darted out of the room, softly shutting the door behind him. He swiftly raced across the hall to his room. For once he was thankful for Benjamin's many idiosyncrasies. If he hadn't spent so much time wiping his feet and turning the doorknob, John never would have made it to his room in time.

Angel received two additional nonverbal, semi-asthmatic phone calls over the next two weeks. She informed Ileana of the calls, but still did not say anything to Jarrod. He had enough on his plate with classes, studies, baseball, and physical therapy. Not to mention that he always made a point of stopping by to see Angel at night, even if it was only for half an hour. He would always ask if she was alright or if she needed anything, forever attentive to her needs and desires.

They were lying on her bed watching television one night when he turned to her and began nibbling gently on her ear. She smiled while closing her eyes and slowly turned toward him. He stopped to look at her, really look at her, and then lowered his head to kiss her. His kiss was soft and gentle at first, turning eager and demanding as the sensual fire between them built to a crescendo. She couldn't help but return his kisses with loving urgency.

As he placed his right hand on her collarbone, he began to softly stroke her shoulder and neck with his fingertips, leaving her breathless. He lowered his head into the crook that formed between her neck and shoulder and began to trail kisses up and down it. While he continued nuzzling her neck, she placed both her hands upon his shoulders as he positioned himself over her body, pressing his onto hers. They both moaned with eagerness and fervor. Taking his time, Jarrod began to unbutton the top buttons of her blouse while giving her featherlike kisses on the parts he slowly exposed. Angel felt like she was going to burst from desire.

Jarrod looked up at her and in a gravelly voice said, "I want to be with you so badly." She slowly opened her eyes and while trying to slow down her breathing to a more manageable level, said, "I want to be with you too…but…"

"But what?" he whispered as he continued to rain light kisses on her cheeks, eyes, forehead, and lips.

"Ohhh…" She responded to his kisses and touch. "I…umm…oh, God, that's nice…"

Jarrod smiled as he noted her response. He loved how she looked when her body was wild with longing. Her face was lightly flushed, her succulent lips pink and swollen from his kisses, and her eyes full of want and need. Her physical reaction to his caresses fueled his desire, and once again his mouth claimed hers as his tongue began its probing exploration that drove her into a feverish madness.

Knowing she needed to slow things down, she hesitantly broke away from the kiss and breathlessly mumbled, "Jarrod, we need to…ohhh…dear God, that feels so good. Yes…yes…no. Wait…wait. We need to stop."

"Angel, let me make love to you. Please…please," he found himself pleading as he continued kissing and caressing her. His hand traveled up along her thigh, making its way near the pinnacle of her pulsating need.

In the midst of this erotic haze she found herself in, she became acutely conscious of the fact that she needed to put a stop to their actions before it was too late. She hated to do so, but she just couldn't let it go any further. It was always better to step on the brakes slowly as opposed to pulling on the emergency brake at the last minute.

She sat up and scooted away from him while she began to rebutton her blouse. Jarrod groaned in despair and turned to lie flat on his back in frustration. He tried to slow down his breathing enough that he could speak.

Finally, when he felt better control over his body, he looked over at her and said, "Why did you stop? I thought you said you wanted to be with me."

She blushed at the memory and stared down at her hands while softly saying, "I do want to be with you. But not here in a dorm room. Not now when Ava is expected back at any moment.

I...I..." She lowered her voice to a bare whisper and turned to face Jarrod before saying, "I want my first time to be special."

Jarrod looked at her for a moment with a mixture of shock and pleasure in his eyes. "Your first time? You mean you've never been intimate with anyone before?"

"No," she said, mortified to be discussing her sex life, or rather lack of one, with him. "You seemed shocked. I'm not my cousin Morgan, you know," she said defensively.

"Believe me, I know. Don't ever compare yourself to her. She's not in the same league as you," he said frustrated. He sat up, leaning against the headboard. "Why would you bring her up at a moment like this anyway? I don't want to be thinking of her when I'm with you."

"I can't help it. I hate the thought of you touching her the way you touch me," she said through tear-glazed eyes.

He gaped at her in blank disbelief and with quiet firmness said, "The way I touched her is completely different from how I touch you."

"How is it different? You made love to her, didn't you?"

"We never made love. We had sex. There's a difference."

"Wow. That makes me feel a lot better," she said sarcastically. "So basically you're saying you found my cousin so hot that you couldn't keep your hands off of her."

"Angel, I'm not going to apologize for having a relationship with her. It's part of the past and now it's over. It was over before you and I ever met."

"Only because she ended it," she persisted.

"I would have ended it eventually. I didn't love her."

He sat up, placed both his hands tenderly on her cheeks, smiled faintly while he gazed into a pair of dazed green eyes, and said, "I'm sorry if it bothers you that she and I were together. But I can't change the fact that we were. I want you to know that what I feel for you and what you and I share is nothing like what she and I had. She was nothing more than a high school passing fancy."

She nodded and through a voice thick with unshed tears, said, "Does it bother you that I haven't any experience...in that area?"

He pressed a feather-light kiss on her lips, drew her close, and said, "I love the fact that you've never been physically intimate with anyone. I love knowing that no one has ever touched you or known you in that way. I love knowing that when we are finally together, I'll be the one to experience that special moment with you." He bent forward and kissed her slowly. "But do you know what I love the most?"

"What?"

"You...I love you," he said as he leaned forward and kissed her again. This time the kiss was deep and languorous.

She gave him the gift he loved more than anything. The smile that no other person on the face of the earth could ever replicate. The smile that made the sun appear dull and gloomy. The smile that warmed his heart and brought him to his knees.

And then she whispered back, "I love you too."

Angel was gloriously happy today. The sun was shining brightly, the birds were whistling a merry tune, and the breeze was softly blowing, causing her hair to tousle in the wind. She sat on the grass and looked over at Ileana and said, "I love him! I love him! I love him!"

Ileana, who was lying on her back with her hands behind her head and eyes closed, simply responded, "Yes, I know, and I'm very, very happy for you. Now shut up."

"He loves me too," Angel said in a singsong tone.

"Very nice. Shut up," Ileana responded in the same singsong tone. She was happy for her best friend. If anyone in this world deserved absolute, pure, arrant happiness, it would be Angel.

Suddenly a dark shadow loomed over the two girls, blocking the sun completely. Both ladies looked up at once and were forced to blink numerous times to make out what, or in this case, who was causing the shadow. There appeared to be a dark silhouette of a man outlined by the light of the sun, which was directly behind him.

"Umm...excuse me...b-b-but...umm...," he faltered.

"Yes?" said Angel as she tried to get a clearer view of the man.

"I was w-wondering if I c-c-could...if I could...ask you a few questions."

"What sort of questions?" asked Ileana.

"I'm c-c-conducting a s-survey for a p-paper I'm w-working on," he responded as he looked down at his notebook. More nervous than he'd ever been in his entire life, it was distressingly presenting itself through his vexatious stammering.

"Are you a student here?" asked Angel a bit nervously.

"Yes."

"No offense, but aren't you a bit old to be a student?" asked Ileana. Now that they had a clearer view of the man, it was obvious he was in his mid, maybe even late, twenties.

"G-g-graduate s-student," he said. He glanced up to briefly look at Angel and then immediately brought his head down again, this time looking toward the ground rather than his notebook.

Ileana looked at the spot of grass directly in front of the stranger to see what it was he found so riveting.

"Graduate student, huh?" she said, eyeing him suspiciously.

"What sort of questions do you have?" asked Angel.

"Just a few. The paper is about how s-s-students adjust to c-college life..."

"What class is this for?" questioned Ileana. Something about this man just didn't feel right. She always felt uncomfortable around people who couldn't make eye contact with her, but this was different. This man flat-out scared the bejesus out of her.

"S-s-sociology," he stated.

Both girls looked at each other, hesitating whether to participate in the survey or not. It wasn't like Angel not to help someone when he needed her assistance, but something about this man made her wary and tense.

"Will it take long?" asked Angel. "We have to get to class."

"No…just a f-f-few minutes," he replied. Her voice was so soft and sweet, just as he had imagined. Her eyes were a beautiful shade of jade green, and her lashes seem to go on forever. She had an air of innocence that emanated from her being, causing him to want to dive into her taintless, merciful soul. Once she was his, truly his in every sense of the word, he would worship her for all eternity. He swore this to himself. Now that they'd met, he instinctively knew they were truly meant to be together. She would become his religion, a religion he would have a blind, excessive idolatrous veneration for.

"Okay, well then, let's speed things up a bit, shall we?" said Ileana dryly as she sat up and started to collect her books, which were scattered about on the grass next to her. She wasn't comfortable with this man and wanted to bring their interface to an end as quickly as possible. She noticed he kept flexing his hands open and shut and shuffling his feet back and forth. He reminded her of a dancer with no rhythm trying to get his groove on with no music playing. His hair was so greasy, it looked as though he had taken a handful of lard and rubbed it on his head this morning. And what was up with those eyebrows? They looked like two furry caterpillars nestled above his eyes.

"What did you say your name was again?" Ileana asked.

"I…d-d-didn't say. It's Benjamin," he stated.

"Benjamin what? What's your last name?"

"Smith," he said.

"And you say you're a student here?"

"Yes." He needed to hurry up. The friend was beginning to irk him. She was asking too many questions. How was he supposed to build a bond with Angelise when her friend continually interrupted them with her interminable questions?

"Where are you…f-f-from?" He directed the question to Angel.

"Bradenton, Florida," she responded. He immediately wrote that down on a notepad.

"I'm also from Bradenton," said Ileana, noting he did not write her answer down. Strange.

"Do you l-l-like it...here?" He once again glanced at Angel when asking the question and then quickly lowered his head.

"Yes. Very much," she responded as she watched him jot her reply down.

"It's alright," added Ileana, noting again that he would only write down Angel's answers. Her brows furrowed in concern.

"What is your favorite m-m-movie?"

"What the hell does that have to do with adjusting to college life?" cried out Ileana.

"The questions are...are...v-v-very general," he said while tugging at his hair.

Both girls glanced at each other and then Ileana abruptly stood up and said, "We have to get to class now, so time to wrap things up."

"Movie?" he said, looking at Angel adoringly for a brief moment before looking down again.

"Um...I don't know. I guess any romantic comedy," she said apprehensively.

"Do you have...a...b-b-boyfriend?" he said, looking up at her immediately, but this time keeping his head up while awaiting the response.

"Yes, she does," Ileana answered as she grabbed her friend by the arm and pulled her up from her sitting position. "A big, strong, muscular one who eats graduate students for breakfast. Time to go, Angel. Now."

"Sorry. Good luck with your paper, Benjamin," Angel called out as Ileana literally dragged her away.

Ileana looked behind her as they walked away and noticed Benjamin just stood there watching them.

"He was weird," Ileana said. "He gives me a bad case of the heebie-jeebies."

"He was strange, wasn't he?" said Angel.

"He was looking at you as if he hadn't eaten in over a month and you were a big ol' cheeseburger platter with a side of fries!"

"Yeah, he made me nervous too."

"If you see him again, make sure to stay clear of him."

"I will. You too," Angel said.

"I have a strong feeling it's not me he's interested in." Ileana glanced back one more time and found that even though he was barely a speck in the distance, he was visibly still watching them. Or rather, watching Angel.

Benjamin stood there watching her walk away and thinking to himself that she was the most perfect being on the face of the earth. Everything about her drew him to her. Her voice, her body, her hair…she was captivating beyond words. He drew a deep breath and whispered to himself, "I l-l-ove you, my b-b-eautiful Angel."

Chapter Twenty-Six

Upon Angel's return to her dorm after her last class that afternoon, she was pleasantly surprised to find Jarrod waiting for her outside the building. Happy and excited to see him, she gave him a big hug.

"Hi!"

"Hi yourself," he said before he pressed a kiss to her lips. He looked at her deeply and thought to himself how beautiful she looked even when she wore her hair in a simple ponytail and wore plain jeans and a modest style T-shirt tucked into them. He loved how she barely wore nor needed to apply makeup, just a touch of mascara and a hint of color on her lips. Her cheeks were naturally tinged with a soft, rose color, and her eyes were so dazzling and brilliant that there was no need to add anything to them to attract attention to them.

"What are you doing here?" she asked happily.

"My class got cancelled, so I thought I'd surprise you. Are you happy I did?"

"Way happy," she said before she tiptoed and gave him another kiss.

⚜ Broken Road ⚜

He grabbed her books and they walked together hand in hand toward the entrance to her building. By the time they reached her room, they were laughing about some story Jarrod had told her about Dave, his roommate.

Angel opened the door slightly and poked her head in. She saw Ava was sitting at her desk studying and said, "Hey, Jarrod's with me. Can he come in?"

"Sure," Ava responded, closing her book. "I've studied enough for today anyway and could use a short break."

Jarrod followed Angel into the room and greeted Ava. He liked Angel's roommate a lot. She was outgoing, sweet, funny, and made friends easily. He only wished he had a friend he could hook her up with. Unfortunately, none of his friends took the time to get to know her and see that there was so much depth to her. They only saw that she was too tall, too thin, and way too blind. She wore glasses with thick lenses, preferring them to contact lenses due to comfort and ease.

Ava smiled at them both and then motioned to Angel's bed, where her mail lay. "Picked up your mail for you."

"Thanks," Angel said.

"No problem. Listen, a few of us are going to the Enigma Rock Cafe tonight. Do you guys want to join us?"

"So you'll be out for awhile?" asked Jarrod with a hopeful gleam in his eye.

Ava immediately picked up on his enthusiasm and quickly said, "Not that long, lover. I have an early class tomorrow."

"Oh." He didn't even bother to hide his disappointment.

Angel smiled at him and then at Ava. She was dying to be alone with him as well, but she was also afraid of having too much time alone. She knew he was hopeful of taking their relationship to the next level, and although she wanted that just as much as he, she wanted it to be in the right setting, at the right time. Well, at least she was almost certain those were the reasons. She still was nervous and unsure about taking such a monumental step. She had always believed and hoped to remain a virgin until her wedding night, but things just felt so perfectly right with Jarrod. She felt confused and torn between what she had been raised to believe was the right thing to do and what her heart and body were telling her was the correct path to take. She had no doubt of the deep, enduring love that existed between the two of them, so why this uncertainty in expressing it physically?

Jarrod sat on Angel's bed and inadvertently began to rifle through her mail. He noticed a large manila envelope with no return address. Written boldly beside her name and address were the words "Be Mine," enclosed within a drawn heart. He eyed it curiously and held it out for Angel to take. When she saw what was written on it, she stopped what she was doing and opened her eyes wide.

"No," she said.

She had become visibly pale, and her hands began to tremble. Ava noticed the change and swiftly helped her sit down on a nearby chair. She rushed to the mini-fridge and retrieved a bottle of water, giving it to Angel to drink. Jarrod had rushed to Angel's side and asked her, "What's wrong?" She didn't answer, only stared at him, obviously frightened.

"Angel, what's wrong? Tell me," he said forcefully.

"It's him again," she responded, distressed, as her eyes began to well up.

"Who?" asked Ava. Nothing had been said to Ava, so she was totally in the dark about the entire situation. Ileana had advised Angel to let Ava in on what was happening, but Angel decided against it, not wanting her roommate to fear every new person she came across. She realized now that Ileana had been right. She should have told Ava, Jarrod, and the police. Perhaps even her parents.

Jarrod didn't wait for a response. He immediately ripped open the envelope and pulled out the contents. Enclosed was an eight by ten photo of Angel and himself taken in the parking lot of the mall. Angel was leaning with her back against the passenger side door, while Jarrod was standing directly in front of her with both his hands on her waist. They were both looking into each other's eyes and smiling. The photo had been taken a few seconds before he had leaned in and kissed her. A bright red heart encircled

Angel's face. A big X was drawn across Jarrod's face in bold black marker. Written below the X was one word. *Die.*

"How many of these have you gotten?" Jarrod asked.

"That's the second one. The first one is in my top drawer." She hadn't looked at the picture that was received today. She was too frightened. Ava, on the other hand, picked it up off of the bed, looked at it, and said, "Oh shit."

Jarrod retrieved the picture from the top drawer. He turned to face her, fury written across his own. "Were you planning on ever telling me about this?"

Ava walked over and placed a supportive hand on Angel's shoulder. "I'll leave you two alone. You okay?"

Angel nodded, so Ava left the room, leaving the two to figure things out. Jarrod just stared at her in angry silence, waiting for her to respond.

"I didn't want to worry you," she said nervously.

"You've got to be kidding me, right? Please tell me that you're kidding." He began to rub his face, concentrating mainly on his forehead as if he could rub away the fear and worry. How could she hide something as important as this from him? What the hell was she thinking?

She didn't answer, so he knew she wasn't kidding. Of all the stupid, crazy, irresponsible things a person could do, this was right up there on the list. "What else are you hiding from me?"

She kept her head low, afraid to look into his eyes. She had never seen him so angry. "I've been receiving phone calls. He doesn't say anything…he just breathes heavily."

Jarrod rolled his eyes in frustration. Angel had never noticed what a big vein he had on his forehead before. Seeing how it protruded now, she wondered how it was she had never observed it. He quickly shook her out of her insignificant thoughts by saying as calmly as he possibly could, "Angel, how many times has he called and how often?"

"Um, about five or six times total. Not every day. It's been going on for almost…a month now." She closed her eyes tightly in preparation for the tirade and tongue-lashing she was about to receive.

"A month! I can't friggin' believe this. I don't understand you. How could you not tell me? This is important. There's some crazed maniac out there stalking you, and you don't say anything? Do you have any idea what kind of danger you may be in?"

She glanced at the picture he had laid on the bed and began to cry. When she saw what was written below the mark placed over his face, she felt as if she had been punched in the stomach, knocking the wind completely out of her. Not only was she in danger, but now, due to her lack of thought and responsibility, she had also placed him in that position.

Between sobs she was able to utter, "I'm sorry...I'm so sorry."

There was one thing that Jarrod could not handle and that was a woman's tears. His anger immediately turned to sympathy, and he pulled her into his arms and held her there until she was able to compose herself. When he noticed she was breathing softly and no longer gasping for air, he tilted her head upward and placed a soft kiss on her lips.

"I'm sorry for yelling at you. I'm just worried sick and wish you had told me about these pictures and phone calls. I have a right to know. I love you...and I want to protect you, but I can't if you aren't honest with me and tell me what's going on."

"I'm sorry. Ile was right. I should have listened to her."

Jarrod's anger suddenly flared up again, but he tried not to let it show. Angel noticed the sudden tenseness in his body as he gritted his teeth and mumbled, "You told Ile, but you didn't tell me?"

Angel pulled back a bit from the embrace. "I was afraid you would get all worried and then want to spend every minute of the day with me. Not that I would mind spending so much time with you, but I just couldn't take you away from all the things you need to get done. You would be distracted and neglect your other responsibilities." She paused and added, "Oh, and you better not let Ile hear you call her that."

At a loss, Jarrod asked, "Call her what?"

"Ile. She doesn't let anyone call her that except for close friends and family."

"What the hell am I supposed to call her then?" he said as he frustratingly tousled his hair with his hand, mussing it into complete disarray. He separated himself from their embrace and began to pace the limited space the dorm room offered.

"Ileana. You have to work your way into her heart before she allows you to call her Ile. It's a familiarity quirk."

Jarrod shook his head in perplexity.

"Getting back to the issue at hand, you should know by now you're my number one priority," he said. "Everything else is secondary. Don't you know that?"

"I do and I love you for that, but it's important that you continue with your studies, rehab, and baseball training," she said vehemently.

Jarrod took her into his arms again. "Baby, I'd give everything up for you. All of it. You mean more to me than my own life." He placed a soft kiss on her head. "When I look into your eyes, do you have any idea what I see?" She shook her head no. With a bent finger, he lifted her chin so she would look directly into his eyes. "I see all the tenderness and love you've brought into my life. And when I kiss you, it's as if you bring a light back into my heart that until I met you was shrouded in darkness." Placing a soft kiss on her lips before pulling her tightly into his embrace, he let her feel all his strength and love and then whispered, "And when I hold you in my arms, I feel a sense of inner peace that spreads throughout my entire body. Angel, I believe…deep in my heart…that you're the reason I was born. I was born to love you forever."

Her eyes welled up, threatening to spill over while she pulled him close. She never knew she could feel all the incredible emotions that he stirred within her. Her heart felt so full and her mind reeled with untapped awareness. She loved him so much that she could no longer imagine her life without him. How was it possible that one man could make someone feel so incredibly loved and cherished?

"Jarrod, I love you so much," she said, crying. "I will love you forever. I'm so sorry I didn't tell you. Can you forgive me?"

He answered her with a kiss. A slow, deep kiss of sweet languor that consumed them both entirely.

Suddenly the door burst open and Ileana came rushing into the room. She hadn't bothered to knock or show any signs of regret at catching them in the midst of their romantic embrace.

"Jeez! Don't you two ever come up for air? Are you okay?" she asked Angel.

Angel turned toward her and said, "I'm fine."

Ileana pulled her out of Jarrod's embrace and brought her into her own.

"I bumped into Ava downstairs, and she told me you received another picture. Please tell me you've told Jarrod everything."

"I have," she said as she gently pulled herself out of Ileana's tight hold and went to sit on the bed. "Jarrod knows everything now."

"So, what do you think about the weird guy at the park?" Ileana asked as she turned to face Jarrod.

"Oops...," said Angel quietly.

Jarrod looked at her, totally exasperated, and then turned to face Ileana.

"Maybe you and I should talk. I think I'll get more information from you than I will from Angel."

Chapter Twenty-Seven

The following morning Angel, Jarrod, and Ileana paid a visit to the University of Florida Police Department. They brought the pictures with them and told everything to the officer in charge. They were asked if they knew of anyone who had shown a divergent interest in Angel and were asked to not rule out those that were considered simply friends or acquaintances. The officer told them that in many stalker situations, those that the victim least suspected were guilty. They all took a moment to think hard, but responded negatively. Ileana made sure they knew about the man from the park, supplying them with his name and description. A quick identity check was run on the computer. There was no listing of a Benjamin Smith as a student, graduate or undergraduate.

"I knew it," said Ileana excitedly as she jumped up from her seat. "Y'see, I knew there was more to him than met the eye."

Angel and Jarrod looked at her in incredulity.

"Don't look so surprised," Ileana added. "I told you I could be right at times."

"I'm just glad you had the intelligence to ask for his last name," said Angel.

"He'd be a fool if he gave his real last name," said Jarrod.

"Damn," uttered Ileana under her breath as she sat back down. "I hadn't thought of that."

"I'm glad you came to us," said Officer Morales. "I just wish you had come sooner. You shouldn't take such things for granted. We'll station a few men outside your dorm, and I suggest you don't go anywhere alone, especially at night. Make sure you always lock your doors and I highly recommend you begin carrying pepper spray with you for defense purposes. In fact, it might be a good idea for you to take some self-defense classes. If you receive any more phone calls, gifts, or pictures, anything at all, you need to contact us immediately."

"Thank you. I will," said Angel. "I promise."

"Hi, Mom," said Morgan as she threw a load of whites into the washing machine. There was one thing she did sorely miss now that she was on her own, and that was having her mother do her laundry. She hated all the sorting, folding, and putting away, but mostly she hated having to come downstairs into the filthy, mildew-smelling, bug-infested basement. Even with all the lights turned on, it still appeared dark and alarming. Knowing spiders, silverfish, and probably mice lurked beneath and behind the hundreds of odds and ends cluttering the floor terrified her.

"Morgan, sweetheart. Oh, honey, how are you?" said Helen as she placed her car keys back on the console table near the front door. She had been on her way out to her second job when the phone rang. She quickly glanced at her watch, knowing she would now be late for work. No matter. It was so seldom that Morgan called, she wasn't about to miss the opportunity to speak to her.

"I'm fine. How about you?" asked Morgan.

"Terrible. I miss you so. You hardly ever call, and I'm always worried sick you're not well," said Helen as she walked into the kitchen and sat down at the table.

"I'm fine. I told you not to worry when I don't call. No news is good news." She jumped when she heard something scampering behind her. She looked but didn't see anything. Just to be safe, she hopped on top of the dryer and sat with her legs crossed beneath her. As she continued her conversation with her mother, she kept a watchful eye out for repulsive, furry critters and their equally disgusting friend, the cockroach.

"I understand that, but it doesn't help with the missing part," Helen said forlornly. "I'm so lonely without you."

"Why? We barely saw each other when I was living there. You were always working," said Morgan in a detached tone.

"You know why I work so many jobs. I want to give you as much as I possibly can."

"Yeah, well whatever. Listen, I need you to wire me some more money." Morgan turned her head abruptly to the left when she heard a loud thud. She couldn't take this a minute longer. She jumped down onto the ground and ran up the basement steps as quickly as possible, slamming the door behind her. She was not going down there alone again. When John returned from work, she would ask him to go downstairs with her to retrieve her laundry. He'd do it. He always did whatever she asked.

"I thought you were working," Helen said fretfully.

"I am, but things are slow at the store, so I've been forced to shorten my hours." She couldn't very well tell her the truth. She could just imagine her mother's reaction if she knew Morgan had cut her hours at the boutique by choice because she was too busy following, spying on, and mentally torturing her cousin.

"I'm barely making enough to cover the rent in this rathole. I'm dying to get out of here and get my own place. Are you going to send the money?" Morgan began to walk back and forth in the living room. God, how she hated it here. Everywhere she looked was some sort of mess. Either empty pizza boxes left out on the kitchen table, dirty clothes strewn across the living room floor, old newspapers piling up in a corner of a room, or dirty dishes left to soak for days on end in the sink. Well, if her roommates were under the impression that she was going to clean up after them, they had another thing coming. She would keep her room clean, but that was as far as the extent of her household duties would go. Maybe just a little further to include the bathroom. She drew the line at having to squat to pee in her own home.

"Morgan, I'm not sure that I can. I don't have much left in the bank and I'm already putting in as many hours as I possibly can."

"Never mind. If you don't want to send it, just say so. Don't come up with lame excuses," said Morgan in a bitter, nasty tone.

"They're not excuses. It's the truth."

"Whatever. I have to go."

"No. Wait. Don't hang up. I'll find a way to send some." Helen didn't know where she was going to find the money, but she would. She always did. She tried willing away an oncoming headache by rubbing her temple with her free hand. Why did every phone call she received from Morgan always have to end up in an argument? The fact that Helen was usually left penniless as well was just par for the course.

"Thank you…so, have you heard from Uncle Willie and Aunt Laura recently? How's Angelise doing?" Morgan asked tentatively while attempting to change the subject. She was wondering if Angelise had mentioned anything to her parents about the flowers and pictures. She walked into the kitchen, opened the refrigerator door, and grabbed the last can of Diet Dr. Pepper. It was John's, but she knew he wouldn't say anything. If it had belonged to Nate, he would make some sort of negative comment about it, and if it was Benjamin's…what was she thinking? Benjamin never had anything to eat or drink stored in the house. He would bring his daily consumption of food, water, soda, and snacks home with him every day after work. He would take his little package of goodies into his room and eat it in there. In fact, he did everything in his room. He ate, watched television, read, and slept in there. The only times she had the misfortune of seeing him was when he would leave his seclusion to make use of the bathroom or to go to work in the morning. In actuality, he was almost the perfect roommate, the kind that was never around. If it wasn't for the fact that he was so weird, she wouldn't mind seeing him on those rare occasions.

"I spoke with your Aunt Laura last week. Everything is fine. Angel loves it at the university and is doing very well. Oh, and guess what?" said Helen, forcing Morgan back into the conversation.

"What?" Morgan responded, trying desperately not to sound thwarted with the news that Angelise was adjusting magnificently to college life.

"Angel met a special young man and they're dating. Sounds pretty serious too. You'll never believe this, but he's from New Jersey."

"Really?" she bit her lower lip as she tried not to show her fury. "What's his name?"

"I can't believe I forgot to ask, and Laura never even mentioned his name. All I know is that Angel told Laura he's wonderful and treats her as if she were made of gold. I'm so happy for her. You don't know how I wish you would find someone special to love. Jarrod was nice and comes from a great family. I wish the two of you had never broken up. His brother says he's doing well—"

Morgan interrupted her mother by saying, "Mom! Hold on and back up a bit. Have you seen Alec?"

"I bumped into him awhile back. Such a nice boy."

"Yeah, he's a real gem," Morgan said sarcastically. She was beginning to get a bad feeling in the pit of her stomach. "Did you happen to mention to him that I was in Florida?"

"I believe so. Why? Was I not supposed to?"

"Mom! I told you not to tell anyone I was here." God, how stupid could her mother be? She may have ruined everything for her. All her hard work gone to waste.

"I don't recall you saying I couldn't tell anyone," Helen said, fearing she'd just awoken the beast and released it from its cave. Again.

"I did tell you. Damn it all. Who else did you tell? Did you tell Aunt Laura?"

"Yes, I did. But I didn't say what town you're in because I don't even know. Which, by the way, I still don't understand why you're being so secretive about it."

"It's a good thing I didn't say what town I'm in, or you would have blabbed that information out to everyone as well. God, you're like the freakin' town crier," howled Morgan.

"What's the big deal? Why don't you want anyone to know?"

"Don't worry about my reasons. Just do me a favor and stop telling people where I am. I don't want anyone, especially the Wentworths, to know that information." Morgan was livid with her mother.

"Alright, honey. Calm down. Please don't be angry with me. I didn't know…I'm sorry." Helen hated it when Morgan was angry with her.

Totally fed up with her mother, Morgan said, "I have to go. Just remember to wire the money to me as soon as possible. You still have the account number from the last time, don't you?"

"Yes," replied Helen softly.

"Good. Oh, and if it's not too much trouble, would you please just shut up about me? I don't want you talking about me to anyone anymore, got it?"

Unavoidable tears were welling up in Helen's eyes as she said, "Fine. Whatever you say. Again, I'm sorry. I love you and please try to call more often. I worry about—"

Morgan hung up.

Helen gazed at the phone for a moment before hanging up as well. She fought back the terrible constriction of pain and tangled mass of emotions she was feeling. She couldn't comprehend how it was possible for Morgan to be so callous and merciless. Helen had done her best to raise her as well as she could, but it never seemed to be enough to satisfy her.

Was it because she worked so much and wasn't able to dedicate as much time to her as she should have? Or was it because her daughter lacked a father figure in her life to help guide and support her? Was she so angry at her father for abandoning them that she took it out on everyone else? So many unanswered questions. Well, there was one question Helen would find the answer to. Tomorrow when she went to the bank to wire the money into Morgan's account, she would inquire as to the location of the bank that housed that particular account. She would find out exactly where her daughter was.

Helen glanced at her watch and jumped up from the chair, knocking it over in her haste to leave for work.

Chapter Twenty-Eight

Jarrod wanted to say something. Angel could sense it. He seemed withdrawn and hesitant, and his mind seemed to be wandering endlessly today. She wondered if he was still upset with her for not telling him about the pictures and phone calls; yet he was still extremely demonstrative in his affections toward her. He held her hand everywhere they went, kissed her passionately when he thought no one was looking, and constantly told her how much she meant to him. If he were angry or bothered, he wouldn't be exhibiting that tender, sensitive side of himself, would he? She decided she should just flat-out ask him about it. There should be no secrets between them, she thought, but then grimaced and frowned when she realized how many secrets she had kept from him regarding her "stalker dude," as Ileana had begun to call him.

"Jarrod?" she said. He was lying on her bed while she folded her laundry at the foot of it. His shoulder was troubling him today, and he had a heating pad on it to try to relax the muscles. He didn't respond, so she repeated his name again a tad louder. "Jarrod?"

He opened his eyes and murmured, "Hmm?"

"Are you okay?" Concern laced her voice.

"Yeah. Just sore. I'll be alright in a little bit." He closed his eyes again, but Angel continued talking, so he grudgingly opened them. The workouts were getting more intense as he got closer to the start of the season, and between training and rehab, his body was constantly aching.

"Is something bothering you today aside from your shoulder?" she asked tentatively.

"No. Why?" He straightened up and removed the pad from his shoulder.

"It just seems like you're worried or that you want to tell me something, but are hesitant to do so." She placed her folded laundry in the laundry basket and then placed that on the floor next to her dresser. She sat down next to him on the bed, and he scooted over to give her more room, which wasn't easy on a twin-size bed pressed up against the wall. He took her hand and brought it up to his lips, palm side up, placing a gentle kiss there, and motioned for her to lie beside him, which she did. She lay on her side, leaning toward him as he put his arm around her. She placed her head gently on his chest and her arm over his rock-hard abdomen. He covered her arm with his and whispered in her ear, "Aside from worrying that some madman is going to hurt the woman I love, nah, not much else going on up there," as he tapped his head with his finger two or three times. He paused a moment and said, "Well, actually... um...never mind."

She leaned up to face him. "You see, that's the fourth time today you've started to say something and then ended the sentence with 'Never mind.' I know there's something you want to say to me, so just say it, okay?"

"Um..."

"C'mon...please?" She pouted.

"I was just sort of wondering if we could...um...maybe spend this weekend together." There, he said it. Now he could breathe again.

"We always spend the weekends together. Actually, now that you mention it, I forgot to tell you my parents are planning to visit next weekend. I'd like for you to meet them, and I know they're dying to meet you. Do you think you could join us for dinner or something?"

"Sure, sure. That'll be nice. Getting back to this weekend, how about it? Can we spend it together?"

"Of course. I just don't get why you're asking. We're always together on the weekends," she said, puzzled.

"I mean *really* together," he said, smiling seductively.

"Not getting your meaning." Angel wondered why he was being so cryptic.

Jarrod thought that this couldn't be any more difficult. How do you ask someone to spend the night with you without sounding like some sex-crazed maniac?

He whispered into her ear, "Remember when you said you wanted to be with me the way I want to be with you, but you wanted it to be in a private setting where we wouldn't be rushed or interrupted?"

"Oh...," she said, placing her head gently back on his chest so he wouldn't see the look of worry and fear that had replaced the look of perplexity.

"Uh-huh," he said, realizing she was finally getting his meaning. "I was thinking that maybe we could go away for the weekend together..."

"Hmmm. Wow. Umm, well..." She began to nervously drum her fingers on his chest. Jarrod didn't say anything. He didn't know what he had expected, but he definitely didn't think she would be so irresolute and tentative. Did he think she would be jumping for joy and ripping her clothes off at the same time? No. But neither did he think she would become silent and uncommunicative.

"What are you thinking?" he asked uncertainly.

"I'm just nervous. It's a big step for me."

"I know. And if you're not ready, then we'll wait until you are," he said while silently thinking, "Please be ready, please... please...please."

She smiled up at him. "But you're hoping I'm ready, aren't you?"

"I'd be lying if I said that I'm not," he said, grinning.

"Can I think about it for a bit?"

"Sure. Take your time." He waited approximately ten seconds before asking, "So, have you made a decision yet?"

She smacked him in the stomach. "You're unbelievable."

"It's just that you're so beautiful and sexy. I'm going nuts here."

"You think I'm sexy?" she asked incredulously.

"Of course I think you're sexy. Especially in that shirt," he said, eyeing her wantonly.

"This is your shirt."

"I know and I want it back. Now," he said in a bold, cheeky tone.

Was he daring her? Hmm...what would he do if she called his bluff? It's not like he hadn't seen her without her shirt on before. They had never completed the act of lovemaking, but they had gotten pretty close. She immediately jumped up onto her knees and straddled him while she slowly and teasingly began to raise the shirt over her head, tossing it on his chest when done.

He didn't say a word. He just opened his eyes wide and leaned forward to pull her atop him. He began to kiss her with earnest desire. She was secretly thinking how happy she was that she had worn that brand-new, silk push-up bra she had just purchased at Victoria's Secret yesterday afternoon. He continued kissing her as he slowly began to lower his head, lower and lower.

"Ohhh...," moaned Angel. He was beginning to lower one of her straps, and she knew she should put a halt to things, but God, this felt so unbelievably good. She loved the feel of his hands on her body, the way his kisses made her feel as if she would explode from pent-up desire, and the emotions he made her feel when he spoke his sweet, loving words to her in that soft, husky voice of his.

Her hands were tangling in his hair, then roaming over his shoulders and back. His hands began to retrace the path where his lips had been. As he joined his lips to hers again, he teased and tormented her with the rhythm he had created with his tongue while thrusting, retreating, and thrusting again as it engaged in an erotic dance with hers.

Suddenly Jarrod lifted his head and said in a frustrated tone, "No…no. No. Not now."

"What?" she said when she realized someone was knocking on her locked door. "It must be Ava. I'm sorry." Angel quickly jumped up, threw on the discarded shirt, and checked to see if Jarrod was composed before unlocking the door. He sat up on the bed, quickly placing a pillow over his lower extremities, and said in a defeated tone, "I'm ready now." She smiled tentatively at him and repeated the words, "I'm sorry."

"Do you love him?" asked Ileana. She had come by after her last class to see if anything new had happened with the stalker dude. Thankfully the answer was no. She sat on Ava's bed facing Angel, who was staring out the window with her arms crossed in front of her.

"With all my heart," responded Angel.

"Then what are you worried about?"

"I don't know. I'm scared. I've never done it before. What if I don't know what I'm doing? What if I'm bad at it?"

"You won't be bad at it. If there's love involved, it'll be perfect. You'll see." Ileana remembered her first time with Heath. It had been Heath's first time as well. With both virgins having zero knowledge in the art of lovemaking, the experience had been somewhat challenging and awkward, but they somehow were able to muddle their way through it and learned over time and lots of practice just how to get it right. She smiled as she recalled those memories.

"What was it like the first time you did it with Heath?" Angel asked as she turned to face Ileana.

Ileana bit her lower lip and hesitated answering. She didn't want to scare Angel more than she already was, but she needed to be honest so she would be prepared.

"Hmm, let's see. The first time wasn't so wonderful. Neither one of us knew what we were doing. And I'm not going to lie, it hurt a little. But the pain does pass fairly quickly. I have to say that after we finally got it right, it really was pretty great. Very, very special."

"Too bad he and his family moved to California. I always liked him. I wonder if he hadn't moved, if you two would still be together."

"We'll never know" responded Ile with a sad smile.

"I'm just so worried," Angel replied as she sat next to Ileana on the bed. Her head was bent low, and she nervously began to fidget with her fingers.

"You shouldn't be. Like I said, Heath and I didn't have any experience. But Jarrod does, right?"

"Don't remind me. The subject sort of came up, and he admitted that he and Morgan had had sex." She so detested picturing the two of them together and immediately tried erasing the image from her mind.

"Yeah, well, that *puta* would have sex with a doorknob," said Ileana.

Angel screwed up her face at the picture Ileana brought to her mind and said, "That's disgusting," causing her best friend to laugh loudly at her reaction.

"Seriously, Angel, don't think about it too much. If you're sure you're ready to be with him and this is what you want, just relax and enjoy it. Having an intimate relationship with someone requires trust and respect, and that already exists between the two of you. The only thing you really need to think about is protection. If he's been around the block, or even if he hasn't been around it all that much, but has been with Morgan, who has been around the block enough times to earn Frequent Flyer Miles, then you seriously need to use a condom. I don't want you getting sick or pregnant. There's no truth to the myth that it can't happen the first time."

"I know. I have been thinking…" She wasn't able to finish her sentence because her phone rang. She stood up and walked over to her desk where her cell phone lay and looked at the phone. She glanced at Ileana and said, "Crap. I think it's him." Based on the grim look on her face, Ileana knew she wasn't speaking of Jarrod.

"Give it to me," Ile said as she grabbed the phone. "*Hola?*" she said in Spanish. Heavy breathing was her only response. "*Hola, quien es?*" she repeated, asking who was at the other end.

Suddenly a woman's voice asked harshly, "Who is this?" Ileana widened her eyes and continued speaking in Spanish, hoping the more she heard the other woman's voice, the better the possibility of remembering and recognizing the sound of it, should the occasion arise for her to do so at a later date.

"*Quien habla?*" Ileana continued to ask who was calling, hoping this person was stupid enough to offer her actual name.

"Do-you-speak-the-English?" the person asked irritably.

"*No inglés. Solo español,*" responded Ileana. The voice sounded somewhat familiar, but she just couldn't place it. Angel was looking at her inquisitively, but Ileana quickly signaled her to be quiet.

"I must have el wrongo numero," said the unknown person. "I try againo. Sorryo."

Stupid idiot. Just because you add an *O* to a word doesn't automatically convert it to Spanish. She hated it when people did that. Suddenly the person hung up the phone.

"She hung up."

"She?" asked Angel in a surprised tone when the phone rang again. Ileana immediately picked it up and answered in Spanish once again. "*Hola?*"

"Son of a bitch," and the person hung up once again.

Ileana hung up and looked at Angel in shock. "I think your stalker dude is actually a dudette."

"It was a woman?"

"Yeah. Definitely. She asked if I spoke English, and when I said no, she said she had 'el wrongo numero.'"

"You hate it when people do that," Angel said.

"I know, right? What a dumbass." Ileana looked down at the phone and pressed the callback key. It began to ring, but there was no answer.

"It's a pay phone," said Angel. "I've tried calling back the other times."

Ileana hung up and stared at Angel. She wished the woman had said more. She was almost certain she had heard that voice before, but just couldn't place it. The few words the woman had said were not enough for Ileana to fully recognize her voice.

"This is just insane. Only you could get a woman to stalk you."

Chapter Twenty-Nine

"Hey, son. How are you?" asked Jim brightly. It had been close to two weeks since he'd spoken to his eldest son, and he missed him terribly.

"I'm good, Dad. Nice to hear your voice. The last three times I've called, you haven't been home."

"Yeah, I know. Sorry about that. I've been working a lot lately. Y'know, that college of yours doesn't come cheap. The scholarships helped tremendously, but—ouch!" Jim yelled.

"What happened?" asked Jarrod, concerned.

"I guess your mom didn't appreciate my comment about the cost of college. She threw a banana at me. It hurt. It wasn't even ripe yet!"

Jarrod laughed while picturing his mom getting mad at his father and tossing the banana at him. He's lucky she didn't have a knife in her hand at the time.

"Man, I miss you guys," he said, feeling suddenly homesick. He sat down on his bed and looked at the framed picture of him and his family that was sitting on his night table. The picture was taken last winter at a Giants game. He smiled as he recalled what a great time they had. Alec had painted his face blue and white and looked like a total idiot, yet he'd cared not one iota. He was far from being the only blue-and-white-faced fan there that day.

"We miss you too. So, tell me, how's everything going?"

"Not bad. Classes are okay. Some are a little on the boring side, but I have to take them, so I will. Baseball's going great, though. My arm is feeling really good."

"Not too sore?" Jim asked worriedly.

"A little. But it's getting better."

"How often do you practice?"

"Every day after classes and sometimes on the weekends."

"You're not overdoing it, are you?"

"Nah. Don't worry about me. I'm fine." He returned the picture to its place and picked up the one of him and Angel that Ileana had taken of them a few weeks ago. Angel was sitting on his lap with her head tilted a bit to the side so that it leaned against his. She was wearing his favorite red shirt that fit just a little too snugly, emphasizing her beautiful bustline, while he had on a plain pair of black shorts and a blue Gators baseball T-shirt. They were both smiling, but Angel's smile outshined, outdid, and outstripped any and every smile since the beginning of time. Well, that was just Jarrod's opinion, but as far as he was concerned, it was the only one that mattered.

"I'm glad to hear it. I called to give you some good news. I just hope you're ready to hear it," said Jim excitedly, yet a bit on the uncertain side.

"Now you've got my interest. What is it?"

"I spoke with Mr. Wyatt today. He called to see how you were doing. Nice of him, huh?"

"Yeah, definitely," Jarrod said eagerly as he stood up and began to pace the length of the room.

"I told him you were doing great and that you're attending college in Florida."

"Did he say anything about baseball?"

"Yup."

"Well?" Jarrod said anxious to hear what Mr. Wyatt had said.

"He asked about your health and recovery. I let him know how you've come a tremendous way in such a short period of time and he was really impressed. I also let him know you made the university's baseball team, that you're doing great, and that your arm is almost where it was when he saw you pitch that day." Realizing he had brought up a memory that might cause Jarrod pain, he added, "Sorry."

Jarrod's euphoria quickly faded as he recalled that day. Yes, it was wonderful that he had pitched so well and that a professional scout for a top-notch league team was there to witness it. But it was also the day he lost his best friend and practically died himself, a day that would be ingrained in his mind forever. He still missed his friend and thought of him every day.

Sobering up, he said to his father, "It's fine. Go on. Tell me more."

"He was happy to hear you're doing so well. Here's the good news. He's going to be in Jacksonsville the weekend of the twentieth and was wondering if you could meet him there. He'd like to talk and see how far you've come along. What do you think? You up to it?"

Jarrod couldn't respond. He stood motionless in the small confine of his room with the phone pressed to his ear, staring into blank space.

"Jarrod? Jarrod? Son, are you there?"

"Huh?"

"You okay?"

"Yeah. Dad, this is unbelievable."

"It is. But—"

"But what?" Jarrod interrupted. Sentences that began with the word "but" never ended well.

"Do you think you're ready? I mean, you've been through a lot, and the accident wasn't all that long ago. It takes awhile to recover fully from something like that…"

"I'm ready," Jarrod said confidently.

"Are you sure?" Jim asked. He didn't want his son to be disappointed if he tried out and wasn't quite ready. It might discourage him from ever trying again.

"I'm sure."

"Do you want me to come down and meet you in Jacksonville? I mean, for moral support."

"Actually, that would be great, if it's not too much trouble. I'd love to see you and, well, yeah, I could use the support."

"Then I'll be there," Jim said.

"Thanks."

"You got it." In a more somber tone, he added, "Listen, Bud, I don't know if I've told you lately, but I'm proud of you. You've been able to achieve something most men wouldn't even attempt. You've never given up, and as your father, I have no words to describe how proud of you I am."

"That means a lot to me," said Jarrod.

"You should be proud of yourself as well."

"I am," he said, smiling. "Um, Dad, I was wondering if you wouldn't mind me bringing someone along."

"Angel?"

"How do you know about Angel?" Jarrod asked, surprised. He hadn't mentioned anything to his parents about her simply because he knew his mother would drive him nuts with questions. She was great at minding her own business when it came to others, but when it involved her two sons, she had no boundaries.

"Alec told me."

"What else did he say?"

"Not much. Just that she's very pretty, seems sweet, and that you're crazy about her. Oh, and that she happens to be Morgan's cousin. How's that working out for you?"

"I don't even know if Morgan knows that we're dating. She threw a conniption when she found out that Angel and I were interested in one another, but I haven't heard from her in awhile and you know what they say…no news is good news. All I know is that Angel and I are doing great. She's special; she makes me very happy."

"I'm glad to hear it. If you're happy, we're happy. I'd love to meet her so definitely bring her along. Wait, your mom wants to say something."

"Jarrod, it's Mom. Are you bringing Angel to Jacksonville?" she asked excitedly.

"Hi, Mom! Yeah, I was thinking about it."

"Great. We'll meet her then."

"Are you coming too?" Jarrod asked cheerfully.

"I am now."

"Great. I'm sure she'll be happy to meet you too. Do you think there's any possibility that Alec can come as well?"

"Sure. It's the weekend, so he won't miss any school. I'm going to give the phone back to your father now. He's tugging on my arm, and I'm about ready to throw the whole damn fruit bowl at him if he doesn't stop. Love you, honey."

"Love you too. Bye."

Jim got back on the phone and said, "Jarrod, first let me call Griffin Wyatt back and get the details as to where and when you two can meet. Then I'll figure things out from this end and call you back, alright?"

"Yeah. Sounds good."

"Alright then. I'll talk to you soon. I love you, son."

"Love you too. Tell Alec I said hi."

"Will do. Bye."

After he hung up, Jarrod immediately sat down on his bed, only to stand up two seconds later and run as fast as his legs would take him to Angel.

Chapter Thirty

"Oh my God," exclaimed Angel as she jumped into his arms, wrapping both her legs around his waist as he twirled her around numerous times.

"Isn't it great?" he asked as he tumbled forward, dropping the two of them onto her bed. Angel lay still with him above her and gently pushed aside a stray lock of hair that had fallen over his eye. She looked into his eyes and said, "I love you."

"I love you more," he said.

"I'm so happy for you…"

"For us."

"For us," she repeated as he bent down and kissed her. Then he abruptly jumped up from the bed and said, "I want you to come with me to Jacksonville next weekend."

Angel sat up and looked at him sadly. "My parents are coming up that weekend, remember? I told you the other night."

He looked devastated. He so wanted her by his side at this incredible moment in his life. It broke Angel's heart to see the distraught look on his face. She walked over to him and put her arms around his waist, bringing their bodies close together.

He slowly wrapped his arms around her waist and gently leaned his head upon hers.

"I'll call my parents and ask if they can postpone their visit," she said. "They'll just have to understand that this is something that is important to you. I mean, to us."

"What do you mean, 'postpone' the visit?" Laura said, displeased.

Angel fully explained the situation to her mother. "I wouldn't ask you and Daddy to postpone the visit if there was any way around it." Even over the phone, she could sense her mother's intense displeasure.

"But we haven't seen you in weeks. You've been so busy at school and with your new boyfriend that you haven't made time to come home and visit anymore." Angel could hear in her mother's voice that she was about to cry. She was getting that raspy, faltering voice with just a hint of a whimper.

"Mom, I'll make it up to you, I swear," pleaded Angel.

"How, Angel, how?" said Laura.

"I don't know, but I will. I promise."

There was a brief moment of silence, until Laura suddenly said, "Well, I know how you can. I want you to come visit us this weekend here in Bradenton."

"Oh." Angel immediately thought about Jarrod's suggestion that he and she go away this weekend. She hadn't said yes to him. Yet. But this might work out. She needed more time to decide if she was ready to take such a big step, and she didn't want Jarrod to feel hurt or offended if she decided she wasn't. She could just tell him her parents insisted she come this weekend; otherwise, they wouldn't postpone their visit to Gainesville. She wouldn't be lying and she would be able to gain more time. Plus, the following weekend they would be going to Jacksonville together, and there was no way they were going to share a room with his family staying at the same hotel. Yes, this was a good thing.

"You got it, Mom," Angel said brightly. "I'll check the bus schedule, and hopefully I can leave right after my last class on Friday afternoon."

"Great!" said Laura enthusiastically. "See, now everyone is happy. Win-win."

Everyone with the exception of Jarrod, thought Angel. "Yup. Win-win." Angel pinched the bridge of her nose, suddenly feeling a migraine coming on.

"Bradenton? This weekend?" asked Jarrod.

"Yes. It was either that or they'd come here next weekend, and then I wouldn't be able to go to Jacksonville with you." She watched him from the corner of her eye to see his reaction.

"But I was hoping you and I would, y'know, be able to go away this weekend. This stinks."

"Don't whine. It's not becoming. Besides, we're going away next weekend."

At that precise moment, Jarrod reminded her of a young child who'd just been informed that Santa Claus didn't truly exist. He plopped himself onto her bed and pouted.

"Yeah, but we're not going to be alone. The whole family will be there."

"Which will be great," she said brightly. "I'll be able to meet them all."

"It won't be great as far as us spending time alone. I mean, really alone." He looked at her to see if she was getting his meaning, but she gave no sign that she did, so he continued by adding, "I mean really, really—"

"I get it, Jarrod." His face dropped, and he looked so sad and disappointed. She bent down to place a quick kiss on his forehead. "Baby, in the immortal words of Mick Jagger, you can't always get what you want. In this case, it's one or the other."

He awkwardly threw himself backward on the bed, then took one of the pillows and placed it over his head. Mumbled, unintelligible profanities could be heard while he punched the bed with one hand and held the pillow down with the other.

Angel raised both her eyebrows at the ridiculous, doltish, incredible, but yet somewhat entertaining display of infantilism. The whining was preferable to the tantrum, but not quite as funny.

Chapter Thirty-One

"Hi, Mom. It's me," said Morgan.

"Hi, love. How are you doing?" Helen sounded tired. She had been cleaning and dusting all day and was readying herself for a long, hot shower when the phone rang.

"I'm fine. I went to the bank today. Thanks for wiring the money, but I was wondering why you sent so little. Last time you sent five hundred."

"That was all I was able to scrape up."

"Three hundred dollars? That's it?"

Helen took in a deep breath as she prepared herself for the ensuing battle.

"Yes, Morgan. That's it. That's all I could afford to send. I still have expenses, you know. I wish you could understand that and maybe, just maybe, have a little more consideration." *Wow, that felt good*, she thought.

On the other end, Morgan opened her mouth in shock, forming a big O. "Listen to you getting all snippy," she said acerbically. "It's your responsibility as a mother to supply your only daughter with what she needs. Just because you've failed miserably at it, doesn't mean that you should take it out on me."

"Listen, Morgan. I don't want to fight. I'm tired of fighting. I sent you all that I could. I'm sorry if it isn't much, but I don't have anymore. Now, can we please change the subject?" Helen was emotionally and mentally spent. Every time she spoke with her daughter, she felt completely wiped out. She was ashamed to admit it, but strangely, when Morgan decided to leave, Helen secretly felt relieved. Every day with Morgan was a constant battle, and things hadn't improved much after she left. Whenever Morgan would call, she was endlessly demanding and nastier than ever.

"Fine. Tell me what's going on over there," Morgan said.

"Nothing new, really. I saw Mrs. Gerbino the other day at the supermarket, and she looks well. She said to say hello when I spoke with you."

"And so you have. Next."

"Umm…" How was it that knowing her daughter as well as she did, she still could be shocked by her interminable rudeness?

"Have you seen any of the Wentworths?" asked Morgan.

"Actually, yes, I have. I saw Jarrod's younger brother—"

"Alec."

"Yes, Alec. He came to the diner last night with some friends. They were all so nice and polite. And handsome. That Alec has grown at least two inches since I last saw him, and he's all muscle now. Very, very good-looking."

"Are you planning on doing him?"

"Doing what with him?" Helen asked naively.

"Never mind," Morgan said, trying desperately to hold back the laughter.

"Anyway, as I was saying, he's such a nice young man. He reminds me of Jarrod a lot. Speaking of Jarrod, their friend Joey mentioned he's doing great. He's practically fully recovered from the accident. Isn't that wonderful?"

"Wonderful," Morgan responded while she skimmed through a bridal magazine she had purchased earlier that morning. She may not be engaged to Jarrod at the moment, but that was just a matter of time.

"But there's even better news. Remember that scout who came to his last game here in New Jersey? Well, it seems that he'll be meeting with him either this weekend or next weekend. I'm not quite sure…maybe it's next weekend…" Morgan quickly stood up, dropping the magazine on the floor.

"Mother."

"Umm…where was I?"

"He's meeting with the scout one of these weekends. Where?"

"That I don't know. Joey didn't say. I just know it's coming up soon. The Wentworths will be meeting him there, so that should be exciting."

"Yes, I'm sure it will be. Why was Joey the one to tell you all this and not Alec?"

"Alec was at the register paying the bill at the time. By the way, they left me a very nice tip—"

"Mom, focus. Did Joey mention anything about Jarrod's girlfriend?"

"He has a girlfriend? I didn't know. No one mentioned that. I guess they were just being considerate, knowing I'm your mother and all."

"Yeah, I'm sure they were all being considerate." Stupid bastards were far from being considerate. They were all probably following instructions from Jarrod not to mention Angelise's name.

"How do you know that he has a girlfriend?" said Helen curiously.

"I just do. I've heard rumors. So you say you're not sure when he's meeting the scout?"

"I'm sure it's either this weekend or the next. One or the other."

"Interesting. I guess he's doing a lot better then. I mean, for him to be meeting with the scout, he must be playing ball well enough to try out for—"

In her excitement, Helen interrupted Morgan with, "Can you imagine if Jarrod were to make it to the big leagues? We could say that we knew him when."

"Yeah, wouldn't that be great," she retorted sarcastically "I have to go, Ma. I have to get to work. I'll call again soon."

"I'd like that. Bye, honey.

"Bye." And she hung up.

Helen had decided earlier that she wouldn't mention to Morgan that she had found out through the bank what town she was in. Something wasn't adding up. Her daughter was being incredibly secretive about where she was. Also, Angel was going to college in a city that was very close to the town Morgan was living in and happened to have a boyfriend from New Jersey. Coincidence? Doubtful. She would have to make a point of asking Alec what college Jarrod was attending the next time she bumped into him. Morgan obviously hadn't contacted Angel, because she had asked about her during their last phone call. If she had been in contact with her, she would have known how she was doing. Why hadn't she called Angel? Also, somehow Morgan knew Jarrod had a girlfriend, but wouldn't say how she'd found out.

Helen had a bad feeling about this. She loved her daughter with all her heart, but she knew deep down she was up to no good. She didn't know what to do or if she should tell anyone. She paced back and forth, biting her nails all the while. Helen didn't want her daughter to get into trouble, but if she said something to the wrong person, she inadvertently might speed up the process of that happening. She went into the kitchen and poured herself a glass of wine. Tonight was her only night off this week, and she planned on relaxing in front of the television with a nice glass or two of wine. She might even start reading that new romance novel she had bought over two months ago.

Later that evening Morgan waited impatiently for Benjamin to arrive home from work. She glanced at her watch and realized he was over an hour late. Where could he have gone? He had no friends to hang out with. Nate or John always did the food shopping, and with a washer and dryer in the basement, there was no need for him to visit a Laundromat. Not that she'd ever seen him do laundry in the basement either. He was never late, but today, when she desperately needed to speak with him, he was.

Hearing a sound coming from the front of the house, she walked over to the window, pulled aside the curtain, and watched as Benjamin stepped out of his car carrying a large brown paper grocery bag. The top of the bag was folded down many times, so whatever he had purchased was small in size. He had it snuggled securely under his arm, so she knew it couldn't be his dinner. Morgan wondered what he might be carrying in the bag, but decided it would be best for her not to ask about it, in fear it would trigger one of his maniacal episodes. Besides, knowing Benjamin, whatever was concealed in the bag would probably disgust her anyway. She waited for him to follow through with his interminable routine. Walk to the back of the house, wipe his feet exactly thirteen times, twist the doorknob back and forth, and then finally enter the house. *The man is a certified lunatic*, she silently thought.

He opened the back door and quietly walked into the house. Morgan waited for him in the living room, but saw he immediately walked straight toward his bedroom.

"Benjamin, we need to speak," Morgan said loudly. He continued walking to his bedroom, opened the door, and placed the brown bag on his desk. He came back out, closing the door to his room behind him. He slowly walked into the living room and stood motionless in front of Morgan. Head down, of course.

Morgan noticed he had left the bag in his room, but once again decided against asking about it. They had more important matters to discuss.

"What's the…m-m-matter?" he asked nervously.

"We have a problem. He's hurting her," she said bluntly.

"Who's hurting…?" he asked as he passed his hand through his greasy hair and then began his annoying habit of clenching and unclenching his fists again.

"Angelise's boyfriend has been hurting her. I overheard her telling her friend today while they were shopping at the store."

"You...you never said she had...had a b-b-boyfriend," he said, looking up.

"Well, she does, but obviously she can't love him. How could anyone love someone who hurts them? She's probably terrified to leave him. He hits her." She watched closely for a reaction.

"No," he said angrily as he began to nervously tug at his hair. Morgan noticed he pulled a few strands out and didn't so much as flinch. As much as the sight of Benjamin self-mutilating himself disquieted Morgan, she continued, knowing if she pushed hard enough, she would be able to convince him to do what she wanted.

"It's horrible. Benjamin, he beats her up, but he's smart about it. He hits her and leaves the bruises where they're concealed by her clothes. When she was changing in the dressing room, I brought her another blouse to try on, and I saw the bruises on her back and upper arms."

"I'll...k-k-kill...him!" Anger flared in his eyes, making him appear demonic. He began to breathe hard and unsteadily while pacing in a circle, forcing Morgan to take a few steps back.

"No...no...you can't do that." She needed to pull the reins in a bit. He was beginning to lose control, and God only knew what that psycho was capable of doing. She didn't want anyone hurt, just scared. "But there is something you can do to help her. That is, if you truly want to help her."

"I'll d-do...anything," he said, coming to a stop directly in front of her, uncomfortably close.

"You need to take her away. She needs to be far away from that monster so he can't hurt her anymore." She noted the sudden gleam in his eyes.

"But she d-d...she doesn't know me. She won't go. I just s-spoke with her once and...and I d-don't think...she liked me. She won't go."

"Make her," she said forcefully. "It's for her own good. You're going to have to take her by force. You have no choice. No one in her right mind would voluntarily take off with a stranger. You have to wear a disguise so you aren't recognized by anyone, and so no one could give an accurate description of you if you're seen. She'll be scared in the beginning, but she'll get over it once she realizes you won't hurt her. The important thing is to get her away from her boyfriend as soon as possible."

"Where? I c-c-can't bring her...here," he said, glancing around.

"No. You're right. You definitely can't do that. I'll figure something out. I'll find somewhere for you to take her. Once I do, I'll give you all the information. You just have to get her and take her there."

"I...I...I'm not s-s-sure."

Hesitation. Not good. Morgan grabbed him forcefully by the arms and said, "Benjamin. Do you care for her or not? He might kill her the next time."

"I c-care."

"Then do this for her, Benjamin. She needs you. You can't abandon her now." Oh, where were those damn tweezers when you needed them? She was putting on her best performance to date, but still couldn't seem to force a tear or two out.

"D-d-do whatever you need to do. I have to protect her... f-from him." He pulled out another strand of hair. If he kept this up, he'd be bald by the end of the night.

"You're doing the right thing," she said, and then she walked away. Once she was in her room, she closed the door and took in a deep breath. It felt like the first breath she'd taken since she started her conversation with Benjamin. All she needed to do was have him take Angelise away for a few days and then release her. She would go running home to her precious mommy and daddy in Bradenton, and Jarrod would remain in Gainesville. Eventually, in good time, he would forget about all about her. He was looking gorgeous. More so now than a year ago. *All that working out brought out muscles on top of muscles, and he was looking mighty fine*, she thought.

She had work to do. She needed to find a place where Benjamin could keep her hidden for a few days. But where? Perhaps a hotel room somewhere. But then he would have to keep her tied up and gagged. If she were to scream, she would alert the other guests or staff. If he kept her untied, she would try to escape. As much as she hated Angelise for her betrayal, she wasn't comfortable with her being gagged and tied. But what choice did she have? It would only be for a few days anyway. All she wanted was for Angelise to be scared enough to leave for good. She needed her out of the way.

What about Benjamin, though? He'd likely be caught and sent to jail if Angelise were able to identify him after her release. And if that were the case, he wouldn't hesitate to throw Morgan under the bus. Benjamin would have to continue wearing a disguise while he kept Angelise captive. Either that, or he would have to keep her blindfolded the entire time.

She would also have to follow Angelise closely for the next few days. Not close enough to be seen, but just enough to keep tabs on her. Morgan already knew her schedule, and if she didn't skip any classes on Friday, more than likely she would be leaving with Jarrod after three o'clock when her last class was done. But what if she wasn't planning on going with Jarrod? Of course she was. Those two were practically inseparable. It made her sick to think she used to have to beg and plead for Jarrod to take her out somewhere. All he ever wanted to do was play baseball or sit in her house and watch television. And even when he did do that, which wasn't all that often, he was constantly glancing down at his watch in anticipation of his departure.

What if it wasn't this weekend they were planning on leaving? Her mother hadn't been sure. The more she thought of it, the more she believed Benjamin should take Angel on Thursday evening. It wouldn't be smart to grab her in the middle of the day, with hundreds of students milling about. No matter. The sooner it happened, the sooner Angelise would be out of her life, and Jarrod's as well. Yes, there was much work to be done. She'd better get a move on it. Thursday was right around the corner.

Chapter Thirty-Two

By Thursday morning Morgan had made all the necessary arrangements. She had checked in for them using the cash her mother had sent and booked the room for Thursday night through Tuesday morning at an offbeat "no-tell motel" south of Archer Road. The main office was a small building separate from the jerry-built, jury-rigged, long, dilapidated building of connecting rooms. With only two levels, there was no elevator, just stairways connecting the ground level to the second.

The tottering building was painted a dull gray and appeared to not have seen a paintbrush in years. The paint was faded and peeling, and the three or four rooms that had air conditioning units dangling from the windows had rusty water stains below from the constant water drip. The motel was perfect for what they needed it for. Unostentatious and distasteful in appearance only meant that the clientele would not be of the highest caliber. Plus, after meeting the proprietor at check-in, she got the distinct impression he would ask no questions. He was overweight, grungy, and sported a curled handlebar mustache, in a look reminiscent of Dudley Do-Right's arch-nemesis, the evil Snidely Whiplash. His outdated and faded red and white Mauna Loa shirt was covered in stains, while his jeans rode so low on his hips that when he bent down to retrieve a pen that had fallen, Morgan's eyes practically popped out of their sockets at the unsightly view.

Even more repulsive was the large gap in his smile caused by a missing tooth. Resourcefully, the man used it to hold secure his lit cigarette, which he would drag hard on every thirty seconds or so. He coughed incessantly and rather than cover his mouth when doing so, he would turn his head slightly, releasing a spray of spittle with every hack. Surprisingly, what threw Morgan for a loop was that he spoke with a British accent. Who knew England had bumpkin hicks? She almost wanted to laugh at the thought.

She had brought cold cuts packed in a cooler, canned food, soda and water, paper plates, plastic utensils, and one of those small electric stoves that had only one burner to it. She also brought Angelise a toothbrush, hairbrush, toiletries, clean underwear, and two days worth of clothing. *As far as kidnappings go, this one earns a five-star rating*, Morgan thought. She had also bought a man's wig, baseball cap, fake mustache, and dark sunglasses for Benjamin that she had already given him the night before. She had spoken to Benjamin about the plans, informing him of all the arrangements. She had also supplied him with precise directions to the hotel, the key to room 241, a roll of duct tape, rope, and a blindfold, instructing him to keep it on her at all times. He was also never, ever to mention her name in front of Angelise.

She imagined Benjamin was as nervous as a cow in a slaughterhouse. Hell, she was nervous. She decided to call him to make sure he hadn't had second thoughts and wanted to back out. She dialed his number and waited for him to pick up. When he did, she simply said, "It's me. Are we all set for tonight?"

"Yes," he said diffidently.

"Are you sure? You have to be sure. Once you start it, you'll have to go through with it all the way. No going back."

"I'm sure. The only thing I'm w-w-wondering about is w-why only for a few days?"

"Because we want to scare her enough to leave Gainesville and go home. Her boyfriend won't follow her there."

"How d-do you know...he won't f-f-follow her?"

"He'd follow her if he thought she was leaving because of him and he'd try to win her heart back. In this case, she would be leaving out of fear for what happened to her. She won't feel safe here anymore and will go where she is safe. Back home to her mom and dad."

"B-but if...if...she leaves, how will she and I ever g-g-get together? I love her."

Love? This man believed he was in love with Angelise. "All in due time. First let's concentrate on getting her away from the abusive boyfriend, and then we'll work on getting the two of you together." That was close. She was getting better at lying than she thought she would. Maybe she should consider a career in acting. She was definitely getting good at it.

"D-do...do I...just untie her and...l-l-let her go?" he stammered.

"No. God, we went over this last night." She needed to calm down and be patient with him; otherwise he would become fearful and nervous and possibly back out. Taking a deep breath, she said, "In a few days you need to release her, but it needs to be done at night when you won't be seen so easily. Drive her somewhere near campus, but not quite there. Untie her hands and tell her to count to fifty before she takes off the blindfold. Make sure to wear the disguise in case she doesn't listen, and get the hell out of there as quickly as you can so that you're gone by the time she gets the blindfold off. Always make sure she thinks you have a gun. This way she won't get all cocky and brave. Understood?"

"Yes."

"If you have questions, leave the hotel room and call me from your cell. Remember, never ever mention my name in front of her. That's important."

"Okay."

"Well then, I guess that's it until we speak later. Call me when you're at the hotel. Not in front of her. Remember that, okay?"

"Morgan?"

"Yes?"

"One m-more thing."

"What is it?" she asked, annoyed.

"I may not want to give her up," he said without stammering, and then he hung up.

Damn. Damn. Damn. She hadn't thought of that. She tried calling him back numerous times, but he wouldn't answer. He had to let her go. Him keeping her was not an option. She didn't want Angelise to be hurt. Damn him for making things complicated. *This is what I get for dealing with a mentally disturbed, psychotic lunatic who should be strapped in a straightjacket and locked up in a padded room,* she thought.

Chapter Thirty-Three

"Will you call me when you get to Bradenton?" Jarrod asked. "No matter what time you get in?"

"Yes," Angel said.

"Promise?"

"I promise."

"Kiss me," Jarrod whispered. As they stood just inside the doorway of her room, she leaned up and gave him one final kiss. This kiss would have to hold them both until they saw each other again on Monday, so she had to make it spectacular. She molded her body into his as she tortuously traced his lips lightly with her tongue. A soft groan escaped from deep within his throat. He inserted his tongue into her mouth, where she welcomed him with her own. She could feel his need for her growing insistent as he pressed his body tightly to hers. She broke the kiss and whispered, "I'm going to miss you."

"I miss you already. I love you."

"I love you more," and then he kissed her again with urgent need.

A clearing of the throat with a follow-up "Excuse me" startled them both back to reality. "If you're going to go at it like rabbits, how about taking it somewhere else?"

"Sorry," said Angel to Ava. "We sort of got caught up in the moment."

"Whatever," she said, smiling. "Will you two lovebirds let me by so I can get in?"

They both moved out of the way to let Ava pass and then Jarrod said, "I guess I should be going. Don't forget to call me, okay?"

"I won't. I'll call as soon as I get there."

They gave each other a quick peck on the lips, and then Jarrod was off. She watched him walk away, feeling a sudden burst of sadness and loneliness. She turned and walked back into the room. As she closed the door to the room, Ava said, "You're not crying, are you?"

"No," Angel said, although it was obvious she was close to doing so.

"It's only for a few days," Ava said sympathetically.

"I know." She sat down on the edge of her bed and lowered her head. Tears began to well up in her eyes. To stop the flow, she jumped up and said, "I think I'll go take a shower now."

"Good for you. I'm going to sleep. I'm exhausted tonight."

"See you in the morning then," said Angel.

A half hour later, Angel returned to the room feeling emotionally stronger and more refreshed. She let the tears flow while she showered, and the effect of the hot water on her tense muscles seemed to revitalize her. As she entered the room quietly, she noted Ava was sound asleep. The television was still on, so Angel walked over to turn it off. That's when she noticed Jarrod had left his cell phone. Picking it up, she quickly skimmed through his contact list and speed dialed the number for his roommate Dave. He picked up and said, "Hello?"

"Hi, Dave! It's Angel."

"Hey, gorgeous! What's up?"

"Not much. Jarrod left his cell phone here in my room. Is he there yet?"

"Nope, not yet," said Dave.

"When he gets there, will you ask him to come get it? I won't be around this weekend, and I know he'll need it. I'll wait for him outside my building."

"Will do."

"Thanks," she said.

"No problem. By the way...how's that beautiful friend of yours, Ileana?"

It was no secret Dave was crushing big-time on her best friend. Everyone knew it, including Ileana. Angel and Jarrod both thought they would make a great couple, but Ileana didn't seem at all interested. She was searching for the perfect man and because of that, all the "almost perfects" were passing her by.

"She's fine. Busy with schoolwork," said Angel.

"Could you tell her I said hi?" he asked dispiritedly.

"I definitely will. Bye."

"Bye."

Angel changed from her pajamas into a pair of jeans and a T-shirt, grabbed Jarrod's phone, and went to wait for him outside.

She should have brought a jacket. It was chilly, and her hair was still damp from the shower. She wrapped her arms around herself, trying to stay warm. It was so dark and no one was around. The silence was oppressive, causing her to feel tense and uneasy. The only discernable sounds were those of the rustling palm tree leaves as they swayed against each other and of the passing cars as they drove by along University Road.

She cast a nervous glance about and quickly realized Security was nowhere in the vicinity. *The guards must be walking around the other side of the building,* she thought. Usually at night there were three of four of them securing the perimeter of the building. She had been waiting approximately ten minutes when suddenly she heard footsteps behind her. She turned to see if it was Jarrod, but could only make out a dark figure walking her way. *Must be security*, she thought as she squinted to try to see whom it was.

The figure was too short to be Jarrod. She turned away and heard the footsteps getting closer. Damn it, why didn't she listen to Jarrod? He had told her never to go anywhere alone, especially at night. Boy, he was going to pitch a fit when he found her outside. Alone. In the dark. She couldn't even call him to let him know she had changed her mind and would leave the phone with Ava. And to boot, she had been in such a rush that she had left her can of pepper spray in her handbag. She pulled her arms tighter around herself, not only in hopes of keeping warmer, but also to stop the incessant shivering her nerves were causing.

"Angelise?" a strange, unrecognizable voice said.

She immediately turned toward the voice and suddenly felt a dreadful shock flow throughout her body. It was quick, yet far from painless. She felt as if her insides had been turned inside out and dropped to the ground, losing her grip on Jarrod's phone, which now lay beside her motionless body.

Chapter Thirty-Four

"Angel? Angel?" Jarrod whispered loudly. Where the hell was she? "Angel?" He whispered more loudly as he paced in front of the entrance to her building. He would give her five more minutes, and if she didn't show up, he would go to her room. He was trying to avoid that because he didn't want to risk getting Angel in trouble by being seen in the building after curfew.

"Can I help you?" asked the security guard who approached him from behind. Jarrod turned, startled by the voice as the overweight officer with the too-tight uniform pointed a flashlight in Jarrod's face, causing him to squint.

"I'm looking for my girlfriend. She was supposed to meet me here to give me my cell phone that I'd left in her room." Jarrod was becoming increasingly nervous with every second that passed.

"Is this your phone?" asked the guard as he pulled a cell phone from his pocket and showed it to him.

"Yeah. That's it," he said as he took the phone from the guard. "Did she ask you to give to me?"

"No. I found it lying there on the ground." He pointed to a spot near the steps. Jarrod stared at the spot and knew

❦ Broken Road ❦

immediately something was wrong. Very, very wrong. Angel would never just leave the phone there. If she had gotten tired of waiting, she would have taken it upstairs with her.

Jarrod began to run up the steps of the building, yelling to the guard, "Come with me!" as he ran through the front door. He continued running until he reached Angel's room and pounded on the door. The security guard eventually caught up to him, completely short-winded, swearing under his breath that he would most definitely begin his diet tomorrow.

"Angel! Open up," Jarrod yelled as he continued pounding on the door.

"Hold on!" screamed Ava from behind the door as she was opening it. "What's going on? Jarrod, why are you freaking out?" She tried to wipe the sleep from her eyes. After placing her glasses on, her eyes fixed on the wheezing security guard. "What's going on?"

"Where's Angel?" he asked, worry strengthening his voice.

"I don't know. I…I was sleeping. She said she was going to take a shower. That's the last time I saw her." She quickly looked at the clock on the wall and realized Angel should have been back from her shower awhile ago. "Jarrod, what's happened?"

"She was supposed to meet me outside the building to give me my cell phone. They found the phone on the ground, but she wasn't there."

"Is this the same girl who recently filed a report concerning a stalker situation?" the officer asked warily.

"Yes," said Jarrod.

The guard immediately picked up his transmitter and called in the information. Within minutes two more police officers were in the room taking down information, while others were immediately dispatched to search the entire vicinity, inside and out. The Gainesville Police Department was also called and notified of the situation.

An hour later Angel could not be found. Ava was crying, and Jarrod sat like a zombie staring into space while sitting on Angel's bed. He was holding her pajama top in his hands. In the hallway a ruckus had developed. All the girls were standing outside her door and down the hallway, trying to find out what had happened.

Jarrod looked at Ava and said, "Call Ileana." She wiped her nose and nodded as she picked up her cell and called her. Jarrod heard the words, but wasn't able to focus on what was being said. He only knew Ava was sobbing and telling Ileana to come right away.

Two officers from the Gainesville Police Department arrived shortly after a detective from the UFPD had shown up. They sat down with Jarrod and Ava and asked numerous questions. Many of them were answered by Detective Anderson of the UFPD, who had grabbed Angel's file and reviewed it before heading over. Suddenly Ileana rushed through the door, pushing aside an officer who was trying, but failing miserably, to keep her out.

"Let her in," said Jarrod. "She can help."

Ileana rushed to his side and said, "Jarrod, talk to me. Where's Angel?"

Jarrod told her what had happened as she began to cry. When she calmed down, introductions were made and immediately she was bombarded with questions. She told them everything she knew, holding absolutely nothing back. They were informed about the flowers, the pictures, and Benjamin Smith, as well as the phone calls, including the call where she spoke to the person in Spanish and heard a woman responding.

Suddenly, like light on glass, it dawned on him. Morgan. *Why didn't I think of her before?*, he thought. Angel had informed him of that call recently, yet the thought of Morgan somehow being involved had not entered his mind. Until now. He turned toward the officers and spoke loudly, instantly bringing silence to the room. "Morgan Billings."

"Morgan?" asked Ileana in a questioning, high-pitched tone. As she considered the idea, she turned away in a thoughtful manner. Slowly she raised her head, her tear-streaked eyes meeting with Jarrod's sad gaze, and let out a small whoosh of air she had not realized she had been holding.

"Morgan," she said bitterly.

"Who is Morgan Billings?" asked Detective Anderson as he wrote the name down on a notepad. He was an older man, probably close to approaching retirement, with a no-nonsense approach to his work. He appeared to be in his late fifties, had a belly indicating one too many beers in his lifetime and yellowish teeth denoting a bad smoking habit. He looked first at Ileana and then Jarrod, repeating his question once again. "Morgan Billings? Who is she?"

In a quavering voice, Ileana responded, "Angel's cousin."

They both went on to tell the detective of their individual personal histories and knowledge of Morgan. The officers who were present wrote everything down as well, while the detective asked interminable questions for the next three hours.

Ava went to get coffee. When she returned, she said softly, "Someone has to call her parents." They faced each other in dejection, neither one wanting to take on that task.

Chapter Thirty-Five

Angel opened her eyes to face more darkness. At least she thought her eyes were open, because she felt her eyelashes brush up against a smooth material every time she blinked. Why was she blindfolded? She wanted to ask someone, but something was covering her mouth and she couldn't move her lips. When she tried speaking, she was only able to formulate guttural sounds stemming from deep within her throat. She wanted to remove whatever was on her mouth, but her hands were tied behind her back. What was going on? Where was she? Who did this to her?

In her nervous agitation, she began to move back and forth in the chair she was obviously sitting in, but she was tied to that as well. Every time she moved, the chair went with her. She started to cry and scream, but she wasn't able to release anything more than loud, inarticulate grunts and sounds.

"Calm down." Angel turned her head abruptly in the direction from which that voice came. Who had said that? She made more indistinct grunting noises and frantically began to twist and turn, trying to loosen the ties around her body as panic set in.

"I said calm down," the voice commanded. She was crying and trying to shake the blindfold off, but it was on so tight, it wouldn't budge.

"You're only making it worse for yourself. You need to calm down. I'm here to help you." The voice spoke to her again and this time it sounded somewhat familiar. She grunted again.

"Listen to me. He won't hurt you anymore. I won't let him. That's why I took you. I'll never let him touch you again."

Who was he talking about? Nobody hurt her. This lunatic was the one hurting her. She was frightened beyond belief. Her throat felt like sandpaper, and she desperately needed water; her hands had gone numb, and the tingling sensation in them was quickly turning painful. She sensed he was getting closer. She could feel his body heat and then he touched her cheek as he tried to wipe away a tear. She moved her head as far from him as she could.

"Stop it!" she screamed out, or at least attempted to, because what came out was, "*Hmmmmm ghh!*"

She had never been so terrified or felt more helpless in her life. What did this person have planned for her? Was he the stalker? Was she soon to become another statistic? How much time did she have left? How would he do it? Would she never see her family and friends again? Oh God, what if she never saw Jarrod again? She needed him desperately now. He would make her feel safe. Her need to see him, to feel his strong arms around her, gave birth to another surge of desperate panic.

"*Hmmm mm!*" Although her grumble sounded the same as before, this time she was yelling, "Help me!" He placed his hand on her shoulder. She struggled to shake it off, but it only made him more determined to soothe her. She grunted her disapproval and continued to struggle to release herself, but it was no use. She couldn't do this by herself. She needed help. Perhaps if she stopped making these noises, he would take the gag off. She was so thirsty. She needed water. She couldn't stop crying and was beginning to hyperventilate. At the same time, she was beginning to feel nauseous. Dear Lord, what if she vomited and ended up choking to death on her own spew?

Calm down, calm down, she kept telling herself. She needed to slow her breathing down. Again and again, she took deep breaths through her nose, taking one breath every five seconds, and then released the air just as slowly. After what felt like an eternity, she was finally able to somewhat gain control of her breathing. Still feeling like a quivering mass of jelly, she tried to loosen her hands from the binding, but it was impossible. Although her hands were bound in the front rather than behind her, she still could not move, due to the binds that held her tightly to the chair. With only the tips of her fingers, she was able to feel the binding. Based on the texture and feel of it, she knew he had used duct tape to tie her wrists together.

She heard his footsteps as he walked away, then he came closer again. He did this two more times, and she realized he was pacing. Then he stopped. Turning her head slightly, she tried to hear something, anything, just to let her know where he stood. Ominous silence surrounded her like a deep, bone-chilling fog, paralyzing her with fear.

Interminable seconds passed before she heard the words, "I'm here" from across the room. "I just w-w-ant you to know I'm sorry. I didn't w-want it to be this way."

This was it. He was going to kill her now, and he was apologizing in advance. She began to grunt loudly again and move her body forward and backward, causing the chair to slightly tip over. He was at her side within seconds and steadied the chair for her.

"Shush…don't be scared. You're s-safe with me. It's him you need to worry about. I would never hurt you the way he d-did." Why did he keep saying someone had hurt her? That voice. She knew that voice. She was positive she'd heard it before. He was behind her now. *No, no, no, please don't shoot me in the back of the head*, she thought as she lowered her head, waiting to hear the "boom" of the gun going off. Yet the only sound she heard was the rapid, loud thumping of her heartbeat. Anger flared in her as she raised her head defiantly and grunted with fury.

"I can't understand you. Listen, if you're a g-good girl, I might consider taking the gag off. Will you be a good g-girl for me?"

Angel sniffled deeply and nodded her head. He leaned forward and gently touched her hair, pulling one side behind her shoulder. Stiffening at his touch, she could feel his face close to hers as he inhaled the smell of her freshly washed hair.

"Ummm...smells like f-flowers," he said as he took another long whiff. Her heart tumbled in her chest like wet sneakers in a dryer while a sudden wave of nausea rushed through her.

He gently began to remove the tape from her lips, and said, "If you scream, I will shoot you. D-do you understand?" She paused in fear and then nodded. He continued to remove the gag slowly. Once it was off completely, she began to lick her lips. He had to step away. Her lips were so beautiful and the licking motion was incredibly sensual. He pulled himself together and said, "R-remember what I said about screaming. I won't hesitate to pull the trigger if I need to." She nodded again.

He was suddenly aware and amazed by the unexpected and swift improvement in his speech. This had happened only once before. When he had finally summoned up the courage to move out of the house he had shared with his mother for over twenty-five years. Unfortunately, the reprieve didn't last long. The stammering returned with a vengeance at the most inappropriate time: during a job interview for a position he knew he was more than qualified for but did not get. When he returned home after the interview, a message had been left on his machine by the employer informing him that his "qualifications were strong, but someone else's were stronger." He was no fool. He had seen how uncomfortable the man had become as Benjamin struggled to speak. The truth was that that man didn't want to deal with someone who couldn't put two simple words together without breaking out in a sweat.

"I'm thirsty," she said hoarsely.

Her voice forcing him back to reality, he stepped away to get a bottle of water from one of the bags Morgan had brought.

He found it, twisted the cover off, and brought the bottle over to her, raising it slowly to her lips. She flinched when she felt the hard plastic against her lips and then realized what it was. He placed his hand on the bottom of her chin to gently lift her face so she could drink. She drank until the bottle was only half full and then pulled away slowly. "I'm good."

"Anything else I can g-get you? Are you hungry?"

She shook her head no. A few seconds of silence passed and then Angel said, "Who are you? What do you want with me?" She wasn't quite sure where he was at the moment, but she sensed he was nearby.

"I c-can't answer the first question for obvious reasons, but I can answer the second. I want you for many reasons. I want you because you're b-beautiful, kind, sweet, strong, and independent, but mostly simply because I love you…I've loved you from the moment I first l-laid eyes on you. I instantly knew that you and I were meant to be together. Y-you are the one I've always dreamed of. I'll love you always and now you can depend on me to protect you from him so he can't h-hurt you anymore."

When he stepped closer to her, he noticed she was listening intently for the sounds of his footsteps, because as he neared her, her body tensed in a manner reminiscent of a hunter sensing his prey within reach, except that he was the hunter and she was his prey.

"Who? Who won't be able to hurt me anymore?" she asked, tilting her head to the side in a questioning manner.

"Y-y-your asshole of a b-b-boyfriend, that's who." He was irritated with the question, she could tell.

"But he doesn't hurt me." He'd begun to pace again, and she was having a hard time following where he was.

"That's not true, and y-you don't have to be ashamed to admit it to me. It's not your f-fault that he's the way he is. He's too d-d-damn stupid to realize how lucky he was to have you. But I'm not stupid. I know how special you are, and I will t-treasure you forever."

Forever? How long was he planning to keep her with him?

"I don't know where you got your information, but my boyfriend is good to me. He would never hurt me...where the hell are we?" she demanded.

"Somewhere safe from him." He slowly walked away from her and then returned.

"I told you that he—" she began, and then he placed the gag over her mouth again, quickly silencing her.

A cell phone rang, and Angel's head turned abruptly toward the sound of it. It continued to ring, finally being answered on the fourth ring. She listened intently, trying to hear something that would give her a clue as to whom this man was, what reason he had for kidnapping her, and what plans he had in store for her.

"Hello?"

"It's me," said Morgan.

"Yes, I know," Benjamin said.

"Do you have her?"

"Yes."

"You haven't hurt her, have you?" she asked nervously.

"Of course not," he said, sounding offended.

"Good. I don't want her hurt, do you understand?"

"I understand completely."

"You sound different."

"Do I really?"

"Yes, you do," Morgan said suspiciously. "Alright, just stick to the plan and everything will turn out fine. Lay low for a few days and then release her. I'll tell John and Nate you had some family emergency to tend to and had to go home for a few days."

"That's fine. Whatever."

"Are you in the room with her right now?"

"Yes."

"Step out of the room so she can't hear you," she commanded.

"Just a m-moment, please," he said as he walked over to Angel and softly stroked her cheek. She stiffened and tried to turn away, but his hand grabbed her chin and forced it back. He held her chin hard and said with intense force, "D-don't you ever turn away from my touch. D-do you understand? Do you?" he screamed. She nodded hesitantly, and the tears began to flow again. "Good girl. I'll be back in a s-second. Try not to miss me too much, alright?"

He stepped away and walked out the door. "You were saying, Morgan?"

"I told you not to mention my name," she yelled.

"Quit w-worrying. I'm already outside. She can't hear a word." He lit a cigarette and took a deep drag, exhaling with profound relief. He hadn't had a cigarette in months. Not that he hadn't wanted one every minute of every day since he decided to quit; but he wanted to have control over something in his life, and he believed that by giving them up, it would be a start. Things were different now. He had more control over his life than ever before. Better yet, he had control over two lives. If that didn't merit a cigarette, nothing would.

"Why aren't you stuttering as much as you normally do?" she asked.

"Excuse me?" he asked.

"You usually stutter a lot when you speak. You're not doing that now. Why?"

"Praise the Lord! It's a m-miracle! Hallelujah!" Amazing what having control over one's life, choices, and decisions will do. He had the power now. No more taking orders; now it was his time to give them. He took another deep, gratifying drag.

"Stop it," she yelled. "Something's up. You're making me nervous."

"I don't have all day, so could you hurry this up, p-please," he said, becoming impatient.

"I heard what you said to her before about not turning away from your touch. Did you say that just to scare her?"

"I mean everything I say, Morgan."

"Benjamin, you can't hurt her. Please don't touch her again. Remember that the only reason we're doing this is to scare her away."

"That's the only reason you're d-doing it. I happen to have other reasons."

"Benjamin, no. Please. I'm begging you. Please don't hurt her. I mean it," she wailed. "She's my cousin. I lied to you. I'm sorry. I made a huge mistake. You have to let her go now. Please. She'll never know who was involved. If you and I don't say anything, it'll be like it never happened. Please, Benjamin, let her go now."

"Please don't bother us again, Morgan. Your b-beautiful cousin and I are going to be busy for a long while." He hung up, removed the battery and SIM card from the phone, and placed everything in his pocket. He would discard them later.

Morgan stared at the phone for a long while before hanging it up herself. What had she done? It wasn't supposed to turn out this way. A tear fell from her eye, and she wiped it away with her fingertips. She stopped to stare at the unfamiliar wetness. She hadn't cried, really cried, heartfelt tears in years.

What was she going to do now? She had created the problem, but had lost complete control. If she went to the police, she would be arrested. But if she didn't, God only knows what Benjamin would do to Angelise. Could she live with that? True, she never cared for her cousin, but nonetheless she was family. Never mind family, she was a human being. Could Morgan stand by and allow her to be hurt or perhaps even killed without doing something to prevent it? Oh, but she didn't want to go to jail. She had such plans. That's why all of this was done in the first place. What about her dreams and goals? Angel's interference was getting in the way, so she had no choice but to make the problem disappear.

What had happened to Benjamin? Where was the tense, anxious, tiresome geek she knew and hated? It was as if the old Benjamin no longer existed and was replaced with this newly confident, self-assured, evil being. How was that even possible?

"We're leaving," the man said as he came back into the room. He shut the door, and she could hear him grabbing bags and placing them near the door.

"Hmmm?" she asked. *Where?*

"Can't understand you...," he said in a bored, monotonous tone.

"Bastard! Then take the damn gag off, and you'll be able to understand me, you stupid idiot." Of course, what he heard was a much different interpretation of that.

"You sound angry," he said. "Be a good girl again, just l-like before, okay?" He waited for her to calm down and then continued with, "We're going somewhere different. We need to leave this place. Now."

She turned away from him and thought that maybe she could find a way to escape. He would have to untie her from the chair. She could make a run for it and scream, or rather, grunt at the top of her lungs for as long as she was able. Someone would be bound to notice.

"You've become quiet all of a sudden." He began his pacing again. "Y-you're thinking that maybe you can escape from my evil clutches during our departure, aren't you?" Silence. "Angelise? Angelise, I'm speaking to you. It's not p-polite to not respond when someone s-speaks to you." Still more silence. "No response, eh? Well, then I'll just have to assume that was w-what you were thinking. But let me just set your thoughts to r-right. No, you will not have the opportunity to run. Do you know why?"

Angelise began to cry again. All that could be heard was a soft whimper.

"I'll tell you why..." He leaned his face so close to hers that she could feel and smell his warm, rancid breath upon her as he whispered, "Because I'll g-get you out the same way I got you in." Suddenly Angelise felt that now-too-familiar shock pulsate through her, and then her body went limp.

Chapter Thirty-Six

"I can't just sit here doing nothing," said Jarrod as he stood up abruptly and went to the window, pulling the curtains aside to look out into the dark night.

"Jarrod, the police are handling things," Ileana said. "There's nothing we can do but sit and wait. I'm going crazy too." She placed her hand on his shoulder.

"I know. I'm sorry. I know this is hard on you too." He turned and upon seeing how utterly distraught she was, he placed his arms around her as she wept. He lowered his head, pressing it against hers, and felt the dampness of his own tears as they softly fell into her hair.

They were waiting for Angel's parents, who had been notified of her disappearance and were on their way. Ava had reserved a room for Mr. and Mrs. Skyler at a local hotel and that was where Jarrod and Ileana were as they awaited their arrival. The police had their phone numbers and knew of their location, so if anything new came up, they would be informed immediately.

There was a soft knock on the door. Ileana stepped away from Jarrod and looked at him sadly. She wiped away her tears, took a deep breath, and walked over to the door. Before opening it, she turned to Jarrod and said, "Are you ready?" He simply nodded.

She opened the door, trying to be strong, but the minute she looked at Mr. and Mrs. Skyler and saw the pain and worry etched in their faces, she dropped her guise and began to cry again. Mrs. Skyler dropped her bag and pulled Ileana into a tight embrace. The two women remained that way for awhile. Jarrod stepped forward and went directly to Mr. Skyler. He offered his hand and said, "Mr. Skyler, I'm Jarrod Wentworth."

Looking sullen and defeated, Willie Skyler shook Jarrod's hand firmly and responded, "Glad to meet you. Just wish it would have been under better circumstances. This is my wife, Laura."

Laura gently separated herself from Ileana and hugged Jarrod tightly. He was a bit stunned, but once past that, he let the comfort of her arms and the warmth of her maternal embrace wrap around him like a warm blanket on a cold winter night. He lost any fragment of control over his emotions and just let the tears flow. In this moment of absolute despair, two strangers found comfort in each other's arms.

In the meantime, after Ileana had greeted Mr. Skyler in much the same fashion, she took his hand and led him to a sofa. They sat and waited for Jarrod to lead Laura to the armchair on the opposite side. Willie leaned forward, grasping his hands together and said, "Tell me everything."

For the next hour, Ileana and Jarrod told Angel's parents everything, as they had to the police earlier that evening. Both parents shared looks of shock, dismay, gloom, and terror, running the gamut of emotions.

Jarrod's phone rang and all four present stood up at the same time. In his nervous excitement, he dropped the phone, immediately bent to retrieve it, and dropped it again. Ileana rushed to his side, grabbed the phone off the floor, and handed it to him.

"Hello?"

"Hi. It's Ava."

"Hey," he said, disappointed. She took no offense, knowing he must have thought it was the police.

"I'm sorry for calling. I know you were hoping it was the police. Have you heard anything yet?"

"No. Nothing yet."

"Will you call me when you do?"

"Yeah," he replied.

"I just wanted to let you know that a large group of students are putting together some flyers and posters with Angel's picture and information on it. They'll be distributed and hung up all around campus and the city by tomorrow morning...I mean, this morning."

"Thanks, Ava. We appreciate anything anyone can do. Thanks for all your help."

"Of course. You know I love her too."

"We know. Thanks again. I'll call you when I hear something."

"Okay. Bye."

After sitting in near silence for over an hour, Jarrod could no longer take it and abruptly stood up and informed them he was going to the police station.

"I'll go with you," Willie said. "I can't stand sitting here anymore." They both left the hotel room, leaving Ileana and Laura to sit, wait, and pray.

For the last four hours, Morgan sat alone in the car she had borrowed from John earlier that day. The car was parked approximately a block away from Angel's dorm and had a perfect view of all that was transpiring there. She had seen Jarrod and Ileana depart in the company of three police officers; had watched as dozens of students congregated, forming a large crowd milling around the building; and had sat by as patrol cars arrived and left at irregular intervals.

She was terrified and confused, not knowing what she should do. At times she felt like giving up, rushing up to one of the police officers, and saying, "I did it. It's my fault. I know where she is!" But then the sickening fear would settle into the pit of her stomach once again, causing her to shake uncontrollably and triggering her inner cowardice to make its vile appearance.

She stared at her cell phone and began to dial. Then she hung up. She threw her head back and allowed the tears that had forsaken her for years to flow. She picked up the phone again, dialing the number of the only person she knew who would not abandon her at this critical point in her life. The only person who ceaselessly loved her unconditionally, even though she had treated her poorly ad infinitum.

"Hello?"

"Mom," Morgan whispered into the phone between sobs.

"Sweetie, what's the matter?" Helen responded worriedly.

"I've done…something horrible. I…I…"

"Morgan, what's going on? What have you done?" Helen knew this moment was coming. Call it mother's intuition or call it a sixth sense, but she knew beyond any doubt that her daughter had been up to no good and that whatever it was she had done, she would now pay dearly. "What's happened?"

"You're going to hate me forever…and I deserve it. I hate myself for what I've done," Morgan cried out.

"Tell me now. Perhaps it's not as bad as you're making it sound." Helen tried to remain as calm as possible, all the while praying that the words she had just said were true and not just vacuous words of comfort. She began to pace back and forth in her nervous angst.

"It's worse…it's terrible…I don't know what to do. Mom, you have to help me. Please!"

"Morgan! You're scaring me," Helen cried. So much for trying to remain calm. Based on her daughter's hysterics, whatever Morgan had done was nothing less than horrendous.

"I…I…had Angelise…I had Angelise…"

"What about Angel?" her mother asked with dread and an ache in her heart.

"I had Angelise kidnapped," Morgan cried out between sobs and gasps.

Time stood still for Helen. It was as if all the planets and their respective moons in the entire spectrum of the universe were brought to an abrupt and final standstill.

"Mom? Mom? " Morgan said. "Mom, are you there? Please say something."

"I'm here," Helen responded in a trancelike state. *This couldn't be happening*, she thought. This was all just a horrible nightmare, and once she woke up, everything would be back to normal. Yes, that was it. It was just a bad dream.

But, it wasn't. It was reality.

"What do I do?" asked Morgan in tears.

"How…how could you do something so evil?" Helen cried. "I don't understand. I don't understand how you could have… where is she? Who has her? What have you done?" She was sobbing wildly now. She rubbed her chest as though she could ease the pain in her heart, which ached with fear, sadness, disappointment, and demoralization.

"Mom, I'm sorry. I'm so sorry. I don't know what to do. I convinced someone to take her. One of my roommates. He's crazy, and now I'm scared he might hurt her. I think…I'm pretty sure he will." She wiped her nose and tears with a napkin she found in the glove compartment and took a deep breath. "I'm so sorry for everything. For what I did to Angelise, and for what I've put you through my entire life. I never deserved you. You were too good and I was…I am…nothing but…" She suddenly remembered what Alec had called her the day she had broken up with Jarrod. "I'm nothing more than a worthless piece of shit."

Helen, amidst a deluge of tears, was able to say, "You have to go to the police and turn yourself in. You have no choice."

"I'm scared," said Morgan desperately.

"You weren't scared when you planned all of this, were you? How scared do you think Angel feels right now?" She burst into tears again, wondering if Angel was even alive to feel afraid. She cried out as she fell to her knees and dropped the phone to the floor. "God, please...please don't let anything happen to Angel."

Nine hundred miles away, Morgan hung up the phone, slowly stepped out of the car, and deliberately dropped to her knees as well. She implored God to help her and to forgive her for what she had done. She even begged for Angel's safe return. She kneeled on the hard pavement for awhile, ignoring the curious stares of passersby, some of whom were concerned enough to ask if she needed any assistance. She morosely shook her head and motioned with her hand for them to go. *I don't deserve help from anyone*, she thought.

A few minutes later, she suddenly felt the presence of someone standing beside her. She looked to her side and noted two black shoes. Not regular dress shoes, but heavy-duty, slip-resistant, leather-upper, tactical shoes. The type of shoes that cops wore.

"Excuse me, miss? Are you alright? Are you hurt? Someone informed me that you looked like you might need help."

She looked up at the officer standing above her, never blinking. She knew what she had to do. For the first time in her life, she would listen to her mother. She straightened up, pushing her shoulders back, lifting her head high, and took a deep breath.

"I know where Angelise Skyler is. I'm responsible for her disappearance."

Chapter Thirty-Seven

The University of Florida Police Department appeared nothing like any of the other run-of-the-mill police departments Jarrod had ever seen. Then again, up until recently he had never really stepped foot in one. He hadn't paid much attention to his surroundings the day he had accompanied Angel and Ileana here to report the original incidences. He found himself essentially noting the similarities and differences between the UFPD and the police stations he had seen on televisions shows such as *Blue Bloods* and reruns of *Monk*.

As he walked into the pristine white foyer, he immediately noticed the large brass lettering above the front desk that read "University of Florida Police Department." The walls were painted a neutral taupe, which imparted a soothing, relaxed feeling. Directly behind the front desk was a large state-of-the-art media room that could be viewed through a floor-to-ceiling glass wall. It housed several computers, security monitors, and additional high-tech equipment. To his left he noted a small room also viewable through a glass partition, with a sign on its door designating it as the private interview room. When he turned to his right, he saw Detective Anderson sitting behind his desk. The detective looked up and upon seeing Jarrod, came out to greet him. They shook hands, and Jarrod introduced him to Mr. Skyler.

"Mr. Skyler, I'm sorry about all of this," Detective Anderson said. "I'm sure you and your wife must be going crazy with worry, but I assure you we are doing everything we possibly can, in conjunction with the Gainesville Police Department, to bring your daughter back to you safe and sound."

"Thank you. We appreciate it. Can you update us on the situation?" Willie asked.

"As of now, unfortunately, we don't have much news. We've run a local check on Ms. Billings to see if we can get an address, but so far we haven't come up with anything. According to Mr. Wentworth..."

"Just call me Jarrod"

The detective nodded and continued. "According to Jarrod, she's from New Jersey, so the Gainesville PD is currently trying to see if they can obtain information from the NCIC—"

"What is the NCIC?" interrupted Willie.

"NCIC stands for National Crime Information Center and is a computerized index of criminal justice information. It's available for federal, state, and local law enforcement. It supplies us with information pertaining to criminal record history and assists us in apprehending fugitives and locating missing persons. If Ms. Billings is newly arrived in Gainesville, she may not have set up a change of address yet or hasn't made arrangements to have her utility bills sent to her home in her name. This sometimes is the case when there are numerous people living in one home.

"Mr. Went—Jarrod—mentioned she may be out here living with a friend, so it's possible this may be the situation we are dealing with. Either way, the NCIC should help us in obtaining an address. It's important for you to remember that we don't know for a fact she was in any way involved, so if we do find her, we can't apprehend her at this point. She would have to come in on her own volition, unless we suddenly find evidence that would implicate her. If she doesn't agree to do so, we'll have officers follow her to make sure she doesn't leave town while we look for evidence of her involvement. Once again, we don't have any concrete proof. All we have right now are the intuitive feelings of her involvement based on the past history shared between Ms. Billings, Mr. Wentworth, and Ms. Mendez. It's definitely enough for us to look into, but—"

Willie interrupted by saying, "Morgan's never been in trouble with the law, so this might just be a waste of time..."

"No harm in trying. We're not going to leave any stone unturned, so to speak, in our investigation."

"Excuse me, Detective," interrupted the officer behind the front desk. "I think you might want to take this call."

"Who is it?" asked the detective as he turned to face the officer.

"His name is John Masterson. He saw one of the posters in town and he says that he may have pertinent information regarding the Skyler case."

"Patch it through to my office," he said. He motioned for Jarrod and Willie to follow him in, but requested they remain silent during the call and not to get their hopes up. He quickly explained that many times, people just want to be involved somehow in a case, or are looking for information they're not getting from the media.

"You also get your idiots who get their kicks out of making calls and having the cops run around like chickens without heads." Jarrod and Willie agreed to remain silent and then the detective answered the call after pressing the speaker button.

"This is Detective Anderson. I hear you have information regarding the disappearance of Ms. Angelise Skyler."

"Yes, sir, I do. My name is John Masterson. I wasn't sure whether to call the Gainesville PD or you, but since this was the number listed on the flyer, I decided to try it first." I have a roommate that I believe may be involved in her disappearance.

"Why do you believe that?"

"He's a strange man. Weird, to be honest. The other day, our house was empty, and since I've always been curious about him, I took advantage of the opportunity and snuck into his room. I found that he has pictures of the missing girl plastered all over his walls. Tons of them. I tried to see what else he might have, but didn't get much of a chance, because I heard him walk into the house, so I snuck out of his room right away."

"How do you know that the pictures are of Ms. Skyler? Have you ever met her?" the detective asked while scribbling information down on a piece of paper.

"No, sir. I saw one of the flyers that are all over the city, and I recognized her immediately. She's got a face that's pretty hard to forget. The girl is drop-dead gorgeous," said John. Jarrod felt a sudden prickling of jealousy at hearing those last words, but immediately quelled them. There were more important issues at hand.

"What is your roommate's name?"

"Benjamin Langdon," replied John.

"Is he home now?" asked the detective.

"I don't know, sir. I'm not home right now. I'm calling from my cell. As soon as I saw the flyer, I called. You should also know that I have two other roommates. I tried calling them both on their cell phones earlier today, but neither one answered. They might be home now, but I'm not sure."

"Give me your address, please," requested Detective Anderson.

"Five Fifty Thirteenth Street, Alachua."

The detective immediately wrote down the address and additional information. Motioning for the officer behind the front desk to come in, he not too subtly threw a small notebook at the glass window to get his attention. When the officer approached him, Detective Anderson covered the mouthpiece of the phone with his hand and quickly instructed him to dispatch two cruisers to the location written on the slip of paper. The officer nodded and looked at the paper as he was leaving the office. Below the address was written "Benjamin Langdon. Have GPD run check with NCIC. Possibly A&D. Look for girl. Two additional people live in house. Careful."

"Detective Anderson?" said John, regaining the detective's attention.

"Yes?"

"Be careful. Like I said, the guy is sort of nuts. To be honest, I always figured he was basically harmless, but I'm pretty sure now that he's not. I have a gut feeling, based on what I saw in his room and after seeing the posters all over town, that he's involved somehow in this."

"Thank you, Mr. Masterson. I strongly suggest that you not go home and ask that you come straight to the UFPD so we can take a written statement."

"I will, but it may take awhile for me to get there. I lent my car to one of my roommates, and like I mentioned before, she hasn't answered any of my calls. I'll have to take the bus to get there."

"Do your other roommates know about Mr. Langdon and the pictures in his room?"

"No. I didn't tell them. We barely see each other, since we all have different work schedules. Now that I think about it, I should have made a point to do so. One of them is a woman. I could kick myself in the ass for not saying something to her. She could have been hurt as well."

"You say you've been calling them, but they aren't answering. Do you have any idea where they might be at this moment?"

"Nate should be getting off work right about now, so there's a possibility he'll be home shortly, unless he plans to go somewhere else first. As far as Morgan goes, I have no idea."

Both Jarrod and Willie stood up at the mention of Morgan's name. Jarrod quickly wrote "Last name?" on a piece of paper, Detective Anderson nodded his head and asked John the question.

"Billings. Her name is Morgan Billings, and my other roommate's name is Nathan Daniels."

Jarrod was attempting to write something down again, but the detective was already aware of the connection, based on his earlier conversation with Jarrod.

"Keep trying to call Ms. Billings and ask her to stay where she is. Just tell her you need to meet with her right away because you need the car. Make something up. Then call us back right away with her location."

"Why? Why just Morgan?" asked John nervously.

"We have reason to believe she may also be involved in Ms. Skyler's disappearance. I can't really say more than that right now. Just tell me where you are, and I'll have a cruiser pick you up," said the detective, inflecting a tone of authority.

"I'm outside the Homestead Diner in Gainesville. But sir, I'm sure Morgan isn't involved in any of this. She just moved here from New Jersey and doesn't really know anybody. There's no reason—"

"Mr. Masterson, she is Ms. Skyler's cousin, and we believe she came to Gainesville with a strong motive: to harm her cousin. Now, please, just stay at the diner, and I'll have someone there in ten minutes to pick you up. Oh, and Mr. Masterson?"

"Yes, sir?"

"Thank you. You've done the right thing."

"I hope so. I really hope it's not too late for the girl."

John hung up the phone and immediately began to dial Morgan's cell phone number. He waited for her to pick up, and when she didn't, he left her a voice-mail message saying he needed to speak with her right away and for her to please call him back as soon as possible. He hung up and sat down on the side of the steps that led into the diner, making sure to leave room for customers to come and go. Why would the police believe Morgan wanted to hurt her cousin?

He remembered how he'd been instantly attracted to the young, pretty girl when he'd met her at a party in New Jersey not so long ago. He had hoped she would call or e-mail him so that they could remain in contact, but she never did, until recently. He was happy when she did and bent over backward to convince his roommates—well, at least Nate—to let her stay. Benjamin never agreed or disagreed, so John took that as an affirmative response. And now here she was, living in the same house as he. He had hoped that by seeing each other on a daily basis, she might possibly consider giving him a shot. Now he thought of what Detective Anderson had said about her being involved in the abduction of the Skyler girl.

Boy, he had crashed and burned numerous times with a multitude of girls in the past. But this time he had not only crashed and burned; he had exploded into a massive ball of fire so gargantuan that it was visible from the planet Mars. He shook his head and tried calling her again while he patiently waited for the police cruiser to come pick him up.

As soon as the detective hung up, he quickly stood up and looked at Jarrod and Willie. "I know you won't want to hear this, but you have to either stay here or return to the hotel. You can't come with me."

"We can't just be expected to sit and wait," Jarrod said. "We have to do something."

"Right now the best thing you could do for Ms. Skyler is to sit back and let us handle things. I can't allow you to go, so don't bother to argue with me. We'd just be wasting precious time."

He left the two of them standing there alone while he rushed out the door, accompanied by two other officers. The atmosphere at the station was beginning to take on a frenzied mode. Officers were speaking to one another in hushed tones, while others were busy at their computers retrieving or entering pertinent data. Just as Jarrod and Willie sat back down in the detective's office, they noticed a big commotion occurring near the main entrance. Two officers entered ahead of someone who was being escorted into the precinct.

Jarrod stood up and walked out of the office to get a better view, but still wasn't able to see anything, because the person who was being led in was much shorter than the officers in the lead. One of the officers yelled to no one specific, "Someone get Detective Anderson!" as they brought this person into the private interview room. Willie now stood beside Jarrod, curiosity getting the best of him. Neither man was able to see past the mayhem as police officers were clamoring around them and inadvertently pushing Jarrod and Willie farther away from the furor.

Finally, when it cleared, Jarrod saw who was being led into the room. She was being told to sit down, and one side of the handcuffs she had on was removed and attached to a steel bar located on the edge of a table in the center of the room. One officer stood behind her, while another one stood to her side, motionless, his hands clasped in front of him. It was Morgan.

Jarrod ran toward the room and pushed open the door. One of the officers grabbed him. Morgan looked up to see his heated face and raging blue eyes. She immediately looked down and away, but that wouldn't stop Jarrod. As the officers were holding him back, Jarrod screamed, "What did you do to her? Where is she, you bitch? I swear I'll kill you if she's been hurt!"

Jarrod was removed forcefully from the room; four armed police officers were needed to subdue him. Willie stood outside the glass looking in. He glared at Morgan, who finally looked up and saw him standing there. This time she didn't look away. Tears were flowing down her cheeks, and she mouthed the words, "I'm sorry" to him. He never looked away. He would not grant her that mercy. He wanted her to witness all the pain and fear he was enduring, hoping that somehow, those emotions would transmogrify to her.

When she couldn't look at him anymore, she lowered her head and let her loose hair fall over her shoulder. A minute later she looked from the corner of her eye, peeking through the strands of her hair to see that he still stood there motionless. She turned her body completely away from him so that she would not be tempted to look again. She could no longer hear Jarrod's voice. She had heard him screaming vile, disgusting profanities at her for a long while, but suddenly there was silence. The two officers still stood their ground in the small room in which she was brought. Nobody spoke. All that could be heard were her sniffles.

She sat there in complete silence for a long while, wondering why no one had come in to question her yet. Her uncle was no longer standing at the glass window, and she wondered where he had gone, but knew no one would tell her if she were to ask, so she didn't even bother.

In the meantime Jarrod and Willie had been brought into a small conference room, where they impatiently awaited for news and for the return of Detective Anderson. Jarrod was secretly happy that the room they were in did not have windows, as did all the others. If he had to constantly see Morgan's face, there would be no way for him to control himself. As it was, he was dying to just rush into that room and strangle all the pertinent information out of her. He and Willie sat there in mute silence for what seemed like forever, both lost in their own personal thoughts.

Finally Detective Anderson arrived. He walked straight into his office, where a police officer joined him to update and apprise him of the new and relevant circumstances. After writing all the information down and giving the officer instructions, he asked that the officer bring Jarrod and Willie into his office.

When they entered the detective's office, he asked that they sit down. Jarrod and Willie looked at each other in apprehension and dread, but did as requested.

"Morgan Billings has turned herself in," he stated flatly.

Jarrod nodded and said, "We saw her being brought in. We had no idea she had turned herself in, though. Has she said anything? Do you know where Angel is?"

"She hasn't been interviewed yet."

"What do you mean, she hasn't been interviewed yet?" shouted Willie as he stood angrily. "She's been here for over two hours."

"I *was* the detective in charge of the case. Nobody could interview her but me, and I just returned from Langdon's house a few minutes ago," said Detective Anderson.

"*Was*? What do you mean by *was*? If you're not handling the case anymore, who is?" asked Willie.

"Detective Lieutenant Jerome Roberts of the Gainesville Police Department. I'm sorry, but as a detective of the UFPD, I can only investigate cases that take place on campus. The case has been led outside my jurisdiction. Only local or state police can handle it now."

"But Morgan's here," Jarrod said. "You're here. Why can't you just interview her and pass the information on to them? We're just wasting time, and we can't afford to do that."

"I understand how you feel. It's aggravating for me as well, but there's nothing I can do. I'm bound by the law. If it makes you feel any better, I will be assisting them in the investigation. Ms. Billings is being prepped for transfer to their precinct as we speak. I'll be heading over there myself as soon as I clear up a few matters here."

"Will you be able to sit in on the interview?" Jarrod asked. "You've been involved from the beginning. You know everything about the case."

"No. I'm sorry. The interview process has to be conducted solely by the detective handling the case. That would now be Detective Lieutenant Roberts, not me. Once again, it's beyond my control. I've already been instructed to have copies of everything we have regarding this case faxed over to him. Plus, as I mentioned before, I will be on hand twenty-four/seven for assistance."

"Can you at least tell us what happened when you went to John Masterson's house?" asked Willie. He was beyond frustrated and needed some answers now.

The detective explained that he, as well as two other UFPD officers, had arrived at the house in Alachua and found only one roommate present at the time, Nathan Daniels. Once he was able to get over the shock of his roommates' potential participation in the case, he was cooperative and led them directly to their rooms. Nothing of pertinent interest was found in either bedroom, aside from the pictures on the walls and a few other items in Langdon's room. His car was in the driveway, so he must have left in either a borrowed, stolen, or rental car. The Gainesville PD was notified. They arrived within minutes of the call and were now handling the case.

"I suggest you both head over to their precinct now," said the detective. "I'm sure Detective Lieutenant Roberts will want to speak to you both personally. If you like, I can have a cruiser bring you over."

"No. No thanks. We have a car," said Willie dejectedly. He didn't know how much more of this he could take. His daughter was being held captive by a madman, and all these people were worried about were policies and procedures. He and Jarrod stood up, shook hands with Detective Anderson, and thanked him for his help. As they left, Jarrod glanced over toward the interview room and noted it was now empty. He had never felt more helpless in all his life, and that was saying a lot, after the horrendous year he had just gone through.

Detective Anderson watched through his office window as they left, and then he slowly turned toward his desk and sat down. He pushed his chair back and leaned forward while lowering his head and placing it in both his hands. While rubbing his head furiously, he took a deep, resigned breath. When he raised his head again, he turned to look at the open file sitting on his desk. Disinclined, but nonetheless under exaction to cede to the infernal rules, he hesitantly closed it and mumbled, "Dammit."

Chapter Thirty-Eight

Less than half an hour later, Jarrod and Willie ascended the steps leading into the Gainesville Police Department. The building was no wider than a large house but appeared to be several stories high. The exterior, especially the front, was covered in gray, chipped cement, and the structure appeared old, a fact proven by a faded bronze sign near the entrance indicating it was originally built in 1919. It was obvious it was under much-needed renovation, as large scaffolding, gray tarps, and numerous workmen surrounded the eastern side of the building. The sound of hammering, drilling, and men calling out orders to one another cut through the cacophony of city traffic as the sluggish day began to break.

A far cry from the modern style and information technology services utilized by UFPD, the interior of the precinct lent more credence to the television shows Jarrod had used in comparison earlier that day. Two uniformed officers stood working behind a large dispatch area. To the left of it was a large staircase leading up to the second level. Practically all the furniture appeared to be made of dark discolored wood, and only the walls surrounding everything were of a light color. The banister was thick and ruddy, matching the steps, which creaked loudly as they carried the weight of those ascending and descending them. The chairs were of heavy, solid wood and must have been at least half a century old. Severely used, but in overall good condition, they would most likely make it to the three-quarter century mark if given the chance. The room was dark, even though the large windows were bare. Even the police officers seemed glummer.

"Can I help you?" asked one of the officers manning the desk as he lowered his glasses toward the tip of his nose while looking over them at the two gentlemen standing in front of him.

"Yes. My name is William Skyler, and I'm looking for Detective Lieutenant Jerome Roberts. I believe he is handling my daughter's case. Her name is Angelise Skyler, and she was abducted last night outside of her dorm." Willie inhaled deeply as he tried to soothe his raw nerves.

The officer turned to look at the female officer who had stopped entering information into the computer when she overheard Angel's name.

"I'll let him know you're here to see him," she said as she quickly jumped down from her stool and passed through a wooden gate that appeared to lead directly into a long hallway filled with offices.

"Why don't you take a seat over there until he comes," said the remaining officer as he pointed toward a small waiting area.

Jarrod and Willie nodded and quietly headed in that direction. They sat in the uncomfortable, but sturdy chairs as they waited.

A tall, muscularly built, dark-haired man who appeared to be in his mid to late forties approached them a short while later and asked Willie if he was William Skyler. Both Willie and Jarrod stood up and Willie responded, "Yes, I am. Are you Detective Lieutenant Roberts?"

"Yes." He stretched out his left hand to shake Willie's and then said, "It's a pleasure to meet you. I'm sorry for the circumstances you find yourself in, and I promise to do my best to recover your daughter safely."

"Thank you. I appreciate anything you can do. This is Jarrod Wentworth. He's my daughter's boyfriend, and I'm sure that he can supply you with any information you might need." Jarrod shook the detective's hand and after exchanging pleasantries, Detective Lieutenant Roberts asked for them to join him in his office. They followed him into the long hallway and entered the third office on the right. It was small, cluttered, but bright, with no dark wood to be found anywhere in his office. His desk was a double pedestal steel desk with a wood-grain laminate top that looked fairly new. Behind it and to the right stood a gray four-drawer steel, vertical file cabinet that had pictures of what Jarrod presumed to be the detective's young children taped to the side.

Additional framed pictures could be found on the right-hand corner of his desk beside the phone. The walls were painted a drab white, and the large, wide window that spanned the length of the office afforded a drab view of the building next to the station.

The detective stood behind his desk and motioned for them both to take the seats that were situated directly across from him. Once they did, he sat down as well. He folded his hands on his desk.

"Once again, please let me reiterate how sorry I am for you both as well as your families. I've spoken to Detective Anderson and he has been and will continue to be a tremendous help in trying to solve this case. Together we are going to do our best to find your daughter, Mr. Skyler. I won't rest until we have her back."

"Safe and sound?" asked Willie.

"I'll do my best," responded the detective. He would make no promises. He'd been at this long enough to know never to do that.

He pulled out a legal-size yellow notebook from the top middle drawer of his desk and pulled out a pen from the inside pocket of his jacket.

♦ Broken Road ♦

"I'll need to ask you a few questions. Detective Anderson has already supplied me with a copy of your statement, Mr. Wentworth—"

"Jarrod."

The detective looked up at him briefly, nodded and then continued. "Jarrod. I have an additional question I'm surprised was not asked when the statement was taken. Let me start by saying I do not mean to offend you by asking this question, but procedure requires that I do." Jarrod nodded and waited for him to ask. "From the time that you left Ms. Skyler's room for the evening and the time that you returned to retrieve your… uh…" He glanced down at the copy of the statement that Detective Anderson had sent him and then added, "Your…uh, cell phone, where were you?" He looked up from the file that lay before him on the desk and cast a quick, appraising glance at Jarrod.

Jarrod responded without any offense taken. "When I left, I stopped at the gas station across the street from her building and got twenty dollars worth of gas. I was there for about ten minutes, and after that I went directly back to my dorm."

"And where would that be?"

"Murphree Hall."

The detective nodded and wrote the information down. Willie was not as inclined as Jarrod to not take offense by the question and said, "Why are you asking Jarrod where he was? He had nothing to do with her abduction."

"It's alright, Mr. Skyler. He's just doing his job. I'm fine with it," said Jarrod.

"No, it's not fine. I don't want time wasted—"

The detective interrupted Willie by saying, "Mr. Skyler, as I said before, questions such as the one I just posed are basic protocol. Based on experience, no one is ever ruled out in a situation such as this. For me to do the best job that I possibly can, I need as much information as I can get my hands on."

"Detective, I have no problem whatsoever with you asking me these types of questions," Jarrod said. "In fact, feel free to follow up and check things out. I have nothing to hide. The only thing I ask is that whatever time or man power that is put into verifying what I've told you, you put the same amount of time and manpower into other possibilities or options. My girlfriend is out there right now, terrified and alone, possibly even hurt, and I don't want everyone wasting precious time verifying my whereabouts, when they can be putting their time and effort to better use in finding her."

The detective instinctively felt Jarrod was telling the truth, but unfortunately he had been wrong more than once in the past when relying on his instincts and he wasn't about to risk the life of young woman by doing so again. He would have one of his men look into it.

"Not to worry," the detective said. "We will look into all possibilities." Just then a police officer knocked on the detective's door and motioned for him to step out. He did as requested, closing the door behind him. A minute later, he returned and informed Jarrod and Willie that Morgan Billings was now in the interview room and that he needed to question her immediately. He also informed them that he might be tied up for awhile, so they should consider returning to their hotel, and he would contact them with any news and updates.

They refused, saying they preferred to stay and would wait in the reception area. Seeing that they were resolute in their decision, he offered them the use of his office. They thanked him, and the detective left the office, stopping first to speak to a plainclothed officer before continuing on to meet and question Morgan.

Morgan sat morosely in the chilly, dank room. An armed officer stood by the door with both his hands folded in front of him. He did not speak; he did not look at her. He stood there frozen and unyielding, staring directly at the wall in front of him. He reminded her of one of the sentries standing guard outside Buckingham Palace, minus the uniform and funny hat. She looked down at her lap and scowled at the sight of the orange jumpsuit she was forced to wear. Orange had never been her color. She could possibly get away with coral or apricot, but never orange.

Suddenly the door opened and a gentleman entered. Without saying a word, he motioned for Officer Gloom Face to leave, which he did.

As he sat across from Morgan, he pulled out a notebook and pen, as well as a tape recorder. All that separated them was a small wooden table made of solid oak. After pressing the Record button, he said, "My name is Detective Lieutenant Jerome Roberts of the Gainesville Police Department." He went on to state the day, date, and time before adding, "Please state your name."

Morgan softly said, "Morgan Billings."

"Please speak up," the detective said.

"Morgan Billings," she said louder, inadvertently leaning toward the recorder.

"Ms. Billings, you are here on your own volition. Is that correct?"

"Yes. I turned myself in."

"For what reason? Why have you turned yourself in?" he asked for the sole purpose of the recorder.

"I helped plan the kidnapping of my cousin, Angelise Skyler." She wiped away an errant tear.

"Where is Ms. Skyler now?" he asked.

She cleared her throat and whispered softly, "Shiny Star Motel off of Archer Road. Room 241."

As Detective Roberts wrote the address down, he said, "Once again, please speak up."

Nervously clearing her throat, she stated loudly, "Shiny Star Motel off of Archer Road. Room 241." Within seconds, the detective stood up and quickly rushed toward the door, grabbing his notebook, pen, and tape recorder. "I'll be back.

We're not done yet." Officer Gloom Face was immediately back at his post.

Soon after, two additional armed police officers entered the room. They instructed her to stand up and when she did, they placed handcuffs on her and escorted her out of the room and back to the holding cell.

Chapter Thirty-Nine

Angelise awoke in a panicky state. Her eyes were still covered, her mouth still gagged, her hands tied behind her back with rope that connected to her ankles, binding her so that she was incapable of defending or protecting herself. She was able to determine that she was either lying in the backseat of a car or in the trunk of one, based on the uneven motion she was feeling. Due to the position she was in, with her hands and feet bound, it was almost impossible to feel above for a trunk hood. Twisting and bending as much as she could, which was not an easy feat, she finally felt something hard above her. She was definitely in the trunk. Beginning to worry about running out of air, she stopped her movements, wanting to take some time to think and figure out how she could get out of this mess. Her thoughts kept bringing her back to the identity of her abductor. Make that plural: abductors. She was certain at least two people were involved in this kidnapping: the man who held her captive and the woman Ileana had spoken to on the phone. If this woman was not involved, then why was she breathing heavily, characteristic of the Stalker Dude, when Ileana had picked up?

Who were they and why two people? If it was just one person, then the stalker theory was plausible, but with a woman involved, it just didn't make any sense. What did she have against her? *Okay, enough of that*, she thought. First things first; she needed to find a way out of the trunk. How, though? Even if she were able to open the trunk, how would she be able to escape, with her being tied up tighter than a Thanksgiving turkey? By the time she was able to get herself into a position of jumping, the abductor would realize what she was up to and put a halt to the escape. And even if he didn't notice, she couldn't just jump out. She was blindfolded, so she'd have no idea what she might be hurtling herself into. What if she were to leap into oncoming traffic in the middle of a highway? She had to think of a way out. Think, think, think…

And then it dawned on her. She had once read an article in a magazine that said the safest thing to do, if one were to find oneself in that type of situation, is to kick out the back taillight. It could be done from the inside of a locked trunk, and then all she would have to do was stick her hand out the opening, and hopefully someone would see it and call 911. It was that simple. Well, at least the article made it seem so. Reality proved to be a different story. She wriggled, twisted, lifted herself, knocked her head four or five times on the top of the hood, lost about ten pounds in perspiration, turned herself around, and finally got herself into a very uncomfortable position to break the light. It took about ten attempts to do so, but she did. She kept waiting for the driver to stop the car to see what the ruckus was about, but he never did. He must have assumed she was just struggling to get loose. It was to be expected.

She lay in that extremely painful position for God knows how long. She was only able to get four fingers to stick out, and she kept wriggling them trying to attract someone's attention. It was obvious the author of the article hadn't ever been in the same exact circumstance that Angel now found herself in; otherwise the "jumping out of the trunk" theory may have been recommended instead. The pain was unbearable. She was feeling spasms in her back, and both her legs and her arms were so numb that if someone were to stab her with a thousand needles, she wouldn't feel a thing. She was fearful to move out of the agonizing position for the simple reason that she wasn't confident she'd be able to get back into it.

She wondered what time it was. It must be daylight by now. Even if she could turn herself around to look through the hole, she wouldn't be able to tell due to the damn blindfold. Someone must have noticed her disappearance by now. Jarrod was supposed to meet her to retrieve his cell phone. He would look into it. She just knew it. He must be so worried. She pictured his beautiful, handsome face smiling down at her, and she felt a sudden sense of peace. He loved her. He would do something to find her. She needed to hang on to that hope. It was enough to keep her fighting for her survival. She just needed to be strong enough to get through this so that in the end, he would be there waiting for her, waiting to hold her safely in his strong, powerful arms and kiss her, pushing her past the point of sensibility.

Suddenly the abductor must have driven either over a large pothole in the road or a small tree log, because the car jolted and bounced a hard jerk, jostling Angel out of position. She cried out in pain. Her body was terribly sore from being in that awkward position for so long, and the sudden hard bounce caused every muscle to scream out in agony. She allowed herself a few minutes to be in another position before attempting to get back into the old one. She could feel he had made a left turn and was now on a more remote road due to its bumpiness and winding feel. They must have been on a highway before. Good thing she didn't attempt the jump theory after all.

She was attempting to get back into position so she could place her hand back in the broken taillight, but found it much more difficult with all the turns he was making. Where was he taking her? She was almost at the point of giving up due to pain and exhaustion when suddenly he began to slow down. Angel stopped and wiggled her body away from the back light, hoping and praying he wouldn't notice it was broken. She felt him bring the car to a full stop, turn off the ignition, and then open and close the driver's side door. She listened for his footsteps to come closer, but they didn't.

He opened another door and she heard his footsteps as they faded away into another direction. A few minutes later, he repeated the entire process. He did this a total of three times before she heard him approach the trunk. He must have been carrying what she assumed to be supplies because she was almost certain she heard what sounded like the crinkling of paper bags. She began to recite the Lord's Prayer in her mind, over and over again.

The trunk suddenly opened, and she felt him bend over and pick her up, throwing her over his shoulder like a sack of potatoes. She moaned in protest, but he ignored her. He carried her about thirty feet and then began to climb one, two, three steps. Three steps that might possibly lead her to hell, if she wasn't already there. She needed to remember every little detail in case the information was to come in handy later. He tried readjusting her while he struggled to open what she presumed to be a screen door, based on the sound of the slam when it shut behind them. He walked another ten or fifteen feet before depositing her gently on a couch. She instinctively stretched out as much as she could. It hurt to do so, but her body begged for extension. She groaned from the pain.

"Sorry. I'm sure it was uncomfortable b-back there in the trunk, but I had to do it. I couldn't place you in the backseat and take a chance that you raise your body up into a sitting position. Imagine what the other m-motorists would have thought at seeing you sitting there b-blindfolded and gagged."

Grunting, writhing, and twisting so hard while trying to free herself, Angel fell on the floor with a loud thump.

"Now, now, Angelise. You need to stay calm. You m-might hurt yourself," he said as he came over and lifted her up, placing her on the couch again, this time in a sitting position.

Why did he call her Angelise? Nobody called her that except for the professors at school and her cousin, Morgan.

Morgan.

Oh my God! If she were able to open her eyes, they would have been wide enough to accommodate the entire Grand Canyon. But she couldn't. The damn blindfold was on so tight this time, she couldn't even open them to blink. Morgan? No. It couldn't be. No. Impossible. She wouldn't.

Or would she?

"Angelise, I need you to be a g-good little girl again, okay? Can you do that for me? Nod if you can."

She nodded nervously.

"Good. Now listen closely to what I'm about to t-tell you. I'm going to remove the gag and the blindfold, but I just want to f-f-forewarn you that even if you were to scream as much as you want and as loudly as you like, there is no one around that can h-help you. The closest neighbor or store is at least ten miles away. Even S-superman wouldn't be able to hear you from here."

Angel dropped her head a notch and then nodded slowly.

He began to gently and slowly remove the duct tape from her mouth. Even with all the care he took in removing it carefully, it still hurt dreadfully. She felt a slight pull on her lip, instantly knowing that he had taken a piece of it with the tape, and she cried out in pain.

"I'm so sorry," he said, sounding sincere. He noted the blood coming from her cut lip and ran somewhere, returning with a cool wet cloth. He placed it on her lip and kept it there a few moments. She was still crying, but not so much from the pain emanating from her lip. She was weeping because she wanted to go home. She wanted to be away from this monster. She wanted to see her family. And most of all, she wanted Jarrod desperately. She never felt such a frantic need for anything or anyone in her life. It was as if there were a big, gaping hole in her chest and no one could fill it but him.

"Stop crying. Please, stop c-crying. I'm sorry." He leaned over and kissed her on the cheek. She immediately turned her head away and let out a meek scream.

Anger flared in him. "What did I tell you about t-t-turning away from me? Didn't I tell you not to do that?" He walked away and began pacing in a strange motion. *Not back and forth, but circular*, she thought. "I d-don't want you to be afraid of me! I asked you to be a good girl and you said you w-would, didn't you? D-d-didn't you?" he screamed. She nodded obediently out of fear. "You've made me mad, Angelise. I d-don't like it when I feel this way."

She heard him pick something up from a nearby table or stand and throw it across the room. Whatever it was, it shattered into a million pieces. She stiffened in terror. He angrily grabbed her hair, pulled it so hard that her head was forced back, and bent down to kiss her on the lips. She automatically turned away in disgust and spat, not realizing what she had done. Suddenly, *bam*! Right across the left cheek. Feeling the awful force followed by the searing pain of the blow, she fell onto the hard floor and cried out in pain.

Benjamin looked at her as she lay on the floor crying. He hadn't planned on hurting her, but she needed to take him seriously. She needed to know who was boss. He was. He was the man; therefore, he was the one in charge. He was sick and tired of women ordering him around, telling him what to do. It began with little Odalys Sanchez in kindergarten and continued all the way through to his last crush in high school, Antoinette Simpson. And it wasn't any better at home. In fact, it was worse. His mother did it to him as well. Do this, don't do that! Eat this, don't eat that! Go here, don't go there! Orders, orders, and more orders! Nothing he ever did was good enough for her. If he brought home straight As and one B, he was chastised for bringing home that B. He was made to feel inadequate in everything.

She made a point of shaming him on a daily basis due to his lack of coordination, which caused him to fail miserably in athletics. She would beleaguer him miserably at his Little League games, yelling at him in front of the coaches, team, and their parents "to take one for the team."

He also remembered, in horrific clarity, that one execrable day when he was only eight years old, arriving home from school to find his wet bedsheet on display outside his bedroom window for the world to see. He had been mortified and teased by his classmates for months. Every day for over a year, he would be taunted during recess with a song that a group of kids had made up. They would chase him around the playground singing "Ben, Ben, the big dumbhead. He's a wittle baby, he wets the bed." When he told his mother what was happening, she laughed out loud and began singing the song to him at home.

Then there was Morgan. Thinking him the fool the whole time, believing he was incapable of getting the girl and keeping her for himself. He let her believe he couldn't do anything without her help, when in actuality he was more than capable. Hey, if she was willing to handle the tedious legwork for him, by all means, go ahead. Less work for him. But he'd love to see the look on her face when she realized that he took her plans and ran with them, literally.

As far as he was concerned, she managed and controlled Part A of the plan, and he processed and executed Plan B. She had the simple task of ordering flowers and having them delivered, capturing photos, making a few phone calls, and making hotel arrangements. He could have hired a secretary from a local temp agency to do what she did. Did she steal the car he and Angelise were now using? Did she find the cabin where they were hiding out? Did she purchase the stun gun and the nine-millimeter Glock he carried in the inside pocket of his jacket?

The answers to all those questions were unequivocally no. It wasn't easy, but he did it. He had to drain his savings account, but no matter. In the end he would have Angelise for himself and that made it all worthwhile. It was amazing what money could buy. Add a little more to the bundle and suddenly questions were not asked. For example, the purchase of the guns. True, he was forced to spend a few tense hours in the seedier, crime-infested part of town, but eventually he was rewarded for his patience by leaving with an untraceable, loaded Glock and stun gun.

The cabin was easy to obtain as well. He knew that a coworker owned a vacation cabin and was always looking to rent it out. Benjamin innocently inquired as to the location so he could check it out, and the owner was more than willing to supply him with that information as well as the keys so he could peruse the interior. It turned out to be quite nice. Warm and cozy. Perfect little hideaway. Naturally, he told his coworker,

"Thanks, but no thanks," and returned the keys. But not before making another set.

Stealing the car was a cinch. He watched a man run in for a cup of coffee at a local donut shop one morning on his way to his boring, mind-numbing job, and Benjamin just put a little excitement into his otherwise dreary, lackluster day by stealing his ride. The man should be thanking him for that favor and for a lesson learned. Never leave an unattended car running. He brought the car directly to Lorenzo's Detailing Shop, located one block from where he had purchased the gun three days earlier, and had the car stripped and painted a dull brown. Nothing too conspicuous. Lorenzo was even kind enough to throw in a set of Wisconsin license plates, free of charge.

Yes, Morgan would be shocked to see how much he'd done on his own. It would serve her right after ordering him around, telling him what to do and when to do it. He'd had enough, and finally he would have his chance to prove to everyone that he was and would remain captain at the helm of his ship. He wasn't about to allow anyone, including Angelise, to commandeer his vessel. There would be no mutiny aboard his ship. Ever.

He looked down at her as she lay bound and helpless on the floor. He picked her up and placed her on the couch again. She was shaking and crying. He whispered into her ear, "I hate that you m-made me do that. I don't want to have to hit you again. You're f-forcing me to be like him. Will you behave?"

"Yes," she said shakily.

"Good. Now, I'm going to remove the blindfold. It won't hurt." He struggled a bit loosening the knot, but was finally able to untie the silk scarf and gently removed it. She blinked many times, trying to clear her vision. She turned to look at him, but her vision was still blurred. She continued to squint and blink until she was able to make out his facial features. It was the man from the park.

"You're...you're the guy from the park. Benjamin?"

"Yes."

She swallowed hard. Her voice was hoarse with dryness.

"I'll get you some water." He walked over to the kitchen sink, filled a glass with water, and brought it to her. He forgot she was tied up and handed it to her, but she said, "I can't take it. My hands…," and she motioned with her head toward her bound hands.

"I forgot." He brought the glass to her quivering lips, and she gulped down the water so quickly he had to tell her to slow down. She did immediately. He was happy to see she obeyed him. Obviously she had learned her lesson. Hopefully he wouldn't have to give her another one.

"Are you hungry?" he asked. She nodded and then said, "My arms are sore." She hesitated and then continued, "Could you untie them for a bit? Just so I can stretch them out. Please?"

He was thinking about it. She could tell. He walked into the kitchen, where he started to take things out of some grocery bags, placing the items on the kitchen counter.

"I'll make you a sandwich first," he said. "Then I'll untie you. But don't get any ideas about escaping. Like I told you before, you're nowhere near finding help." He pulled out his gun from inside his jacket and showed it to her. "Besides, I'd hate to have to shoot you in the back." She gasped in fear, but nodded.

While he made the sandwich, she took advantage of the time to study her surroundings. It appeared to be a weekend lodge of some sort, based on the fact that it contained only the bare essentials. The living room had a sofa and matching loveseat with hand-knit afghans draped over them both. An old television set in the corner of the living room on a faux wood stand. On top of it was a DVD player with various movies stacked on it. There was no coffee table, only a stained, threadbare circular area rug that had seen better days.

Above the sofa hung a large landscape portrait framed in cheap wood, the kind a person finds at a garage sale or flea market. There were also two large windows, one situated on each side of the front door. Deer, bear, and moose decorated the outdoor-themed, heavy, green curtains that hung on thick, wooden rods above the windows. Angel began to wonder how long it would take for her to reach the door once he untied her. She estimated she could make it there in less than five seconds, but by the time she unlocked and opened it, he would be right on top of her. And then he would be angry.

She shifted her glance toward the kitchen, where Benjamin stood. It had plain wooden cabinets and an ancient oldfangled white refrigerator with a large silver handle reminiscent of the ones seen in old black and white movies. The stove was fairly new but cheap looking. A small black microwave nestled in the corner of the L-shaped counter. It reminded her of the one in her dorm room. Small, but practical.

The dining area was directly across from the kitchen. There wasn't much to it. It contained a small red and silver oval-shaped Formica table with four matching chairs, one placed on each side. Had the table been in better condition, it might be nice, being that retro fifties-style furniture was now the thing. There was no centerpiece, no paintings on the wall, no windows. Just a table and chairs.

To the right of the dining room was a door situated between that area and the living room. The door was closed. She assumed it was the bedroom.

The bathroom was to the left of the kitchen, but the door was not open wide enough for her to see in it. She wondered if there was a window in it. *Please let there be a window in it*, she thought. He would eventually have to let her go to the bathroom, and now that she thought about it, she did need to go.

"Benjamin?" she called out meekly. "Is that really your name?"

"Yes."

"I need to use the bathroom badly."

"I'm sure you do. It's been awhile."

"Please? I need to go now. I'm in pain."

With an exasperated sigh, he dropped the knife into the mayonnaise jar and came toward her, stopping directly in front of her. She prepared herself for his touch and secretly vowed not to flinch away. He bent down onto his haunches and said, "I'm warning you. Don't t-try to escape. You can pee in the bathroom, but you have to keep the door open the entire time. W-wide open."

Angel looked at him in shock. "I can't use the bathroom with you right there watching me. I need privacy. Please don't degrade me that way...," she said pleadingly as her eyes began to well up once again.

"I won't stand there w-watching you. I promise to have my back to you the whole time. But either you go with the d-door open or you can just pee in your pants. Rather a simple choice, d-don't you think?"

She agreed grudgingly, and he began to untie her. As soon as her hands were loose, she brought them forward and began to rub them together to ease the stiffness and numbness. Once they felt better, she moved to her shoulders while she turned her head in a slow circular motion to work out the kinks in her neck. While she was doing all this, Benjamin worked on removing the binding around her ankles. He was having trouble with the knot, and she was so desperate to get to the bathroom that she said, "Let me, please? I really need to get to the bathroom."

He nodded and stepped away while she brought her legs up onto the couch, bending at the knees and leaning forward to work on the knot. She was much quicker than he was. She jumped up so quickly from the couch that her body protested violently from the abrupt movement. She cried out in pain, but quickly recovered herself. Quickly glancing at the semi-open door near the kitchen, she turned to Benjamin and said, "Is that the bathroom?" He nodded and directed her to it with a simple pointing of his finger.

"Keep the d-door open," he reminded her.

"Turn away, please," she reminded him and he did. She could see his back the whole time. She quickly glanced around the bathroom, but did not see a window. She glanced quickly at Benjamin again and saw he was still facing the opposite direction. Although the bathroom appeared clean, she wasn't about to sit on the toilet seat, so she hovered over it in a squat position and leaned to the side a bit to reach over and gently pull the curtain aside to sneak a peek behind it. She hadn't gone to the bathroom in such a long while that her flow was still going strong, so he wouldn't question her delay. She pulled the curtain open a bit wider and saw there was indeed a small window.

She let go of the curtain and smiled. Her first smile in God knows how long. Her first smile since she'd said good-bye to Jarrod. The smile quickly faded as she accepted the reality of where she was and the situation she was in. She was done and took some toilet paper to wipe herself with. She pulled up her pants and turned to flush the toilet. She was washing her hands when she sensed he was near. She turned and found him standing in the doorway, his glasses on his head holding back his greasy, disheveled hair.

"I'm coming," she said.

"I hope you like b-bologna and cheese."

She nodded, although she absolutely detested bologna. At this point she realized that beggars can't be choosers and she was hungry enough to eat a dead man's toenails.

He placed the sandwich and drink on the small table. He pulled the chair out for her, and she looked at him hesitantly before sitting down. Angel tentatively picked up her sandwich and nervously took her first bite. After another bite, hunger took over, brandishing her trepidation aside like a hammer-wielding Thor. Eating as quickly as she could, practically shoving the sandwich down her throat, she swallowed and followed it with a long sip of the warm soda. Bologna had never tasted so good.

He wasn't eating. He just watched her while she ate. Neither one of them spoke. When she was done, she asked if she could stand up and walk around the room a bit. Her body ached and she needed the movement. He agreed as long as she kept her distance from the front door. He watched her assiduously as she roamed the room, keeping his hand firmly on the gun, which he had made a show of placing on the table. Finally she broke the silence.

"Why?" she asked.

"Why what?"

"Why did you kidnap me?"

"I guess you h-haven't looked in the mirror lately. You're beautiful," he said, smiling.

She blushed and said, "Normally I would thank a person for a compliment such as that. But I don't like you very much at this moment, so I don't feel the need to be polite."

"Feisty. I strongly suggest that you try very hard to r-rein that facet of your personality in a bit." He got his point across.

She sat down on the edge of the sofa and softly said, "I'm sorry."

"Good girl. I forgive you. You should go to sleep now. You've had a l-long day."

"I have more questions. Why aren't you stuttering as much as you did that day in the park? How do you even know me? Do you have a partner?"

He looked at her and said with authoritativeness, "No more questions."

"But—" she continued.

"*I said no more questions!*" he screamed. She recoiled and instinctively covered her face, which she could feel was now swollen in the cheek area from his last fit of temper.

"I'm sorry...I'm sorry," she said, keeping her face covered.

"Get in the bedroom!" he hollered. "N-now!"

No. No, please don't let him hurt me, she thought. She looked up pleadingly into his eyes, her own brimming with tears. "Please don't hurt me. I promise not to ask any more questions. Please, just please, don't hurt me."

"I'm not going to hurt you," he said, annoyed with her weak and constant apologies. "Just go to s-sleep."

"Where?" she asked, still shaking from his outburst.

"In the bedroom. Where else?" He noted her surprise and sudden eagerness to leave. He grinned at her and she wondered why. "I know what you're thinking, but you can f-forget it. The windows have been boarded up inside and out. You have no way to escape. Sleep t-tight."

She walked into the bedroom and closed the door, expecting him to yell at her for doing so, but he didn't. She pressed her ear to the door and heard clearly when he locked it from the outside. She turned on the lamp and quickly went to the windows to verify if what he had claimed was true. Well, he may be a kidnapper, but he certainly was no liar. They were double boarded and nailed solid into the frame. She tried pulling on them, but they wouldn't budge. She quickly looked around the room and checked the drawers of the dresser and night tables to see if she could find something—anything—she could use to pull the boards out. But there was nothing. She checked the closet, but again found nothing she could use.

On the bed laid clean clothes, undergarments, and toiletries. This crazy man thought of everything. But he might have missed something. There was no such thing as the perfect crime. Everyone slips up. She'd seen enough *CSI* shows to know that. She tried looking around again; this time she bent down to look under the bed and behind the dresser, but still came up with nothing.

Frustrated and frightened, Angel lay down on the bed, not even bothering to get under the covers. She had no idea what time it was. Whether it was day or night, she had no way of knowing. There was no clock in the bedroom, and she hadn't bothered to put on her watch after her shower last night. Or was it two days ago? Who knew? The only things she was certain of were that she never felt so alone in her life and that she desperately wanted and needed Jarrod.

Jarrod. The thought of never seeing him, hearing his voice, or feeling his soft touch again sent glacial shivers down her spine. She closed her eyes and felt the warm tears saturate the pillow under her head. She felt herself slipping away and welcomed the safety, warmth, and refuge she found there.

Chapter Forty

Jarrod had left the detective's office in search of the men's room. As he passed one of the desks where a plainclothed officer talked on the phone, he couldn't help but overhear a portion of the conversation. When the officer mentioned Angel's name, Jarrod froze. He noted he was writing what appeared to be an address, phone number, and some information on a piece of paper and carelessly and unintentionally left it where Jarrod could see it. Jarrod quickly scanned the information and then walked over to the watercooler, taking a cup, filling it, and then slowly drinking the cool water, all the while nonchalantly listening to the one-sided conversation.

He continued to listen as he looked around and noticed that Mr. Skyler was still in Detective Lieutenant Robert's office, pacing and talking on his cell phone. He seemed upset and was beginning to raise his voice to whomever he was speaking to. Jarrod couldn't clearly make out was being said, due to the fact that he was also trying to focus on the conversation that the officer was having regarding Angel; nonetheless, he sensed something was wrong. He saw Mr. Skyler hang up the phone and sit down angrily in one of the chairs.

Jarrod oscillated between staying where he was or returning to the detective's office, but the decision was made for him when the officer hung up the phone. Before entering, he knocked on the open door. Willie looked up and saw it was Jarrod and motioned for him to come in.

"Everything alright, sir?" Jarrod asked.

Willie gave Jarrod a worn-out, tentative smile and said, "I think with all we're going through, you can go ahead and call me Willie."

Jarrod simply nodded. He stood in the doorway, not wanting to intrude on his privacy. Sensing Willie felt the need to speak or vent, he waited for him to initiate the conversation. After a long pause, Willie took a deep breath and said, "I just got off the phone with Helen. Morgan's mother."

"That must have been hard."

"It was…it is…" He took another deep breath. "I feel torn. I know she had nothing to do with any of this, but I almost feel as if she did. If she hadn't spoiled Morgan the way she did — if she had only disciplined her once in awhile, just said no every now and then — maybe Morgan wouldn't have turned out the way she did."

He hesitated before going on while Jarrod took a quick glance behind him at the officer who had taken the call concerning Angel. The officer was on another call, and although Jarrod was anxious to speak with him about what he had overheard, Willie began to speak again, forcing him to abruptly turn away from looking at the officer and to face Willie.

"Helen is my wife's younger sister. They've always been close. She's a good woman that was burned big-time by her ass of a husband. She tried hard to be a good mother, maybe too hard. She gave up a lot so she could offer her daughter the best, a fact Morgan never appreciated. My niece always wanted more; no matter how much Helen gave her, it was just never enough. At one point Helen took on three jobs to support herself and Morgan, but my niece never gave a rat's ass. We tried to help out every now and then, but there was only so much we could do. We're not exactly rolling in the dough either, and with two kids, a mortgage, car payments…"

"You don't have to explain, sir. Both my parents work, and still they struggle to make ends meet. Um, did Mrs. Billings know what Morgan did? I mean, did she know about Morgan's involvement in Angel's disappearance?"

"Yes and no. She wasn't aware of what Morgan had been planning. If she had, I know she would have forewarned us. She loves her daughter, but she would never have allowed for Angel to be in any sort of danger. She loves Angel as if she had given birth to her herself." He looked out the window again and said, "If there was any way at all of preventing this, she wouldn't have hesitated to do so. Helen found out when Morgan called her and told her of her involvement right before turning herself in. Helen didn't even know she had done that. I told her."

"How is she?"

"Upset, to say the least. She's crying hysterically."

"Is she flying out to be with Morgan?"

"Next flight out."

Jarrod took a deep breath and glanced behind him again. The officer was no longer at his desk. A uniformed officer was standing beside it, sifting through the messages.

Jarrod frowned and said, "Excuse me a moment," as he walked out of the office and went straight to the desk. "Excuse me, Officer?" The officer's name tag indicated his name was Sergeant Powers. "Sergeant Powers?"

"Yes. Can I help you?"

"I was wondering if you could tell me where I can find the officer who was sitting here just a few moments ago."

"Detective Bradley?"

Jarrod simply shrugged and said, "I didn't catch his name. He was sitting here on the phone before."

"If he was sitting at this desk, it would be Detective Bradley. His shift is over. He's gone home. Is there anything I can do for you?"

Jarrod was disappointed to hear the detective had left. He looked down at his watch and noticed the time. God, it felt as though it had been forever since he'd last held Angel, kissed her, told her that he loved her. How did all of this come to be?

She was supposed to be in Bradenton, happily spending the weekend with her family, and he was supposed to be sitting in his dorm room drowning in his sorrows because he missed her so much. He was definitely not supposed to be sitting helplessly in a police precinct waiting for news on her safety. He lowered his head in anguish and began to rub his face again.

Sgt. Powers cleared his throat and repeated, "Is there anything I can help you with?"

"Sorry. Ummm…when Detective Bradley was here, I heard him speak on the phone to someone, and I saw him write down some information. I—"

"What is your name?" the sergeant said as he continued shuffling through the stack of papers.

"Jarrod Wentworth. My girlfriend is Angelise Skyler."

"The missing girl?" he asked flatly as he looked up.

"Yes."

Now giving his undivided attention to Jarrod, he said, "I'm sorry about the situation. But I can't pass any information on to you without speaking to Detective Lieutenant Roberts first. Detective Bradley would have told you the same thing. The only thing I can tell you is that we've been receiving a lot of calls with information and are checking out each and every one of them. Every call is being taken seriously."

"Any leads yet?"

"Not yet. Sorry. We've checked out a few, but unfortunately they've all turned out to be bogus calls. As you can see…" He pointed to a stack of loose sheets of paper with writing on each, "We've gotten a lot of calls regarding her case."

Jarrod nodded and saw that the sheet with the information Detective Bradley had written down was on top of all the others. Something about that call made Jarrod uneasy—sort of a gut feeling he had that that particular call wasn't bogus. He had heard the detective ask the person on the line, "You say you work with Langdon?" Jarrod needed to find out where Benjamin Langdon worked. He thanked Sergeant Powers and started heading back toward Detective Lieutenant Roberts's office when he noticed three police officers escorting a handcuffed Morgan toward the holding cell.

Jarrod quickly walked toward them and said to the officer in the lead, "Officer, my name is Jarrod Wentworth. I need to ask her something important."

"I'm sorry, but Ms. Billings is being taken to the holding cell in the back. She's being processed, and no one can speak to her now until Detective Lieutenant Roberts is done with her."

"What is it, Jarrod?" she asked.

The officer said, "No questions" as he started moving forward with her and the other officers in tow.

"Please wait. This is important," said Jarrod to the officer. "I just need to know where Benjamin Langdon works."

"I said no more—"

"Elite Enterprises. He works in the warehouse," Morgan said quickly and loudly.

"Ms. Billings," said the officer.

"I'm sorry," she said and then was led away with her three police escorts. As she passed Jarrod, she quickly said, "I'm so sorry for everything. I'll do whatever I can—"

"This way, Ms. Billings," said the officer again as he impatiently grabbed her by the elbow and began to pull her firmly away. She looked toward Detective Lieutenant Robert's office and stopped for a brief moment to look at her uncle, who was staring back at her through the open door. She was unable to wipe away her tears because her hands were bound together behind her, but she mouthed the words, "I'm sorry" and then was forced to continue past the office. He simply turned away from her.

Soon after, Detective Lieutenant Roberts entered the station and headed straight for his office. As the detective entered the office, he immediately sat down behind his desk. He motioned for Willie to sit and Jarrod as well, who had followed him and was now standing in the doorway. Sergeant Powers came in with the messages and informed him they were leads that were called in and that four of them had already been looked into and turned out to be false. The detective nodded and asked him to close the door on the way out.

"Let me update you on what's going on. As you may already know through Detective Anderson, we went to Langdon's house earlier today and found his other roommate, Nathan Daniels. There are a total of four people living there. He showed us into Langdon's room and you wouldn't believe the amount of pictures he had of your daughter," he said to Willie while shaking his head.

"It was like a shrine dedicated to her. We tore the room apart, but found nothing else. Fingerprints are being lifted, photographs are being taken, and items that could possibly be used as incriminating evidence have been seized." He hesitated for just a moment and then said, "I spoke briefly with Ms. Billings. As soon as she informed me where Ms. Skyler was, I left." Jarrod and Willie both stiffened and leaned forward at the same time. "She gave us the name of the motel, but when we got there, Langdon had already left with Ms. Skyler. We found a note, but nothing more. I also left men there and the same steps are being taken there as at the house. We checked with the owner of the motel, and he said that a woman had booked the room until Tuesday. Based on his description of her, I'm assuming it was Ms. Billings. That can be easily confirmed."

"What did the note say?" asked Willie.

The detective looked at him sadly and replied, "It said 'Follow us and she's as good as dead.'"

Willie turned his head away and covered his face with his hand. Jarrod heard the sound of a choked sob and placed his hand on his shoulder for support.

"Why was the room booked until Tuesday?" Jarrod asked as he tried valiantly to shake the fear that was tearing him up inside.

"I don't know yet. I'm going to continue questioning Ms. Billings in a few minutes and hopefully I'll get all the answers we need. In the meantime, I…uh…I understand how anxious the two of you must be, but I honestly think it might be best for you both to return to the hotel. There's nothing either one of you can do here. Mr. Skyler, I'm sure your wife must be desperate and in need of your support and comfort right now. I promise as soon as we find out anything, we'll let you know. Go back to the hotel and get some rest."

Both Jarrod and Willie looked at each other hesitantly and then finally agreed it would be the best thing. They shook hands with the detective, thanked him, and then walked out of his office.

Once they reached the main entrance, Jarrod turned around and saw Detective Lieutenant Roberts step out of his office and head down the long hall. The message taken by Detective Bradley just kept nagging at his mind. Acting on impulse, he quickly informed Willie he had left something in the detective's office and needed to go back to retrieve it. He also said he needed to take care of something important that could not wait and would meet him back at the hotel soon after he completed his task. Willie raised his brows in surprise, for he couldn't imagine what could be more important than the disappearance of his daughter, but he decided against prying and nodded. They parted ways, with Willie heading toward the lot where his car was parked.

Jarrod nonchalantly walked back toward the detective's office and immediately noticed that most of the police officers and detectives, with the exception of Detective Lieutenant Roberts, were convened in the communications room. This was his perfect opportunity to retrieve the information that was given to the detective earlier. He had been able to memorize the name of the caller, but did not have time to obtain the phone number. He casually walked toward his office and was able to slip in without being noticed. Quickly glancing out the door to make sure no one was watching, he swiftly grabbed the paper and wrote down the information on a blank slip he picked up from the corner of the desk. He placed the original back in its place and slipped his copy into his back pocket. As he turned around, he noticed an officer coming out of the communications room, heading directly toward him.

"Can I help you?" he asked in a firm voice. "What are you doing in Detective Lieutenant Robert's office?"

Jarrod hastily came up with the excuse that he had left his cell phone in there and did not want to disrupt the meeting taking place in the other room. The officer eyed him suspiciously and asked, "Where's your phone?"

"I have it now." He pulled it out of his front pocket to show him. The officer still wasn't sold and began to ask him another question when another officer interrupted them by saying, "What's going on, Galanti?"

Officer Galanti told him he had seen Jarrod walking into the detective's empty office and came out to find out what was going on.

"I had left my cell phone in his office. I just came back in to get it, and I saw that almost everyone was in a meeting." Jarrod motioned toward the windows of the communications room. "I knew it would only take a second to get it, and I didn't want to interrupt to ask permission to go in. I'm sorry if it's caused a problem."

"No…no problem at all. Galanti, it's fine. You just came on shift a little while ago, so you don't know. Detective Lieutenant Roberts had offered them the use of his office while he conducted the interview with the Billings girl. Go back into the meeting. I'll rejoin you in a minute."

"Yes, Captain," he said as he left, but not before giving Jarrod another suspicious once-over.

Jarrod thanked the captain and left. *That was close*, he thought. He ran down the steps and rushed toward the parking lot when suddenly he remembered he had no car. Damn. He had left it at the hotel, deciding to ride with Willie in his car. Well, it wasn't that far to the hotel, he tried to convince himself. He began to run fast and hard, as if his life depended on it. No, as if Angel's life depended on it, which was likely. Keeping that thought in mind, he continued to run, not allowing himself to feel the soreness in his still not fully recovered leg or the constricting pain in his chest from trying to take air into his lungs. He wouldn't permit his body to give up; he had never pushed it as hard as he did now, mainly because nothing had ever mattered as much as it did now.

He finally reached the hotel parking lot after an intense two-mile run. He saw that Willie's car was parked right next to his. If Jarrod had the strength to kick himself in the ass for not riding back with Willie, he would have. He slowed his run down to a jog and made it to his old, reliable Neon. He took a moment to catch his breath before unlocking the door and settling into the driver's seat. He made sure he was breathing at a normal rate before he began to dial the number on the paper. He listened as it rang once, twice, three times before it was picked up.

"Hello?"

"Hello. May I speak with…" He quickly glanced at the name on the paper in his hand. "Nick Scott?"

"I'm Nick Scott. Who are you?"

"This is Lieutenant Wentworth of the Gainesville Police Department. I'm calling because a message was left at the station that you have some information pertaining to the missing Skyler girl case." Jarrod detested the sound of his voice when forced to speak in such an uncaring, impervious manner.

"I do. I don't know how relevant it is, but I thought the police would want to know anything and everything that might somehow pertain to the case."

"We appreciate that," Jarrod said as he leaned over and took out a small notebook and pen from the glove compartment. "What can you tell me?"

"Well, Benjamin and I are coworkers—"

"Where do you work?" Jarrod asked in anticipation.

"Elite Enterprises on University Avenue."

Jarrod closed his eyes in relief. He had desperately hoped he would say that. "Go on."

"As I was saying, he and I work together. We're not buddies or anything even near that. To be honest, he doesn't have any friends at work. Real strange guy. Keeps to himself a lot…"

"Go on, Mr. Scott," Jarrod said, wanting him to get to the point, but not wanting to appear too anxious.

"Ummm…where was I?"

"You work together, but you're not friends and the guy is weird. What else? Is there anything more you can tell me?" Although he didn't want to seem unprofessional, he just didn't have the time or energy to squander on obtaining information he already had. Aside from a catnap here and there, he hadn't slept much in over twenty-four hours and was beginning to feel the effects.

"Yeah, there's more. About two weeks ago, I was having lunch with a group of friends in the lunchroom. Benjamin was sitting alone at a table next to us, and he overheard me telling my friends I was looking to rent out a small cabin that I own for weekend getaways and such."

Jarrod's eyes opened wide and his brows shot up in hope and eagerness.

"Where exactly is this cabin located?"

"Georgia," said Mr. Scott.

"Excuse me?"

"Georgia. Thomasville, Georgia."

Jarrod felt his stomach drop. He hadn't been living in Florida long enough to know how far or even how close Thomasville, Georgia, was to Gainesville, but he did know that Georgia was not right around the corner.

"He came over to the table and asked a few questions about the cabin. Mainly he wanted to know about its exact location. He asked how far it was from the nearest highway and town, and he also wanted to know how close the nearest neighbor was. He made it obvious he was looking for someplace secluded, out of the way. I answered all of his questions and he seemed really interested, but then he said he wanted to check it out first."

"Didn't you find it strange that he would be willing to drive so far just to check out a place for a weekend getaway?"

"It's not that far, really. I mean, a person can make the ride there in less than three hours. Plus, he said he was looking for a place to spend his two-week vacation this summer. I figured what the hell? I could make a good amount of money renting it out for two whole weeks."

"Did you take him to see it?"

"No, sir. Every time I picked a date, he said he was unavailable. Then he just asked if he could borrow the keys and check it out on his own. I didn't see what harm there would be in doing so. The guy seemed so harmless."

"So you just gave him the keys," said Jarrod.

"Yeah. I also charged him a hundred bucks just in case he decided to spend the night and told him that if he did, he would have to leave the place in the same condition he found it in. He agreed and gave me the money right there and then. He brought the keys back after the weekend and told me he wasn't interested in the cabin. I asked why, but he just shrugged and walked away. I told you, the guy is nuts."

"Could you please give me the information you gave him? I need the address and detailed directions to the cabin from here." Jarrod silently whispered a quick prayer that his car would make it to Thomasville without a problem.

"Sure. You have to get on 441 South, then…"

Nick Scott went on to give Jarrod all the information he needed. Jarrod thanked him and hung up. He immediately turned on the ignition and shot out of the parking lot, leaving skid marks in his wake. There was no time to waste. Not even to call Angel's parents or the police. He needed to get to her as soon as possible. He drove continuously at the same intense, demanding level, stopping only once to fill up with gas and to relieve himself. He hadn't eaten anything in as long as he hadn't slept, so he grabbed a ready-made sandwich and a couple of high-caffeinated energy drinks from the attached convenience store, paying for them as well as for the gas with the emergency credit card his father had given him when he had left New Jersey.

He placed the key in the ignition and turned it, but immediately noticed that even with a fully loaded tank of gas, his old, reliable Neon, was beginning to lose some of its reliability. It faltered, shook, and made a high-pitched sound that disappeared as quickly as it came.

"C'mon! Please don't fail me now! Not now." he screamed to the car. He turned the car off, leaned his head against the steering wheel, and said a silent prayer to God, pleading with him to let everything be alright. *Please let Angel be at the cabin unharmed and please let the car start again without any problems. Please…please…please.* He took a deep breath and wiped away the tears of anger, worry, and frustration that had formed.

He saw his phone on the passenger seat and decided he should call Angel's parents and tell them what he was doing. They in turn could contact Detective Lieutenant Roberts and inform him as well. That was one call he didn't want to make.

He knew he had been wrong to go out on his own without informing anyone, and he just didn't want to hear or deal with their diatribes. He picked up his phone and soon realized the battery was dead, not having been charged in days.

"Son of a bitch. What now? How much more do you want me to take?" he screamed toward heaven. "I can't handle much more!"

He was starting to feel sorry for himself. Why did everything have to be so damn hard? What did he ever do in his young life to deserve so much pain and sorrow? He was a good person. He always followed the rules, never hurt anyone intentionally, and treated everyone with respect. Why then? Why did his best friend have to die? Why did he have to be so badly injured in the same damn accident that claimed Dante's life that he was left not knowing if he'd ever be able to achieve the only goal he had ever set for himself?

And if he isn't able to play ball, what then? What was he supposed to do with his life? All he ever wanted was to play ball professionally. He worked his ass off all his life to attain that dream. For what? What was the point of all that hard work? So he can become a gym teacher in some blasted grammar school in New Jersey and watch kids play dodgeball all day long? And now the absolute worse had occurred. The only woman he had ever loved needed him desperately and here he sat, alone in a beaten-up car with a cell phone that was dead and useless. What more?

He repeatedly banged his head against the steering wheel in frustration and let the pent-up tears flow. He cried hard, releasing all the anger and bitterness and letting it flow out of his body until he was exhausted.

When he finally felt in control again, he leaned back and took a deep breath saying one last prayer before he tried starting the car again.

"Please, God, I'm begging you. Please let the car start and let me get to Angel in time. I love her. I need her…and she needs me right now. I have to get to her soon. Please don't take her away from me too. I can't handle anymore loss. Please."

He closed his eyes tightly, turned the key slowly, and whispered again, "Please. Please." The car started without a hitch. No shaking, no hesitation, no noise, nothing. The gentle roar of the engine was music to Jarrod's ears. He smiled serenely, looked up toward the heavens, and simply said, "Thank you."

He contemplated using a pay phone or going back into the convenience store and asking if he could use their phone to call Angel's parents, but he just didn't have the time to deal with that or the hassle of using his credit card to make the call. Besides, he was afraid he would be pushing his luck by turning off the car and risking the possibility he wouldn't be able to start it again. He needed to get to Angel as quickly as possible. He didn't know exactly what he was going to do once he got to the cabin, but he'd figure something out. He drove out of the lot, continuing to pray they would be at the cabin when he reached it and that Angel was alright.

He made it to Thomasville in record time, reaching it in just a little over two hours. He drove the entire time with all the windows open and the radio blasting in hopes of that keeping him awake and alert. His back, neck, and shoulders ached from the long, stressful drive, but it didn't matter. He knew in his heart he was close to Angel now. Nothing could stop him from getting to her. He wondered if that bastard had fed her. Was she cold? He could just imagine how frightened she must be. It tore at his heart to imagine the terror she must be enduring.

He quickly glanced down at the directions again and continued on the winding road he was on. The first thing he was going to do once Angel and he were back home safe and sound was invest in a GPS, he thought. He was forced to slow his speed down to only ten miles over the speed limit on this curving, dark road that had absolutely no street lighting. He could barely see two feet in front of him, and the fog that was unfolding was only making it worse. Based on the directions Nick Scott had given him, a narrow, hidden driveway that he would need to turn on to would soon be approaching. Supposedly the driveway was close to a quarter mile long. Jarrod would have to leave the car toward the bottom of the drive to avoid being seen.

"I'm coming, Angel," he whispered to himself. "Just hang on a little longer, baby."

Chapter Forty-One

Morgan sat patiently in the interview room again. She was informed that Detective Lieutenant Roberts would join her in a few minutes, but that had been close to half an hour ago. She looked toward the two-way mirror and wondered who was sitting in the room behind it, watching her squirm.

In the meantime Detective Lieutenant Roberts and Detective Anderson of the UFPD stood motionless, staring back at her.

"Do you think she'll cooperate?" asked Anderson.

"Yeah, I do," Roberts said. "I was with her for only a few minutes earlier today, and she immediately supplied me with the hideout location."

"Too damn bad they had already left."

"Yeah. Well, then it would have been too easy and we both know from experience it's never easy. Alright, let me get in there and do my job."

"Let me know if I can be of any help," Anderson said. "By the way I don't know if you've been informed yet, but her two other roommates, John Masterson and Nathan Daniels, are here and are currently giving their statements."

"Yeah, I know. Can you stick around a bit, or do you have to get back to your department right away?"

"You couldn't pry me away. I'm interested in knowing what the hell she has to say," responded Anderson solemnly. Detective Lieutenant Roberts nodded in acquiescence as he walked out of the room, closing the door behind him.

Upon entering the interview room, the detective motioned for the officer who was standing guard to leave them alone, as he had done earlier in the day. In fact, his entire routine was executed exactly as before. After sitting down across from Morgan, he pulled out his notebook and pen and pressed the Record button on the tape recorder.

"Sorry about the interruption earlier today, but I had a defenseless, terrified girl to rescue. You may have heard of her. Angelise Skyler. Sound familiar?"

"Is she alright?"

"She wasn't there. The motel room was empty," said Roberts matter-of-factly.

Morgan looked truly shocked. "I swear I didn't lie. I booked a room there for them until Tuesday—"

The detective held up a hand, stopping her mid-sentence. "Tuesday? Why Tuesday?"

Morgan drew in a deep breath. "The plan was for him to release her on the side of the road, any road, on Tuesday. I never wanted her to be hurt. I just wanted her to be scared enough to leave Gainesville and Jarrod. I figured a couple of days of being held hostage would do the trick."

"Jarrod? As in Jarrod Wentworth?"

"Yes. Jarrod is, I mean *was*, my boyfriend. He's now Angelise's boyfriend."

"Cousins sharing boyfriends? Now I've heard everything."

"Not by choice. He and I had broken up a few months ago, and when Angelise came to visit my mother and me in New Jersey, they met at a party and somehow hooked up here in Florida. Detective, I didn't lie to you about the motel. That's where they were supposed to be."

"I believe you. A note was left behind."

"What did it say?" she asked.

"Something to the effect that she would be killed if we were to pursue them."

Morgan let out an anguished sob. "I'm so sorry. If I could take everything back, I would. I don't know what to do…"

"You can supply us with as much information as you can. Make it easier for us to find them."

Wiping her nose with her sleeve, she said, "I'll tell you everything I know."

"Based on what little you've told me so far, I'm assuming you were the brainpower behind the whole abduction. Who took her? Give me a name," he boldly stated. He sat up straighter as he glared at her, making her wince.

"My roommate. Benjamin Langdon. But, Detective, I swear I didn't think he would hurt her. He might not. I just don't know anymore…""

Just answer the questions. Why did you plan your cousin's abduction?" he asked.

She began to sob hard while gasping for breath. He remained silent, allowing her time to calm down. It was taking a supreme force of will on his part not to grab her by the shoulders and shake her hard until she gave him all the information they needed. When he became a cop over twenty years ago, he felt as though he had hit the lottery — decent salary, great benefits, excellent pension plan, and early retirement. Little did he know that over the years he would become a hardened man from being exposed to and having to deal with such deep-seated malice and acerbity on a daily basis.

Between sobs she uttered, "I…I was blinded…I just wanted Jarrod. I just wanted to be with him so badly. I hated her for having…having him. I didn't know…what else…to do."

"So you approached your roommate with plans for him to kidnap her?" he asked.

"Not at first. I told him that…that she was a customer in the store where I work. I told him I had overheard her telling her friend that she liked him. I knew he…he wanted someone to like him. So bad that he would…he would do anything. He believed me."

"Because he wanted to believe you."

"I suppose," she said as she wiped her nose again.

"Then what?" Roberts asked.

"I took a picture of Angelise and showed it to him. He thought she was beautiful, so he kept asking for more."

"And you kept supplying them to him, ultimately feeding his hunger. How did you get the pictures?"

"I took them," she said quietly.

"You were following her?"

"Yes," she said, remorseful and shamefaced.

"Were you the one calling and sending her pictures, or was it him?" he asked sharply.

"I did everything," she admitted regretfully. "In the beginning he did nothing. As I brought him more pictures, he would just stay locked up in his room for hours on end staring at them."

"What about the flowers that were sent to Ms. Skyler?"

"Me."

"Was Langdon the man who approached her in the park? The man said his name was Benjamin, but gave a different last name."

"It was him," she said. At least they now had a name to go with the face, a face that Ms. Ileana Mendez would be able to identify.

"Do you have any idea where he may have taken Ms. Skyler?" he asked.

"No.

"Do you have any idea what car he's driving?" he asked.

"I would assume his," Morgan replied.

"Wrong assumption. His car is sitting idle in the driveway at your house."

Once again, she was stunned. Who would have thought Benjamin would ever be capable of thinking on his own? He obviously had his own personal agenda and had gone on to make plans and arrangements in furthering his involvement in the scheme.

"I don't know. I had John's car, so I know he wasn't able to use his. John is my other—"

"I know who John is. He's here."

"Why?" she asked. "Detective Roberts, John had absolutely nothing to do with any of this. Neither did Nate. It was just me and Benjamin, I swear. Why is John here?"

"It's not your time to ask questions. It's mine. So just answer whatever questions I throw at you, got it? Why and how did you convince him to kidnap her?"

"Things weren't moving fast enough for me. I kept trying to convince him to go up to her, but he wouldn't. I figured if she met him and saw how weird he is, she would put two and two together, and realize he was the one sending flowers and making the phone calls. He was her stalker. I thought maybe then she would be afraid and leave. But it didn't work out that way. Then he told me he finally followed her to the park one day and went right up to her and asked her all these questions, but nothing came of it. I got desperate so I lied and told him that her boyfriend was physically abusing her. I told him she needed his help and the only way he could do that was to take her away from him. I convinced him that if he took her and then released her in a day or so, she would be too afraid to stick around and would return home, far away from her boyfriend."

"Yeah, but far away from him as well. Didn't he ever ask you about that?"

"He didn't say anything until after he had already kidnapped her. To be honest, I was glad he hadn't. I don't know what I would have said. I probably would have just winged it. I seem to lie better when I don't think things through first. I'm a good spur-of-the-moment liar."

"You don't give yourself enough credit. You're a good liar, period," he said disgustingly. "What was it that he said to you after he kidnapped her that made you think that he might deviate from the plan? Did he mention where he might take her?"

"No. He never said anything about taking her somewhere else. He agreed to the plan. He was to release her on Tuesday. But when I spoke to him the other night..." She paused and looked at him.

"What?"

"I called him to make sure he was all set and wouldn't back out, and he said…"

"Said what?" Roberts said with growing impatience.

"He mentioned something about not wanting to give her up. He made it sound as if he might want to keep her."

"It seems as though he finally realized he needed to keep her close to him and not let her leave." Detective Lieutenant Roberts glared at her with such anger and disgust that she found herself cowering in her seat like a defenseless mouse forced into a corner by a big, fat house cat.

"And you didn't think to put a stop to the whole thing? Maybe fess up and contact the police? If you had contacted us right away, we may have been able to get to them while they were still at the motel. Oh wait, I'm sorry. I forgot. You're the one who wanted her out of the picture in the first place. Why would you give a damn if he raped, beat or even killed…"

He stopped. Just saying the words out loud made him sick. Nauseatingly sick. For the first time since he had sat down to speak with her, he showed signs of losing control. He leaned forward, placing both elbows on the table and began rubbing his face brusquely with both hands. Then he passed them roughly through his hair, returning to his face when done. Morgan sat quietly watching him. She knew better than to speak. Jarrod did the same thing whenever he grew frustrated or angry. It would not be a smart move to say anything right now. She would remain silent and hope it would pass soon.

After a minute or so, he pulled himself together and uttered, "What else? What else did Langdon say?"

"I heard him…umm…talking to her when he was on the phone with me. He threatened her."

"How? What exactly did he say?" Aside from being infuriated, he was overwrought with worry and concern for Ms. Skyler's safety.

"It wasn't so much what he said; it was how he said it. He told her never to turn away from his touch, but he said it angrily and I could sense he was threatening her. I told him not to hurt her and reminded him that the only reason we took her was so that she would be scared and leave Gainesville. I didn't want her to be injured in any way. But…but he said…"

Her hesitation worried the detective. He wasn't sure he wanted to hear what Langdon had said. Morgan continued by adding, "He said that may have been my reason, but it wasn't necessarily his. And then he told me to stop bothering him. That…" She began to weep softly again. She took a stabilizing breath, wiped her nose, and said, "He and Angelise were going to be busy. Oh God, Detective. I'm so sorry. I'm…so…sorry. I'll do anything, I swear, anything to help get her back safely."

The detective turned his head away from her because he couldn't stand to look at her any longer. He turned off the recorder, grabbed his notebook, and walked to the door. As he turned the handle to leave, he stopped a moment to look back at her.

"By the way, according to the law, you're just as guilty of the crime as Langdon is."

She simply nodded and whispered, "I figured."

Two hours after Nick Scott had hung up with Jarrod, alias Lieutenant Wentworth, his phone rang once again.

"Hello?"

"Hello. This is Detective Lieutenant Jerome Roberts of the Gainesville Police Department. I have a message that you called earlier today with information concerning Benjamin Langdon."

"Um…yes sir…but I already spoke to someone about that. He called a few hours ago," Scott said, perplexed.

"Hmm. That's strange. There's no note of it written here on the memo. Who did you speak with?" The detective was just as puzzled as Scott was.

"Lieutenant Wentworth."

"Lieutenant Wentworth? We don't have a Wentworth here. Did he say if he was with the University of Florida Police or the Gainesville PD?"

"Gainesville."

"Are you sure?"

"Yes, sir. I'm positive."

"Wentworth?" he said, scratching his head as he tried to remember why the name sounded so familiar, but knowing Gainesville definitely did not have a Wentworth on the force. "Wentworth, huh?" Suddenly, it dawned on him. "Son of a bitch. That stupid, stupid kid," he yelled at no one in particular. He jumped out of his chair and began pacing as far as the cord on the phone would allow.

"Did I do something wrong?" asked Scott, alarmed.

"No...no...not you. Mr. Scott, I need for you to tell me exactly what *Lieutenant Wentworth* asked you and what you told him. Do not leave anything out, understood?"

"Yes, sir. Well...uh...he asked how I know Benjamin..."

Scott told Detective Lieutenant Roberts the entire conversation, holding nothing back. Roberts thanked him and hung up the phone. He immediately rushed out of his office and yelled to the only officer not on the phone, "Get me the Thomasville Police Department on the phone right now."

"Thomasville?" the officer asked questioningly.

"Thomasville, Georgia."

What the hell was that kid thinking? The kid was going to get himself killed going after that madman. Not to mention how much more danger he was putting his girlfriend in by trying to be the damn hero and attempting to rescue her.

"Better get the FBI on the line as well," he yelled.

"Willie, I can't take it anymore," Laura cried. "Why haven't they called us with any news?"

"Sweetie, I don't know. Maybe there is no news." He took Laura into his arms. He was just as nervous and worried as she was. Somewhere out there a crazed man was holding his sweet, defenseless daughter hostage. It was killing him that he wasn't out there hunting the man down, but he knew the police were doing all that they could. He had spent the last few hours watching the news with his wife and Ileana, but there were no updates. The same information was still being given. They would show pictures of Angel and of her abductor, Benjamin Langdon. They would say he was probably armed and dangerous. That he had a history of mental illness.

His neighbors were interviewed, but all they had to say was that he was a strange man who mostly kept to himself. Didn't anybody ever think that maybe he was trouble in the making? That he was a walking time bomb? No. Everyone just minded his own business and kept away from him. Now this maniac was out there alone with his daughter. Willie swore to himself that if Langdon laid a hand on her, he would rip his throat out.

"I wonder why Jarrod hasn't come back," Ileana wondered aloud.

Willie walked toward the couch with his wife still clinging to him. They sat down and he took a deep sigh.

"I have no idea where he might have gone," Willie said. "He said he needed to take care of some things, but that was a long time ago. I don't know what could be more important than this."

Ileana noticed the annoyance in his voice and immediately came to Jarrod's defense.

"It must be something extremely important that just couldn't wait. Jarrod is madly in love with Angel, and —"

The phone rang. All three jumped up, but Willie got to the phone before the others.

"Yes?"

"Mr. Skyler, this is Detective Lieutenant Roberts. I'm just calling to give you an update on what's going on."

"Finally. We've been going crazy over here," he said, not caring if he sounded rude or not. He was sick and tired of sitting around waiting for news.

"I understand, but we've been busy," said the detective.

"I know. I'm sorry. It's just that this is so hard."

"I'm sure it is," said Roberts sympathetically.

"What can you tell us?" asked Willie.

"Let me start by saying that we believe we know where your daughter is. Please don't get your hopes up yet. We've contacted the police in Thomasville, Georgia, and they're on their way to a remote cabin in that town."

"Thomasville, Georgia? I don't understand."

"Turns out one of the phone leads we received looks to be valid. A gentleman called and said he works with Benjamin Langdon..." The detective went on to explain all the details, leaving Willie flabbergasted. As Roberts explained, Willie would have to stop to repeat what he was saying for Laura and Ileana's benefit. They were practically pulling him off the phone trying to hear what was being said on the other side.

Finally, the detective said, "By the way, I have a question for you. I'm almost positive your answer is going to be no, but I would love to be pleasantly surprised by you saying yes. Is your daughter's boyfriend there with you right now?"

"Jarrod? No, he isn't. Why do you ask?"

"Yup. I thought so. Any idea where he might be?"

"No. He said he had some things to take care of and that he would meet me here at the hotel when he was done, but that was hours ago. I honestly do not have any idea where he might be. Is there a problem?"

"Yes, indeed. There's a big problem."

"What is it? What's wrong now?" asked Willie.

"It appears Mr. Wentworth may have decided to take matters into his own hands and is currently on his way, if he isn't already there, to Georgia."

"Oh shit."

Chapter Forty-Two

Angel woke up disoriented and starving. She lay in the bed, motionless, taking in her surroundings. The house was quiet and she still couldn't tell if it was day or night. She didn't even know how long she had slept. Was it just a nap that she had taken, or did she sleep the whole night through? She couldn't stand this anymore. She slowly lifted herself into a sitting position, her back up against the headboard, her legs crossed at the ankles. She remained that way for a few minutes until she had no choice but to get up and inform Benjamin that she needed to use the bathroom. She hated the idea of having to see him again, but nature was knocking, or rather pounding, on the door and she needed to answer.

She stood up and knocked on the bedroom door. No response. She twisted the doorknob a few times, and not surprisingly, found that she was still locked in. She knocked harder until she heard him stir and groan. *He must be sleeping on the couch*, she thought. She began to pound heavily on the door.

"What do you want?" he screamed, obviously annoyed.

"I have to use the bathroom."

"Hold it in," he yelled back.

"I can't. I need to pee now. I'll just keep pounding until you open the damn door!" And she did exactly as she said she would.

"Fine. I'm c-coming. Just stop making all that racket!" But she didn't until she heard the clicking sound of the door being unlocked. As soon as he opened the door, she pushed her way past him and hurried to the bathroom, slamming the door shut and locking it.

"Hey, what did I tell you about c-closing the door?" he yelled.

"Screw you!" she yelled back. "Now leave me the hell alone while I pee in peace!" She began to relieve herself, taking her time. She was surprised by her sudden burst of courage and defiance, yet regretted it just a little at the same time. The last thing she wanted to do was make him angry, but it was so difficult pretending to be meek and obedient when all she wanted to do was spit in his face and dropkick him to the floor.

She should have listened to that police officer who suggested she take self-defense classes. She should have listened to a lot of people. Ileana had advised her to inform Jarrod right from the get-go of all that was happening, but she didn't because she didn't want to burden him. Then, once she finally did, he had insisted she not go anywhere alone, but she did anyway, and thanks to her inability to follow simple instructions, she was now being held captive by an unbalanced, deranged lunatic. No more. No more would she sit back and just let things happen. She wasn't going to just sit there and wait and pray for something to happen. She was going to make things happen herself. She would start off by getting herself out of this mess. She would do whatever it would take to get the hell away from this madman.

Angel wiped herself dry and flushed the toilet. At the sound of the flush, Benjamin knocked on her door and said, "Are you done?"

"Not yet," she responded.

"Open the d-door."

"No. I want some privacy. All I'm doing is freshening up. Now, will you please go away and leave me alone."

"Don't try anything. I boarded up the bathroom w-window from the outside, so if you have plans of trying to escape, think a-again."

"Shut up," she said, once again regretting her insolence.

"You better w-watch yourself. Looks like I might have to remind you of what happens when you don't b-behave," he said as he walked away from the bathroom door and sat down on the couch.

Angel quickly looked behind the shower curtain and attempted to open the frosted glass window as quietly as possible. She was able to open it about four inches and checked to see if he had indeed boarded it up from the outside. For a second time, he'd spoken the truth. She was able to determine it was dark out, based on the fact that only weak slivers of light shone through the cracks between the wooden planks. If it wasn't late at night, then surely the day was nearing dawn. She slammed the window shut in frustration, not caring if he heard or not.

"Told you," he laughingly mocked from outside the door.

She looked in the medicine cabinet to see what she might find. Perhaps there might be a razor in there that she could store in her pocket for later use. No razor. All she found were a few stray travel items someone must have left behind after spending a few days at the cabin. She picked up a small trial-size bottle of hair spray and pocketed it. It may not be pepper spray, but it could come in handy. She pictured herself aiming it toward his eyes and missing her target. With her luck, all she might accomplish in her attempt to defend herself would be to set his greasy, unwashed hair into a hard hold guaranteed to last all day.

She closed the cabinet and looked in the mirror. Her cheek was slightly swollen and was already taking on a purplish gray coloring. She gently touched it and cringed at the soreness.

"What's taking so l-long?" he hollered. "Thinking of a way to f-flush yourself out of there?"

"No. I was just sitting here wondering how long it's been since you've seen the inside of a shower curtain," she responded loudly.

Damn it. She better stop articulating every thought that popped into her mind. He didn't respond. Maybe he didn't hear her. That would be a good thing.

She brushed her teeth with the toothbrush she had grabbed and placed in her back pocket before leaving the bedroom and attempted to comb the knots out of her long, thick hair, but the comb she found in the medicine cabinet snapped in two after just four strokes. What now? She lowered the lid on the toilet and sat down cross-legged. She leaned forward, resting her chin on the heel of her hand, while rhythmically drumming her fingers on her good cheek as she stared at the ceiling, then the walls and lastly, the floor. She contemplated barricading herself in the bathroom, but she knew that was unfeasible. Besides, she would be much more comfortable if she did so in the bedroom. Too bad it didn't have a bathroom. She would have to make a point of not taking in too many liquids. The less time out of the bedroom, the better.

It was so quiet outside the bathroom. Too quiet. He hadn't responded to her comment about the shower. Maybe he had stepped out. She stood up and quietly unlocked the door. She opened it slightly and poked her head out, looking for him.

"Benjamin?" she called out softly. No reply. "Benjamin?" she tried again, this time with more force. She stepped out and calmly walked into the living room area. She was standing silent and motionless in the middle of the room when suddenly she sensed an oppressive feeling that she was indeed not alone. Her worst fear was confirmed by a long shadow looming directly over hers. Slowly she turned and there he stood, a mere inch or two behind her. She jumped back, but he grabbed her arm, forcing her forward again.

"You w-want to repeat that comment you made regarding a shower?" he said menacingly.

Although quaking within, she lifted her chin high and said, "Go to hell, you fucking asshole."

Glaring at her with intensity so profound and volatile that she instantly regretted her words, he pushed her with such force that she fell back and landed on the hard floor. Scuttling away from him, she tried to scramble to her feet, but he continually pushed her back down with his foot.

"You're just like the rest of them. You're no different."

"Stop it," she cried. "You're hurting me!"

"S-stop it. You're hurting me!" he said, mimicking her in an exaggerated high-pitched tone. He grabbed her by the front of the shirt and pulled her up, tearing the shirt. She stood and covered herself as quickly as she could by placing both her hands over her chest. She started to back away, but he kept coming toward her, his eyes gleaming with fury. She glanced behind her and saw she was only a few feet away from the bedroom door. If she was able to reach it before he caught her, she could barricade herself in the room until he calmed himself down.

As she turned to run, he grabbed her by the hair and pulled hard. She screamed and fell backward. He jumped on top of her and covered her mouth with his hand, muffling her screams. She tried to bite him, but he pulled away and slapped her hard across the face. Once, twice, three times in a row. She shrieked in pain. He bent down and tried forcibly to kiss her, but she twisted her head away from him and screamed as loud as she could.

"Stop screaming!" he yelled as he punched her with his closed fist.

In desperation she tried to fight him off, but he was more than twice her weight and was smothering her. She felt herself losing the battle as she continued to push, kick, and fight her hardest to get him off, but she only seemed to tire and weaken, while he seemed to gain strength and become more aggressive.

"Help!" she screamed. "Help!"

He punched her again and grabbed her by the throat with both hands, trying to silence her. He held his grip tight.

"I was never good e-enough, was I? You couldn't just accept me for who I was. Always wanting more. Always wanting b-better!" He tightened his grip more.

Angel was gasping for air. She tried to scream, but nothing came out. Her eyes began to close as she felt the room darken. The sound of Benjamin's voice became fainter and fainter...

It was dark when Jarrod neared the cabin. As he approached it, he saw lights were on, but the curtains were closed and some of the windows had been boarded up. He lowered himself into a crouching position and hid along the side of the car that was parked in the driveway. He placed his hand on the hood. The engine was cold. Just as he lifted his head to look inside the car for signs Angel had been there, he heard a loud, piercing scream. A scream for help. He recognized the voice immediately. It was Angel.

Jarrod stood up and ran toward the cabin. He heard her scream again, and then he heard a man yelling loudly at her. Her cries for help suddenly stopped, and all he could hear was the man hollering in rage. Jarrod ran up the steps, never slowing down as he rammed the side of his body with great force into the door. When the door burst open, he would never forget what he saw. Benjamin was straddled over Angel with his hands pressed firmly on her throat. She wasn't moving.

Benjamin had turned to face the door when he heard it crash open. Jarrod jumped on top of him, knocking him off Angel. They thrashed about on the ground, rolling over and over. Jarrod was able to get from under him and stood, grabbing Benjamin by the shirt and lifting him easily off the ground.

"You son of a bitch!" he screamed as he pulled his fist back and let loose, hitting him squarely in the nose. Benjamin fell to the ground, knocking a lamp over. Suddenly the room was pitch black. The only light that entered the room shone from the moon outside and streamed through the cracks of the boarded-up windows and open door. Jarrod moved forward, his eyes quickly adjusting to the darkness. He found Benjamin's form and grabbed for him. They struggled, and Jarrod felt something cold and hard in his assailant's hands. A gun. He grabbed for it, and they continued to struggle like fury. Suddenly a loud shot rang out.

Jarrod knew he hadn't been hit. Benjamin hadn't slowed down, so he hadn't been shot either. The bullet missed them both. They continued to struggle, the gun still in Benjamin's hand. Jarrod fought with all his might, thinking of Angel the entire time. Somehow he was able to turn the gun when suddenly it went off again. A deafening silence filled the room. Jarrod felt a cold wetness on his hand that was still clutching the gun, as well as Benjamin's hand. The smell of rusty iron permeated the air. They both stopped struggling, and Benjamin's body went limp and fell to the ground, taking the gun with him.

Jarrod stood for a second above Benjamin, alert to any movements. When he was satisfied there were none, he rushed over to Angel.

"Angel, are you alright?" he said as he scooped her up. "Baby, answer me. Are you alright?" She didn't respond.

Jarrod was kneeling and holding her in his arms when he suddenly felt the cold wetness again. It was so damn dark, and he couldn't see well, but he knew instantly what it was and felt an immediate sense of foreboding. Blood. She must have been hit by the stray bullet.

He lifted his hand to look at it and began to scream.

No! No!" He held her tightly and began to rock her unmoving body in his arms. "Angel, please...please don't leave me," he pleaded as he cried. "Please, baby. I need you. I love you. Don't go. Fight. Fight it!" Driven by fear and desperation, he clutched her lifeless form tighter against his chest and whispered softly, "You can do it, baby. I know you can. Fight it. You can't leave me. Please."

He loosened his hold and looked at her pale, ashen face, caressing it softly with his hand. Her eyes were closed and he leaned forward to place a tender kiss on her forehead and a gentle, lingering one on her lips. He wiped the tears from his eyes and took a sharply drawn breath, releasing it slowly.

"My life is nothing without you. You're what makes my heart beat," he whispered shakily.

Suddenly a bright light shone from the doorway. Jarrod looked up through his tear-stung eyes, but couldn't tell what it was or why it was there. For a moment he recalled the lambent light he had seen during his enigmatic twenty-five-second passing. Was the presence of this light an indication he was dying as well? He hoped so. He wanted to be with Angel, no matter where she was. Be it alive, here on earth, or be it dead, in heaven. It didn't matter as long as they were together for all eternity.

But the feeling wasn't the same this time around. Where was the sensation of peace, calm, and serenity? He couldn't feel the warmth or the love that emanated from it the first time. All he felt now was emptiness coupled with pain and sadness.

The light abruptly turned toward the loveseat, and Jarrod turned his head to follow it. Standing there, clearly, he saw Benjamin holding a gun directly at him. When Benjamin saw the light focused on him, he turned the gun toward the light and shot once. The light fell to the ground, along with a loud thump. Immediately two other lights shone brightly on Benjamin, and four loud, consecutive shots were fired. With the light still on Benjamin, Jarrod watched as he recoiled with every shot and finally fell to the ground.

Chapter Forty-Three

As Angel was placed into the ambulance, Jarrod stood zombie-like while a police officer wrapped a blanket around his shoulders. As soon as she and the paramedics were settled in, he jumped in beside her. They immediately took off for the hospital with the lights and sirens blaring. As they headed down the driveway toward the main road, Jarrod watched through the small back window as a truck passed them heading in the opposite direction. He read the words written on the back doors as it continued on toward the cabin. *Coroner's office*. Benjamin's ride had arrived.

Several hours passed as Jarrod impatiently waited at the Thomasville Medical Center for Angel's parents to arrive. Angel had been brought to the ER, where doctors had worked feverishly on her. She had taken the stray shot directly in her left shoulder, but fortunately the bullet passed all the way through. He held her hand at her bedside while she slept. He lifted her hand and kissed it gently as he looked at her bruised, swollen face and cut lip. *She still looked beautiful*, he thought.

"I love you," he softly said to her. Her eyes began to flutter open, and she squeezed his hand tenderly.

"I love you more," she whispered, barely audible. He smiled at her, stood up, and leaned over her, placing a soft kiss on her lips. She smiled back at him as she closed her eyes again and quietly fell asleep, breathing softly.

When Willie, Laura, and Ileana finally arrived, emotions were high. Tears of gratitude for her safe return flowed interminably. Laura leaned in a half-sitting, half-lying-down position on the edge of the bed and wouldn't let go of Angel, even when she opened her eyes for a moment and told her she could barely breathe.

"You can breathe later," Laura said. "Right now I need to hold you for awhile." But mercifully she did lessen up on her clinch a bit.

They all returned to Gainesville a few days later. The doctors had told Angel and her family she could resume her daily activities as long as she took things slowly in the beginning and rested.

Solemn and exhausted, they all entered Willie and Laura's two-room suite at the hotel and immediately sat down on the two couches in the living room area. After a few minutes, Jarrod stood up and went directly to the pitcher of water that sat on the dresser and filled an empty glass for Angel. He took out two pills from a small envelope the hospital had supplied them with and gave them to her. She looked at him with questioning eyes.

"They're for the pain," he said.

"But I'm not feeling that much pain," she replied.

"Thanks to the two pills you took earlier today. Take them, and then I want you to go lie down for a bit," he said. She took the pills without argument and thanked him.

Ileana stood up from the couch and placed her hand on Angel's good shoulder. Angel smiled up at her from where she sat.

"Do you need anything?" Ileana asked.

"No, I'm good. Thanks." She covered her friend's hand with her own and added, "Thanks for everything, especially for being my best friend."

"My pleasure. But if you don't need me, and I do believe you are in great hands, then I'll be on my way. I'll call you later, okay?"

"Okay," said Angel.

Ileana said her good-byes and headed toward the door. Before opening it, she looked over at Jarrod and said, "Take good care of our girl, alright?"

Jarrod nodded and said, "You have nothing to worry about, Ileana."

"Just call me Ile," she said.

A few minutes after Ile had left, Angel stood up and asked her parents if it would be alright for her to speak privately with Jarrod for a moment. She asked permission to take him into the bedroom. Both parents looked at each other and nodded. Willie stood up and said, "Before you do, there's something I'd like to say to Jarrod."

Jarrod walked over and stood facing him.

"Yes, sir?" he said.

"Willie, remember?"

Jarrod smiled and said, "Willie."

Willie cleared his throat and through his oncoming tears said, "I want to thank you again…thank you for what you did. Thank you for saving my little girl." He choked on a sob and took a deep breath before continuing, "What you did was incredibly brave. Not many men out there would attempt it. You put your life at risk to save Angel. Laura and I will forever be grateful to you for what you've done…thank you."

He pulled Jarrod into a deep embrace. Laura sat watching the two men behind tear-glazed eyes. She then stood and pulled Jarrod out of Willie's arms and folded him into hers. She held him for a long while that way. Suddenly Jarrod uttered, "Mrs. Skyler?"

"Laura," she said quietly.

"Laura… I can't breathe," he said.

Laura took a deep, invigorating breath and whispered softly, "You can breathe later."

Angel led Jarrod into the bedroom and closed the door. She sat on the edge of the bed and motioned for him to join her by patting the spot next to her. He did and then he took her hand that was not confined in the sling and enclosed it in both of his. A lone teardrop fell from her eye, and he leaned over to kiss it dry.

"I want to thank you too," she said as she gently pulled her hand away for a brief moment so she could wipe her nose with her sleeve. She realized it was the sleeve of the jacket he'd given her to wear and she smiled at him shyly and said, "Sorry." He smiled back. She returned her hand to him again and he held it tightly.

"You're welcome," he said softly.

She looked at him in awe and said, "You saved my life."

"All in a day's work," he responded, and they both chuckled at the memory of what the injured police officer had said in Thomasville when he had come to visit Angel. Luckily, Benjamin's shot was off and had only nicked him in the arm, not causing any severe damage.

Jarrod became serious all of a sudden and said to Angel, "I need to ask you something, but I don't know how to do it."

"You can ask me anything."

"This is tough, though."

She slowly turned to face him, scrunching her face a bit from the discomfort, and said, "Don't be afraid. Go on and ask me."

"I want to know if…well, umm…did he…did he touch you? I mean besides the… hitting." Every time he thought of that bastard touching her, he felt a renewed burst of fury.

Angel realized what he was getting at. He wanted to know if Benjamin had forced himself on her. Jarrod had lowered his head and kept his eyes on their clasped hands.

"Look at me," she said softly. He slowly lifted his head and looked directly into her eyes. "No. He did not rape me," she said.

Jarrod took a deep breath and leaned toward her to kiss her tenderly on the lips. He looked up toward the heavens as he had done in his car that fateful night so long ago and silently said, "Thank you…again."

Two days later the Skylers were still residing at the Embassy Suites and were continually arguing with Angel that she needed to return to Bradenton with them. Angel was adamant that she remain in Gainesville and continue with her studies. She explained she was no longer in any danger, with Langdon dead and Morgan sitting behind bars awaiting her trial. They weren't comfortable leaving her, but Jarrod promised to keep a close, protective eye on her, which made them both feel much better. He was, after all in their eyes, Angel's personal guardian angel.

They left the following day. As they hugged outside the hotel lobby, Angel promised they would visit soon. Jarrod stood with his hand gently pressed against the small of her back as they waved good-bye to her parents. They remained there until the car could no longer be seen.

"You okay?" he asked.

She nodded. "Just a little sad, I suppose."

"I'm sure. Your folks are great people. I like them a lot."

"Well, they're absolutely in love with you. Talk about making a good impression."

He chuckled and said, "Hey, I never did ask. What about your little brother? Why didn't he come?"

"This wasn't exactly a pleasure trip, y'know. He stayed with our neighbor. They have a son that's the same age as Luca, and they get along really well."

"That's good. I guess I'll meet him when we go to Bradenton."

"He'll love you. He's a real baseball fanatic. Loves the Red Sox."

Jarrod rolled his eyes and groaned in misery. Not another one.

That night, as they lay in Angel's bed in her dorm room watching television, Jarrod leaned toward her and whispered, "I love you." She smiled the smile of his dreams, nestled closer to him, and whispered back, "I love you more."

They lay motionless for awhile, savoring their love and all the wonderful feelings of warmth and tenderness it brought.

"I've made a decision," she said.

"Hmm? What decision have you made? To love me forever?"

"That goes without saying. Forever and ever and ever…"

"That's a good decision," he said as he leaned over and kissed her warmly on the lips. He was still being careful with her. Her bruises were fading, no longer a deep purplish blue, but rather more of a faded greenish yellow. Nonetheless, they were still tender to the touch, and he didn't want to hurt her unnecessarily. The gunshot wound didn't seem to bother her as much as he thought it would. She kept her arm immobilized in a sling, but every now and then, if she turned or bent down to retrieve something, forgetting she needed to be careful, she would feel a sharp pain. Other than that, she was doing wonderfully.

"Seriously, I've made a decision, and I want you to be the first to know."

"Does Ile already know?"

She hesitated and then said, "Like I said, I want you to be the second to know."

He laughed out loud. God, how he loved her. She was everything to him. He could not ask for anyone more perfectly suited for him. She was beautiful, sexy, sweet, loving, smart, and funny. There had been so many times in the past year when he'd thought he would never be able to laugh or smile again, and yet she always seemed to find a way of making him do so. Time and time again.

"Alright, tell me about this decision."

"I'm going to make love to you," she said.

Jarrod became silent. "I thought you had already made that decision."

"Not really. I knew I wanted to, but I wasn't sure if I was ready."

"I thought you were ready, except for the whole timing and the right setting issue."

"I know I said that, but truthfully, I just wasn't sure if I was ready to take such a big step."

"And…you're ready now?"

"Yes."

"Right now?" he said hopefully.

"Not right at this very moment," she said, seeing the gleam in his eye. "I would like to look sort of presentable, maybe a little on the sexy side, when the time comes. I'm not exactly feeling pretty with these bruises on my face and this stupid sling on my arm."

"I think you're beautiful, with or without the extra coloring. Plus, the sling is removable," he said and then added, "for short periods of time." He knew he needed to add that last line. She was dying to stop using the sling, and if he gave her any indication it wasn't necessary, off it would be within seconds.

"Very funny," she said sarcastically.

Jarrod sat up on the bed and faced her directly. "Look, I love you and I will wait as long as it takes until you're ready. I'm not going to lie, I hope it's soon, but if it isn't, I'll accept that. I'm not going anywhere, and I refuse to be one of those boyfriends who pressures you and forces you to do it out of guilt. I want you to come to me because you want to be with me as much as I want to be with you. Remember one thing, though. Between you and me, it will never be just sex. Every time, for all time, it will always be making love for us."

She nodded and he lay down next to her again. He took her hand in his and caressed it gently with his thumb. They were quiet for a moment when Jarrod suddenly said, "I can't believe Ile knew before me." Angel rolled her eyes and smiled inwardly.

A few hours later, Jarrod announced he needed to leave to make a few phone calls and that he would come by early in the morning to check on her.

"Why don't you just make them here? It's still so early."

Hesitating, he said, "I'd rather not."

Her curiosity sparked, she asked, "Jarrod, what are you up to? Who are you going to call?"

"Mr. Wyatt and then my parents."

"Why don't you want to call them from here? I don't understand. You're just calling to confirm the appointment for Sunday, right?"

"Not to confirm... to cancel."

Angel jumped into a sitting position, groaning from the pain, and exclaimed, "What? Why? You can't cancel. You have to go. This is too important...you've worked so hard for this opportunity! You can't cancel. You—"

"Hold on. Stop talking for a moment, okay? Let me explain."

"But—"

"Shush. No talking. Just listen."

She nodded, but it was apparent it was killing her not to speak. She looked like a balloon ready to burst.

"I can't leave you alone and you're not well enough to come. I'll call Mr. Wyatt and see if we can reschedule something for the next time he's in Florida. It's not a big deal."

"Yes, it is. No...there is no way I'm letting you cancel this appointment. I am well enough to come and I'm coming, like it or not."

"Baby, look at you. You're all bruised and sore, plus the doctor said you need to take it easy—"

"I don't care. I promise to take it easy there. I will."

"You need to rest."

"No resting. I've done enough resting. We're going. End of discussion."

"Angel—"

"No. Now you shush. I love you and I am not going to be the cause of your dream not coming true. This is what you've always dreamed of and this is your opportunity to make it happen. If you do well, which I'm sure you will, you could be playing for the Red Sox someday."

"Hey. No need to get nasty about it."

"You know what I mean. Please, please don't argue with me. You know I'm right. Please, Jarrod…please." She began to cry onerously.

"No…no tears! That's not fair."

"Please, Jarrod," she pleaded once again as she wiped away a fresh onslaught of tears.

Jarrod stared at her in disbelief. She was serious about going. It didn't matter that she was still in physical pain. What did matter to her was that he take advantage of this once-in-a-lifetime opportunity and do whatever it took to realize his dream. She was putting his dream, vision, and goal for the future ahead of herself.

"Jarrod?" she asked again, fearfully awaiting his response.

"Do you promise to take it easy?"

"Yes."

"That means lots of rest and the minute you don't feel well, you'll speak up."

"Yes. Yes, I promise. I'll speak up."

Jarrod took a deep sigh. "I'll call the doctor and if he says it's alright for you to go, then we'll go. But, if he says no, then we stay. Both of us. Deal?"

"No deal. If he says no, then you still go. I just hope he says yes, because I want to be there when the scout tells you you're going to be a professional baseball player."

She stood up slowly and went into his arms, hugging him as tightly as she possibly could without hurting her shoulder.

"Thank you," she said.

He pulled back a bit, kissed her full on the lips, and said, "No, thank you."

Chapter Forty-Four

The next morning, bright and early, Angel waited for Jarrod to pick her up. She no longer took chances and waited in her room rather than outside. When he knocked on her door, she asked who it was and when he responded, she opened the door.

He burst out laughing at the sight of her. There she stood, wearing enormous black sunglasses that seemed to cover half her face and a gargantuan, wide-brimmed hat that practically covered the remaining half. She frowned and said, "What are you laughing at?"

"You're crazy," he said, laughing heartily.

"I may look like an idiot, but at least you can't see my bruises! Can you grab my bag?" She walked out the door with her head held high.

A few hours later, they arrived at the hotel in Jacksonville and checked into two separate rooms. Jarrod checked to see if his parents and Alec had already checked in, but the desk clerk informed him they had not. He left a message for them to call him in either his room or Angel's when they arrived.

While taking the elevator to their rooms, Angel ignored the curious stares she was receiving. Unlike his girlfriend, Jarrod felt a bit ill at ease with all the gawking and gazing that was being shed on the shorter, dark-haired version of Paris Hilton. Nonetheless, he was proud of the woman he knew was hidden behind the eccentric cover-up.

Once they reached her room, she immediately took off the hat and glasses and leaped into his arms. He held her tightly, but not too tightly, and kissed her profusely.

"I wish I didn't have these bruises. I'd attack you right now, if I didn't have them."

"Ahhh, don't tell me that. I've barely got a hold on my control as it is."

"They're starting to fade fast, aren't they?" she said animatedly as she tenderly touched one of the bruises on her face.

"Uh-huh...," he said as he gently kissed every single one. He moved to her mouth and parted her lips with his tongue. She moaned aloud in pleasure while leaning into his body and pressing her hips into his own.

Desire quickly built into a crescendo as they tumbled backward onto her bed. She moaned slightly from the pain and he asked if she was alright. Smiling and nodding, she lifted herself up and began to remove the sling.

"What are you doing? You need to keep that thing on," he said.

"Not right now," she said. "I feel fine. It barely hurts anymore." She was lying, but she wanted him to hold and kiss her so much that she would deal with the shoulder discomfort for a little while. *It would be well worth it*, she thought. She gently lay back down next to him and tilted her head up to receive another kiss. His arm tightened around her and he pressed his hips gently into her. Again she moaned, but this time from pleasure.

His mouth slanted over and over hers, all the while his tongue taunting and maddening her with longing. His hands slowly slid up and down her body and then discreetly under her blouse. Her soft skin felt like silk against his hand. Angel was breathing heavily and placed both her hands on his shoulders and then around his neck, bringing him closer. She inwardly grimaced at the soreness she felt from lifting her arm, but made sure he did not notice, or else he would stop doing all those wonderful things he was doing. She wrapped one leg around his, trying urgently to pull his body as close to hers as possible. Jarrod began a slow rocking motion that was driving her crazy.

"Oh God!"

Her words of arousal drove him over the brink. He lifted himself up and quickly yanked off his shirt over his head. He began to unbutton her blouse but was having difficulty, so she swiftly took over. She sat up and removed her blouse and bra slowly, her gaze never leaving his. He gently pushed her back against the mattress and began kissing her in earnest, all the while exploring her body with his hands. Angel moaned into his mouth when he cupped one of her breasts. His body began to throb as he pressed himself against her. He began the rocking motion again and it was almost her undoing.

"Angel," he pleaded.

"Yes...yes," she said, barely able to breathe.

He began to unfasten his pants when suddenly the phone rang, startling them both.

"Ignore it," he said as he continued to kiss Angel. "Just ignore it and it'll stop." He continued unfastening his pants, but the phone's incessant ringing abruptly brought Angel back to reality.

"Jarrod, no. We have to stop. It's your parents and they know we're here. I don't want them to think we're up here fooling around. They'll think badly of me."

"No, Angel. Please. I can't handle much more of this. I want us to be together."

"I do too. But not now. Go answer the phone. Quick!"

He stood up, not bothering to refasten his pants. They barely stayed on as he walked over to the phone, answering with a hostile, "Hello."

"Hi, honey," said Janet brightly.

"Hey, Mom," he said while rubbing his face and releasing a deep, aggravated sigh. Angel watched him as she pulled out a fresh, unwrinkled blouse from her suitcase and began to put it on. She smiled at him, but in his frustration, he did not smile back.

"We're here. Come meet us in our room. We're on our way up. Room 450. I can't wait to see you. Bring Angel too. I'm dying to finally meet her."

"Alright." He looked down at his still-unbending display of passion and said, "Just give me…I mean us…about ten or fifteen minutes, okay?"

"Make it ten." And she hung up.

As Jarrod and Angel walked hand in hand toward Room 450, Jarrod looked at her and said, "Could you at least remove the hat?"

He was in such a foul mood after having to abruptly stop their lovemaking that she didn't want to agitate him any further, so she agreed. She pulled the hat off and tucked it underneath her arm.

"Smile," she told him.

"I can't," he responded sourly.

"You mean to tell me you were able to fight off a gun-toting, psycho kidnapper, but you aren't able to bring a simple smile to your face to greet your parents?"

"I wasn't sexually frustrated when I fought off the gun-toting, psycho kidnapper." He turned to face the door and knocked heavily on it.

A minute later Janet opened the door wide and squealed with delight when she saw Jarrod standing there.

"Oh, my baby, look at you," she said as she pulled him into a big bear hug and wouldn't let go.

"Mom…," he whined.

"You just look so handsome!" She looked over and saw Angel standing in the doorway, immediately noticing the large sunglasses she was hiding behind. "You must be Angel. Come in, sweetheart," she said as she gently led Angel into the room. She gave her a hug but was careful not to squeeze too tightly. Jarrod had already called them to inform them of what had happened, plus they had kept abreast of the situation via CNN and Headline News. Angel had had so little recovery time that she knew that her body must still be extremely sensitive and sore to the touch.

"I'm so happy to meet you and so very, very glad to know you're alright after what happened," Janet said. "I hope you don't mind that Jarrod told us," she said belatedly, not knowing whether she had just gotten her son into trouble for telling them.

Smiling timidly, Angel said, "No, not at all. Unfortunately, it's been on all the news programs, so basically the entire nation knows by now anyway."

"I'm happy to meet you too and am equally ecstatic that you're fine," said Jim as he came over and hugged her. "This is our youngest son, Alec," he said, motioning for Alec to come forward.

"We've already met," he said. "It's good to see you again. Glad you're okay."

"Thanks, Alec," she said as she leaned over and kissed his cheek.

"Come in and sit down," Jim said to both Jarrod and Angel. They all sat on the two couches that were in the room. Alec remained standing, simply because there was no room left on the couches. Jarrod took about half the couch himself.

"Angel, I love your sunglasses," said Janet. "They make you look mysterious."

"Hmm, mysterious. I think I like that," Angel replied. "Maybe I'll continue to wear them after the bruises have disappeared."

She looked at Jarrod, who simply shook his head and said, "I don't see that happening." They all smiled at his no-nonsense response.

"It must have been so difficult for you," said Janet in sympathy.

"It was. But thank God it's over," Angel said with a deep sigh.

"Mom, why don't we talk about something else? It's still a little soon for Angel to discuss what happened."

"I understand and I'm sorry," Janet said.

Giving Jarrod a stern, if not reprimanding look, Angel said, "It's fine, really. I don't mind talking about it. I'm just incredibly relieved that it's over and I'm alive. Thanks to your son. By the way, thank you for having him."

"You're quite welcome," said Janet cheerfully. Initially, she was shocked and angry at Jarrod when he had first told her what he had done. It wasn't that she didn't feel an incredible amount of pride in his immense display of courage, but she was sorely disappointed in his decision to attempt a rescue without notifying the police first. He could have easily been killed. How could he have done something so rash and impetuous? Feeling a knot form in the pit of her stomach every time she thought of how the scenario could have played out, her body gave a quick shudder when she pictured him lying helpless on the ground, slowly bleeding to death while his attacker stood over him, smiling wickedly.

She gave another tremble and shook her head, trying to push the thought out of her mind. Although she knew that the reality of the outcome was infinitely better than the one she constantly imagined, she still could not stop the horrific thoughts from passing through her mind.

Alec noticed his mother's sudden change in mood and attempted to change the subject and atmosphere.

"So, are you ready for tomorrow?" he asked Jarrod.

Jarrod gave him a grateful look and said, "I hope so. We're supposed to meet him at two o'clock at the Baseball Grounds."

"I hear that ballpark is nice. New too," said Alec.

"Have you been able to keep up with your training and rehab schedule?" asked Jim.

"Not this week. I've been a little busy." The room became uncomfortably silent, until Angel asked, "Does a week of not training make a big difference?" The continued silence and various frowns and reactions answered her question.

She looked at Jarrod sadly and said, "I'm so sorry."

"Why? It's not your fault," he replied, sincerely surprised she would even feel that it was.

"Yes, it is. If I had only listened to you and not left the room alone that night, Benjamin never would have had the opportunity to take me."

"Yes, he would have. Morgan and Langdon had already planned the abduction. Exactly when and how it would have happened, we still don't know, but it would have happened." He hesitated, then said, "We didn't say anything to you, but it turns out that Detective Lieutenant Roberts spoke with the warehouse supervisor at Elite Enterprises, and Langdon hadn't shown up for work in four days. We're pretty sure he'd been following you that whole time, just waiting for an opportunity. Eventually, regardless of you being careful or not, it would have occurred."

Angel sat silently, trying to absorb the information. "Why didn't you want me to know that?"

"You've been through enough. Willie and I talked about it, and we just thought it might be best for you not to know. It's over. You don't need to keep thinking about it or dwelling on the what-ifs. The only reason I'm telling you now is because I don't want you to feel bad and think it's your fault if things don't work out tomorrow."

Angel tried to wipe away a tear, but her sunglasses got in the way. Janet saw her struggle and said, "Why don't you take off the sunglasses when you're with us? You'll be more comfortable, and you shouldn't be embarrassed by how you look. Bruises fade."

"Only the one's on the outside," Angel responded as she removed the glasses, exposing her still slightly swollen cheeks and the scarcely visible bruises to Jarrod's family. She expected to hear gasps or be subjected to looks of sympathy, but she received neither.

They smiled tentatively and then Alec said, "Still gorgeous as ever. You're a lucky guy, Jarrod."

Jarrod put his arm around Angel and gently pulled her close. "Don't I know it."

Chapter Forty-Five

That evening, after they had all gone out to a very enjoyable dinner at a local Italian eatery, Jarrod walked Angel back to her room. As they stood outside the door, he gently removed her sunglasses and kissed her softly on the lips as he bid her good night.

"If you need me, either call me or just knock on my door. I'm only three doors down."

She nodded and said, "I'll always need you. I love you."

He smiled at her and kissed her again, this time with more urgency. He would have continued if he hadn't heard the elevator door open and heard people chatting animatedly as they hastened out of it. He stepped away and said, "I love you more. I'll see you in the morning, unless you need me during the night," giving her a slight wink and walking toward the room he was to share with Alec.

When he reached the room, he used his key to get in and immediately noticed that the room was a mess. Alec was lying on his bed with most of his formerly neatly packed clothes strewn across the foot of it, as well as the chair next to it. Hotel visitor guides and brochures were littered across the desk, as well as two empty soda cans and an open bag of barbecue potato chips.

"Dude, the dresser has drawers," Jarrod said. "They're there for a reason—put your clothes in them." Jarrod picked up the empty cans of soda and tossed them into the garbage can.

"It's easier this way. I don't have to rummage through drawers to find what I want. Stop picking up after me. What are you, Mom?" Alec's eyes never left the television screen.

"No, but if this is what you have her doing at home, then I'm beginning to sympathize with her."

"This is me. This is who I am," Alec said morosely.

"What's that supposed to mean?"

"Let's see...it's what differentiates me from you. You're the star athlete, the kid who gets good grades, the good-looking one. Oh, and let me not forget, the one who always gets the gorgeous girlfriends. I'm just the invisible kid brother of the star athlete, the kid who gets good grades, the good-looking one. Oh, and let me not forget, the one who always gets the gorgeous girlfriends. Plus—and this is where I get to stand out—I'm the slob."

Jarrod was surprised to hear the hostility in his brother's voice. He looked at him, stunned, and said, "Something the matter? Do you want to talk?"

"What could possibly be the matter? My life is perfect, or haven't you heard?"

"Alec, what's the matter? I know something's wrong. Spill."

"Just forget it, Jarrod. Just concentrate on baseball, okay? I'm fine. I'm also tired, so I'm going to sleep now. Good night." He turned off the television set with a click of the remote and quickly maneuvered himself under the covers, turning his back to his brother.

Jarrod didn't know what to make of Alec's attitude. He would need to find some time alone tomorrow with his parents and ask them about it. He was worried. Alec was usually such an easygoing, happy-go-lucky sort. It wasn't like him to seem troubled and depressed. He wondered to himself how long this had been going on. Looking at Alec worriedly once more before heading into the shower, he thought he saw him tremble slightly under the covers. Like someone who was trying hard not to cry.

Three rooms down, Angel paced back and forth in her room. Alone. This had been the first time she had been alone since the abduction. Since being rescued, she had been surrounded by her parents, Jarrod, Ileana, or Ava. At certain times, all of the above.

Sitting on the edge of her bed, she turned on the television set with the remote and flicked through the channels, finally settling on *The David Letterman Show*. She smiled recalling how Jarrod would sometimes Skype her on the computer, and they would watch the show together but not together, laughing and commenting on the host and his celebrity guests.

She stood up and went to the window, pulling the drape aside. She looked out into the darkness searching for anything that looked remotely suspicious. There was nothing. No shadows, no movements, and no sounds other than the soft rustling of the swaying palm tree leaves and the whoosh of the passing cars along the highway. It dawned on her that those were the same quiescent sounds she had heard just seconds before reeling from the massive shocking sensation that left her feeling as though she had fallen from a two-story building.

Pulling the drape closed, she walked over to the door to make sure it was locked. She checked it twice and also made sure the bolt was secure. Looking down, Angel noticed the "Do Not Disturb" placard on the doorknob. Fixating on the sign and suddenly enduring an onslaught of thoughts as they drifted through her panicking mind, she felt her heart begin to palpitate rapidly and her breathing become labored. Trying in vain to take in deep, steady breaths, Angel began to feel as though the room were closing in on her. She placed one hand along the wall and felt her way toward the bed. Once there she sat down and placed her head between her legs until she was able to slow her breathing down. Finally gaining control, she stood up to turn off the television but stopped suddenly as she passed a mirror. For a brief second she almost did not recognize the reflection staring back at her.

She slowly began to trace with her fingers the indications of the brutal beating she had taken, and tears sprang to her eyes. Lowering herself onto the floor, she began to cry with earnest. She couldn't seem to stop the flow as the tears cascaded from her eyes like a small waterfall. Blindly reaching up onto the desk, she felt around until she found her cell phone and speed-dialed Jarrod. He picked up on the second ring.

"Miss me already?" he asked lightheartedly.

"I need you," she said between sobs.

"I'm on my way." He jumped up from his bed where he'd been lying listlessly for the last twenty minutes worrying about Alec. Wearing nothing but a pair of shorts, he quickly grabbed one of the shirts Alec had left on a chair and pulled it on as he rushed for the door.

Alec, hearing the phone ring and the short conversation that followed, poked his head out from under the cover and said sleepily, "What's up?"

"Angel needs me," Jarrod said as he rushed out the door.

The door closed and Alec lay motionless on his bed, looking up at the ceiling.

"Have to remember to add knight in shining armor to his résumé," he said softly for no one's ears but his own.

Jarrod reached Angel's door and tried turning the knob, but it was locked. He knocked softly, not wanting to attract attention, but she didn't respond. He knocked a bit harder and said in a hushed tone, "Angel, open up. It's me. Open the door, baby." He could hear her moving in the room and then the sound of her unlocking the door. She opened the door as far as the bolt would allow and peeked hesitantly to assure herself it was indeed Jarrod.

"Open it," he said again. She closed the door slightly so she could remove the bolt lock and then opened the door for him to enter. He quickly made his way in and closed the door. She was already standing in the middle of the room with her back to him. He walked over to her and wrapped his arms around her small waist, pulling her tightly against him.

"What's wrong?"

She took a deep breath and said, "I'm so scared. I don't want to be alone." She began to cry again and Jarrod slowly turned her so that she now faced him. He pulled her into the safety and warmth of his arms and held her while he stroked her hair and laid soft kisses on her head. He felt her tension ease away and her breathing slow down to an almost normal rate.

"Are you better now?" he asked, concerned. She nodded and smiled shyly.

"I'm sorry," she said.

"Don't be," he responded. "I told you to call me if you needed me. Good girl for listening."

At the mention of the words "good girl," she tensed up and tried to pull out of their embrace, but Jarrod held her still.

"Don't say that. Don't call me that."

"What? Good girl?"

"I said stop," she said, raising her voice and finally pulling away from him brusquely.

"Angel, what's wrong? What's the matter? Tell me."

She turned her back to him, not able to face him in her humiliation. "*He* kept telling me to be a good girl, and if I wasn't...if I wasn't..."

"If you weren't, what happened?" he asked uneasily.

"If I wasn't, he would hit me...hard," she said tearfully. "I tried to be good. I swear I did. I tried so hard not to flinch when he would touch me, but I was scared. Every time he touched me, I'd cringe and he'd get...he'd get so mad." She slowly turned to face him, but kept her head lowered.

"He did rape you, didn't he?" he asked furiously.

Looking up, she said, "No. No, I swear, he didn't. He would touch my face or try to kiss me and I hated it, so I'd turn away and that would infuriate him. But I swear, I wasn't raped. Please believe me."

"I do," he said as he pulled her back into his arms. "I do believe you, baby. I'm sorry. It's just that every time I picture that ass hurting you, I wish it was me who had pulled the trigger of the gun that killed him."

"Don't say that."

"It's true. If I'd been the one to do it, then I think I'd feel some sort of relief."

"No. In time, you would eventually feel regret. I'm glad you weren't the one to kill him. But at least you got the chance to beat the living crap out of him first."

"Yeah, that did feel good," he said, smiling at her. He led her toward the bed so she could sit down. Her room was quite small, having only one queen-size bed, a small desk, and one armchair. The television was on the dresser directly in front of the bed, with a small mini-bar next to it. He walked over to the mini-bar and took out a bottle of water and handed it to her.

She shook her head and said, "Are you crazy? That's a seven-dollar bottle of water. I could buy six bottles for that price at the grocery store across the street."

"Well, I'm not going across the street to get a bottle of water, so here. My treat," he said, smiling at her. She took the bottle, opened it, and took a long swallow. She eyed the bottle and said, "I still have about five bucks' worth left."

He chuckled and said, "I'm glad to see you're joking around. Feel better?"

"I always feel better when you're with me. I'm sorry I bothered you. I have to get used to being alone, but it's my first time since... well, you know."

Sinking down onto his haunches, he took her hands and asked, "What triggered it?"

"You'll think I'm crazy."

"Try me."

"I went to make sure the door was locked, and I looked down at the 'Do Not Disturb' sign. Suddenly I went into panic mode. I thought to myself that I should place it on the outside, so if somebody wanted to break into the room to steal something, they would know someone was in here and it would stop them. Then I thought, well, if I do and they're looking to hurt someone rather than just rob the place, then they'll know I'm in here and—"

She was rapidly spewing these thoughts out to Jarrod, and he noticed she was precipitately becoming anxious again, so he cut her off by saying, "I get the picture."

"Crazy, huh?" she asked timidly.

"Nope. You've been through a lot. It's going to take awhile before you begin to feel safe and secure again. But you will. I promise. You're like a flower in the rain. Every day you'll grow stronger and more resilient."

"Like you after the accident?"

He nodded and said with a slight grin, "Yeah, I suppose so. Although I'm not too keen on the idea of being compared to an itty-bitty flower."

"Sorry, macho man. You're like those big trees that grow in California. With time you grow stronger and tougher. Better?" she asked.

"Yup. Much better," he responded as he jokingly flexed his biceps.

She laughed and asked, "What are those trees called? I forget."

"I don't remember. Alec would know. He's good at that kind of stuff. He's like a walking encyclopedia of useless information. Dante used to call him Professor Wentworth," he said. As he thought of his friend, he face became somber.

Angel quickly noticed the change in him and said, "I wish I had met him."

"Yeah. You two would have gotten along great."

"You miss him a lot, don't you?" she asked sympathetically.

He nodded and said, "You have no idea. He was like a brother to me." He smiled tentatively at her and then said, "Alright. Let's change the subject before I get all wishy-washy and you have to resort back to comparing me to a flower. I don't want to lose my macho man status."

She chuckled at his feeble attempt to lighten the mood and said, "Thank you for coming to my rescue. Again. I'm fine now. You should go back to your room so you can get some rest. Tomorrow's a big day, so you need to be well rested and in top form."

"I'm not going anywhere. I'm staying with you tonight."

"No. You can't. Your parents would freak if they found out."

"First of all, they won't find out. I'll sneak out early in the morning before they wake up. Second, they just wouldn't freak out. Angel, it's different for a guy than it is for a girl. They wouldn't be disappointed or shocked if they knew we were together. I suppose they expect it."

"Still, they'll think badly of me."

"No, they won't. Besides, like I said, they won't even know. As far as they're concerned, they know you have your own room. It's not like we're going around announcing anything."

"What about Alec? He'll know something's up if you don't return to the room tonight."

"He won't say a word."

He moved to sit beside her on the bed and turned to look at her. Mesmerized by her beauty, he leaned forward and gently pressed his lips to hers. She responded immediately, searching, grasping for more intimate contact. He gently lowered her into a lying position and positioned himself next to her. She was starving for contact.

Angel was already breathing heavily and pulling him closer and tighter to her body. Her hands found the broadness of his shoulders as they crept up to encircle his neck. As tenderness merged with passion, he threaded his fingers through her soft, silky hair. He laid himself atop her, trying not to press his full weight upon her. Their tongues danced to a soaring tempo, their kisses rendering them senseless, all the while sending rushes of desire and fervor throughout their bodies. Jarrod slowed his pace by softly lifting his lips off hers and tenderly raining gentle kisses upon her neck and lower as his hands lovingly roamed her body under his fingertips.

"Take your top off," he said, and she obediently followed his instructions. He stared at her, in awe at the beauty of her naked breasts. "Everything about you is perfect," he said. He continued to explore her body with his hands, causing shivers to flow through her. His lips followed the path of wherever his hands had been. Nipping, licking, and gently biting. She felt as if her body were on fire; the heat was so intense, she thought she'd explode.

"Jarrod...Jarrod?"

"Hmm?" he asked as he began to pull her lower clothing off.

"We need protection."

Jarrod felt as though a bucket of ice water had been unceremoniously dumped over his head. He stopped what he was doing and looked at her in pent-up frustration. He began to rub his face.

"I don't have any," he said miserably. Why, for the love of God, did things always go wrong when they were so close to consummating their love?

"I do."

"You do?" he asked, shocked. "How? Why would you—"

"Ile put condoms in my handbag, just in case."

"God bless her," he said as he jumped up from the bed to retrieve her handbag. "I owe her big time for this."

Angel laughed as she sat up, not the least bit embarrassed by her half-nakedness. As he lay down next to her, she softly asked, "Would it be alright with you if we turned off the lights? Just this one time. I'm a little nervous, and I—"

"Whatever you want. I want this to be perfect for you, and I promise to take it slow and do my best to not hurt you. I love you," he said as he bent his head down and kissed her again. Then he leaned over her and turned off the lights. "I love you here...and here...and here...and here...," he said after every kiss he placed on her body, leaving a trail of passion and lust.

They made love for the first time that night. Angel had never felt so loved or desired, or more beautiful in her life. Jarrod had vowed to make it perfect for her and he had more than surpassed his objective. Although he was not able to prevent the quick, sharp pain she felt when he seized her innocence, he did his best to ease it by comforting her with tenderhearted words of love.

Chapter Forty-Six

Angel awoke at five a.m. and turned to look at the man she loved lying beside her, naked and beautiful. *He was exquisite looking*, she thought. She placed her hand gently on his back, feeling the sinewy muscles along them. So strong.

Jarrod opened his eyes slowly as he felt her touch. "Again?" he said happily, but quite shocked. She smiled and said, "No. It's time for you to go."

"You're tossing me out?" he said groggily. "Damn. I feel so cheap and used."

She laughed and smacked him on the back while saying "That's right, mister. I've had my way with you, and now I'm done, so go."

He stood up and stretched in his naked glory while Angel gazed at him in utter admiration of his toned and firm body.

"Very nice," she said while smiling alluringly.

"Oh, no you don't. Don't you dare look at me in that sexy way. I'll never leave if you keep that up."

She laughed again and said, "Get dressed. Hurry up."

He did as she said while she wrapped herself in a bathrobe. When he was done, she walked him to the door, where he kissed her long and hard.

"I'll see you downstairs at nine thirty for breakfast, okay?"

"I'll be there. But we better call down to the chef and forewarn him to cook a lot today. I worked up a tremendous appetite last night."

"Me too." He hesitated and then said somberly "Are you okay? I mean, I hope I didn't hurt you too badly last night."

She smiled at him and said, "If you did, I wouldn't have asked for seconds, would I?"

"Or thirds," he said jokingly.

"You're the one who asked for thirds."

"Ahh, but you were more than willing!"

"Go," she said laughingly as she pushed him out the door.

"I love you," he whispered as he leaned forward and kissed her again.

"I love you more."

The Wentworths and Angel met for breakfast at precisely nine thirty. Jarrod and Angel were not kidding when they joked about having large appetites. They ordered their meals and yet continually picked from each other's plates as well. In addition Jarrod ordered extra sides of bacon, sausage, and toast, which they quickly polished off. When Alec attempted to grab a slice of bacon, Jarrod smacked his hand with his fork, never even bothering to look up when doing so.

After breakfast they decided to head over to the ballpark a few hours early. Jarrod needed to warm up his arm after not practicing at all the past week. He grabbed his gear and as they headed toward the rented mini-van, he whispered in Angel's ear, "I need a few minutes with my mom, okay?"

"Sure. Is everything alright?"

"Yup. I just need to talk to her about something that's bothering me about Alec." He quickly gave her a peck on the lips and ran over to his mother, who was standing in the middle of the parking lot, looking for the key to the car in her handbag.

"Mom, can I speak to you for a minute?"

"Sure. What's up?" She found the keys and started walking toward the car. Jarrod gently held her back by grabbing her elbow and steering her the other way.

"Jarrod, what's wrong?" she asked worriedly.

"I need to ask you something. Is everything okay with Alec? He seems…well, umm…different to me."

"How do you mean 'different'?"

"He just seems…I don't know…not as easygoing or carefree. He seems bothered by something, but he doesn't seem to want to talk about it."

Nodding to indicate she understood, she said, "I've noticed a change as well. I think, or rather, I'm hoping that he's just maturing and realizing that things change as you get older. Your dad and I have spoken about it, and we're hoping he's just going through a phase, a sort of 'growing pains of the soul' phase."

"Have either of you spoken to him about it?"

"We've tried, but he just shuts us out. He tells us he's fine and not to worry about him. I don't know what else to do. I've even resorted to going through his private things—"

"Mom—" he interrupted.

"I know, I know. Invasion of privacy and all that crap. Well, let me tell you something, bud. When you have a teenager someday, and you notice a sudden dramatic change in his or her personality, I can guarantee you'll be doing the same exact thing I did. I did it because I'm worried and I want to find a way to help him and—"

"Alright, alright, Mom. I got it. Did you find anything?"

"No. Not a thing. I ransacked his room and went through his backpack, but zilch. I'm at my wit's end."

"I'll try talking to him to him again. I don't know why you and Dad didn't call me."

"You have so much going on in your life, we didn't want to add more to your plate. Besides, you have to witness and experience it, not just hear about it to fully comprehend the changes in him."

"Have you noticed anything else that's different about him, aside from his attitude?" he asked.

"Only that he spends a great deal of time at Cameron's house."

"He always spends a lot of time there. They've been best friends since the second grade."

"I know, but he's there more than he is at home. He doesn't even come home straight from school anymore. He's always there. He eats there, does his homework there…he might as well sleep there, with the amount of time he spends at Cam's."

"I wouldn't worry too much about that. We all know that Cam is a great kid."

"I suppose you're right. I guess I just miss seeing him and then with you gone…well, maybe I'm just suffering from a slight case of empty nest syndrome." She sighed and then said, "Your dad says it's all just a part of getting old."

Jarrod wrapped his arm around her, giving her an encouraging squeeze, and said, "You're not old. You're perfect. You always have been." Just then Alec called to them from outside the car, saying, "C'mon already. Let's go." Both Janet and Jarrod headed toward the car at a slow pace. Janet latched arms with Jarrod and said, "Let me know what he says when he talks to you, alright? Dad and I are both worried."

"I will if he opens up to me and I think there's something we can do to help. Otherwise, if there is absolutely nothing we can do and he forces me to promise not to say anything, I won't."

"Jarrod."

"No, Mom. I won't betray him that way. The only possible reason I would even consider doing something like that is if I feel that he's in some sort of danger."

They reached the car and she pulled him back a few steps.

"Fine. I won't ask you to betray your brother. But just promise me you'll do whatever you can to help him, if that's what he needs."

"I promise," he said.

"Thank you," Janet replied, then adding "Now, I have a quick question for you regarding you and Angel."

"Sure. What?"

"Are you being safe?"

"Mom!"

"Don't 'Mom' me. I need to know that you're being safe and responsible. You're too young to become a father, and I'm sure as hell way too young to be a grandmother."

"Yes, yes, yes. We're being extremely safe," he said, flushed red with embarrassment.

"Good. Just remember that your father and I raised you to be a gentleman and to always be respectful. I'm not stupid and naïve. I know you're a young man with needs, so I don't mind you doing the dirty deed, as long as you are smart about it and practice safe sex." She walked away from him to get inside the car. Jarrod stood there dumbfounded and completely mortified.

Chapter Forty-Seven

They reached the ballpark in Jacksonville in just a few short hours. As they stepped out of the car, Jarrod took a moment to take in the sight. It was a beautiful ballpark. As far as minor league parks went, it was one of the most modern and impressive ones he had ever seen.

Jim put his hand on his eldest son's shoulder and asked "Are you ready?"

"Since the day I was born."

Angel removed her hat and tossed it into the open trunk, where Alec was removing Jarrod's equipment bag. She smiled at Alec while doing so and he humbly returned her smile, turned his head away, and mumbled under his breath, "You looked silly in it anyway." Angel wasn't able to clearly make out what he had said, but based on the look he gave her, she felt it might be better not to know.

"Hey," she said to Jarrod, beaming brightly.

"Hey back," he said as he kissed her sweetly on the top of her head. *She was such a tiny little thing*, he thought. So small, delicate, and beautiful, reminding him of a dandelion puffball just as the seed heads would float away like thousands of graceful, gentle pixies on their way to making someone's wish come true. He never tired of looking at her. With every day that passed, he found himself loving her more and more. He adored her gentleness and sensitivity. Admired her strength and profound ability to see past the negative. Regarded her tenacity and courage. Respected her ideals and morals. He marveled at her capacity to forgive and her strength to move forward. She wasn't envious or resentful, ill-tempered, or hurtful. She truly saw the good in all and somehow had the capability of spreading the feeling of warmth and compassion into the hearts of those she met. He would forever be thankful God had placed her in his life and knew in his heart that in Angel, he had found his eternal soul mate.

"Let's play some ball," said Alec, grinning as he moved past them carrying two equipment bags, one over each shoulder. Now there was a smile he hadn't seen in awhile, thought Jarrod happily.

They entered the south gate and walked toward the field through the interior of the stadium. As they approached the field, Jarrod stopped to revel in the sight, smell, and sensation of the field that lay before him. There was nothing like the smell and look of the freshly cut grass cut in the form of a curved diamond, with the dirt in the infield helping to sketch its design. The field was a place of hopes and dreams for all who were fortunate enough to grace the hallowed diamond as they ran the bases.

He took a deep breath, smelling a combination of the grass, spilled beer on the concrete, the lingering aroma of hot dogs, pine tar, and the sense that summer was right around the corner. If he closed his eyes, he could almost hear the whistling sound of the ball as it approached the plate, the crack of the bat as it made contact, and the earsplitting roar of the crowd. He suddenly thought of Dante and how he would rip him to shreds for thinking in such a sappy manner. He smiled as he thought of his best friend calling him a "cornball, dewy-eyed mush."

Jarrod noticed a few other players practicing on the field. He couldn't help but wonder if they were there for the same reason. Perhaps these men, at this very moment, were sharing the same fears, thoughts, and hopes as he. But then again, there was also the possibility that these men were professional players for the Jacksonville Suns and had already been where he is now and were well on their way making it to the show. He took a deep breath and turned to Alec.

"Want to help me warm up?"

"Didn't bring my equipment bag for nothing, y'know," Alec replied. He seemed to be in a lighter, more jovial mood. Jarrod smiled, thinking that not even Alec's existing disagreeable disposition was immune to Angel's pleasant demeanor. She'd spread that good-natured amicability once again, just like the sun had the ability to find its way through dark clouds on a stormy day.

They walked out onto the field and began throwing the ball back and forth. With every toss, they would both take a few steps back, forcing them both to throw harder and farther each time. They did that for awhile and then moved on to pitching. Alec donned a catcher's mask, chest protector, and leg guards. His gear was mostly red with dark blue scattered within the foam crevices, making him look like Spiderman on the attack when he would squat to catch one of Jarrod's pitches. Angel was amazed at how hard and fast Jarrod pitched. Jim was standing behind Alec and would call out "strike" or "ball" after every hurl. She was also impressed with how easy Alec made it appear to catch the balls.

They soon moved on to hitting, but weren't at it for long. Angel noticed a man approach and stop. He watched Jarrod intently and would continuously write things down on a clipboard he carried with him. Angel looked over to Janet and tapped her on the shoulder. When Janet turned toward her, Angel motioned with her head toward the man. Janet looked at the man, leaned her head toward Angel, and whispered, "That's him. That's Griffin Wyatt."

Angel closed her eyes and said a quick prayer. The man began to walk onto the field and stopped when he reached Jarrod. They shook hands and exchanged pleasantries while

Jim left his position behind Alec and joined them on the mound. Alec stood up, removed his mask, and came to join Angel and Janet.

"How'd he do?" said Janet to her youngest son.

"Pretty good. He's not throwing as hard as he used to, but still hard enough for me to feel the sting under the glove."

"Accuracy?"

"Not bad. A few balls, but mostly strikes."

"Consistency?" she asked. Angel was impressed with Janet's knowledge of what sort of things one needed to look for. As far as she was concerned, if one didn't hit the batter with the ball, it was a good pitch.

"Getting better. I just wish he'd practiced more this week. I can tell his arm was tiring already, and this was just a warm-up." He glanced at Angel and realized he might have said the wrong thing in front of her. "I'm sorry, Angel. I didn't mean—"

She stopped him from completing his sentence. "It's alright. Don't worry about it. I know Jarrod says if he doesn't do well, it's not my fault, but I know the truth. It will be. If I had listened to him and stayed in my room, the abduction wouldn't have happened that night, and he would have had the week to practice."

Janet looked at her sadly. "Angel, if it didn't happen that night, it would have happened eventually. You heard what Jarrod said about how it was well planned out. For all any of us know, it would have happened later in the week or maybe even this weekend. Then we would have had to cancel the entire appointment. So you see, it was more convenient for us that you were kidnapped last weekend."

Alec and Angel stared at her temporarily speechless, both equally dumbstruck. Janet, on the other hand, continued watching the interaction between the scout, Jarrod, and her husband as if what she had just said was as trivial as discussing the weather.

Hours passed as they silently watched Jarrod pitch, field, and hit. Jim had joined them on the bleachers and was nervously biting his nails the entire time. One of the men who had been warming up on the field assisted Jarrod as a pitcher and catcher whenever necessary. Mr. Wyatt kept a stopwatch with him and would time Jarrod in just about everything. He also stood nearby with a radar gun to record the speed of his pitches. Once again he would continually jot things down on his clipboard. Angel noticed on a few occasions, Alec would express his thoughts aloud by either saying "Yes!" when pleased with what Jarrod had done, or by letting out a profanity when not pleased. His mother and father did the same.

Finally Mr. Wyatt said, "Alright, Jarrod. That's enough for now." Angel, Alec, Jim, and Janet all stood up simultaneously, trying to read Griffin Wyatt's expression while he wrote down a few more things. They couldn't tell whether he was pleased or not. He walked over to Jarrod and spoke with him for a brief moment, and then they both walked toward the visitor's dugout. They sat there speaking for what seemed a lifetime, not just a quarter hour. Suddenly they both stood. Jarrod climbed the steps back onto the field and headed toward his family and Angel.

"I can't tell if he's happy or sad," said Janet.

"Neither can I," responded Alec.

Angel and Jim said nothing. Their nerves were beyond fried, and Angel noted that Jim began to rub his face. *So that's where Jarrod got the habit from*, she thought.

When Jarrod reached them, no one dared to speak. There was a veiled cloud of doom hanging over them, and each one was afraid to say anything for fear of it fissuring and soaking them in disappointment.

Angel looked to where Mr. Wyatt had gone and saw he was still sitting in the dugout, speaking to someone on his cell phone.

"I need a few minutes alone with Alec, if you don't mind," Jarrod said as he motioned with his head for Alec to follow him. All were in shock, and Angel had to nudge Alec to move. He slowly moved forward and followed Jarrod toward right field. They stood there speaking to each other, but nothing could be discerned from their reactions.

※ Broken Road ※

"I can't stand this," said Jim. "What could they be talking about?"

"This is driving me nuts," responded Janet as she looked at Angel, who had removed her sunglasses, yet was shielding her eyes from the sun with her hand.

"You in a hurry to leave?" Jarrod asked Alec.

"No. Why? Jarrod, what's going on? What did Wyatt say?"

"He wants to see what you can do."

"Huh?"

"He saw you when you were catching for me and was impressed. He wants to see what else you can do."

"Shit. God, Jarrod, I'm so sorry…what about you? You're a thousand times better than me."

"Nah. Don't be sorry. This is a good thing. He thinks I need a little more time. He noticed a difference in speed, accuracy, and power from the last time he watched me, but said he expected it. I mean, it hasn't even been a full year since the accident. In fact, he said he expected a lot less from me and was impressed with what I've accomplished so far. He wants me to continue with the training and rehab, play for the university's team, and then meet with him again next year."

"That's not too bad."

"No. I'm fine with it. Really, I am. But now it's your turn, if you're interested."

"Shit, I don't know. I mean, yeah, of course I'm interested. But I feel bad. This is supposed to be your day, not mine."

"Alec, it was never 'my day.' It was 'our day.' The whole family. What Mr. Wyatt told me about my playing isn't bad news. He never said, 'Hey, kid. Sorry, but you suck, so it's time for you to pack up your gear and quit baseball.' He just told me that I'm not ready yet, but to keep at it. I still have hope. You, on the other hand, have a great opportunity right now. Don't waste it. Go out there and give it your damnedest. Make me proud, but more importantly, make yourself proud."

Alec grabbed his brother into a big hug and held him that way for a good minute, then pushed him away. They were both laughing as they returned.

"What just happened?" asked Janet.

"I have no idea," said Angel. "But they look happy."

"Boys, get over here now," hollered Jim. Lowering his voice, he turned to Janet and asked, "Did you bring my blood pressure pills?" She nodded and began rummaging through her handbag.

Chapter Forty-Eight

That evening they all went to dinner and ate, laughed, and celebrated for hours. Alec had tried out and was basically told the same thing as Jarrod. Mr. Wyatt was interested in them both and wanted to see them again next year. He was extremely impressed with their skills and knowledge of the game. He just felt they were both not ready at this point, but with hard work and determination, could be by the following spring. He gave them both his business card and asked them to keep in touch. He also mentioned he had a good feeling about the Wentworth brothers and would love to see them someday play for the same team.

Jarrod's body was aching. His shoulder throbbed, and Angel promised to give him a rubdown when they returned to the hotel. Janet gave Jarrod a knowing glance, and he quickly lowered his blushing face.

Once at the hotel, they all said good night to one another in the main lobby and headed to their individual rooms.

"Will that rubdown Angel promised you take all night, or should I expect you back?" Alec whispered to Jarrod.

"I don't know. My shoulder really, really hurts…," he said, smiling.

"Lucky bastard," said Alec as he stopped in front of his and Jarrod's room and opened the door. "Good night, Angel," he said.

"Goodnight Alec," she responded. "Don't wait up for Jarrod." Well, that answered his question.

They entered Angel's room and as soon as Jarrod closed the door, Angel wrapped her arms around his waist and hugged him tightly. They held each other for a long while without speaking. Then she took his hand and led him to the bed. He sat down on the edge while she climbed behind him on the bed. On her knees she began to pull his shirt off while he lifted his arms for her to pull it over his head. With only one hand, due to her healing wound, she slowly began to knead the tight muscles in his back, neck, and shoulders, concentrating more on the last. He moaned from the sheer pleasure of her hand roaming his body, easing away all the tension and exhaustion from his weary muscles.

"You're spoiling me," he said with his eyes closed.

"You deserve it," she whispered in his ear. "Lie down on your stomach." When he did, she straddled him from behind and began to put all her weight into the press.

"God, that feels so good," he moaned.

She smiled and said nothing. She wanted him to relax, and if she continued the conversation, it would defeat the entire purpose of the massage.

After a good twenty or so minutes, her hand and arm became tired, so she stopped. She lay down next to him and asked, "Feel better?"

With his eyes still closed, he mumbled, "Yes. Thank you."

"You're welcome."

He turned onto his back and placed his arm out so she could scuttle her body into it. She fit so perfectly. He looked at her as she stared up at him. "How can someone be capable of loving so much?" he asked her in a soft voice.

"I just am," she said.

"I wasn't talking about you. I was talking about me."

"Oh…"

"I never thought a person could feel so much. It's like my heart isn't big enough to take in all these emotions. Saying 'I love you' just doesn't seem to cover everything I feel for you. I just feel that the words aren't enough."

Angel eyes began to water. She knew exactly how he felt. "You show me every minute of every day how much you love me." She placed her hand on his cheek and softly caressed it. "I'll love you forever, Jarrod."

He leaned over and began to kiss her. "I want to show you how much I love you tonight, but I'm worried it'll be too much for you."

"I'm fine. Show me. Show me how much you love me."

They made love over and over again that night. And later, as they lay awake fully sated, Angel leaned over and whispered to Jarrod, "Thank you again for saving my life."

"No. Thank you for saving mine," he said as he placed a lingering kiss on her lips as a prelude to what they both knew would become another mind-blowing, earth-shattering stretch of lovemaking.

Epilogue

Relaxing in his father's favorite lawn chair, Jarrod sat back and watched as his dad cooked burgers, hot dogs, and chicken on the grill. Alec was running around chasing their three little cousins as they screamed in horror of being captured by the big, hairy, ugly monster he was pretending to be. He caught the littlest one, four-year-old Stella, and picked her up in his arms while twirling her around as she squealed in delight. Janet, who was standing right smack in the middle of all that chaos, hollered for Alec to stop before poor little Stella threw up.

Jarrod looked to his left and watched Angel as she sat at a picnic table, drinking a Diet Coke while speaking to her Aunt Helen, who had hesitantly agreed to attend the gathering that his parents had decided to throw in honor of Jarrod's return for the summer. Well, at least part of the summer. The remaining portion would be spent in Bradenton.

He looked up at the sky and savored the warmth of the sun and the gentleness of the soft breeze they were fortunate to have today. He was happy today. It was great to see everyone again. He had missed them all, but hadn't realized how much until he saw them again. Alec's unpredictable mood swings continually concerned the family, but he refused to speak about what might be troubling him, insisting he was fine and just needed space. Jarrod and his parents spoke privately about the situation and agreed to keep a watchful eye on him while still giving him the time and space he greatly sought.

Brendon and Joey looked well and seemed to be doing great. Both were attending college, Brendon at Seton Hall and Joey at Rutgers University. They saw each other most weekends when they came home. Just two days earlier, they all went together to visit Dante's grave. Joey brought along a portable CD player and they listened to their friend's favored music softly in the background as they sat around, talking and reminiscing about things they had once done, scrapes they had gotten into, parties they had gone to, things Dante had said. They laughed until they found themselves wiping tears from their eyes. Joey's mother had put together a beautiful scrapbook of photos and articles she had collected over the years of the five of them. They passed it around and smiled, laughed, and softly cried when they reached the page devoted to Dante's passing.

"Hi, hon," said Janice Malone, abruptly bringing Jarrod out of his reverie. He immediately stood up and gave her a hug and a kiss on the cheek. "How are you doing, sweetheart?" she said.

"I'm good, Mrs. Malone. How 'bout you? Please sit down," he said, offering his seat. She shook her head no and replied, "I'm fine...fine. It's so good to see you. You look well and I hear you're doing great in baseball again."

"I can tell you've been speaking to my mom," he said laughingly. "I'm on the pitching rotation list and we're doing really well."

"Are you still enjoying the sport?" Janice asked, already knowing the answer.

"Can't live without it."

"We miss you around here, you know."

"I miss you too. How are you and Mr. Malone doing?" he asked.

"As well as can be expected. It's always going to be difficult," she said as she looked away. "We miss him terribly."

"Me too. He was always there for me."

She nodded, took a deep sigh, and said, "You were always there for him as well." Looking over at Angel, she added, "Your girl is beautiful. You might have had some competition if Dante were here." Although she had said it in a joking manner, there was an aura of sadness behind it.

He chuckled and said, "No competition. I would have lost her to him in a blink of an eye."

She smiled briefly and then became serious. "I'm sure you already realize it, but the anniversary of his passing was just a few weeks ago. We wanted to wait for your return to hold a memorial service."

Jarrod nodded solemnly. He could never forget that fateful night. It was the beginning of the worst era of his existence. He involuntarily shuddered as he recalled the two most horrific days of his life—the day he lost his best friend and the day he almost lost Angel. The memories would forever be seared into his memory.

"Now that you're here, we'd like to hold a service and were wondering, if you're feeling up to it, if perhaps you could say something…"

Jarrod pulled her into his arms and said, "I'd be honored."

She leaned up and patted his cheek gently and said, "You're such a good kid. We're proud of you."

"Thanks," he said shyly.

"Come visit me and Mr. Malone before you leave, won't you? We would love the company."

He felt her loneliness and heard it in her voice as well.

"How 'bout this Sunday? Maybe you can make your world-famous spaghetti for me."

"Oh, I'd love to. That would be wonderful. I'll even make some bracciole," she said excitedly. "Bring your sweetheart and Alec as well. I'll make meatballs for Alec." She kissed him again and ran off to tell Mr. Malone they would be coming over on Sunday. Jarrod smiled and made a mental note that he would have to make a point of visiting them a few times before he and Angel left.

As he stood there for a moment glancing at Angel and silently thanking God for the millionth time for bringing her into his life, he was approached from behind by Cameron, Alec's best friend.

"Hi there," said Cameron.

He turned and smiled at the person he had grown to love over the years as another sibling.

"Hey, gorgeous. How are you?" he said as he pulled her into a deep embrace.

"I'm good. I'm so glad you're home. I've missed you," she said brightly. Cameron was the epitome of goodness, sweetness, and kindness. She would get along well with Angel. Two peas in a pod.

"I've missed you too," he said as they separated. "You look great. Wow, look how long your hair has grown. Looks good on you." The last time he had seen Cameron was last year, when she wore her highlighted, blonde hair stylishly short. Now it cascaded just below her shoulders with a soft, undulating wave. Her bluish-gray eyes sparkled with spirit and energy. He had witnessed her bloom from an awkward, ungainly tomboy with wiry hair, courtesy of some really bad home perms, and braces into this alluring young lady, resplendent with beauty, grace, and femininity.

"Thanks," she said as she unconsciously ran her hand through it. "You look great too. I see you've been working out. Check out those guns." She gently squeezed one of his biceps. They both laughed.

"So, tell me what's new? What plans do you have for college? Harvard, Princeton, or Yale? I'm sure you were accepted to all three," he said. Alec had just informed them the other day that Cameron had been selected as the valedictorian of their graduating class. "By the way, congrats on being selected valedictorian. I'm really proud of you."

"Thanks. Now I have to work on a speech. I'm not looking forward to that. You know how I hate being the center of attention." Jarrod nodded, knowing full well how nervous she must be.

"You still haven't answered my question about college," he said.

"Not really sure yet," she said nervously as she bit her lower lip.

Jarrod playfully scowled at her and said, "That's not like you. You've always been so decisive."

"I know, but things have changed a bit. I've...I've met someone."

"Really? That's great, but what does that have to do with your decision as to what college you're going to attend?"

"He lives abroad. He's from London and we met in the city a few months ago."

Jarrod looked at her skeptically and wondered where this was going. She appeared agitated as if hoping not to disappoint Jarrod. She had always looked up to him and truly valued his opinion of her.

"He's an actor and was in the city auditioning for a lead role in a movie. I bumped into him, literally, on the street, and he stopped to help me pick up some things I had dropped. One thing led to another and he's been traveling back and forth over the last few months to audition for roles and to spend time with me. He's so charming and smart and—"

"It's the accent," he interrupted.

"Excuse me?" she asked.

"The accent. It always makes the Brits seem charming and smart. He could be depriving some English village of its idiot, but will still seem smarter than Einstein because of the accent."

"That's really deep," she said as she rolled her eyes in annoyance and exasperation.

"Anyway, go on. So you met him in the city and now what? You're in love and planning on leaving everything behind to go follow him to London or something?"

"I don't know yet. I haven't made a decision. You sound like Alec," she said sadly. "He's so angry with me."

"If he's so angry, why is he always hanging out at your house?"

"I don't know. Maybe to prevent me from spending time with Ian. Whenever Ian is in town, that's when Alec is stuck to me like a remora fish."

"Ian? Sounds hoity-toity," he said, chuckling.

"He's not. He's really wonderful. And handsome. And talented."

"Did he get the role he was auditioning for?"

"No," she said morosely.

"Hmm…," he said, silently thinking that if Ian was so talented, he would have gotten the part.

Cameron noted Alec was approaching them and quickly whispered to Jarrod, "Shhh. Alec gets upset when Ian's name is mentioned, so don't bring him up, okay?"

Jarrod nodded and when Alec approached them, he said, "Hey, Cam was just telling me about Ian." Cameron quickly turned and glared at him.

"So she told you all about her Prince William wannabe?" said Alec as he placed a protective arm around Cameron's shoulder. She gently shrugged it off and said to Jarrod, "I think I'll go over there and introduce myself to Angel. Maybe I'll share with her a few stories I have about you. I know exactly which one she'll love hearing. I think I'll tell her about the time you dug a hole into an apple with a spoon, and I caught you practicing how to French kiss on it." She smiled wickedly at him and flitted away.

"Hey! Don't you dare," Jarrod yelled as Alec placed a hand on his arm to stop him from chasing after her.

"She won't say anything. She's just goading you. Don't you know her by now?"

Jarrod realized he was right and said to Alec, "So, why don't you like this Ian character?"

"He's not good enough for her. She deserves better. Just wait 'til you meet His Royal Pain in the Hine-ass. You'll know what I'm talking about."

"How well do you know him? Maybe he is on the up and up."

"He's not," Alec said determinedly. "He's too good looking, too charming, too suave. I don't trust him. Do you know that the jerk calls her by her middle name, Snow? Not Cameron; not even Cam like the rest of us do. No, that's not good enough. He says her name is too 'androgynous,' so he chooses to call her Snow. What an asshole. The dude thinks he's a couple of notches better than the rest of us, but what Cam doesn't realize yet is that she's the one who's too good for him. She's beautiful, sweet, kind, loving, smart, sensitive...,"

He went on describing all of Cameron's merits, but Jarrod stopped listening. All at once he realized what Alec's problem was. He now understood why Alec had turned so sullen and morose over the past few months. His brother was in love with Cameron. After all these years of being constant, devoted companions, Alec had suddenly fallen head over heels in love with his best friend. And now she was planning on leaving everything, including him, to follow her new boyfriend to London. No wonder he was so upset.

Jarrod interrupted his brother by saying, "I know why you hate him so much," as he placed his hand on his brother's shoulder in a show of support and empathy.

"I know you do," Alec responded after a deep sigh. "I'm dealing with it. You don't have to worry about me." He began to walk away, but added, "Jarrod, please don't say anything to anyone about it. I mean it. Not a word. I kept your secret—now it's time for you to return the favor."

Jarrod nodded and sat back down. After a few minutes of being lost in thought over his brother's troublesome predicament, his mother came toward him, dragging another lawn chair with her. She sat down next to him and smiled.

"Are you enjoying your party?" she asked.

"Yup, very much. Thanks again," he said, returning her smile.

"No problem," she said. She looked over at Angel, who was still speaking to her aunt, and said, "I'm glad Mrs. Billings came. It's nice for Angel to have someone here that she knows."

"Yeah. She feels bad for Mrs. Billings. This has been so hard for her."

"I can just imagine."

"Things are looking up for her though. She was recently promoted to day manager at the diner, so she was able to quit her second job. Plus, now that she has her nights free, she told Angel that she plans on taking a computer course at Bergen Community College."

"That's wonderful. I'm so happy that things are turning around for her. How is she handling the whole Morgan situation though? That can't be easy."

"It's been tough, but I think having Angel here has helped. She seems stronger and is holding up pretty well. Angel had the opportunity to speak at the sentencing, and she pleaded with the judge to be as lenient as possible when determining Morgan's sentence."

"I give Angel a lot of credit. I don't think I could do that."

"I'm not sure I could do it either. I have to admit, I was pretty angry with her when she told me she was planning on doing it, but I suppose she made me understand. She explained to me about Morgan's past, things Angel's father had only touched on. She feels Morgan's past had a big influence on how she turned out and why she made certain unfortunate decisions. Plus, Angel loves her aunt so much and couldn't stand to watch her suffer. She wanted to do whatever she could to help her."

"Angel's name truly suits her," Janet said.

"She's more like a saint, I think," he replied. "Speaking of names, did you know that Cam's middle name is Snow?"

Janet nodded and then said, "Yup. I think it's because she was born during a big snowstorm or something like that. Anyway, so tell me what happens now to Morgan?"

"Let me put it this way. It'll be a long time before she steps foot out of a prison courtyard."

They remained silent for a moment before Janet said, "Long, hard year."

Jarrod sighed and said, "That's an understatement." He said nothing while he contemplated the past year. "Mom, can I ask you something?"

"Of course."

"Remember when Alec and I were little and you told us about the three paths that life offered?"

"Yes, I do. I'm glad you remember."

"Well, I know about the 'good,' the 'bad,' and the 'need to make a change' paths, but…" He hesitated.

"But what?"

"What about the fourth path?"

Giving him a quizzical look, she asked, "Fourth path?"

"The path where you feel lost and uncertain. Terrified and alone. The road where you can't help but think you'll never find your way off, because no matter how hard you search, you can't seem to find an escape. You feel like you're climbing a colossal mountain, trying desperately to reach the summit, but then you realize you can't because it doesn't even have one. You've lost everything you've ever wanted or fought for and feel like no matter what you do, you'll never be able to recover any of it."

"Ahhh…you're referring to the 'broken road.' The good thing about that road is that it's entirely reparable. It just takes a lot of hard work, determination, strength, and most importantly, faith. You need a tremendous amount of faith to find your way off that road. And as far as that mountain goes, there absolutely, beyond any doubt, is a summit. It's hard to reach, but when you do get there, you'll find there is no place in the entire world with a lovelier view."

She took a deep sigh and glanced sadly at her son, knowing how difficult this year had been for him. He gave her a meek smile in return and then turned his head to look at Angel. Suddenly it was as if his entire mien changed from pensive and dispirited to blessed and halcyon.

"It's a difficult path to be on," Janet said. "Terrifying and terribly lonely, as a matter of fact. But it is possible to find your way off of it. You did." Just then Angel, as if sensing that Jarrod was thinking of her, looked over at him, and they smiled brightly at each other. Janet glanced at the two of them, smiled as well, and simply said, "And sometimes you just need someone to point you in the right direction."

The End

About the Author

Broken Road is Elizabeth Yu-Gesualdi's debut novel. Originally from New Jersey, Yu-Gesualdi moved to Connecticut in 2005. For the past sixteen years, she has been a stay at home mother for her two sons, Jarrod and Alec. Shockingly, outside of an A+ in high school creative writing, her captivating debut novel is her first writing experience. Aside from writing she enjoys reading, reality TV shows, online shopping and spending time with her family. She currently lives in Connecticut with her husband, David, and their two children.

Made in the USA
Lexington, KY
26 June 2013